The Traitor's Penalty

Written and Illustrated
By
Levi Hyatt

Raised by a group known as the Jackals, Kaiźer has only lived by the sword. His world has been shrouded in darkness & sadness since the beginning. Born of royalty, he knows not of whom he is & is raised as an orphan. He had not family excepts his closest friends, but even they are far away.
It has been over one hundred years now, but when old enemies come out of hiding, Kaiźer is forced to protect the reincarnation of the one he loves, even though she knows nothing of him. Calling on his allies, will he be able to defeat his old nemesis once again?

Levi Hyatt
Grants Pass, OR
lmhyatt98@gmail.com

Dear Reader

"To the ones who dream of other worlds beyond their own, enjoy the mortal realm and her Five Kingdoms as well as her neighboring realms of astral and daemonic decent"

Chapters

Kaizer

Prologue: a Deadly & Mutable Council

With Fire and Ice, is thy Bound! Let not Air, nor Earth release thou till thy time have come.

The First Unseen One
The Age of Echelons

2514 A.B; just north of Ascaria

Kaiżer finally felt at home. A fire burned in the hearth, and the scent of pine and cedar filled the small two-story cabin with its sharp scent. The freshness, mixed with the flames' crisp heat, created a feeling he prayed would last forever.

Standing before the hearth, he stared into the flickering flames and thanked the gods for his blessing. He cradled a hot mug of tea in his hand and, taking a sip, he let the hot liquid warm his chest.

His wife, Abika von Morningstar, was an artisan in the kitchen, and he cherished the fact. He tried to remember what he could have done to deserve such a woman. How had he been lucky enough to win her heart despite being who he was? He considered it a miracle and knew that despite his many flaws, she loved him back, and even as he thought of her soft touch, her hand glided over his shoulder and around his side to embrace him softly.

Pressing herself into his back Abika reached around and linked her hands over his stomach. "Is everything like you thought it would be?" she said, nuzzling against his back.

He chuckled and placed his free hand over both of hers. "I wouldn't say no, even if it wasn't."

He ran his thumb along the back of her hand, enjoying the feel of her soft skin against his. "It's peaceful, which is all I ever wished for."

His wife hummed her approval, and he pulled her around with grace to stand before him. She looked up at him, and he caressed the elegant curve of her cheek. Dipping his head, he lifted her chin, even as she rose to meet him. Passionate and soft, her lips merged with his. He didn't need to say a word, for she understood his contentment and cherished it. Nothing stood between the two of them.

Breaking away, she dropped back onto her heels, and his breath caught as the firelight circled her figure in rays of light. She was his, and she was beautiful, so beautiful it made him ache. He remembered his vows and of how, at that moment, her breath had caught upon hearing them. "*I promise to walk with you through this life and the next. If ever we are pulled apart, I will search for you through a thousand lifetimes and a thousand worlds.*" Such was his promise to her, and he meant to keep it.

"Kaiźer?"

"Yes?" He focused his gaze on her and looked into her eyes. She was striking with the firelight upon her fiery hair, the strawberry highlights clashing with the burgundy streaks to create a torrent of living fire around her.

"What of Maliki? Did he understand?"

He didn't need to think twice. "Yes, I believe he did. I know him, and if he'd had the chance, he would have given us his blessing."

Abika smiled and closed her eyes. Her head fell to rest on his chest, and she relaxed to the beat of his heart. It was intense and steady against her ear as she breathed in the smoky scent of the man.

He was unlike anyone she had ever met, and she got the feeling no one would ever measure up to him. She cracked an eyelid and looked out the window, where the setting sun was beginning to vanish behind the mountains. She wanted to end the day, but she couldn't help but wonder if it was time yet. Kaiźer was so relaxed she didn't want it to end.

"Abika?"

She heard the word as it vibrated from within his chest, reaching her with a sensation that sent shivers down her spine. Every time he said her name, her legs turned to jelly.

The single word oozed intimacy, and she couldn't help but grow warm inside. Unable to quell the urge, she looked up into his dark blue eyes, eyes that were swimming with a passion she had only read about in stories.

She had to lick her lips as her mouth went dry and looked at him intently. She struggled to keep from jumping up and down at that moment. "I have something to show you."

As he began to pull her away from the hearth, his words sent shockwaves through her. She felt an intense heat in her chest as she fully realized what was happening.

Were they finally going to—after so long on the run? She'd been planning to do just as much herself, but the moment was gone. She had lost her chance. Now he was taking the lead.

Across the many miles, they had fled, they had never had the time to settle down, just the two of them. Her cheeks grew hot at the idea that finally, they were alone.

The day had been long, but here they were. Was she seriously having second thoughts? It had been so long since the last time, and yet she craved the idea of Kaiźer sharing her bed. They had only gotten here today and hadn't had time to relax. To think they were about to do that after so long!

However, Kaiźer took a beeline towards the front door at the last second. Blinded by the setting sun, she let her heart settle as they stepped outside. She felt a breath of sudden disappointment while at the same time letting out an involuntary sigh of relief. The evening air touched her skin, and even as a warm breeze, it sent shivers down her body as it clashed with the sudden change in temperature from the house.

They were moving towards the forest edge, and she was unsure of what he had in mind. Still, she couldn't help but be curious. What could he have planned? *Could he have set a surprise dinner, chilled wine with a multitude of candles as they fed each other small treats, perhaps?* The idea had her drooling for more than treats. However, if not that, then what? She was burning with questions, but she knew nothing would make him talk. She would have to wait and find out.

They moved through the trees at a leisurely pace, and she came to walk beside him. He held her hand in just the right way to make her feel safe but not trapped. He knew just how much pressure she could handle. Her hands were so small compared to his. It made her feel like a child when he held her like this. She giggled at the thought.

Looking down at her, he grinned. "What do you find so funny?"

She shook her head. "Oh, I was thinking of how—compared to you—I'm small! I feel like a child."

He grinned, and it grew until it looked like it would become stuck. Seconds later, he lost all composure. His laughter echoed through the trees, and despite no one being around for miles, she flushed.

"It's not funny, I'm serious," she said in a forced whisper even as she punched him in the arm, essentially feeling like she had just hit a wall. He wiped a hand over his face to hide his grin and to give himself a moment to catch his breath. "Oh, I had no idea. I beg your forgiveness, my child."

She raised an eyebrow as she looked at him again. "Ha, ha, ha. Very funny," she said sarcastically

He chuckled.

"So, where is this surprise you have for me?" She had to know. It was killing her inside, not knowing, and she knew that he knew this, which only made her feel all the more irritated.

"It's just up ahead," he said as he took her hand in his again and pulled her along.

Kaiźer had finally confessed his feelings just one year ago, and now here they were walking through an unknown forest in a strange land, their hands intertwined as one. The trees showed the change from summer to fall, their leaves shifting from a lush green to the reds and yellows of autumn. No longer was there a need to hide their true selves, and no longer was there an air of awkwardness present. It made her feel free.

She was so lost in her thoughts that she didn't notice they had arrived at a clearing till Kaiźer called her name. She looked at him, then at her surroundings, and let out a soft gasp as she saw where he had taken her.

Covered in a sea of flowers, the grass she found herself treading upon swam with color. It was so beautiful and unbelievable she couldn't hold back the tears that pressed against her eyes. Her vision swam as she moved through the rich grass, a hand rising to cover her mouth. There were so many different colors around her, their many shades blending into a vast blanket of color.

"Kaiźer, it... it's beautiful." She turned and, fighting the tears that threatened, closed her eyes to the sight before her. It was too much. It was unreal. She stood there for only a second before his arms encircled her. The movement broke her control, and she wept as he held her. Before long, her tears ebbed, and she sniffed, pulling away to look at Kaiźer in the low light of the night. The sun had set while he had held her, and she hadn't noticed. Gods, she was hopeless. Here she was, breaking down over a bunch of flowers.

She felt Kaiźer put a finger under her chin, and he raised her eyes to his but was shocked as his lips met hers. He barely feathered them against hers, and she caught a hint of the spearmint tea she had made. It laced his breath like a fine wine, and she grinned against his mouth.

"What are you doing?" she giggled.

"I'm giving you your anniversary present."

She gasped. *You remembered! oh, what a sly man you are!* "With a kiss, really?" she raised an eyebrow at him.

He grinned. "Is it not what you wanted; can I not kiss my wife?"

"Oh, that's not the problem. It's just the way you do it. Why do it teasingly when you could do it like this." Standing on tiptoes, she pressed her lips to his as she clutched his shirt in her hands and pulled him to her. His hands slid over hers, and he spoke against her mouth.

"I want this moment to last for eternity, but the kiss wasn't your present."

She paused against his lips and opened her eyes a moment before he opened his. "What more could you have to give me?"

"This!" He stepped away, and she gazed at his retreating form. She felt an odd sense of loss as he moved away and didn't consider that she could see him despite the lack of moonlight till the fog that had submerged her lifted.

As if seeing for the first time, she looked at the sky. She watched the stars as they appeared above her and, glancing at Kaiźer, dropped her gaze to the ground once more, and froze.

All around her, the flowers that had once colored the meadow now glowed with a sea-blue light. They spread out around her, creating a mirror image of the night sky above.

She was speechless, unable even to think. She could only feel, and the sensations that overcame her were so intense they overtook any thoughts she had of crying again. She looked at Kaiźer, and he smiled his warm smile she knew was for her alone. He held out a hand, and she moved through the sea of blue light to place her hand in his. Moving her fingers up, he brushed them against his lips and closed his eyes. He was at peace.

"Do you know how long I have looked for you?" he whispered.

"No..." She whispered back.

"Since the beginning, for years, I feared I'd never find you."

Her breath came faster as her heart sped at his words. It was the same for her but to hear it from another. She needed to understand. Was he saying it had been fate? If so, she agreed wholeheartedly.

"Kaiźer, it's the same for me. I..." She struggled to find the words. She had known him from a distance throughout her childhood and had never once said a word to him. At least not until he was about to complete his training. Only after a year, things had gone by so quickly that it was amazing to look back and think, man!

Right now, with him mere inches away, she wanted him to take her right here in this meadow, but she didn't dare to make a move. His eyes were-- they were looking past her. Here she was, and he had the balls to ignore her? She opened her mouth to berate his ass when she saw his expression. She looked over her shoulder.

In the distance, she saw what had caught his attention. Lighting the night, it flickered from beyond the trees. It wasn't a steady light, and she got a bad feeling. It looked as if--

"The House!" she shouted even as Kaiźer took off into the trees. Taking off after him, she ran, her dress trailing around her legs until she passed out onto the vast stretch of grass around the burning house. Wholly consumed, the two-story building was already collapsing from the damage inflicted by the flames. How had this happened? There had been nothing near the hearth to cause such a fire, so how?

She watched as Kaiźer emerged from the flames, but as he looked at her, she was too late in noticing his rage as it appeared at the sight of her. Before she could cry out, her world went black.

Kaiźer was too late; he emerged from the burning house to see the dark figure flicker into visibility behind Abika, striking her as it did.

He had gone into the house to retrieve his sword upon seeing the flames when he should have stayed at his wife's side. Such a costly mistake, and he hadn't thought twice; such a fool he was.

Kaiźer gripped the hilt of the sword he had chosen over his wife, gritting his teeth all the while, but forced himself to stop mid-draw.

Held at Abika's throat was a knife he thought he recognized. Steady and sure, its owner restrained her from behind with leather-clad arms. Overall, it made him want to pull Kaín out the rest of the way, but as his wife stirred, he froze. She was conscious, if only barely. Her eyes became apparent, and she soon stared at him in terror.

"Let her go! She's done nothing to you." He held the hope of the figure dropping her so he could attack, but the man did nothing. He had a hand laid across her throat, knife hovering too close for comfort.

"Oh, but she did. She stole you from us, didn't she?"

The voice was one he had heard many times, the gravelly tone like a plague to his ears. Throughout his childhood, that voice had given him orders and commands while at the same time giving praise for the things he accomplished, especially if they had involved the death of another how he had grown to ostracize that voice. He detested it with a passion, and now...? Hearing it come from the one holding his wife's body made him throb with rage. He knew he had recognized the knife. He could feel his sword mirror his feelings of recognition, and he fought against the demands it gave to spill blood. He knew if he succumbed, Abika would die.

"Why are you here?" he asked, his voice tight with restraint.

The cloaked figure shook his head as if in disappointment, and when the man looked up at him, his eyes flashed a violent green. "Isn't it obvious? We're here to take you in. After all, you committed treason of the highest order, and your sentence was to hang!"

He had known that things were not over. His master may have forgiven him, but that didn't mean the court had as well. He looked at Abika, memorizing her face, her hair, her figure, all the while knowing they would never share a life. She would hate him for this, but he didn't want her to die because of his honor.

"I will go with you, but only under one condition."

The black figure tilted his head slightly. "And what is it you desire?"

Kaiźer took a step forward. "I only ask that you let her go. She is no threat to you or the order."

The dark figure tilted his head as if thinking. Kaiźer knew him to be a man of his word, and if the man agreed, he knew he could trust the outcome; but the answer he had hoped for didn't come.

"Hmm, I want to believe you, but I can't decline such a succulent kill." The words hit Kaiźer like a wall, and he watched as Abika's throat turned red in a flow of fresh blood. He watched her crumple to the ground, delicate skin slit in a clean line. She looked at him with eyes of pure terror as she struggled to breathe. He didn't look away even as tears blurred his vision. He watched her breath catch and sent reassuring thoughts to her even as he despaired. Her face settled, and she nodded as she gave him a small smile. As she did, her eyes glazed over, and she slipped into an endless sleep.

He stumbled forward and falling to his knees before his wife's body took her in his arms even as his heart shattered. His worst nightmares were coming true before his very eyes. He didn't even react as Ryeznya came to stand before him.

"She was a mortal"—the man wiped his bloody blade on his shirt—"she would have died anyway."

He had nothing to say to this man. His will to fight was gone, and what little strength he had remaining vanished, seeping from his limbs like water from a broken vase.

"Well, My King told me to take you in and that if I couldn't, that I was to kill you." Ryeznya went around and stood behind him. "I'd thank you for not fighting back, but it only disappointed me. You used to be the best."

Kaiźer heard the steel of his sword sing behind him as Ryeznya picked up the black blade he had dropped as he'd rushed to Abika and recognized the sound of Heavens Bane as he slid free from his sheath. He waited. All too slowly, time crawled by right before the blade pierced his shoulder and punched through his heart. Two words filled his ear as the life flowed from him in flickering waves.

"You lose."

Always a competition, even with death as the judge, I see that you haven't changed. Kaiźer doubted there was anyone here with his uncle. Besides the dagger, Repidar, he guessed the man had come alone. He felt a chill creep into his limbs as the blade withdrew from his flesh. He wondered how he was still alive; usually, Kaín shattered a person's soul once it pierced their heart. He took a stuttered breath and looked up at the man who had taken everything from him. Ryeznya tossed away the black blade and pulled off the leather cowl that masked his face. His lips pulled back in a triumphant smile as he looked down at him. Twirling his dagger around him, he spoke again, the words dripping with scorn. "You could never have replaced me; I am Maliki's brother, and yet he adored you and ignored me."

Ryeznya kicked out, and Kaiźer flew backward. "But not anymore. I'll leave your corpse for the buzzards. Enjoy the afterlife, Nephew." Turning away, Ryeznya left him in the mud and soot.

The fire burned around him, but he didn't feel the heat; he didn't feel anything. Spread eagle on the ground, he looked at his beloved, lying just a few feet away. She gazed at him with dead eyes, and he felt a dull pain in his chest. He would keep his promise; he would not let death stop him from finding her. *May we join in the afterlife, my love!* The words swam through his mind, and as the world faded to black, he clung to his vows. They were his only lifeline.

Heat turned the air thick, its cloying scent clogging the wind around the remains of the small farmhouse. Besides the crackling of the last remaining flames licking at the wooden beams that still stood to mark the skeleton of the once small two-story cabin that had sat proudly in the soot-stained clearing, Kaiźer heard nothing outside of his ragged breathing.

The living realm was there, but under it all; the shadow realm sat as a mirror image of the land under it.

Kaiźer walked in this realm of shadow, tears running down his face. He felt nothing; he was nothing. He had lost everything, and here he was stuck between mortality and immortality, cursed to live again and again while those he loved perished. He had thought things to be suitable for a change finally, but no. His uncle had taken everything from him once more, his wife, life, and freedom. He was nothing. Even his vows had gone unanswered.

He walked along with the dark weaves of the fold and wondered how things would have gone if he had stayed by her side? Kaín would have been fine; he was a magical being, immune to the scourge of time. He berated himself for choosing that which he had.

He fell to his knees and slammed his fists into the grey ground. He was useless. It had been his fault. He had thought he could live a peaceful life away from the war of man, but it had followed him despite his best efforts, and now here he was, trapped in a land of timeless obscurity with no idea of where his path would lead.

He sat there for he knew not how long, upon the ground, with only his thoughts to comfort him. However, when a soft sound of musical soprano graced him, he looked up as it carried past him on a phantom wind. It rippled through his hair and caressed him with the softness of a lover's embrace.

Do not think of yourself as such. There is still much to be done, and your beloved would want you to keep going. You will find love again, this, I know. Now wake and make your choice.

He felt pressure on his chest, and soon it grew until it felt like his heart would cave under pressure. He coughed, and everything flashed white.

Kaiźer sat up, breathless, and grasped at his neck. He found the wound where Ryeznya had stabbed Kaín into him, but as he ran his fingers over it, the sliver of sore skin began mending itself together until it was whole once more.

Dropping his hand, he looked around and found his beloved where Ryeznya had left her. Her throat was red, and he stood slowly, tears running free once more. He felt them hot against his skin, and his throat constricted when he knelt beside his wife's limp form.

He cradled her in his arms and rocked back and forth in anguish. He was surprised to find himself once more upon the mortal realm, just like always. Usually, when Kaín stabbed a person, he shattered their soul. All the same, he wasn't happy. His immortality hadn't failed him despite his desire for it not to.

Looking around him, he stared at the crumbling remains of his home and felt rage boil within him. He would avenge his wife's death, even if it took him eons to do so. The words on the wind had said he would find love once again, but he knew better. Love was an illusion that had no place in his life. He had tried to hold its hand twice now and had had it taken from him each time.

I vow that I will take the life of the one who had taken everything from me. I promise to protect the people my brothers and sisters hunt, keeping them from harm. I swore to set aside the way of the Hunter, but I vow now to use my skills against the very people who have given them to me. I am a Jackal, and nothing can change that.

Part 1:

Kaizer

chapter 1: Reunion of Past & Present

The enemy grows strong but the weaves that the mother creates, will be met with a fatherly touch to teach the new ones of courage to be.

The Wise Sage of Genesteria
The Age of Echelons

3921 A.B. Present Day

The room smelled of stale tobacco and cheap perfume. Kaiźer eyed the patrons mulled about the tables and couches that took up the first floor's entirety. A lot of them smelled of rich wine and sex, but that didn't hold his attention. Just a few moments ago, Kaiźer had watched an old friend walk through the door.

Dressed in a merchant coat, the man had aged since last he'd seen him, but he still held himself the same. Shoulders back chin low and eyes twinkling, he looked as if he had a secret he wished to share. All the same, Kiyle Ross seemed different, more mature, almost put together, complete. Looking at him now, Kaiźer nearly didn't recognize his old friend.

Kiyle had walked in the door with a wide grin on his face, and Kaiźer had watched him mingle with a multitude of people, most of them female. Right away, it became apparent his old friend hadn't changed much when it came to the ladies. Despite the man's attitude, Kaiźer couldn't place what was different about him. Moving through the tables, he had had only one sole intention: getting a lady of the sheets on his hip.

However, when Kiyle saw him finally, his mission fell away, and his face lost its happy glow, becoming a mask of pure shock. He forgot about the woman he was talking to and turned to face him. Stumbling forward, he passed through the room, completely unaware of another lady who called out to him. When he didn't reply, she gave him a rude gesture, spilling her drink in the process. The lady he had been talking to saw this and went to confront her.

Kiyle didn't even notice. Everyone who did get his attention only got waved away without him even looking their way. It was hard, knowing what was going through his mind as he approached, but Kaiźer shut the man's thoughts out of his head and waited. Soon coming to stand at the bar before him, his old buddy looked at him in disbelief.

"Caine..." he asked softly, still unbelieving. "Is that you?"

The question was expected but, Caine? It took a minute for him to remember. It had been the name he'd used in the military ten years back when he'd decided to learn about the world he'd left behind. After spending the last thousand years on the run, he had needed to catch up, so to say. He'd meet Kiyle during training one day, and the two of them had hit it off, quite literally. Kiyle had been overconfident in his abilities with a sword, and he had nearly lost his head to Kaiźer's blade. After that, Jokan, the blade master at the time, had put them on the same shifts for a week; served the lord Vermilian his wine and meals as punishment. All the same, during that time, they quickly became close friends.

It was no surprise that Kiyle was in denial at what he saw; he did look the same as he had ten years ago. Nevertheless, with him staring at him so intently, it was beginning to get awkward.

"Dude!" he snapped. "Would you stop staring? It's getting weird. You're acting as if I'm going to grow horns and a tail. Are you trying to find out where I keep my pitchfork?"

With a grunt, Kiyle looked down and stared at the counter.

~That was what I'd been thinking precisely, if not in that context. Why now? Why this day? There was no way this man can know my secret~

These thoughts reached Kaiźer, but he ignored them. The man's secrets were his and his alone. He had no reason to know what kept his friend up at night.

"You are Caine? Aren't you?" The words came out in a whisper as Kiyle looked back up at him, still unbelieving.

"I helped you prank Jasmine in our first year. The mice were a bit much, but the girl's screams were worth it."

At the memory of their prank against the princess, Kiyle's face brightened, and he smiled from ear to ear. Not an ounce of awkwardness remained, and the two of them become lost in conversation. They sat at the bar for hours, only catching up on what had happened since they'd last seen each other. Kaiźer learned that his old friend had settled down and gotten his place. It explained the mature air about him. He didn't say much, only talking about the past year and how he now lived in the middle-class part of town.

After a while, things calmed down, and the two of them sipped their drinks in silence. They observed the crowd of people, Kaiźer watching as Kiyle eyed a watery-eyed lady as she dealt with a rather nasty group of ruffians who wouldn't keep their hands to themselves. She was returning his friend's gaze here and there, but she didn't leave the table. She was interested in his friend; that was clear but was most likely too shy to say anything. Besides, being a green forest nymph made it hard for her to connect with people. Also, she probably didn't want to anger the fellow who kept fiddling with her dress.

"Hey bud, that lady you keep staring at seems to be in a bit of a pickle."

Kiyle looked at him, then back at the lady. Kaiźer saw him sparring with the decision to go or not. He kept wringing his hands and adjusting his collar but still, he didn't get up.

"Gods!" he groaned. "Just go already!" Gripping Kiyle's arm, he pulled him to his feet and gave him a shove. Stumbled forward, Kiyle quickly regaining his balance and shot a stern look over his shoulder. Kaiźer gave a wave in response, all the while grinning like a fool.

Kiyle turned away, squared his shoulder, and walked towards the brothel's far side where the lady sat. She glanced up, and upon seeing Kiyle approaching, a pink blush filled her cheeks, and he knew his buddy was in for a struggle, and sure enough. When he arrived, the men who were sitting at the table looked up at him as one. Kaiźer wondered how his friend would handle the situation, so when Kiyle spoke up and the man who had his hands on Jessíca shot to his feet, Kaiźer did nothing. His friend didn't even move a muscle in response, though, and Kaiźer grinned behind his glass of beer. The man's buddies joined him, standing to either side of brute number one.

Still not moving a muscle, Kiyle directed a question at Jessíca, and she nodded, eyes wide. Brute number one looked between the two of them, and it was then that Kiyle moved.

Dropping slightly, he rammed his fist into the big guy's gut, doubling him over. As the guy gripped his middle, Kiyle kneed him in the face, breaking his nose. Jessíca let out a small squeak, and Kaiźer chuckled at the sight of the big man now on the ground, clutching his broken face.

Kiyle pushed the downed man away and faced his buddies. He did nothing to egg them on, standing with his hands at his sides, only waiting, and he didn't have to wait long. They bull-rushed him as one, and he became a blur of color, striking vital points on each man in quick succession. Passing through them, he came to a stop behind them and stood straight, not even bothering to see if they were still awake, let alone alive.

His attack had put them all on their faces in one go. Not even a minute had passed since the fight had begun, and already, the six goons lay unconscious. Kiyle was the top commander to the king, but no one knew his face or name, and he liked to keep it that way. Kaiźer would make sure no one said a word of this once outside the doors. From what he had learned about Kiyle during their talk, the man hadn't sat idle since last they'd met. He hadn't risen through the ranks till he had become who he was today with ease.

Jessíca stood at the table in shock. She had yet to move since Kiyle had landed the first hit, and as the goons landed on the hardwood of the floor, she jumped at the impact. Looking at Kiyle, she babbled till he went and placed a finger against her lips to quiet her.

Suddenly the lady threw her arms around him and squeezed him tight. Kiyle's shoulders sagged in relief, and he let her pull away before he spoke up.

Jessíca's eyes went wide, and she nodded quickly. Had he... yep, Kaiźer was sure the man had just asked what he knew he himself would have asked.

Backing away, Kiyle just about bumped into a table, nearly falling over in the process. Jessíca giggled, and Kaiźer watched his friend smile in embarrassment as he turned and walked away quickly. Arriving back at the table, Kiyle fell into his chair with a huff. "I feel like a total fool," he mumbled.

Kaiźer shook his head and laughed. "You are no such thing. I'd dare say she was happy for the help. Those men weren't going to stop anytime soon, that was for sure."

"Yeah, I know. You sure the lady was happy with me, interfering?"

"Oh, yeah. I'm positive."

Kiyle smiled and took a sip from his beer. "I was sure I'd botched it at the end there."

"I doubt that."

Smiling, Kiyle held his hand out. "I did get this, though," he said. In it was a small slip of paper. Scribbled on it in neat bubbly handwriting were a name and address.

Kaiźer grinned. He had always thought Kiyle to be quite the showboat and what had just happened proved that. "I will warn you," he said in a quiet voice. "Jessíca's a little shy when it comes to meeting new people."

Kiyle raised an eyebrow but nodded as his mind registered the fact. "Got it!"

"Now, on that note, I wish you the best of luck because I have to get back to work.

You have a good rest of your night, bud."

"Back at yah," Kiyle said with a salute of his beer, quickly draining it in turn.

With a sigh, Kaiźer rose to his feet and moved back behind the bar. He began to clean the counter and back shelf while keeping an eye on Kiyle as he ordered a couple more beers.

Jessíca joined him, and Kaiźer hid a smile by turning back to the wall that held the drinks. Turning back around, he filled two kegs of beer and slid them down the bar to where two men sat, looking into their empty mugs as if they had just learned their mothers had died. They looked up at him, and he raised his tankard in salute. They cheered and grabbed the new beer mugs. Kaiźer chuckled at their renewed enthusiasm.

Just then, the waitress Kiyle had gotten away from the inevitable disaster came up, drawing his attention away from the boisterous patrons. He looked at her questioningly.

"Did you know that man, the one who came up to me?"

He smiled. "Yes, he's an old friend. Why do you ask?"

Jessica blushed and, with a shrug, spoke in a shy whisper. "It's just that you were sitting with him and"—she paused in thought—"and I know how you don't have a lot of friends. I was just wondering what you thought of him?"

He looked at her with a small smile. "What did you think of him?"

"I thought he was cute"—she covered her mouth to hide a smile—"and he seemed nice if only a bit flustered." She took a breath and spoke suddenly. "Do you think he'll visit me?"

Looking at him with big eyes, Jessica looked as if she weren't sure he'd say yes.

"He'll visit you, I'm sure. Don't you worry," he said as he booped Jessica on the nose. "Now, you need to get to work; I see a young man over there that needs a refill."

Giggling, she took off, skipping towards the man he'd mentioned. Jessica was a nice girl. She had a lot going for her. He knew she'd like Kiyle.

Turning away, he began to take inventory of the remainder of their stocks. The night had been long, and the drink was running low. He would need to go into the back and grab a new Rum keg before he left, but just as he was writing down that they would also need the refill of wine and whiskey, a familiar scent assailed his senses. he suddenly smelled peppermint underlain with cinnamon, which was quite extraordinary as it wafted past him. He knew whom it had once belonged to and as he looked around, he prayed he didn't imagine things.

He could see her in his mind's eye, hair a strawberry red, eyes like diamonds, and skin like pure white marble. He didn't need to look up to confirm the vision. She appeared, and even among the wide assortment of customers that the nightclub attracted, she stood out among the otherworlders and humans as a virtuoso. She was just as he remembered, despite her hair being tied back in a loose bun. She was all business at the moment, but as she sauntered through the club —passing the people on the open floor of which swayed together as one giant mass to the fiddle— the black dress she wore could not hide her feminine charm. She drew the eyes of multiple people, even a few females, as she passed. She was so similar yet so different from the lady he had known.

Stepping up beside him, Mike, the brothel's head of staff, spoke over the music. "I'd be careful with that one; everyone knows the boss tends to let her appetites get the better of her."

Turning back to look at her, Kaiźer put her face with a name, the Lady Sin'ka. He felt a slight twinge in his chest as Mike called her the boss. Abika had been very dependent herself, but she would never have thought of running a House of Sin. Sin'ka, with her fiery red hair, was a mirror image to his first love, and despite learning that she ran the Lover' Bite, he was still awestruck. So far, fate had oppressed him, and now of all times, it had decided to grant his only wish and his only promise?

Looking back up to where Kiyle sat, his mug raised as he took deep swallows from the thick ale. Jessíca rested on his knee, and the old commander was looking into her eyes as he answered something she had said. She laughed and stood to take his hand in hers. She pulled him to his feet and started to lead him through the tables. Kiyle shot a look over his shoulder and saw him watching. A wide grin had taken over his face, and Kaiźer gave him their old military salute from back during their days on the force. Two fingers against the center of his forehead, then the lips, before changing into a fist. Finishing with a flourish, he met that fist against his chest. Kiyle disappeared into the back hallway before responding, but Kaiźer knew he had recognized the old signal.

Just then, the scent of mint drew his attention once more. Sin'ka was coming his way. She looked around, catching the eyes of a few well-built men throughout the club. They returned her stare boldly, despite her scowl, which made him feel a twinge of anger as their lustful thoughts shouted in his mind's eye. The men of today's age had no respect for women. It made him sick just thinking about how things had become.

As a few of them drew the courage to try to approach, he took his chance, heading towards the end of the bar. As he drew close, the men who saw him quickly changed direction—he smiled inwardly—they had a brain at least.

Coming to stand behind the redhead, he cleared his throat. "What can I get you, Miss Sin'ka?"

Glancing up, she looked into his eyes and froze as if awestruck, not looking away for a long minute. She was staring, her mouth opened as if to say something, but no words came out. For a few long moments, nothing happened.

"Uh, Miss?"

She recovered and looked away, mumbling her request as she blushed. With a grin, Kaiźer turned to prepare her order. Most women had similar reactions to him. At first glance, most of the women called him beautiful. The first time he'd been told such, it had felt weird, but after a time, he'd grown used to it. Now to have his boss look at him as she had, he knew he was in trouble. He was watching the past repeat itself before his very eyes. Abika had loved the taste of Genesteriana wine, so he wasn't shocked at the request, but it still shook him to his core.

Now, where was--

Ah there! Reaching up, he grabbed the bottle of Genesteriana wine. Made from the vineyards of Genesteria on the Elder Mountain's foothills, it was an amber-colored sweet dessert wine. Made from sun-dried grapes of the varieties Xynisteri and Mavro, it was often a fortified wine, its production method often reaching alcohol levels around fifteen percent, even before fortification. It represented an ancient wine style documented back to the First Age. It had the distinction of being the world's oldest named wine in production, with the name Genesteriana dating back to before anyone had even discovered the Land of Nypheriam.

Whistling softly, he grabbed a crystal glass from under the bar and, pouring a small portion, took a sip and let it swirl around for a bit before filling it and setting the crystal before Miss Sin'ka; but she wasn't there.

He found himself looking into the gaze of someone he knew to be long dead.

With warm eyes and a more amiable smile, the lady he'd cared for raised her arms, reaching out to him, her fingers spread wide as if she expected him to come into her embrace. Her clothes were in tatters, and dried blood stained her cheeks, but she either didn't know or didn't care.

Shutting his eyes tight, he shook with the effort not to roar in anger. *No! I watched you die; you aren't real.* His thoughts swam with the memory of the blade that had sliced through her flesh. In a red stain of severed skin, her blood had carved a crimson path through the air in reply to splash onto the surrounding area.

Forcing himself back to reality, he opened his eyes to see Miss. Sin'ka back where she had been. She was facing back out at the floor, watching the people as they danced to the frenzied music of the fiddle. He wondered what could have caused such a strong vision. Was there something he was missing here that he had yet to see? As he pondered what it could be, he reached out and tapped Sin'ka on the shoulder. She turned with a start but relaxed the instant she saw him. She murmured her thanks when he slid her drink towards her.

Glancing back at the dance floor, she looked at him with a quizzical glance.

"Did you see that?"

"See what?" Confused, he wondered if she had seen what he'd seen.

"The man with the red hair, he had it tied back... No?"

He shook his head, letting out a mental breath as she asked him. She had seen someone else. Not a vision, then.

She must have seen one of the patrons; most people in this region had red or burgundy colored hair, so it wasn't much of a surprise. He asked her if she knew him, but she didn't answer straight out, so he told her about the security crystal in the back office, pointing her in the right direction. He felt like a fool instantly after. She owned the place, for Christ's sake. He should have just kept his mouth shut.

Thanking him, Sin'ka turned to go. When she was gone, he faced Mike. The man had been watching the exchange from the sidelines, and Kaiźer didn't want the man to pester him. "I guess I'm not on her list of appetizers," he said sarcastically.

Mike shook his head before going over to a young man who looked barely old enough to drink despite his thick stature with a grin. Kaiźer could see his eyes swirled with a dark light. The man had years of knowledge despite his age. His attire made him a death dealer by trade, and most of the men and women who took up such a profession lived complicated lives. The two of them had something in common.

Coming back, Mike gave him the boy's order. Not surprising, the drink was simple, and after filling a mug with beer, Kaiźer slid the tankard down the bar to where the boy picked it up with a smile. He knew the kid would have control, but he would still make sure he only got one glass this night.

The last remaining hours of the night passed by quickly, with only a few mishaps. They were nothing he couldn't handle, and soon enough, the night was at its end, and right before the break of dawn, he reached his apartment and, without changing, flopped into bed. He was asleep before his head even hit his pillow.

Sin'ka Finsaria hated blood! She grew faint at the sight of it, its color, its texture, and its flavor. She gagged at the very thought of it, or she had since her turning two hundred years prior. It was then, with a lover's embrace, the darkness enveloped her.

Emerging from the memory of her birth, she fell back to reality. Looking out over the sea of lights, she remembered how the city before her had grown. It's busy streets bustling with people when before, but a few would travel its roads at a time.

During times of great distress, she has recently found herself searching for a place to think. She'd soon found a place within the royal castle of Nypheriam, a lone tower in the west wing. It faced the ocean and was the highest place in the city. She enjoyed the feeling of the wind in her hair and the fresh scent the air carried.

At times she found herself imagined that the drop was daring her to test its open void.

This night, she accepted the challenge, and with a whisper, the air moved with a hint of smoky leather. Mist curled around her as she flung her wings out to their entire expanse. Standing slowly, Sin'ka looked out at the sea of buildings that carved curving lines and pools of darkness throughout the city. Drinking in the cold air of the night's expanse, she leaped into the night with a snarl.

Too long had her thirst been denied! With no moon and no stars to light the night, shadows overlapped shadows, and only with keen eyes did Sin'ka finally find her target.

Dropping for the sky, she landed but a few feet from her prey. Silently she watched as the boy's breath came heavy and labored. She listened to the youthful beat of his heart, and from deep inside her, the beast she hated with a passion rose to bare its fangs, which made her physical fangs elongate.

As she moved towards the young man, he stirred suddenly, rising to look around. His eyes were bright with awareness, and they fixed upon where she stood. Even within the darkness, she froze.

"Clary, Is that you?"

When he spoke, Sin'ka let out a breath she hadn't known she'd been holding. Then she noticed what she hadn't before; a hint of liquor laced the young man's breath.

Moving forward, she ran a hand through his curly hair. Doing so, she caressed his cheek with a slim finger as she whispered into his ear. His pupils dilated, and his heartbeat picked up, letting her know he was hers.

Nuzzling his neck, she slowly pulled his head to the side and, straddling him, trailed her lips along the beating vein that was pulsing with his arousal. His breath came quicker, and with smooth precision, she sank her teeth into his neck and drew upon his lifeblood with slow pulls as she drank. As the young man relaxed, his heart slowed, and she fought to find satisfaction, slowly retracting her teeth and licking the wound. Her saliva activated his healing properties, and the evidence of her feast slowly faded.

She pulled away, looked into his eyes, and seeing the passion that resided deep within them, couldn't help but grow cold inside. She couldn't help but think, *"who can love a beast such as I?"* She stood up then and delved into his mind, whispering to him in a soft voice.

"You will remember nothing of this,"—as she spoke, she pulled a fistful of silver marks from her pocket and slipped them into his coat pocket—*"rest now and when you awake, take this and find your way home."*

His eyes fluttered with sudden drowsiness, and he nodded sluggishly.

She let her control over him fade, and his eyes closed. He fell into a deep sleep, and watching him rest once again, Abika suddenly became overcome with a strong sense of anger and sadness. Frustrated, she turned and walked to the ally's end, where the door to her destination lay hidden in the shadows.

As she approached, a phantom of her nightguard, Hex, appeared. "Welcome, Lady Sin'ka, you look just as beautiful as always." He was always sweet, but more so when in a foul mood, and she could see he was irritated, although he wasn't usually this upset.

"Hex, what troubles you?" she asked in a calm voice. His response came with a bite not directed at her, but she still felt its sting.

"I have had multiple attendants walk out drunk beyond words, and their words were not too kind themselves," he huffed. "The humans these days have no honor."

"I'm sure they don't mean to insult you directly, my friend."

Hex gave her a warm smile. "You are not like them, this I see. You are kind, Lady Sin'ka. Are you here to stay, or did you want to talk to me?"

She looked over at the wall. "I came to stay."

"Then, don't let me keep you. Enjoy your stay, Lady Sin'ka."

He stepped aside, and the door materialized, opening to reveal a blood-red light. Smoke leaked out, trailing around her legs like phantom serpents, and she stepped forward past their hazy grip to become enveloped by the spicy scent that came hand in hand with the Lover' Bite. She owned the place, but she had only used it to carry out her side hustles so far. She was moving through the brothel, listening to the beat of the music when she heard a man speak. She was about to move on when the topic of his words caught her attention.

"I'd be careful with that one; everyone knows the boss tends to let her appetites get the better of her." She looked at whom it was who had spoken, but it was only Mike. Still, he was talking to a big man who looked new and familiar. She had to guess he'd been staring. She wasn't surprised. He was a big man, bigger than most but she had more pressing matters to attend to, so casting the big man from her mind, she headed to one of the back tables, sitting down to face the man she had come to meet. She eyed him carefully. The man, dressed in casual clothes, didn't stand out much, but his face gave a different story. He had a scar across his left eye and had another x-shaped one carved into his left cheek. She'd known him since her turning, and as she had grown up, he had helped. However, on the side, he found her suitable clients that had a fancy for the dramatic.

"Did you find what I requested?" she asked.

Sliding a file across the table, Ba'ile spoke so those around wouldn't hear. "The client is upstairs. What's in this file is all I could gather on him, nothing out of the ordinary. He's clean."

"I'll be the judge of that"—closing the file; she looked at him—"which room?"

Ba'ile slid a key across the table. "I know you're not one to listen much, but I have to say it."

She met his gaze when he didn't let the keys go. "Then say it."

Ba'ile let out a slow breath. "You cannot simply shut down this type of business. You have seventy-five houses throughout the city, and if you still plan on leaving, you're going to need to find someone to take over once you're gone."

Sin'ka looked at the table. He was correct, but she didn't know anyone who would be able to keep such a path. She had had to deal with men and women who thought a knife was better than subterfuge when it came to trying to get their money back after they either abused one of her girls or tried to walk away without paying their fee. She didn't know anyone who could handle such.

Looking back up at Ba'ile, she put on a fake smile. "I know, and I will figure it out when the time comes."

Picking up the keys, she winked and, without a backward glance, was gone. She hated this part of her life, but she had known the risks when she started. Men would never change; they all had their hidden fantasies that they didn't want to tell their wives about; it was these men who came to her. Tonight, she would have to deal with a man who had an engrossment in role-playing. She was going to need a few drinks before she went up.

Walking towards the bar, she glanced around to meet the eyes of a couple of young men. Scowling, she hoped they wouldn't bother her, but even as she sat down to wait for Mike to arrive, she got the feeling it hadn't worked.

"What can I get you, Miss. Sin'ka?"

It wasn't Mike who spoke; The voice was too deep. Deep enough to send ripples through her. Looking up, she found herself captured by the bluest of eyes. They danced with specks of silver and green while alongside them, red streaks mixed to form and complement the dreamiest eyes she'd ever seen. She found herself drowning in their depths; it was the man she'd seen earlier. The one who'd been with Mike!

"Uh, Miss...?"

With a start, she crashed back to reality. Looking down, she blushed as it dawned on her that she had been staring. She felt like a little girl after her first kiss. He was so gorgeous and so familiar. Looking back into those eyes of his, she drew in a quick breath.

"Genesteriana wine...please."

He turned away, and she let her breath out slowly. Enhanced senses were one of the side effects of being ShadowFolk, but they weren't always a blessing. She had to see everything, hear everything, and she missed nothing unless she forced her mind to shut it out. With this man before her, she struggled not to watch the broad muscles of his back as he moved around. Therefore, turning away from the bar, she fought to clear her mind of him instead of taking in the sweat and hormones from the open floor while at the same time listening to men as they flirted with her girls. Awe damn, those things only made her mind race even more! Looking up at the magic-infused lanterns, she sharpened her sight to take in the ultraviolet rays as they bathed the writhing bodies flowing as one on the open floor. It mixed with the warm heat of the countless humans and otherworlders, stirring the fresh blood in her veins.

She needed to stop thinking before the heat building in her core made her do something she would regret in the morning! She closed her eyes and shut everything out, she shut out the music, and she shut out the people. She shut it all out and paid attention to the rise and fall of her chest. Her heart hadn't beat for two centuries, and yet she felt more like a vampire than she had as a human.

However, despite her efforts, she lost what control she had when she looked up. And into two cold eyes, eyes she'd hoped never to see again.

His face, carved like the purest alabaster, held a beauty immune to time. His hair stood red against the black of his clothes. Moreover, his lips were as pale as an ocean under a grey sky. And to make matters worse, in his hand, a blade shone with a deathly light, countering the beauty before her. Moreover, as his lips curved to form a cruel smile, he brought that blade up and drew it across the red flesh of his lips, piercing the skin. At that moment, she knew it wouldn't matter if that blade were to be her corruption once again. Taking slow steps towards her, the man who'd turned her into the monster she was today held the knife out, tip dripping with red blood, his lips moving to form one word.

"*Drink...*"

It came out as a whisper, touching her mind like a shadow of its former self. She shivered and closed her eyes, wishing for her creator to disappear.

Just then, a tap on her shoulder made her turn with a start. She held her breath as she expected to find Julian there, but it was only the bartender with the gorgeous eyes to her relief.

"Here's your drink, miss." Smiling, he slid the glass of Genesteriana wine in front of her. Murmuring her thanks, she lifted the wine to her lips as she turned to confront her creator. However, she couldn't find him anywhere. Turning back to face the bar, she set the glass down and, after glancing at his nametag, asked Kaiźer if he'd seen a red-haired man with pale skin and a black suit come into the brothel.

"I'm afraid not ma'am, is he by chance a friend of yours?"

"Oh, heavens, no! Just a..."—she hesitated for a second—"an old acquaintance of mine."

Flicking a thumb over his shoulder, Kaiźer pointed behind himself to where a surveillance torch hung. "But if you wish to know where he went, you're welcome to check the footage in the back office. You do know the place, Miss. Sin'ka?"

"I do indeed. Thank you, Mr. Kaiźer, and quit the Miss; I'm not your mother." Picking up her drink, she circled her way to the back.

Once she reached the hallway that led to her office, she sank into its shadowy embrace, becoming wrapped in not just its darkness but in its past sins as well. Opening the office door, she flowed from the hall's black shade into the soft grip of the small room's single lamp. The circular chamber lit with a single torch, and in the center of the room was an enormous mahogany desk. Upon it sat a silver orb of clear glass. Alongside it was an assortment of papers and folders, but she ignored those. Sitting gracefully in the chair behind the desk, she laid her free hand atop the glowing sphere as she nursed her wine. She summoned the footage she needed.

Sorting the last couple of hours, she searched the mental images that rushed to the surface. She finally found the desired footage; and focused all her attention on the torch, which hung behind the bar. However, upon seeing the images thrown her way, she lost her hold on her glass, and it fell and shattered against the lush carpet.

Her thoughts swam as she sat back in the chair and stared at the low ceiling. Where Julian had stood before her, the camera showed nothing. No one was there; had she imagined it then? If so, why? It has been years since he'd crossed her mind. Why now? She needed to find out what had happened to him.

Kaizer

Chapter 2: The Garden Eternal

I do not know about you but I love how, during the clearest of nights when the wings of the ethereal flow peaceful and secure, the stars of the night skies appear at their brightest.

Unknown King
The Age of Heroes

Kaiźer didn't wake all day. Only when the sun had set, and the moon hung high did he finally rise from his slumber. He called in letting Mike know he would be taking a trip for the next few days. He knew everything would be fine at the Lover's Bite in his absence, and after a quick bath, he cleaned up and left. He had to give a visit to the forest. Not a cloud stood in the sky, and looking up, he strolled through town, passing the shops and markets that were closed during the snow. Today was the winter solstice; he could sense it through the freshness of the land. It sang with new life. He could feel it in the air and even beneath his feet as he walked. The snow was whiter, and the sky was bluer despite the weather. As he passed out into the countryside, he moved through the hills at a leisurely pace, thoroughly enjoying the peace. Silence surrounded him, and as soon as the city's lights faded over the horizon, he let his mind open. With a flicker of shadow, he jumped.

He appeared in a deserted clearing utterly void of trees, and raising his face, he looked at the sky and stared. He let his body relax, and taking a deep breath, watched as the stars twinkled above him like fairies trapped, unable to do anything but show their beauty to those below.

Kaiźer had just traveled to the one place that would never see a human until the end of days. Nestled in the Ascarian forest center, it was well hidden, and within the Kingdom of Light, it was miles from where he had initially been standing.

He activated his sight and began to follow the pulsing of the land. Visible as a liquid trail through the soil, the maña that ran thick after the solstice was visible to him like it was every year.

Passing through the trees, he came up upon a circle of stones that stood tall, their weathered faces wrapped with years of green growth. Moss dotted their sides, and the greenery, coupled with red and green vines, wrapped around the bases of each uneven pillar. The elves treated this place with care, but they had always believed in letting the land do its thing. What even they didn't know was what lay below the soil. He ran a hand over the rough stone and listened to the magic as it whispered through the land. It all converged here within what the ancient texts called an Eternal Pool. In the heart of every forest, desert, and tundra throughout the five kingdoms, lay a convergence. No one today remembers their purpose, but he alone had learned much over the last few years.

He had found this one five years ago during the summer solstice, and he'd felt its healing properties firsthand. Each time mother Gaia renewed her land, all leftover maña gathered here was flushed away. The pathway was a mystery, the writings around it long lost to Father Time.

Since he had found this place, he had learned much about how Mother Gaia renewed herself. Each solstice, he had come here, and each time he watched the eternal pool churn. Once again, Kaiźer moved to sit in the stone pillars' center and let his spirit merge with the surrounding area. Falling into a deep trance, he left his physical body and walked the astral plane once more. Within the whole area, maña of all types were getting sucked towards the ground surrounding each circle's pillar. Letting his body fall into the ground, he let the flow of magic lead his journey. Each year the path was different and took many turns until it reached the cave that sat many miles below the surface.

His astral form sank through the ceiling, and he settled into the traditional lotus position beside the Eternal Pool. The rock, comprised of a pit, curved like the barrel of a gun and ended with a small spire. The rock then stuck up from the center to thrust into the ceiling above. The magic within was in liquid form and glowed a warm icy blue.

Five diamonds shone brightly within the roof of the small man-made cavern, and from them came streams of all types of maña, each with its very own texture and color. When Kaiźer had first found this cave, he had questioned the natural set of the uneven jewels against the man-made structure of the cave itself. It was proof that mankind had once known of this place. However, any entries that would have led in and out had been closed off ages before.

Laying his hands within his lap, he watched the flow of energies as they sank into the pool to merge as one. He felt his form pulse as the pit pulled at his unused magic. He watched as it slipped from him in tendrils of reds and yellows. Like all the others, his maña's texture was dissected and pulled apart until it was pure arcane magic once more, with no shape or purpose.

He gathered his magic, so no more was taken, and helped the pool break down the collected magics. He saw both Divine and Demonic energies alongside the four Elementals, and as he worked, he let his mind roam. Did this pool gather all magic and break them open to their nucleus? Did that mean it went to Gaia? He could try to ask her, but his mortal mind would most likely not understand. Gaia was the oldest immortal and rarely walked the mortal realms, and what if the magic didn't go to her? Did it go to some undiscovered domain?

Unweaving the list of mental links that had once been the workings of a mortal man's mind, he contemplated the idea of someone older than Gaia. One hour had passed since last he'd stood, and as the remaining magic got pulled into the pool, he sighed in completion. He bowed his head and spoke in the ancient language a prayer of eternal cleansing.

Once he finished, he let his spiritual form dissipate and flow back to his physical body. He merged with his flesh, opening his eyes to the moon as it shone down upon him from high above. He stood, and eyeing the circle of stones; he centered his magic. Cleared of all negative energy from the Eternal Pool, his body felt rejuvenated, happy even. Every time it was like waking up from a satisfying nap and knowing everything would be right.

In a headspace of complete satisfaction, Kaiźer turned and passed from the center of the clearing and merged with the forest's skeletal embrace, passing under branches hanging heavy with white snow. He jumped back to the outskirts of Nypheriam and headed north. The high woodland was rich in its color, and as the leading resource for the kingdom, it had dwindled in size over the years. Merging with its entrance, he passed through the trees.

As he drew near to the center of the forest, a sound alerted him of another. He dropped his gaze from the stars to look around him. He let his magic bloom, invisible within his hands, but as he did so, the scent of peppermint assailed his senses. Shocked, he gazed through the trees to where a beautiful lady stood. Her skin, wrapped in the moon's glittering sight, stood out as white as the purest marble. Standing stark against her fair skin, the lush red of her full lips and the dark shade of her thick lashes captured him. It was unbelievable. She was precisely the same, all the way down to the way she held herself. He started towards the thick green grass of a clearing between them and soon came to stand beside her. When he did, he mirrored her gaze and looked up into the sky once more. Even though the wind was soft, its path whistling through the trees as its embrace rustled the leavings around him in a calm shimmer of noise, he could hear the sounds of the many creatures as they filtered through the trees.

"Do you come here often, Mr. Kaiźer?"

Watching a small star streak across the sky, he faced Sin'ka. "Please, just Kaiźer and only on the rarest of nights do I come here."

Dropping her head, she looked at her hands then back at him through her lashes. Like diamonds, her eyes shone, their color striking and mesmerizing, but as he gazed into them, they flooded red. He blinked, and just as quickly, it vanished.

"What was that?" Backing away from her, he rolled his wrists on instinct, but he already knew that his daggers were not there. He'd given that life up a long time ago.

"What was what?"

"Don't play coy with me," he snapped. "I know the red of a vampire's eyes."

Turning away, she stared at the ground. "How could you know that? Only a..."—her head snapped up in horror—"you're a Hunter! You're here to kill me, aren't you?"

How does she know about the Jackals? With a sigh, he looked at the sky. Dark clouds were forming. Thunderheads, by the looks of them, shame, and the night had started quite nicely. "No, I gave that life up a long time ago. You need not fear me"—glancing up again, he felt the air pressure drop—"I think it best if we leave, a storm is coming, and I wouldn't want to get caught in its anger."

Nodding her agreement, she turned hesitantly. Pushing away from the tree unconsciously, Kaiźer followed her. However, as they passed through the middle of the glade once more, an uneasy feeling came over him. It sent shivers running down his spine, and he looked up at the sky to watch and listen to the sounds of the coming storm. A crash sounded, and he watched the sky flash with ethereal light.

Lighting struck thrice.

Nothing lasts forever. Winter turns to spring; small things become big. If the world is our mother, then time is our father. Nature makes us into who we are, while time teaches us what to make of it. Our mother is kind, but our father is strict. He teaches us discipline, but afterward, we run for our mothers' embrace in the hopes of finding comfort. With every passing day, the need for Mother Nature grows smaller and smaller, the reasons being that we are growing used to the lessons of time.

However, there is still a place only Mother Nature controls. Its name is known to only a few, and sitting outside of time, she has yet to let any mortal man, woman, or child feel its embrace. The Garden Eternal will always be a capricious place.

Birds chirping, branches swaying, leaves crackling. All the familiar sounds that walk hand in hand with nature. Nevertheless, under it all, something extra, something wrong, roars for control.

The rattle of carriages, the thunder of construction, and a sprinkle of molded stones overpower what was once a thriving jungle but is now just a tiny forest, home to a few wild beasts.

Running his hand along the wood grain of the trees he past, Kaiźer waited for an answer, an answer to his rising problem with the world around him. It was changing too quickly for Mother Nature to handle. With his eyes closed, he breathed in the scent of the forest he'd once known during its prime.

Straightening the collar of his coat, he started on his way. Tears fell along his cheeks, and he wiped his face in frustration. Now was not the time for him to get all weepy. His life was going to shit, and finding out his boss was a vampire didn't help any! If he weren't just beyond the outskirts of the city, he would have had second thoughts—no, that wasn't true—he wasn't a killer. He'd vowed to put his past behind him. The Jackals were no longer his family. He was alone, and he liked it that way. If he killed Sin'ka, he'd only be proving his master right; *once a Jackal, always a Jackal,* his master had used to say—if only to get him back on track with his training.

As he was reaching the center of the glade, he looked up at the rumbling sky. Kaiźer thought back to his graduation when he'd become a full Jackal. He remembered how proud he'd felt, how excited, and how it had stopped him from seeing the true nature of what it meant. As his first assignment, his uncle had taken him up into the mountains where the two of them had tracked a lone sky nymph. Wild in spirit and hard to follow, it had been like an adventure for the eighteen-year-old. However, when they had finally caught her, his uncle had slit her throat before his very eyes. His following words, Kaiźer had never forgotten, *"They're nothing but abominations, an infestation of another realm. Remember this, my son. Don't let them live. If you find one, attack them first because if you don't? They will!"*

Those words and stuck with him since, but he has never accepted them. The time soon came that he finished his training, and he chose to leave the Jackals Court, never to return. Ever since he had had to deal with his decision and all its consequences, but never once had, he had second thoughts. If he had to do it all over again, he would make the same choice.

He broke from his thoughts as he came to stand in the middle of a glade once more. An uneasy feeling came over him then, and he felt shivers run down his spine as he looked up at the sky to watch and listen to the sounds of the coming storm.

A sudden boom from above caught his attention. Looking up, he listened as the sky gave an angry challenge and watched as it crashed with lightning clash.

Three bolts of lightning bloomed just above him, and as they shot down, time slowed to a crawl. As one, the lightning bolts descended around him. He watched them flow in an erratic pattern as they fell from the sky with grace outside of time. He was witnessing a sight that he knew none had seen before. The lightning curved around him, dancing a slow circle towards him, when as suddenly as it had started, it all ended. The skies rage shot into his chest, and entering his heart, sent bolts of burning energy throughout his body until he passed out from the pain.

For what felt like an eternity, he floated weightless, with darkness as his only friend.

With a start, Kaiźer sat up to warm blankets and fluffy pillows. He rubbed his eyes and--

Wait, pillows? Looking around, he found himself in a room carved from the heart of a tree. Lifting the blankets that covered him, he sat up and swung his feet out to sit on the edge of the bed. He was shocked as he looked around the room.

Everything he saw came from one piece of wood. The bed was in the same state. The mattress, however, wasn't. Comprised of... he didn't know for sure. He could say the same for the blankets.

He stood up, walked over to the small closet, and found a set of clothes folded neatly on one of the shelves. He dressed quickly, dawning the baggy pants and high boots before slipping on the shirt. The cloth hung loosely from his muscular frame, and as he put on the leather vest left for him, he frowned. The garments were new, and they smelled fresh. The leather felt cured, but he couldn't tell if it was or not. He didn't recognize the material of his new clothing at all. Looking around once more, he began to question where he was for the first time. He noticed the door then, and with a glance out of one of the windows, he took a step forward. He couldn't see anything but a white expanse outside, but he didn't see anything threatening, so hell.

Walking towards the door, he opened it to a world only the gods would recognize. Eyes widening, he found himself standing in the middle of the open sky. All around him, clouds flowed freely while on the horizon, a forest out of legend stood tall, its trees reaching high, their bark a variety of colors and textures unknown to him.

Walking forward, unhindered by the concept of falling through, he crossed the expanse of pure white clouds, looking down at the world below. He recognized the land and could see the lights of the five great cities far below. He could even see the lone mountain island that sat out at sea. He wondered how high he was.

He soon reached the forest edge, and he left the open sky behind, stepping onto rich soil. Time flowed with the seconds and years intermingled to cause a feeling of everlasting comfort. He forgot all his questions and stood in the forest's green embrace, his mind at ease.

Moving forward, he watched as the plants turned with his passing, following his movement even as animals of all shapes and sizes joined him. He trekked towards the center of the forest as elk, mythical birds, and mighty lions guided him through rays of sunlight that bathed the air in mystery.

Looking around him, he watched the very spirits of the trees and streams rush past in a wild dance that made him want to join in. He didn't know why, but intense joy filled him at the thought.

Entering a glade, he turned in a circle, watching the forest move—as if with a life of its own—in dance. Looking into the center of the glade once more, he noticed a woman he hadn't before. Her hair, clothed in light, shone white while stained with soil; her hands were pristine. Around her, bright, colorful flowers rose from the ground, their petals blooming. Turning around, the woman looked into his eyes and smiled. When she spoke, it reverberated through the forest bringing with it new life

"Kaiźer," she hummed. "It's been too long."

Confused, he spoke in a soft voice. "Do I know you?"

The lady smiled. "We met once, and recently, many years back, the fold thinned enough for me to see you and help you once more."

Body quivering, his mind struggled to figure out when he had met this lady as he watched her move around the glade. She walked with a watery elegance, and her eyes glowed with hidden joy, and from behind her, the grass grew thicker, and the flowers grew brighter in reaction to her passing. His eyes followed the slow flow of her dress, and he watched its near translucent material move along her figure like smoke. He even caught a hint of olive skin through a slit along the side, and trailing his gaze along the inner curvature of her breasts, he stared at the fine lines of her collarbone, following them up to the slim curve of her throat.

His sight moved along her jaw, drawing in full rosy lips, a dainty nose, and big watery eyes. Eyes so beautiful and bright he couldn't decide what color they were. Shifting from silver to emerald to gold, he watched as azure, maroon, cobalt, platinum, bronze, and orange, each flashing as a myriad of colors one after the other. They swam in the depths of her eyes, occasionally rising to become prominent. Those eyes, framed with thick black lashes, captured his own. He watched as her lips moved and listened while her voice washed over him. Its sound was refreshing, rejuvenating, and cleansing in its passing. "Do you know why you're here, Kaiźer?"

He said nothing.

The lady smiled. "To understand your visit, you must first understand this gardens meaning"—she turned and spread her arms wide—"to start, this place we now stand in, is a realm between the worlds you know as the lands of the living and the lands of the dead. Think of it as a fence of sorts."

That caught his attention. "So, I'm dead?

"Not exactly, you are near death's doorstep, and our time is limited. Sin'ka is attempting to save you as we speak"—she gestured to his heart—"as a vampire, you know what she is, but as the reincarnation of your first love, you have yet to know what she will be. I'd advise you to protect her. The Jackals Court led you to believe your life's goal was to wipe out her kind as well as those similar"—the lady motioned to the forest around them—"you found that to be wrong. As a Hunter, your job is to protect the very people you hunt. This place reacts to those who behold it, and for you, it sees a pure man of heart and soul. Heed my words, and don't forget," Putting a hand over his heart, she stared into his eyes. "Sin'ka is someone who needs you. You are not a Jackal. You're a warrior, and a warrior protects the weak"—she gave him a soft push—"now wake."

With an ethereal sound, he grew weightless once more, moving parallel to the land and sky. He watched as the stars above morphed. As if captured in a kaleidoscope, they rippled and moved as he sank into the soil. Breaking into icy shards, the grass and the land shattered around him. His clothes unraveled from his figure, and with a flash of light, his sight became white. Fading through grey and black, his very soul screamed as his body burned with energy too strong to contain.

Becoming aware of soft grass tickling his backside, he awoke with a start, letting out a snarl befit a beast. Flashing white, his body drained of the power it struggled to contain. He slumped after a few seconds, falling back onto the grass beneath him. Taking deep breaths, he listened to the stron heart, feeling his chest heave with its n realized; ragged breathing overl ened his eyes in confusion and f el hovering above him.

Staring bac m, she knelt over him, her clothe and he felt her place a hand on his existence.

"You're alive," ng, Kaiźer suddenly watched her eyes fl apsed. He wrapped his arms around her as she on his chest, quickly lifting her. Glancing at her unconscious form, he took in her fiery hair, delicate shape, and mature features and thought about what the lady in the garden had said. He looked at her then as both, Sin'ka the ShadoWalker and Abika, his love from days past. Nuzzling his chest, she slept as he turned east.

Kaizer

chapter 3: the Hunted Becomes the Hunter

True love is unknown to me but I feel its heat with each greeting I see. She knows not that I exist but still I crave her hand upon my cheek.

Prince Skyler of house Vermilion
The Age of Knowledge

Stepping into his small home, Kaiźer carried Sin'ka to the bedroom. He set her atop the sheets and pulled the pillows out from under the blankets. He then lowered her head onto them. Moving slowly so as not to wake her, he checked her wounds. At first glance, he was confused. She didn't have the depth of damage he was expecting, but at closer inspection, he watched as a few of her wounds faded before his very eyes. He marveled at her healing capabilities. Even with a full feeding, most ShadowFolk took hours to heal, some even days. She was something else, but to think, a vampire. He would never have guessed. Laying a blanket over her, he blew out the single candle that sat beside her upon the bedside table as he stood up and turned to go. He was grateful, but he didn't think he was ready. Once Sin'ka woke up, he didn't know what would happen. He stopped in the doorway then, lost in thought, and stood there for a long moment, caught between going through with what he was about to do and walking away.

Frustrated, he closed the door with a soft click and headed to the kitchen. Moving to the center island, he dropped his head into his hands and let out a heavy sigh. He rested his arms on the cherry wood and looked through his fingers at the bedroom door, behind which Sin'ka lay. She had been hurt by his hand, and he felt a pain in his chest that wouldn't go away. He had promised never to injure Abika, and Sin'ka was her incarnate, so his promise carried to her as well. He dropped a fist onto the pressured tile without another thought. Releasing the countertop, he uncovered the hidden compartment inside the island.

Picking up the item within, he lifted it out, walked into the main room, and sat down in its center. Same as during his visit to the Eternal Pool, he settled in the traditional lotus position and faced the far wall. Placing the item in front of himself, he ran a hand along its length.

Made from Dragonstar alloy, its pure black blade was impervious to damage. Etched along the hilt to flow up to its length, the engraving that gave it its name glowed incandescently. The engraving depicted the dragon spirit trapped inside centuries before and flowed from deep within the blade. Its incandescent hue was lighting the very air around the blade's edge as if trying to break through the metal.

As he gripped the hilt, the dragon's eyes flashed and moved to look at him. Filling his mind, the voice he'd come to find comfort in spoke.

~So, you still run from your destiny, young warrior~

"You know I hate killing," he said, tightening his grip.

~I also know that you know that I know that you know, you can't turn away from the only thing you know. Take what the seer said and use it. You're not a Jackal anymore, so be something more~ it stated in response.

Before his master's master had constructed the black blade he held now, his companion had run rampant in the world.

That had been seven thousand years ago. Thinking back to the day he'd found the sword, he smirked at his ignorance back then. What he'd thought to be a standard sword had been a mighty prison. It had sucked his spirit inside itself, and he'd spent the next three days in the blade's cage side by side with Kaín Algoria, a black dragon once mighty—but now slave—to the blade's magic.

After releasing him, his master had told him that he had decided to let him stay in the blade for a time with his snooping. His master had been behind him at the time of his mistake. He guessed his master thought it a fitting punishment for him to stay in the sword to teach him not to mess with things he didn't yet understand.

~Hehehe, I remember that. I immensely enjoyed your company. It had been a long time since I'd seen a fellow human~

"You tried to devour my soul!"

~I rest my case, quite enjoyable indeed~ Kaín chuckled.

Standing up, he turned in a slow circle, his movements controlled. He swung Kaín in a wide arch, going through moves he hadn't done in a long time. It was calming in a way, the blade's comfortable weight causing his muscles to bunch and ripple with tension.

~Ha, at this speed, I feel like I'm floating. Still got your steady hand, I see~

Butting into his concentration Kaín began to whisper a multitude of strategies long forgotten to time. With smooth precision, he flowed through them, striking falcon in water, heron bending past crane, sweeping fire to turning sea, and so on until he felt his mind calm and his body relaxed. As he moved, Kaín whispered a group of combinations designed to let the user strike out at the opponent while keeping up an unbreakable block, and he remembered on whom he'd last used the fighting style.

With a start, he dropped the sword as if it had burned him. Kaín had been having him run through the killing blows he had used to fight Darzíel, while his friends had sealed him in the mirror dimension.

He dropped to his knees as hot tears filled his eyes. Letting them flow down his face, he turned his gaze to the ceiling. Kaín lay beside him, a reminder of what he had lost.

"Why did you do that?" he growled.

~You need to face your demons at some point, Kaiźer!~

"Gũnder and Meagän gave her lives because they had no choice in the matter,"—he cried out in agony, falling prostate as the words fell from his lips—"You Know That!"

~They knew how you felt, ~ Kaín said softly. *~They did what they did because it was obvious you couldn't stop him if they didn't ~*

"If I had known, I would have—"

~You would have what? Tried to stop them? You need to stop punishing yourself because of what happened in the past!~ Kaín shouted back

"Shut up!" he snarled, wiped a hand across his face. "Just shut up,"

Silent, Kaín retreated from his consciousness.

He didn't know how long he sat there on the floor, but when a loud creak sounded behind him, he straightened his back, sitting up abruptly. Standing in the doorway to his bedroom, Sin'ka stood silent with a worried look in her eyes.

He turned, hiding his face. "How long have you been there?" he asked.

Moving forward, she came to sit behind him. "When you shouted, I came to see what was wrong. I didn't expect to find you like such. I'm sorry." Putting a hand on his back, she traced a hidden design on his skin. He had yet to put a shirt on, and he blushed at the contact.

"It's fine," he said softly.

Sin'ka shifted behind him, but she didn't move. He didn't move either. He didn't want to scare her. She thought him a Hunter and didn't know of his vows, so he let her examine his back, breathing slowly as her soft touch sent shivers down his spine. It had been years since he had felt a woman's touch.

"When did you get this scar?" Sin'ka asked suddenly. "It looks painful." Her fingers were trailing along his back lightly, and he realized after a second that she was tracing a dragon. Starting at his right shoulder, it traveled down his back and flowed along his hip to disappear under his jeans.

"Such a scar never lay upon my skin... it must have happened when the lightning struck me."

He began to tell her about his visit to the mysterious garden, telling her what the seer had said about the two of them minus the part where she was Abika's reincarnation, and as he talked, Sin'ka shifted to sit in front of him. Closing his eyes with a hand, she started to shadow her fingers over his face. With a soft touch, she trailed her fingers over his nose, lips, and jaw to find his old battle scars. In 3570 A.B., he had been following a wild banshee that had been on a killing spree. She'd caught him unawares and had dealt a deadly blow, slashing across his throat, cutting him from his left ear to his right collarbone. He had been near death when he'd stumbled into the streets of a nearby town. He had been lucky to survive.

Sin'ka followed it down to the Y-shaped scar he'd received just the day before when a wild forest daemon had tried to cut out his heart. Jagged and still sensitive, he flinched at her touch. Pulling away, she apologized. He was about to tell her not to worry when her hands grazed his hip suddenly. She'd found it, huh. Moving along its length, she let her fingers delve under the lip of his slacks. He shivered at the sensation as her hand followed its entirety.

"How did you get this one? It looks different than the others."

As Sin'ka followed the scar that fell beneath his jeans, kaiźer watched her closely. At her question, he softly took her hand in his and moved it down his leg. She blushed at the contact but didn't pull away.

"During my... training," he stated, "I would go out to gather and cut firewood. One day I was deep in the woods when I stumbled upon a lone demon. Being alone, I went for my sword, and she attacked, but she wasn't there to kill me."

Sin'ka looked at him in shock. Slowly a smile grew on her lips, and she looked at him with a twinkle in her eyes.

"What did she do?"

Grinning, he looked at her and, with a supple accent, began to tell her the story.

Kaiźer lay in the dirt, his sword out of reach, as she straddled him. She was wearing a silk sash that hung from her hips, its ends tied at her sides. Her breasts were bare, and being only sixteen years of age, Kaiźer was struck dumb at the sight of her. He'd never seen a naked woman before today, and she took full advantage of that predicament.

Kaiźer couldn't escape. She had him trapped by her beauty. It was like a flame that burned within his sight. Kaiźer was lucky to remember that he had his knife hidden in his boot.

Grabbing it, he stabbed the Witch in her abdomen with a flourish. No hesitation was given as he acted, for he knew no ordinary woman walked around with skin of violet, her ears tipped with red.

As he did so, a small flame appeared within her chest and burst from her skin to float weightlessly without a source. It mesmerized him as it flickered, so when the Witch began to shake and shudder, he didn't notice.

With a cry, he watched the flame grow and realized too late what was happening.

He tried pushing her off of his chest, but she was glued to him. He began to panic, throwing his hips up as he grabbed her arms and twisted her to the side. Still, she did not budge! Watching the flame pulse, he despaired when it doubled in size suddenly.

Throwing his arms up, he shut his eyes tight. But not a second after, an intense rushing sensation ran through his gut, and his eyes snapped open.

He found himself being dragged away by an on known being, and with a grunt, he heard a blade slide free of a sheath and saw the metal of the dagger flash right before it was thrust into the temple of the Witch.

She convulsed atop him and, with a cry, separated from him. A boot flashed into his vision, and the lady blasted away, her ribs cracking under the impact.

"No! He's Mine!"

Her cry reached his ears, the words escaping from her lips as a fire lit within her throat, and Kaiźer's eyes went wide as her skin began to broil from the inside out. Her body self-combusted as he was pulled away by the stranger.

As suddenly as she had vaporized, Kaiźer watched, unable to do a thing, as his knife was hurled free from her body towards him. Its blade slashed into my leg, entering mid-thigh to slice up and bounce off my hipbone.

So painful was the wound, he gave a roar and felt his magic abrupt from his skin with a frenzy.

So sudden was the outburst, he blacked out.

Sin'ka gasped in horror and, looking down at his leg, stared in wonder. She looked back up at him with bright eyes, and he grew uncomfortable. Her eyes hinted at what he had been feeling since yesterday. Abika had always found his stories fascinating with how he told them, but now he felt awful. Such feelings were all wrong. She didn't know him as he knew her.

He stood up abruptly. "I think I'm going to go, and uh... are you hungry by any chance?"

Sin'ka looked stunned, but after a second, she nodded slightly. "Oh, uh sure, I could eat something. What were you thinking?"

Stumbling for something to say, he looked around, suddenly lost. "I don't know, uh, what about, uh. I have tea and some cured meat in the cellar?" He blushed as the words stumbled out of his mouth. Mortified, he stuttered as he tried to find a way to clarify.

Sin'ka became lost in stitches. "You look a the mouse that's just been caught by a canary. Don't worry, I'll fix us something to eat. Do you want to help?"

Nodding, he followed her into the kitchen.

Stay calm, Kaiźer; you're a trained warrior. You held your cool with Abika. At least you did, partly. You can do this!

At least he hoped he could.

Kaiźer was shocked at first. He'd been told the only thing that a ShadoWalker could consume was the blood of others. Sin'ka proved that false! It held no nutritional value and didn't affect her physically, but all the same, the rumor that food tasted like dust to her kind was not valid.

Watching Sin'ka dice up many colorful foods, he was soon entranced by her fluid movements as she danced around the kitchen. From memory, she created a multitude of dishes and afterward finished with effortless cleanup. In record time, they were settled down in the main room.

He started by explaining why he was no longer a Hunter, telling her how he'd moved around a lot after leaving the Jackals Court, but Sin'ka kept her thoughts to herself even after telling her about his vows. She didn't say much when she did speak, her words short and to the point, till they soon sat in silence while they ate.

Taking small bites, he watched as she fiddled with her food. Unable to take it, he broke the silence.

"What am I to you?"

Looking up, Sin'ka raised an eyebrow.

"I mean, after..."—he looked at her from the corner of his eye—"after what happened?"

Sin'ka gazed at the wall for a bit, her mouth opening and closing. She didn't know what to think. He'd been struck by lightning, and nothing had happened. She had seen a few things since her turning worthy of such, but what had just happened? It far outreached anything she had seen so far. He was unscathed except for the dragon that had been burned onto his back. She was at a loss for words.

"I..."

He smiled as if knowing her thoughts. "You're wondering why I'm unscathed."

Could he read her that easily? Usually, it was the other way around. However, she couldn't read him at all. He was a black hole for her. It was as if she'd been hidden from sight.

"Yes."

"Well, that is something you will have to find out on your own."

Sin'ka looked at him in shock, but he only smiled. He had her. She wouldn't stop till she learned his story. This he knew from experience. "On another note, how long have you owned The Lover' Bite?"

She dropped her gaze and stared at the floor. "About twelve years now... although... it's about time I moved on. People are starting to notice my age; I should be forty-three by now."

"Hey, you don't age! You should consider yourself lucky. You're immortal and get to experience the world from a completely different perspective compared to a mortal."

"Yes, but such a life has been lonely."

He stood and gestured to the window. The sun was gone, but the moon was bright, and it glowed against the night sky. "You're what, 200 years old?"

"Something like that?"

"Okay, now what if I told you that I'm just under 1,500 years old."

Sin'ka gasped. "No way!"

"Yes, way! You travel a lot, I'm guessing?" so I can easily say in total confidence that I know full well how lonely immortality can be without spending it with people.

She nodded. Kaiźer could have said it without hesitation. Most immortals can't live in one place for long if they're not with a companion. Most who tried ended up losing something of themselves. He knew from experience and remembered the soul tearing sensation of abandonment.

He could see Sin'ka through the ages, changing with the times, but he compared her to Abika. So far, she was a perfect match in every way, all the way down to the way she smiled.

"If you traveled, I imagine you found someone you relate to, right?"

"I guess..."

He frowned. "You guess?"

"Well, she isn't exactly your average walk-in-the-park kinda person."

He smiled at that. "That's okay, as long as you felt alive?"

"You can say that."

Sin'ka grinned, and he mentally cheered. She had someone who had been there for her then, and it was a lady friend to boot. He hoped that didn't mean the woman he loved was gay.

"She gave my life a sense of meaning. It was as if I was meant for something. You know what I mean?"

"Yep, I do." *Please be but only friends.*

Sin'ka looked at him, and he smiled. She was glowing, and it was rubbing off. He felt like he had back in the day when things had been right with the world.

"You know..."

Sin'ka raised an eyebrow. "Know what."

"You don't look a day over 100."

She looked at him for a second, and he began to fear he had said the wrong thing when she doubled over in laughter. Her hiccups came in heaves, and it was so sudden he sat there for a moment, not knowing what to do. Was she okay? He had been sure that...?

Sin'ka sat back up and, giggling, hid behind her hair. "That's not funny," she finally heaved with a long breath.

Grinning, he looked at her. "Not funny? Why would I try to be funny? You are beautiful, and if you think I'm kidding, then I'll show you just how serious I am."

Leaning forward over the table, he kissed her. Looking down, she didn't see him till his lips touched hers. At first, she didn't move, and he feared she might pull away and slap him, but slowly she relaxed, moving to kiss him back. Their lips mingled, and he tasted peppermint. He gathered her into his arms, lifted her over the table, and rested her in his lap.

Pulling away, he looked at her. "If I thought you weren't beautiful, would I have done that?"

Eyes glazed and half-lidded, she was leaned forward slightly; her mouth opened as if about to speak. She had lifted off Kaiźer somewhat, and slowly she focused her gaze as he smiled at her, but what he saw made him freeze in place. The silver of her eyes was flooded red in her passion. He knew the fact, but he still thought of the blood lust that usually came hand in hand with that passion if she lost control.

Sensing his hesitation, Sin'ka fell back onto her legs and, with eyes now silver, looked at him with worry.

"Are you alright?" she asked, placing a hand on his cheek. He jumped at the contact, not registering her question. He was too deep in memory.

Screams filled his mind; blood swam thick, its sticky texture surrounding him from past kills, and in a flash flood, it tormented him.

He stood in a dark room, surrounded by old allies, their bodies still holding their mortal wounds. A heavy object filled his hand, and looking down, he found his hand grasped around the black blade he'd come to call a friend.

"Kaiźer?" a female voice said fearfully. Looking up, he saw Sin'ka cowering before him, her hands covering her mouth.

However, she melted away, becoming replaced by his uncle. Looking at him with cold eyes, his old teacher stood before him, covered in thick leather, his dagger dripping with blood, his wife's blood. His rage peaked, and he rushed forward, catching him by the throat.

"You, why did you betray me? Why did you betray Maliki?" Seeing his uncle was bringing it all back. "You killed my beloved! We could have found a way that wouldn't have involved her death."

He raised his arm unconsciously, placing his sword to his uncle's neck. "Only a demon would torment me so. Tell me why I shouldn't kill you now," he growled.

His arm suddenly flashed, and his sword heated. Materializing next to him, a man with reptilian eyes and long wild hair stood gripping his shoulder.

~You can't kill her, Kaiźer!~ Kaín said insistently. *~Wake up! This isn't Ryeznya!~*

"I must avenge her death," he yelled at him, tears rolling down his face.

Kaín's words were clear as flames bloomed in the palm of his hand as he pulled his arm back. *~If you don't listen to reason, then via pain, I pray you will!~*

With a flash, Kaín threw his hand into Kaiźer's chest, burning a ruin into his breast. Crying out, his vision flashes white as his chest sizzled from the magic. When his sight returned, he was back in his apartment.

Realizing what had happened, he followed his arm to where he held Kaín hot and glowing against Sin'ka's throat. With a soft cry, he let go of her, stumbling back in shock.

He flung the black blade away and fell to his knees, staring into Sin'ka's eyes as she stood against the wall, her arms held aloft like she was fending off a wild beast.

He sat silent, unable to speak after what he had almost done. Voice shaking, he finally said.

"You need to go," he said, his voice hoarse. "I think it best if you... you can't be here."

Stepping forward, Sin'ka moved towards him, her mouth open as if to say something. He didn't let her.

"Don't!" he snapped. "Don't come near me...."

Closing her mouth, Sin'ka purses her lips, wounded. She turned away and rushed for the door. She gripped the handle but, at the last second, turned. "I know your pain. If you need, I will be here." She pulled a card from her jacket and set it on the table beside the door. Doing so, she slipped out into the night without another word.

He sat in silence, tears threatening to run free; she had seen his dark side and yet, hadn't been afraid. Another similarity he noted from times long past.

After he assembled his thoughts, he rose and retrieved his sword from the floor. Walking back to the kitchen, he set Kaín down on the center island and waited without taking his hand from the hilt.

~She's a wonderful woman that Sin'ka. Be thankful I'm a part of you because if I weren't, I wouldn't have been able to force you from that vision~ Kaín finally said.

"I almost killed her," he said as he turned a dial counter-clockwise twice and then clockwise once to open the hidden compartment in the wall. Silent and swift, the wall swung open. Pulling the door open fully, he grabbed the contents within before shutting the door, letting it seal shut with a small puff of air. The wall became whole, leaving not even a tiny seam. If someone looked, nothing would be visible but blank stone.

~Yes, but you didn't ~

Dressing quickly, he dawned his dragon scale armor and strapped his gauntlets on. He closed the safe, turning as it slid back into place, the oven racks falling back into place silently.

Facing the island, he slid Kaín into his sheath. Strapped to his back Kaín chuckled. *~So, you're taking what the seer told you to heart?~*

"She told me that my people hunt the very people they should protect. It's about time I made up for past sins. Besides, Kurai Aka Hoshi is still out there," he stated.

~Then let's go, Kaiźer von Maliki~

Opening the kitchen window, he looked out over the city, his hair whipping around in the wind as the lights below lit the night sky.

~ Let's hunt!~

The two of them jumped into the night's dark embrace.

Jumping across a broad ally Kaiźer landed in a tight roll. Popping up, he didn't even lose speed. It had been years since he had done this, and as he had expected, he had stumbled over the first few rooftops, his lands a bit shaky occasionally. Kaín commented on his lack of practice, but he ignored him; he didn't need the guy's two cents to know he was rusty. He was running through the slums of Nypheriam with his senses on high alert, and he couldn't afford to miss even one small detail. Moving with the shadows that draped across the buildings, he passed over the city like a wraith. Reaching the upper-class side of town, he dropped into a thin ally, landing in a low crouch.

Gathering his magic, he cloaked himself in the alley's shadows, gathering them around himself. The trick was simple enough, allowing him to hide from sight even in a well-lit room. He could stand in a dark corner, and no one would notice until he moved. It came in handy when eavesdropping. He recalled that he had been curious to know what the clan's women did in their meetings. Chuckling slightly, he recalled how he had walked out with a deep blush on his cheeks. Not only had the woman talked of battle, but they had also spoken of their men as if they were talking about knitting; it had taken a while before he had been able to meet their eye whenever he had seen them after that.

Grinning, he stood flat against the wall and peeked out from behind the stone. Right now, he had other reasons for using his ShadowStep; he needed info.

Civilians passed by unaware as he stood there wreathed in darkness, and his target, a tiny man in a lord's coat and breeches, was walking down the street just a few yards away from where he waited.

The man, or should he say, the *Demon*, wore a disguise and an expensive one from what he saw. As an assassin, he usually took jobs for the people in the higher-ups. From what he knew, the man had worked with Darzíel for a short time, and he hoped that he would spill what he knew about the Fallen with a bit of grilling.

As the guy passed by, he swiftly yanked the guy into the shadows and covered his mouth, placed Kaín against its spine as he did.

"If you move, you're dead. If you shift, you're dead. All I wish for is to know about Darzíel's whereabouts," he stated quietly.

"Oíe, watch da skin!"

He growled and twisted the blade slightly. He didn't have time for this

The demon raised his hands. "Chill, man, if I tell ya, will ya let meh go?"

He pushed on the sword. "If I let you go, will you keep following the young lady you've been tailing for the last twelve blocks?"

The man froze but didn't answer.

"If you agree to stop following her, then I'll let you go, but only after you tell me what I want to know."

"Yeah, whatever ya want, pal, ya got it."

"That's what I want to hear. Now about Darzíel, tell me!"

The demon took a breath and started talking. "I can't say for certain; da guy moves round a lot. But I do know dere to be a gathering at the docks in an hour from now. If ya hurry, ya might still catch da show."

"What kind of show?" he asked.

"How shou I know, agh! Fine. Some low-level demons are summonin' the guy. They wish ta strike a bargain with im."

"A summoning you say...."

The demon nodded enthusiastically. "Yeah, now can ya let meh go—

Ignoring his words, he thrust the sword between the demons' ribs, puncturing his heart. He burst into flames, and his essence was sucked into the black blade. He wouldn't be coming back anytime soon.

He cleansed the area of his scent as well as the hellfire scent of the demon's death, and after one final check, he cast a cloak over himself and merges with the passing crowd. To anyone who looked, he was an average man in jeans and a t-shirt.

He had a show to watch.

Moving over the docks, Kaiźer reached the place he was looking for and, jumping up, landed on a stack of massive crates in a low squat. Just a few paces away, the group of demons his *friend* had mentioned sat in a small circle on the lower dock.

They flowed as one with their arms locked. They were chanting with mixed voices, and not too soon, Kaiźer cursed. He barely dropped behind the crate in time when the portal opened in a blast of magic. Peeking out from behind the now twisted metal of the container, he looked at the group.

Ruins burned around them from the portal's forced opening and glowing red-hot; the ethereal anomaly hung within their circle like a canvas of writhing darkness. Kaiźer watched the gash ripple slightly and waited until just as the demon had said, Darzíel arrived, stepping out like the immortal he was. With wings of the purest black spreading out behind him, the man looked just as he had a hundred years ago, the only difference being the scar Kaiźer had given him just before sealing him away. It had healed, but the skin was raised slightly and stood out against his eye.

Everything else of his screamed elegance and masculinity, even his eyes, which were something he wouldn't long forget. Hidden under long white hair that hung loose and tangled, they glowed with an inner fire and looked to be carved of stone.

Although he frowned at the man's clothing choice, he should say total lack thereof since it was nonexistent. He glared at the man's arousal, still quite the cocky one, huh.

Pushing his irritation aside, he hid his presence as quickly as possible, essentially blocking both his physical and spiritual body from prying eyes. It would do no good if he were spotted now.

Darzíel had yet to move and stood before the demons, his face a mask of nonchalance. He looked up when the demons grew restless. He watched as one of the miniature monsters broke away from the others.

"Oh, Great One, we wish to serve."

Looking down at him, Darzíel said nothing, and the little guy fidgeted under his gaze. Even Kaiźer began to feel antsy. Was the Fallen just going to stand there in all his apparent glory? The demon who'd spoken up was about to speak again, and Kaiźer craned his neck in anticipation as Darzíel broke the silence.

"You shall serve...."

The demons breathed a sigh of relief, but it was short-lived as Darzíel spoke up again.

"...as my entertainment!" he continued, pooling fire into his hands before his last word was even complete.

The demons broke ranks, all attempting to escape Darzíel's path. One after another, he killed them, leaving piles of smoking ash in their place. Kaiźer watched it all from his high vantage point without a drop of despair for the little buggers. With each demon he killed, Darzíel sucked their escaping spirits into his body, strengthening himself with their essence. That wasn't a fun fact to know, but he could do nothing without letting his presence become known. He could only watch and wait.

When everyone was gone, Kaiźer surveyed the area's aftermath as the Fallen reopened the portal with a wave of his hand.

When he did, Kaiźer took a chance and drew on his magic once more to study the portal in the magical spectrum. When he passed through into a low realm of the Underworld, though, he frowned. What business could Darzíel possibly have in the Underworld? He had looked too long already, he knew, and quickly released the magic, but it was too late.

Darzíel turned around in a blur, and even as he let the magic go, Darzíel looked directly at him. He froze.

He'd been spotted! His fear was fleeting, however. When Darzíel looked up, his gaze continuing past without pause. Letting out a slow breath Kaiźer didn't move a muscle as the Fallen stepped backward into the swirling portal. As soon as it closed around him, Kaiźer slumped to the stone of the docks. His hands shook with adrenaline, despite everything. He'd been prepared to fight for his life if need be. However, with nowhere to put his energy, he shook from the aftershock. It had been a narrow escape. If he hadn't cut off his magic when he had, he would have been spotted for sure.

Moving down to the dock, he walked over to the smoking remains of the demons. They had been reduced to piles of ash, some of them not even that much remained. Pulling Kaín out, he began to chant. Magic bloomed along the blade, and with a prayer, he cleansed the area. Once it was complete, he turned and, without a backward glance, headed home. He had work to do. Besides, he knew he would need more manpower to get it done.

He needed Oníx.

Sinka

chapter 4: the past returning

Remember my command. Know my law. Follow my last order and know my name, for the Queen will never forget; a rule to be broken.

First Adviser to the House of Starasix
The Enchanted Age

Walking into her house, Sin'ka slammed her door in frustration. She couldn't help but think it had been something she'd done, but how could she have known something like that would happen. And to think she had told him she would be there for him. She was an idiot! He'd clearly become lost in some horrid vision and hadn't wanted to worry her. Why else would he have made her leave like he did?

Leaving the foyer, she moved down the hall and headed to her room. She moved without thinking, undressing as she went. She kicked her shoes into the closet as she threw her clothes onto the bed. Not stopping, she stepped into the adjoined bathroom and headed straight for the clawfoot tub near the back of the large bath. She turned on the hot water and listened as it ran hot.

As she stood there waiting for the water to heat, she thought back to what had transpired before at Kaiźer's place. He had been so strong and masculine. He had made her warm inside, and she had been lost for words, as they had eaten. It had been a shock to have him kiss her so suddenly too, but when he had lifted her up like she had weighed nothing, she had felt herself throb inside with both arousal and bloodlust and his lips had only made it worse. Gods! Ridding herself of her undergarments, she stepped into the water; and let herself sink into its depths. A soft sigh escaped her lips as the hot water warmed her cold skin. She was soon flushed from the heat, and grabbing the soap, she washed the grime of the night free from her limbs, her mind still going over what happened at Kaiźer's.

Why had he seemed afraid? He was huge, a warrior, and that sword he'd held? No Otherworlder or human alike had the skill to craft such a weapon. She'd never seen anything like it, but more so, the man behind the blade. To think that such a man was out there. He'd seemed so familiar to like she'd know him. The way he'd moved, the way he'd spoken, all of it gave her a tingling sensation all over. She would have known if such a man had been in her life and she had for sure never met anyone like him in the whole two hundred years she'd been alive. Submerging herself, she let the suds wash free of her. She could hear the surface splash from under the water as it grazed the edges of the tub. She could have stayed this way for hours, submerged, but as she floated just below the surface, her mind picked up on how hungry she was.

After only a slight hesitation, she emerged and stepped out onto the lush rug that circled the floor around her tub and grabbed her robe before walking into her wardrobe. Vast and full to overflowing, it had everything you could think of, but what she wanted wasn't on a hook or a shelf but in a hidden room behind the entire floor-to-ceiling mirror she had at the very back of her closet. Moreover, only after pressing the trigger to open the small compartment and retrieving what she desired did she return to her room, sitting on her queen-sized bed, item in hand. Opening to its first page, she read the words that had changed her life.

"This book is the property of
Julian Alexander the IV"

She'd taken the book to remind herself of who she was and had learned a lot from its pages. It covered in detail what a vampire was and how Julian had come to be one. His findings were written down, starting with how he'd been turned and how to create another like himself. It talked of how he'd learned to control his thirst and of how, when he had chosen not to feed, he'd gone crazy, slaughtering his whole village. She had taken what he'd learned and used it herself. What he had failed; she'd accomplished. She had yet to lose control because of the book she held before her. She also knew of the ShadowFolk, those born to the vampire bloodline, true-bloods that lived within the Kingdom of Twilight. They were said to have changed others into ones like themselves, but it had been a lost knowledge for the last three ages.

Closing the journal, she ran a hand over its cover. Lifting it to her chest, she fell back onto the bed. *Is Julian out there still? He said he'd protect me... so why did he leave?* These questions had been in her mind since the club, but she hadn't the answers to them. He was *changed* and had written everything he learned as he went. But not once in his writings was there a word that spoke about the ShadoWalkers.

Dropping the book onto the bed, she rose and stretched, shrugging the warm robe from her shoulders. Looking down at her physique, she took in her pure alabaster skin. She had always loved the way her hair stood stark red against her pale complexion, and moving to stand before her polished silver mirror, she gazed along with her shapely figure.

She ran her gaze along the flat contours of her belly, following the round curve of her hips. She moved her gaze along the smooth curves of her firm thighs as well as her calves until she reached her dainty feet. She wiggled her toes with a smile.

So far, she'd been immune to the scourge of time, and as a vampire, the only change had been her change into womanhood. As the years had passed, she had slowly aged to full maturity. She was no longer the sixteen years of age she'd been. Therefore, when looking at herself in the mirror now, she marveled at her figure. She looked to be in her late twenties, early thirties now, with the rosy cheeks and full lips she had once envied her mother for.

She turned away; the idea of home was challenging. She still got homesick at times. She walked out onto her balcony, which overlooked the rocky mountainside that her house sat upon. Standing within the wind, she let her hair move about in the slow breeze. Closing her eyes, she tilted her face heavenward. Drinking in the wind, she let everything fade from her mind, leaving only the feeling of the cold air and the feeling of freedom… at least up until her portable source link went off.

With a start, she rushed inside. Flashing into the bathroom, she dug her magic shell out of her pants before looked at the codex. It was most likely the man she'd been supposed to meet the day before. However, it said unknown, but that was normal; most of her clients used private numbers.

"Hello? Gregaren? Listen, I'm so sorry about yesterday. I was distracted by… well, it doesn't matter. What matters is that I left you hanging."

"I don't know who this Gregaren is, but he shouldn't be mad at you. It's been too long; how have you been, my dear?"

If she hadn't heard it, she wouldn't have believed it. Could it be? How long had it been?

"Onix?" she practically squealed. "Oops, sorry, oh my god! I'm doing well; what about you?"

"Sorry about the abruptness," Onix said smoothly. "I'm doing well. It's good to hear your voice after so many years."

"Why the sudden contact? I thought you were out of the country on a dig?"

"I was," Onix said quickly. "But an old friend of mine called and said he'd found something he knew I'd be interested in."

"And were you?"

"Let's just say I've been looking for it for some time. So yes," Onix stated. "But before I tell you about it, I'd like to know what you're wearing?"

Looking down at herself, she stared at her bare breasts. "Why do you want to know?" she asked.

"Because I love your choice of clothes—oh!" Onix's voice merged with the room as she suddenly walking through her door. Turning, Sin'ka stared as Onix stopped before her, her eyes taking in her nubile body appreciatively. "Actually, on second thought, I love the new look." She grinned wickedly, her eyes twinkling.

She gasped, "Onix!" Covering herself, she blushed.

"Oh, don't flatter yourself. I've seen you naked countless times. But I don't think I've seen you in this kind of lighting before; it's quite... sensual," Onix said seductively.

Her blush deepened.

Suddenly Onix grew severe. Seeing the change, Sin'ka forgot her nakedness. "What's wrong?"

Onix looked at her. "I didn't come here to simply visit; I came to ask a favor."

"I'm listening."

"My friend and I can't do the new job alone. I came to ask if you'd like to join us. We could use your help."

She nodded. She didn't need to think twice about her answer; Sin'ka knew what she was going to say before Onix had even finished.

"I'd love to help in any way I can."

Giggling, the two of them danced around the room like two young girls before their first Midsummer Gala. Oníx smiled and took her hands in her own. She was glad to have Oníx home again. It felt like things were looking up for a change.

"So, who's this person who asked you to come back to the Five Kingdoms?" She asked as they danced around. "Have you known him long?"

"You can say that he's older than me, actually."

"Really?" she said in shock. "What's the man's name?" Oníx's answer, however, came as a shock. Sin'ka could see her friend hiring a big hunk as a business partner. He was most likely big and muscular with brains to match. However, the guy could very well be gay. Oníx was more into the ladies, and she would insist on working with someone who wouldn't flirt with her 24/7.

"Kaiźer."

"Uhhh,"—she stepped back—"what!"

After the surprise visit from Oníx, things become a jumble. Everything Sin'ka had been planning to do all flew out the window. She soon found time to grab a robe and gave Oníx the grand tour of her place. Simple yet well-decorated, her house was two stories: a living area, a dining room, a well-stocked kitchen, four bedrooms, and two baths. While the second floor had one bathing area, it was taken over by a single large room with two adjoining rooms on the north side, connected by a door between. She had commandeered the room for her training and had placed polished silver mirrors on every wall. It was basically an atelier of sorts. After seeing the house's entirety, Oníx settled in the living area while she went and got dressed.

Now here she was, sitting on her couch, watching Oníx move around the open floor of the room. It seemed unreal. Oníx looked just as she had a hundred years ago when

Sin'ka had met her in Londinium. She'd been working as an herbalist at the time. She had always had a knack for plants and took up the profession before turning, so naturally, it was something she had continued. Even now, with the turn of the century, new discoveries were changing the world for the better. Back then, the Kingdom of Sand had been alive with healers. Until the Jackals had come through with a purge, slaughtering anything otherworldly in the search for a traitor. There had seemed to be no reason behind the mindless killing, and the folks had packed up and moved away and or sailed to the old world of their ancestors. Even with what was happening, Sin'ka felt that she and Oníx weren't going to change much.

Oníx more so than her, she was still dressed in the traditional elven hunting attire, which consisted of a wrap covering her bust and a pair of tight slacks and high black boots laced up past his knees. Her skin, which was always tanned from all the geological digs she handled, gave her an Amazonian look, which in turn made her eyes stand out against its olive hue. Bright green, those eyes shone with an inner light, making her seem like she was always up to something. Her hair was still raven-black, though; it was longer than last she remembered. It seemed to shine in the light of the fireplace, too, as she browsed through her collection of books. She sat on the couch, her knees drawn up. She had put on a loose shirt and a pair of black pants that hung baggy around her legs.

Oníx soon flopped down beside her after browsing her bookshelves and held up a black-covered book on necromancy. "Do you mind if I borrow this?"

Sin'ka shrugged, unfolding her legs to sit cross-legged before Oníx as the book vanished over her shoulder. It disappeared through a small portal with a flash, and Sin'ka bit her lips as Oníx seemed to examine her. Sin'ka took a deep breath and tried to stay calm. Her mind swam with ideas of what the two of them would do if she asked her the one question that burned at the forefront of her brain.

Sitting here on the couch with her, she was barely in control as Oníx sat before her. She felt her chest heat, and afraid of Oníx seeing her arousal, she wrapped her arms around herself. "So..." She droned uncomfortable, looking at Oníx out of the corner of her eye.

She just kept studying her. The seconds crawled by, and Sin'ka began to feel self-conscious. She squirmed under her friend's intense gaze wondering the whole time what she could be thinking.

Oníx squealed suddenly, and her eyes lit up. She hopped up and down on the couch and clapped her hands excitedly.

"You have a thing for Kaiźer! Don't cha?"

"What! No... I mean... I don't know," she mumbled.

Looking at anything besides her friend, she fiddled with her shirt, and Oníx grinned.

"You do!" Oníx squealed again. She could feel her ears burning as she fiddled with the hem of her shirt. Looking down, she twisted the fabric, a smile growing on her face. "It just happened, we ran into each other, he works at one of my many high-end houses of all things, and then later I saw him in the woods outside of town. He was beautiful and ravishing with his blond hair and icy blue eyes. He was, oh, gods! I can't...." She trailed off, lost in her fantasies.

"I agree; he is quite ravishing indeed," Oníx breathed.

"Yah..." she sat obliviously, lost to the world. She imagined Kaiźer with his curly hair as it hung damp with sweat. She could see his muscles as they gleamed, bulging huge above her. Moreover, his eyes, oh his eyes, utterly full of passion and lust as he leaned down, his mouth capturing hers...

"Uh, Sin'ka, greetings to Sin'ka, come in Sin'ka! Is anybody home?" She heard Oníx saying.

She gasped, realizing what she had just been thinking about. She covered her mouth to hide her grin as she blushed, hoping Oníx hadn't noticed.

"It looks to me like little old Sin'ka needs to get laid! I bet he's been a gentleman and has yet to make a move."

Not quite, but damn, why did you have to notice? Mortified, she sat with her head in her hands, wishing the world would end.

"Don't worry, I think it's cute," Oníx said happily. Grinning, she punched her in the shoulder, "Now I think we should go out and have a bit of fun. It's been like what, twelve years since we last saw each other?" Oníx grabbed her hand and pulled her off the couch to drag her towards her room.

"Where are we going?" she giggled.

"We're going to get dressed," Oníx stated. "It's time to go blow off some steam."

She let Oníx pull her into her room, turning up the light of the lamp as she dragged her into her vast wardrobe. She had a wide selection of clothes to choose from, ranging from sunny and bright to Goth and gloomy. For years, she'd collected the most beautiful and fancy trends that the five Kingdoms had to offer. She had an insane love for shoes, which showed, taking up a good part of her closet.

And as she passed, Oníx grabbed a pair as she sat her down on one of the many stools, continuing to hold whatever else that caught her fancy. She soon had a heaping pile worthy of a queen, and Sin'ka sat watching her flutter about. Oníx soon stopped before her and held up a thin black dress that was form-fitted, with a long slit on one side

Facing her, Oníx held it up. "What do you think?"

"It's not really my color," she stated.

Putting the dress aside, Oníx moved towards her with a small smile. Raising a finger, she beckoned her forward, so she stood with a false huff of irritation and went to stand before the mirror. Tracing a hand down her back, Oníx took hold of her shirt and told her to raise her arms. Lifting the shirt free, she tossed it aside.

After pulling the drawstring on her pants, she stood nude before her friend and let her admire her appreciatively. It felt good to have someone see her like this. It was... comforting if that made any sense. It sounded awkward, but it was true; she reveled in her friend's gaze, and now that she thought about it, she wondered what Kaiźer would do if he saw her like this? Would he have the same look in his eye, or would he look at her in disgust and tell her to put her clothes back on. Gods! She was totally fucked. She most definitely expected his resignation on Monday, and he'd been such a great employee.

Still musing, she watched as Onίx picked a red dress from the pile, but she didn't turn till she had a pair of matching lace undergarments. Choices in hand, Onίx had a Cheshire grin on full display as she sauntered forward and presented them to her. Sin'ka shook her head in amusement but put them on all the same.

She soon stood in front of the mirror, looking at her reflection once more. The dress was a dark burgundy and made her skin glow. It was elven in design, hugging her figure like a second skin. Comprised of multiple layers of cloth, the fabric rippled in the light as she moved, and she did a twirl, letting Onίx enjoy her handy work.

Turning from the mirror, she saw that Onίx had yet to change. Raising an eyebrow, Onίx looked at her questionably. Gliding gracefully forwards, she went up to her and, placing a finger to her lips, whispered in her ear, "your turn."

Unraveling the wrap from around Onίx, she let the fabric fall to the floor. The material hadn't been tight, but as she was exposed to the cold air of the room, Onίx let out a slow breath. Sin'ka had always envied Onίx for her slight bosom, and she grew even more envious when she saw how dark the skin beneath the cloth was. She had been out in the sun; that was clear.

"Oníx, you're such a slut, been giving the boys at work an eyeful, have you?"

"Maybe..."

She knew better. The girls' skin was tanned; not a single color break was visible. She took the dress Oníx had been admiring earlier and held it up to herself.

"I think you should wear this tonight," she said softly.

Taking it from her, Oníx bit her lip as she looked at it admiringly. "Are you sure?"

Nodding, Sin'ka urged her to put it on. Grinning, Oníx slipped the black dress on and let it settle around her. It hugged her figure nicely, and she was able to see every curve as it clung to her like a second skin, even as it fell around her legs in silky waves.

Oníx stood before her, her eyes gleaming mysteriously, "What do you think? Is this sexy enough for you?" She ran a hand down her side and cocking a hip, shadowed her hand over the round curve of her rear, she gave a teasing smile. Next, she winked and blew a kiss as she did a twirl.

"I'll try my best to keep my hands off tonight."

"Awe, that's no fun; why would you say that?"

She just grinned and gave a quick shrug. "Oh, it's nothing personal. What now?"

Oníx grinned. "Time to hit the party,"

With that, they both ran outside, giggling the whole way, right up to the point where Oníx stopped, and turning away, held two fingers up to her lips and gave three sharp whistles. Dropping her hand, she turned her gaze to the sky and waited. Sin'ka came up beside her and looked at the heavens in anticipation.

Not long after their call, a streak of light flashed down from above and came to a dead stop, not inches off the ground a few feet from them. From within the blaze, a carriage materialized and from within, out stepped a toad-looking creature. With a wet sound, it smacked two fingers against the center of his forehead and then its lips before making a fist that he swept in an arch to meet against his chest that was the traditional meet and greet among the Nypherians.

Sin'ka held back a giggle at the man's attire and let Oníx shuffle her into the carriage. As the door shut, she waited as the gremlin hopped upfront. She hated traveling by *Rakariage*, but it was faster than her wings. Therefore, taking a deep breath, she readied herself as they became weightless, but too soon, her stomach rolled into her throat as they shot into the sky.

Coming out from the mountain pass, they roared into the bay area of Londinium. Passing through the city, it was only a couple minutes until they came to a stop in front of a house of sin called *The Red Fountain*. Known for its fine wines and scantily clad waitresses, its main entrance was packed with people trying to get in. They stopped in front of the main entrance just as a well-dressed young man came out. He opened the door to the carriage, and Sin'ka stepped out with a smile. The boy was dressed as a bellhop, and as Oníx came around the side, he openly gawked at them with an innocent eye. Just a boy Sin'ka had to assume he rarely saw such elaborate attire very often.

"Is the owner around?" she asked him.

The boy nodded slightly without taking his eye off Oníx, and she grinned at the look in the boy's eyes. Oníx's dress was definitely not something you got to see every day. Made from Gandian silk, it looked transparent in texture despite its dark color. It was a trick of the light that had been mastered by the merfolk, and it had been a gift from the lady Suk'reana during her stay in Ascaria two decades back. She noticed a few others besides the boy who gave appreciative glances in Oníx's direction. The two of them soon headed inside, their hips swaying as they moved past the two guards that stood on each side of the door, emerging through the hazy light to pick a table near the back of the room. Drinks were brought to their table, and

Sin'ka looked up at the lady as she set the glass before her. Dressed in a thin shift, she left nothing to the imagination, and Sin'ka wondered what kind of owner let their girls walk around half-naked. It wasn't proper, even for a place like this.

Sipping the creamy liquid, she just about choked as the spirits hit the back of her throat. She coughed to clear her lungs, but they cleared up before she could cough a second time. She was just taking a second sip when a striking man who looked to be in his forties came to their table. Oníx stood to meet him, and holding out his hand, she shook it slightly. It was a traditional greeting within the Kingdom of Sand, but she didn't see anything that would have showed him to be of such birth. He looked odd, but she couldn't place why. His skin was too light, hair too dark, and his eyes were violet in hue, and when he spoke, the deep baritone of his voice made his accent thick. After the introductions were done, he faced her, and she stood warily.

"Do not be frightened, Miss Sin'ka; Oníx here says you are a good judge of character, and I mean you no harm."

She could hear the truth in his words, and his heart didn't change in beat, but she still couldn't shake the feeling that something was off. "Pleasure," she said as he took her hand in his.

"Such flawless skin for one such as yourself," the man commented as he shook her hand. "Where are you from, if I may ask?"

Taking her hand back, she smiled shyly. "Why, thank you, I don't usually hear such compliments often. I am from Sha'arda."

The man paused for a second but recovered just as quickly as Oníx pulled up a chair for him. Sitting down across from her, he was joined by Oníx, but he seemed not to notice.

"Of course, such beauty is rare indeed. I did not see it at first. Most ShadoWalkers don't have hair of such... wild nature." He said with apparent unease. "The names Draghi, I own this fine establishment."

She gave a quick nod of her head in acknowledgment, but he had already let his attention get drawn away. He feared her for some reason. Most didn't bat an eye when she told them that she was from Sha'arda. So why was this man breaking out in a cold sweat at the mention of her origin? Was it why he felt off? Was he hiding something? She couldn't know unless she asked but now was not the time or place.

He seemed to have forgotten her, though. He was talking with Oníx as if Sin'ka were not even there in front of him.

"When you called to make reservations, I was delighted to please." The man was saying.

"Well, your services came recommended," Oníx said to him. Leaning forward slightly, she placed a hand on his chest, "and I wasn't just talking about the wine."

Swallowing, Draghi opened his mouth but said nothing. Sin'ka smelled his sudden arousal and rolled her eyes. Picking up her glass, she took another sip and cringed as they burned a path down her throat.

She listened to Oníx laugh and knew that her friend was simply playing with the man. She continued to sip her drink and heard from the sidelines, seemingly unnoticed until Oníx ended her teasing.

"—I must compliment you for trying, but I must inform you that I am taken."

Draghi laughed. "Well, I apologize for anything I may have said that upset you."

"Oh, don't worry, I think you're cute."

"Of that, I am glad to hear, but alas, I must bid you ladies a goodnight. Do enjoy yourselves." Draghi had been frowning towards the front of the club as he spoke, but she couldn't see what he was looking at, and as he stood to go, she noticed that his heart was racing.

Once he was gone, Sin'ka drained her glass, looked over at Oníx as she came, and sat next to her. Ordering a refill, her friend gave her a look that said *I hate that guy.* The waitress from before came and refilled her glass, and the two of them sipped their drinks—she couldn't stop her face from scrunching up each time she took a sip.

"I know you're not taken," she said finally.

"Not true; I'm with you right now, so technically, I am taken," Oníx said as she turned to face her.

Looking up at the second story Sin'ka watched as a few of the ladies who worked the establishment took the men courting them by the hand and led them away and out of sight. "Oníx, what does Kaiźer need your help for?" she said suddenly before looking over at her. She watched her face for some telltale sign of something, but her question didn't derive any physical reaction. Oníx turned back at her with a swivel of her chair and met her gaze with a frown. Oníx hadn't wanted to tell her before. She looked to be in the same mindset now, but Sin'ka wasn't going to let her keep her in the dark. She knew something big was going to be going down, and she wanted in. If it was a search for an ancient artifact, she knew her nose might come in handy.

"Come one, tell me. It won't kill me, right. If I can help, I will"—Sin'ka said as she took another sip from her spirits—"Oníx, if it's that bad, I don't mind. I know the kind of stuff you deal with daily."

Oníx scoffed. "You have no idea."

That came as a surprise. Oníx's sarcasm was so misplaced Sin'ka questioned its existence. Why would she say such? Was there something more profound to what Kaiźer had asked her to help with? If so, she wanted to know everything. It might even tell her a little about him. "Oníx, you know I can handle my own skin right. If you think I can't take it, I assure you I can."

"Oh, I know that," Oníx stated. "It's Kaiźer that I'm worried about. He..."—she paused as if unsure of what to say—"he doesn't want anyone else involved."

Sin'ka frowned. "That doesn't make sense. What's the big deal? Is there like some ancient curse involved?"

"No... sorta."

Sort of? That didn't convince her at all. Oníx was hiding something, and she was going to find out one way or another. She stood from her stool and was picking up her glass when a loud crash drew her eye. She looked up towards the back of the room.

With an explosion of wood, a body came flying through the wall. Limbs flailing, the guy sailed past to smash into the wall behind her. Peering through the hole he had left, she gasped when she saw who it was. Dressed in a silver suit, now torn and shredded, Draghi was slumped in the mud of the alley that sat outside, his face plastered with blood. Despite his ragged appearance, he looked the same as he had before except for one thing. His ears were curved to sharp points, and his skin was washed out. He looked like a walking corpse or an unconscious one, at least.

Oníx followed her gaze and gave a quick bark of laughter. "About time someone called him on his bullshit.

She looked at her friend with wide eyes and pointed at the guy. "His ears! He's not human; what is he?" she snapped in horror. She had been right when she had thought the guy had been hiding something. He had been wearing glamour! She mentally hit herself for not recognizing the scent before.

Oníx looked at her and was about to speak when a voice hollered from behind them. Echoing in a rich baritone, it reached her ears, and she raised an eyebrow at its familiar depth.

Turning, she gazed into the crowd of people that were trying to see what had happened. Standing among them was a tall blond mountain of a man. His clothes seemed ordinary, but when she sharpened her gaze, she thought she saw something hidden under them. But she couldn't really tell what she was missing. She let her sight relax and watched as Kaiźer stepped out of the crowd, and made his way towards them slowly.

Coming to stand beside her, he peered through the wall and raised his eyebrows in a questioning way. He had clearly been the cause of this and was playing the ignorant sideliner.

"What did he do to you to deserve such?" she asked him.

He smiled grimly but didn't answer, making it clear he wasn't going to say. Sin'ka gave a huff and stomped over to Oníx, who, in turn, scowled at Kaiźer. He met their stares with a blush, but just as quickly, it vanished, and before she could say anything, he stepped through the hole in the wall. As he disappeared from view, she was just about to look outside to see what he was doing when she felt her skin prickle, and at the same time, a bright flash of light appeared beyond the wall. The crowd of people fell back with cries of fear and awe, and she didn't know why but she got the feeling that something terrible had just gone down but had left the world better off for it. She shook her head and opened her eyes to Kaiźer, stepping back into the room. She came forward and looked past him but, in shock, found the alleyway empty! Draghi was gone! She looked at Kaiźer, and he averted his gaze.

"Let's go get a room in the back," he said abruptly. To the rest of the crowd, he raised his voice as he said, "nothing to see here. Drink and be merry, love your woman, and give a coin to thy drink!" He shouted.

The crowd roared in agreement, and he turned back to face them. He gestured to the back of the room with his chin, and she saw a few open spaces that were unoccupied. They were for VIP only, and with the manager missing, she wondered if it would be alright to use one of them? She followed after Kaiźer while thinking this and soon let her worry go as he let them inside and shut the door behind them with a soft thump. Looking around, Sin'ka eyed the queen size bed with its red satin sheets and feather-stuffed pillows. Against the wall, a desk sat with nothing on it, and beside it, a cushioned chair sat alone. Compared to the rest of the building, the room was fit for a queen or a king, she thought with a quick glance at Kaiźer as he cracked the door and slipped back into the hall. She sat down on the bed and waited as Oníx settled herself in the chair beside the desk. Kaiźer, still outside, could be heard speaking to someone. Sin'ka figured he was making sure they weren't disturbed, but she couldn't be sure of anything after what had just happened—

When he finally stepped through the door, he didn't sit down; he froze and turned slowly to face Oníx with a frown.

Kaizer

chapter 5: Triangle Gathering

Thy skin burned with desire of a single touch of thou eyes. Passion peaked with a single touch and thou fire heated thy loins with such.

A Lady of the Sheets
The Enchanted Age

Kaiźer stood silent. He and Oníx had yet to move or say a word. Sin'ka thought they looked like statues made flesh, unable to move. Oníx sat, her arms folded over her chest, legs crossed. She oozed sensuality and power, despite her stature. She felt it, and her skin tingled because of it, and yet, Oníx was looking at Kaiźer with a blank expression, and he, in turn, watched her, face equally expressionless and standing like a statue, his arms hung at his sides.

Sitting there, she simply gazed down at the table, all the while wanting to be invisible. Sadly, invisibility was not on her list of ShadoWalker gifts. In fact, neither was the ability to shapeshift. It had been a bit of a disappointment at first, learning of what she lacked when it came to what a naturally born ShadoWalker could do, but as she had learned of what she could do. She'd soon forgotten what she couldn't. She was just as strong as most of the ShadowFolk, and she was able to walk in sunlight despite what the stories said, though she still got quite a nasty burn if she went too long under the sun. Another up and up was her ability to read a person's thoughts and even change them if desired. It came in handy once and a while.

Being here next to Oníx, although it was impossible. Both were having one of the most intense stare-downs in history, and it was starting to grow awkward. They were just standing there, for heaven's sake, sedentary like statues, not saying anything. She couldn't take it anymore.

Looking up from the floor, she opened her mouth to tell them that they should just make up, but the words died in her mouth as she caught sight of Kaiźer.

He was smiling, just a little, but it was there, twitching at the corners of his mouth, and slowly but surely it grew, becoming prominent until he was flat out grinning like a fool. Finally, Sin'ka watched as he lost the last of his composure.

Bursting, Kaiźer doubled over in laughter, a hand over his stomach. "Oh, you never disappoint." He stood back up, eyes twinkling with amusement. "Even now, you can hold your own against me."

Confused, she looked over at Oníx to see her smiling slightly.

"Well, I was taught by the best," she said

"We both were," Kaiźer told in return.

Frustrated, she shot to her feet, knocking the bed into the wall behind her in her haste. "I don't understand; all you two did was stare at each other for eternity! And what's all this about being taught something because I sure didn't see anything."

Kaiźer looked at her in shock, and Oníx sat unmoving as she stood there fuming. She covered her mouth in embarrassment and mumbled a quiet apology. She let her hair fall over her face to cover the deep flush that overtook her face.

"Sin'ka... what you just saw was indeed Kaiźer and I staring at each other. Granted, we weren't moving, so to someone untrained like yourself, nothing seemed to be happening? But if you had been looking, you would have noticed small telltale signs that would have given away the battle that was being waged—"

Kaiźer crossed his arms as she looked between the two of them. "—it may be a slight change on the tone of our skin or our hair may move as if in a slow breeze"—he gestured to his face—"maybe even a bright glow that lights the eyes. It all depends on the nature of the struggle—" He explained to her

"—and what you didn't see was our inner struggle for control over one of the other's minds. This kind of battle is rarely fought, but when executed, both your opponent and you must be ready, or there won't even be a struggle." Oníx finished

The two of them spoke in soft tones weaving their story together like a well-oiled team. It was fascinating to watch. It was as if they knew what the other was thinking and finishing each other's sentences. Sin'ka still couldn't see the point, though.

"Wait, a battle of the mind? She asked them. "You mean like telepathy?"

"Close, but yes"—Oníx nodded—"when Kaiźer first arrived, he instantly attacked my mind; thankfully, my mind is always open and alert. The two of us were trained to keep our minds like such for multiple reasons."

Moving to the side a bit, she let Kaiźer sit down beside her on the mattress. She felt like she got the idea. What they had done was a little like her mind-control trick. Cool! She had been told that all Hunter's used telepathy, but to see it firsthand was nowhere near the same. Kaiźer soon came back, and continuing from where Oníx had left off, he sat down.

"The goal of such an attack is to break into the mind of the other. The first to do so wins."

"So, who won?"

"I did, and quite easily, I might add," Oníx said with a frown. She was staring at Kaiźer as if daring him to explain.

"But you two sat there for an eternity!" she protested.

"Yeah, I lost, but I also have yet to win against her." Sitting beside her, Kaiźer had his eyes closed and didn't see Oníx roll her eyes. "Besides, you both look... you distracted me!"

Oníx laughed. "What? Big strong Kaiźer distracted by the beauty of a woman, how would you hold up if a female demon attacked you then? What would you do then, hmm? You'd probably just stare at her."

Kaiźer's eyes grew cold.

"I'd stop her from doing something she would regret," he said softly.

For some reason, that shut Oníx up, and Sin'ka watched as she leaned back, her eyes suddenly sad. From his reaction to Oníx mentioning a female demon, she wondered if the daemon Kaiźer had told her about before—the one that had tried to kill him—was what had crossed his mind at that moment, and why was he acting like he was tormented with regret when she had wanted to kill him? The plot thickened.

"I'm sorry, that was wrong of me. It wasn't my intention to bring up bad memories; please forgive what I said."

Kaiźer accepted her apology with a nod. He gave a quick glance towards her, dropping his gaze as he did, but he blushed after only a second and looked away just as quickly.

Looking down at herself, she saw nothing wrong. *Does Kaiźer... like how I look?* She was sure that was what it was, but she could be wrong. Was it because he didn't care for her attire? If not that, she didn't know what else?

Obviously embarrassed, he cleared his throat. "Well, I must be going. I don't want to intrude any more than I have." Getting up, he faced them and gave a slight bow before leaving quietly, closing the curtain back up behind him.

After he left, the two of them didn't say anything for a long while. They sat in silence, merely enjoying the muffled peace of the booth.

"Are you still mad at me?" she asked. It was out of the blue, and she knew it, but she had to ask.

Leaning on the wooden back of the chair, Oníx shook her head. "No, I'm not. I know it wasn't your fault. It's nothing to worry about.

She gave a mental frown at that. Yep, something was going on that Oníx didn't want her to know. *Did something terrible happen?* She had to find out what was causing this worry. She sat up about to head outside when Oníx was in front of her. She pushed her back down onto the bed and went to sit behind her. Oníx then began to knead her shoulders. It was excellent, and she needed it, but she couldn't stop her mind as if it ran rampant, cooking up a multitude of scenarios not respectable as a friend.

"So," she started. She was surprised when her voice didn't shake. "What happened to that Draghi fellow? He wasn't human, so where did he go?"

Oníx looked at her from above and let out a heavy sigh. "He didn't go anywhere fun. That's for sure. If I had to guess, Kaiźer killed him."

"Killed him?" she sputtered. "I thought Kaiźer didn't do that anymore."

"Wrong. Kaiźer goes after otherworlders still, but only the ones who break the law. Besides, Draghi wasn't from this realm, so he was fair game."

Sin'ka looked at her friend and contemplated the idea of her as a Hunter. No, that was preposterous. There was no way her Oníx was a killer. She was too sweet and laidback. Her character said differently, but so had Kaiźer's. She'd had no idea a Jackal had been working for her security detail for the last three years! He didn't act like in the stories. By all accounts, he was an ordinary man! But still, she was having trouble with the idea that he was a Hunter of Old. Oníx met her gaze but looked away just as quickly. Sin'ka wasn't going to get any more out of her than she already had. She would have to ask Kaiźer himself how—with being a Jackal—what he did during his free time, but with him gone, the only other thing on her mind was this demon lady. She couldn't help but ponder.

"So," she droned. "Kaiźer has a female demon as a friend."

Oníx perked up, and Sin'ka saw her face flush as she spoke.

"Don't take it the wrong way. She originally tried to seduce him, and when it didn't work, she took what she wanted. So, he was forced to kill her." Oníx moved a hand up and started rubbing her neck.

"Then how did they become friends?"

"That's where the story gets interesting. Apparently, a male mage turned Kaiźer into a mountain lion, and he was stuck in the forest for a time. Oníx chuckled.

"Wow. That sounds somewhat harsh. What did Kaiźer do to deserve that?" She slipped her shoes off and tucked her legs under her. She wondered how Kaiźer would look like a mountain lion. She envisioned silky black fur over strong muscles as he slinked through trees of old, eyes aglow in the dim light of midnight.

"I don't know, but when he was stuck as such—killing the mage after he was changed—the succubus, whose name was Kurai Aka Hoshi, found him. Kaiźer usually calls her Kira, by the way.

"It had been ages since their first encounter, and she had only been back in the realm of the living for a few days."

"Is this the same succubus that attacked him when he was sixteen?" she interrupted. Oníx looked at her in surprise.

"Yes, she is. How do you know that?"

She blushed. "Kaiźer told me."

"And when did he have the time to tell you this?"

"Just a couple hours before you arrived, I was at his place recovering. He'd been struck by lightning, and I got the backlash, so to say."

Oníx blinked in surprise. "Wait, what...? You know what? I don't want to know. I don't care how he got struck by the lightning of all things. It's like he's a walking magnet for trouble."

Sin'ka could believe that. He did seem to attract a lot of trouble. Every time she'd been with him, something terrible had happened.

"What about you though, you say you got the backlash; what do you mean?"

"Oh, it was nothing, just a few small scratches."

"Okay... as long as you weren't hurt. You're sure you're okay?"

"Yes, I'm sure. Now back to Kurai Aka Hoshi. I want to hear the rest of what you have to say."

Oníx combed her fingers through Sin'ka's hair and continued from where she'd left off. "Anyway, she ended up breaking the spell on Kaiźer, returning him to his natural state. At first, they didn't recognize each other, so the two grew close after a couple of days. It was only after remembering their first meeting that things got bumpy, but even then, what they had grown into a friendship despite their violent past."

Her face heated. They had been close? She thought after what the lady had done to him all those years ago, he'd have sent her back to the Underworld.

"Why did they become so close? I thought they'd have hated each other because of what happened?"

Oníx shrugged. "I would have thought the same if not for what Kaiźer told me."

"What did he tell you?" she urged.

"Kurai Aka Hoshi had been ordered to gather energy from others. At first, he'd thought it normal for her. Her kind did gather energy, but of their own free will, so upon hearing she'd been ordered to give away the energy she gathered, he changed his mind about her and decided to help," as she spoke, Onix filled her hands with liquid heat and ran them over Sin'ka's shoulders once more.

"She was on a leash, and her orders didn't originate from the Underworld. Can you guess who was pulling on that leash?"

She shook her head. She didn't have a clue, "Who?"

Oníx shifted, standing up slowly. "You wouldn't know him, but he goes by the name of Darzíel." She turned to face her.

She knew very well who that was. She'd read about the angel in her family's old library. He was said to be an angel that was charged with protecting the innocent. "He's a guardian angel. Why is he trying to kill you?" she whispered.

"Even gods can go bad," Oníx whispered.

"So Darzíel became a Fallen and charged Kurai Aka Hoshi with killing Kaiźer?"

Oníx nodded, confirming the fact. "Kurai Aka Hoshi had been ordered to take Kaiźer's life energy, but when she found him, she couldn't drain him. He had too much maña for that. He captured her and made her confess. Of course, Darzíel didn't like what Kaiźer was doing, so he took her back."

Sin'ka leaned forward. "What did she do after that?"

"She rebelled, escaping multiple times with Darzíel on her tail each time. Kaiźer tried his best, but he soon couldn't protect her. She was taken right out from under his nose. I've been searching for her ever since."

Sin'ka let out a breath she hadn't known she'd been holding. Falling back into her seat, she wondered what had happened since. "That's quite the tale." She breathed.

"So, what about you and Kaiźer? When he arrived, you tensed up. Did something happen between you two?"

"In a way, yah; after we got back to his place, we got..."—she paused to think—"we got close."

Oníx grinned, "You did not!"

"Yah... no... not really? We were... you know... when his eyes glazed over suddenly. He changed then and started talking about avenging... his beloved,"—she shivered as she remembered what had happened—"It was scary."

"What? Did he attack you? Was he acting as if in a trance?"

She looked at Oníx. "Yeah, how—"

"It's a long story. Only Kaiźer could tell you what really happened, but good luck trying. He rarely speaks of his past. From what I know, his uncle took her life and tried to take him as well, but I don't know for sure. You'll have to ask him yourself, but like I said, good luck trying."

She knew all about what it was like to lose someone you loved. After her first kill, she'd not fed for a week, and Julian had had to force her to go back out to hunt. Unable to age, she had also had to watch her family die, one after the other. She understood where Oníx was coming from. Kaiźer had regrets, and he was running from his past.

"Anyway, he may have a few issues, but I'm sure he makes up for them in other ways." Oníx nudged her in the shoulder and wiggled her eyebrows comically.

"I'm sure," Sin'ka grumbled.

Oníx grinned. "Okay fine, we'd better call it a night."

She nodded. "Yeah, I think that's best."

An hour later, they arrived at Sin'ka's house. She had been forced to summon the *Rakariage*, thanks to Oníx being slightly drunk, and it had been a hard ride home. Things grew worse when they arrived at her house, and her friend began trying to undress her. She pushed Oníx's straying hands aside and led her into the living room, and set her on the couch. Oníx fell onto her back and giggled when she waved her hand, and the hearth flashed in a rush of flames. Blazing bright, they lit the room with a warm glow, and Sin'ka turned to Oníx in shock. Being drunk was not a good thing when you could control fire. She would have to watch Oníx close or risk her burning the mansion to the ground. She had to go and fetch some blankets, though, so she crept out for a second and grabbed some from down the hall, but of course, she came back to find Oníx standing before the hearth.

Her dress was gone, and Sin'ka blushed when she saw her friend. Her figure was framed by firelight, her skin lit with an orange blush, so it shone golden bronze.

Taking a breath, she came up behind Oníx, intent on covering her with the blanket when she turned to face her. Out of the blue, Oníx began to feather her lips over her. She felt her skin heat and couldn't stop herself as she kissed her back. Oníx ran her hands along her skin, and out of the blue, she felt her core heat.

There was neither a warning nor a buildup. Sin'ka just peaked from the contact. In fact, she crested in waves, her vision going white from the strength as what was apparently sex magic coursed through her. She went rigid as it passed into her endlessly.

After what felt like an eternity, she collapsed into Oníx's arms, limp as a rag doll. Oníx lowered her to the floor, and she lay limp, her body unable to respond to her demands. She was shocked at how powerful the rush had been.

"Oníx," She breathed. "Why did you do that?"

When there was no response, Sin'ka looked up. However, she was struck frozen by Oníx's own gaze.

"Uh, Oníx... You're looking at me funny."

Smiling, Oníx slid a lock of her hair behind her ear and bent down to capture her lips in a soft kiss. Breathing deeply, Sin'ka took in Oníx's spicy scent, letting it overwhelm her senses. It had been so long since last, she'd been touched. Even with it being Oníx, she craved more. Common sense flew out the window, and she let her friend caress her cheek with a hand. She sighed at the sensation and closed her eyes.

Raised as a lady, her current life would have shocked those she'd grown up with. For the past five years, she'd basically been a lady of the sheets, and now, with Oníx, she'd done things she had once found repulsive. But oh, the pleasure she felt, it was addictive.

"Oníx..." She whispered.

Purring in response, Oníx slid a leg up along her thigh, skin smooth against hers. Soft as silk, Oníx knelt atop her, clenching her thighs against Sin'ka's hips.

"Did you enjoy tonight?"

Sin'ka looked at Oníx in shock. No longer did she sound drunk; in fact, she didn't even sound tipsy. Had it all been an act? She felt an odd sense of guilt suddenly. What would Kaiźer say if he saw her now? Would he agree with her actions? She'd seen him at the Lover' Bite. Then he'd seen her with Oníx at the Red Fountain.

Both times he had looked at her as if knowing her fully? Did he know what her life was like? Would he disagree with her actions despite such? Her thoughts were not clear, but neither were they straight. A yawn wracked her body as she struggled to gain control of her limbs once more, but the aftermath of Oníx's attack was still rolling through her, and she couldn't concentrate with her brain all foggy. She was tired, so tired. Her world was going dark; she couldn't keep away the dark depths of sleep any longer.

Watching Sin'ka, Oníx waited until her breath came to a stop. She envied her. Still in the adolescence of her immortality, Sin'ka had yet to know the pain the rest of them had endured.

She'd used her magic to heighten Sin'ka's sexual sensitivity to make her pass out from the pleasure, and it had worked perfectly.

If she had let Sin'ka get her chance to please her, in turn, they would have been here all night. She didn't need her friend turning her into a puddle of sexual desire because of arrogance. Sin'ka had no idea what she was and was oblivious of the outcomes of such.

It hadn't been a surprise when she had become the head of all the prostitution within Nypheriam. Her heritage demanded as much after all, even if the girl didn't know it herself. When she had learned of Sin'ka, the lady had worked as an herbalist and still did such, just not openly.

Sin'ka controlled all of the spice trade that passed through Nypheriam without even knowing she was doing such. By selling spices and herbs in her establishments, she had unknowingly created a network that had grown independently.

As Oníx wondered how to sit Sin'ka down and tell her what she had done in the last year, her mind-link magic signaled a call, and sensing the ID, she answered it without a second thought.

"Oníx..." Kaiźer's voice resonated in her head.

His words were slightly incoherent, sounding as if to be underwater. *Damn, there must be iron nearby.* Oníx looked around the room, but she could see none, which meant it was on his end.

"How'd you get my source link?" she asked him.

"You weren't the only one who won something during our fight. I thought it would come in handy. Besides, you don't carry a portable *codex.*"

Oníx rolled her eyes. The man had balls. "What do you want?"

Kaiźer's voice lost its teasing tone. "We need to talk."

Straight to the point, hmm, he hadn't changed. Good.

"Tomorrow, at noon, I'll meet you at the Enchanted Lagoon. Don't be late." She ended the signal, cutting their connection. She had to get cleaned up.

Kaizer

chapter 6: an old Enemy Returns

Magic is the pseudoscience of life. It comes and it goes, taking many forms and many faces, but never once does it change its origin.

The Elemental Alchemist
The Enchanted Age

Kaiźer had woken this evening expecting another boring night to unfold. Little had he known that his boss would turn out to be a vampire? He also hadn't expected her to turn out to be the reincarnation of Abika. His blood felt like it was churned and boiled within his body at the thought of her. It fought to overwhelm him in its succulent call, making it nay impossible to think straight.

All throughout last night, he'd gone out to hunt, questioning anyone he knew to have connections to Darzíel. He didn't enjoy what he did, but to find and protect his family, he would do whatever was needed to accomplish such. Besides, Darzíel had been a thorn in his side since day one, which meant he needed to protect those he loved twice more.

Also, his surprise when he'd run into Onix right after talking to her had topped the cake. He'd expected her not to come and to find her with Sin'ka of all things? Now that had been a shocker. He wondered how they knew each other. And what had they been doing at that Red Fountain anyway; he'd been there to question Draghi when he'd run into them.

Could Sin'ka know Draghi? He hoped not; if she consorted with his sort, he didn't know what he'd do. Onix was most likely to blame—the demon had hesitated at the mention of her, and he had to give it to her; she knew the worst of the worst. Sin'ka didn't seem like the type. If she were anything like Abika, she helped when needed, but Sin'ka was not Abika, so he couldn't know for sure.

After leaving the Inn, he had decided to stop by The Lover' Bite to clean up and get the place ready for the following night, and so now, here he stood, in the middle of the club... not knowing what to think of the last few hours. And it bugged him.

Wreathed in shadow, the underground brothel was silent. Activating the lanterns, Kaiźer did a quick sweep of the place, sending his consciousness into every nook and cranny till he was sure the area was empty. He would need to knock up his paranoia a few notches if things were going the way he thought they were.

He renewed the weave around the musical instruments that sat in the corner of the room and ensured they would activate when the place opened.

Checking the phantom lanterns that decked the corners and walls, he transferred to the security ward. He sent the original to the main codex that held the building's vital information and security info.

Anything that was to be kept confidential was stored in the Orb. Once within, it became inaccessible to anyone but the owner. Tweaking the Fire Weave that lit the hearth with its phantom light, he grinned at how much the place relied on magic.

Moving behind the bar, he started on the list of kegs stored in the back storeroom. The storage would require a new shipment of spirits based on what was left; he realized that he sent the bill to the brothels Orb with a quick tying of weaves.

Sin'ka would see it in the morning when she arrived, he knew. The place was not out of order, he knew, but he couldn't stop himself from stopping and giving the area a second glance. He did a sweep-through of the stage and then checked the rooms before feeling satisfied with the place's equity.

However, as he was heading towards the back exit, a noise drew his attention. Stepping slightly, he infused the soles of his shoes with magic and quickly drew one of his daggers as the sound came again louder this time. He stepped out into the back hall and moved along the wall until he reached the doorway that led back into the main lobby. *The place is supposed to be closed, so why can I sense the maña of another?*

~*Who could it be?*~ Kaín whispered.

"Why are you whispering?" he hissed.

~*It could be the boogieman. You know how much I hate that guy*~

He smirked at the idea of being the boogieman, but the energy he was sensing was not the same. It was female. Peeking past the doorframe, he cast the shadows around himself and waited. The intruder was almost at the doorway.

"Kaiźer, are you in there?"

At the voice, he let out the breath he realized he'd been holding; it was Jessíca. Moving into the room, he let the shadows go, and they sloshed from him as she stepped into the light.

Jessíca was standing near the main entrance, and at the sight of him, she smiled in relief. "Kaiźer, I thought it was you. What are you doing here at this hour? The club is closed right now."

"I could ask the same of you. Why would a lady such as yourself be out at this hour?"

Jessíca blushed. "Oh, I was just meeting Kiyle, but he isn't outside, so I thought I'd check to see if he were inside. The lights were sort of an incentive, but it's just you"—she looked around—"is he here with you?"

Kaiźer frowned at that. She must be the trusting type to let his friend—who was still a stranger to her in his eyes—meet her alone here at two in the morning.

~I bet they were going to get it on. Right on this bar, too~

Ugh. Gross. He did not need that image in his head. *~Thanks a lot for your two cents, you dick~*

~ You're welcome~

Even though the guy didn't have a face, he could see Kaín's smug grin.

~Shut up!~ He shot at Kaín even as he answered Jessíca's question.

"Nope, I haven't seen him. In fact, I hadn't heard from him since I last saw him, which was when he met you."

Jessíca frowned. "I wonder where he is. He said he would be here as soon as he finished up at practice."

He cocked an eyebrow, "Practice?"

Jessíca gasped. "You didn't know? When he isn't guarding the Queen, Kiyle plays the cello for her. He's part of the Royal Orchestra!"

He nodded in understanding, but even as he thought about his friend playing an instrument, he paused, sensing a strong aura. Its power permeated the air, growing more extensive and more menacing till the club reeked of it.

Turning around, he moved out from behind the bar and stood beside Jessíca. He prayed it was just his imagination, but he knew his luck was starting to run short nowadays.

"What is it? It is Kiyle?"

It wasn't Kiyle. But she couldn't have known that.

They had a guest!

On the typical day of the ordinary life of the orchestra's regular band members, the practice was indeed unusual.

It continued as usual; the band played in the small amphitheater within the Queen's gardens. Covered in mirrors, they practiced the typical set of wholly original ensembles, very usual indeed up till the abrupt stop of a single cello.

The abrupt stop probably could have been a usual thing had the man not shot to his feet, causing his instrument to nearly hit the woman next to him. She curtly inquired *what the fuck* his problem was, which was not a usual thing for her to say. This unusualness caused everyone else to stop and stare at them, also wondering, *what the fuck...?*

The cellist, one of the usually quiet social attitudes, did not utter a single word. He just stood there, clenching his bow in what seemed an unusually tight grip to the others. The others would note his eyes were glazed over, glossy, almost shiny. They were metallic, reflective.

Kiyle Ross began to stalk forward, trancelike, somehow not bumping into anything or anyone on the tightly packed amphitheater. He descended while they watched, also silent. Bow in hand, Kiyle walked around and went up to the sizeable, hammered copper mirror that made up the side of the castle wall behind them. Kyle raised the hand that held his bow as if to play, yet he had no instrument. The others sat silent, now dumbstruck by the unusual behavior he was exhibiting.

All at once, Kyle raised the bow and began to saw at his neck. Shouts and screams erupted in the morbid confusion. Several of those watching sprang forward to halt their friend's actions.

The cellist was sawing away so fast that by the time they reached him, blood was gushing, covering the large mirror in a crimson flood. One man grabbed Kiyle's arm that held the bow in an attempt to stop him from severing his carotid artery but only got an elbow in the face instead. Those near him heard his nose shatter. Letting go, the man staggered back, his hands covering his face, whimpering.

Kyle kept at it for a minute or so before abruptly stopping, this time collapsing to the floor, eyes no longer glossy but glazed over in death.

The castle guards came soon after and ushered the group that stood around the man away, assuring them that everything would be taken care of, but everyone knew; nothing was okay. A man had just gone mad, and word would get out no matter how hard the guards tried keeping what had happened quietly. The gardens were secured, a guard was placed at each entry. All the same, it didn't halter the Hunter that paid the palace a visit among all the confusion. To the patients within the palace's security, this was a typical act of insanity. Still, Ryeznya did not miss the small detail they missed that proved that conclusion of events was false.

Simply put, the mirror that took up the side of the castle was clean, while the floor wasn't, which told the Hunter one thing!

Mirror Demon!

Mirror Demons are indeed a freaky species of the damned. They pretty much are constantly watching the mortal realm from their dimension. The mirror dimension is often used and worshipped by a group of mortals who called themselves the mirror lords even though they weren't really *lords* over anything in the mirror dimension. Still, the demons within tolerate their disturbance for but one reason; their meddling opened the veil.

The myriad dimensions within the shadow realm are more commonly known as planes, and these many planes hold energies that sorcerers, mages, and witches draw from to fuel their powers. All dark magic uses the different planes' energy to manifest in our reality, whether used for good or evil or old or new.

The mirror dimension isn't part of the shadow realm per se; it is a middle-lower plane that closely *mirrors* the shadow realm. There are plenty more than demons in the mirror dimension, oh by far, worse things indeed. Luckily for humanity, said terrible things can't pass into the mortal realm nearly as quickly as the lesser demons can; they only require a small output of energy to do so, unlike the greater daemons, which needed large amounts to pass through.

In theory, all Hunter's know all about the planes; Ryeznya certainly did. He's been a Hunter for thousands of years and was considered *the Slayer* by most other Hunter's, mainly because Ryeznya didn't hunt his prey; he just effectively murdered anything and everything he chose to track.

Of course, the new information about him investigating the mirror dimension was very much going to complicate life; indeed, so much so he resolved to hunt down his old nemesis, the disciple of Maliki. Known by very few, the man was a regular at a brothel known as The Lover' Bite within Nypheriam; it was a club for humans and otherworlders alike, which seemed like the perfect place for him.

Ryeznya slowly ventured to The Lover' Bite, but after checking the supernatural bounties... it was not too far from the Queen's palace, Ryeznya found his current destination; the Lover' Bite. It was a relatively decent-sized brothel he found, considering it was basically hidden beneath a hotel, and only those who knew of it knew it was there.

One could search thousands of dark allies and never find the door to the club. Even though some would argue the Slayer didn't need to know where the entrance was, it was now right in front of him.

Ryeznya knocked on the wall at the back of the ally and waited. He didn't have to wait long. The keystone in the arch above opened, flickered for a second, and then turned red and closed. The *eye* was a magical ward linked to someone's mind, and that someone had just denied Ryeznya admittance to the clandestine house of sin.

His eyes flashed a violent green with one final *knock*, promptly destroying the magical ward, obliterating the wall and *the door* that had been hidden. It flew past the security lobby to slide across the floor in shambles. He heard a stifled scream and grinned. It was after hours, and the office was vacant. Even the front entrance of the lobby was empty. That suited Ryeznya just fine all the same—though he had hoped to find the place busy. He walked through the double archway towards the tables all the same...

As would be expected, the tables were empty after hours and the large stage in the back. However, there was music coming from the corner, odd. Looking for the source, Ryeznya found an assortment of instruments playing themselves. Floating in the air as if held by invisible people, they were spouting a pleasant melody. The reason the Slayer had come was standing in front of a bar. He was in the opposite corner to the left of the instruments that were playing themselves. Standing in the entrance, Ryeznya saw that his prey wasn't alone.

Ryeznya's smile was perhaps a bit murderous as he stalked towards the man he sought; Kaiźer waited patiently, all the same, holding the pretty blond at his side. She must have been to one who'd screamed.

"*Γεια σου αγόρι*—hello, boy" Ryeznya took a seat at the bar. Kaiźer said nothing. Silently hoping that Ryeznya was just another illusion from Darzíel, he met the man's gaze...but those red eyes were unmistakable. It was he.

"Greetings to you too, *friend*"—Kaiźer emphasized the word friend—"drink?"

"Of course, chilled rose wine if you please."

"Coming up!" Kaiźer declared, obviously eager to look away. Kaiźer paused to consider what kind of murderous immortal Hunter ordered a monarchs' drink of all things but quickly cast the thought aside just in case Ryeznya was probing his mind. With Ryeznya being well trained, Kaiźer's head would be easy for Ryeznya to get into now, but only because of Oníx, he admitted regrettably.

Kaiźer led Jessíca to the bar and told her to stay silent as he cared for their guest. Delivering the drink to the man who'd tried to kill him, Kaiźer tried to sound civil as he asked the murderous demigod what brought him.

"You," that was his answer, simple... no emotion.

"Uh... okay. How have I brought you to?"

"My artifact."

"Oh." *Shit*. Kaiźer didn't know how Ryeznya would react to the truth. He didn't have it, well; he'd lost it in a way, as it definitely wasn't reachable from this plane of existence. It had been a part of the sealing ritual Oníx, and he had used it to trap Darzíel.

"The artifact!" Ryeznya barked, snapping Kaiźer back to reality. When his eyes returned to the conversation, the Slayer continued. "I need The Mirror of Retribution. Something has come up."

Kaiźer realized there was no backing out of this. His uncle would not let up now that he had caught his prey. "I used it to seal a Fallen."

The patrons' eyes flashed that violent green again, and a glass cauldron behind Kaiźer shattered. Jessíca let out a small squeak as the glass shards fell to the floor.

"It's gone, is it?" Ryeznya said quietly, knowing Kaiźer could literally smell the hate in his words. "Gone is very much a problem."

"Well, it was a good idea at the time," Kaiźer stated. "Despite requiring a human sacrifice, it had been the only option. What has come up anyway? You know I search for you? There is still much you, and I need to settle."

"What has come up is a huge problem, and there is nothing to settle between us," Ryeznya said in a snarl. "But I will simply tell you the truth... old friend? Your past is saying hello. The mirror lords have decided they are not done with you yet."

Reality fell away, and images filled Kaiźer's mind of the day he'd finally finished off the mirror lords. He had paid in blood, and the losses had been significant. Now, if *they* were back, then Darzíel was free as well, which meant everything had been for naught.

"Wait," Kaiźer snapped, "The mirror lords were after Oníx. Why am I on their radar? And honestly, those fools have little when it comes to power."

"Because you know the most; they watch and the see. The mirror lords are probably working to free this *Fallen* once and for all. If you and your friends used *The Mirror of Retribution* and a willing sacrifice, it shouldn't be easy to break out of such. Though judging by your reaction, it is obvious he's at least split the seal, I'd assume partly so by my estimation.

"My opinion, whether it matters to you, is that, given the fact that they have already killed three of your past acquaintances, I would say the mirror lords are collecting life energy from others to finish off what remains of your seal. In fact, here's a file on the latest assassination." Flicking his wrist, Ryeznya summoned a brown folder that was tied with a red string. The cover was stamped, *Property of the City Guard*. Kaiźer digested what he was being told, nearly vomiting as he realized the darkness at hand. Three of his past acquaintances had been killed. Damn it! Who could have died? He took the folder from off the bar and undid the string to open it. Inside were three pictures of the crime scene and a written statement. Looking at the pictures, he knew who it was. Drained of blood, the man's face was ashen and sunken. He wouldn't have even guessed it was him if not for one of the pictures, which showed a class ring. It was Kiyle's. Looking up, he glanced at Jessíca. She watched his face and frowning, slowly approaching him to take the folder. He watched her as she looked at the pictures. Her face drained of color, and with a cry, she clutched at the file.

"No... no, no, why? He... we..." Jessíca trailed off, tears streaming down her cheeks. He took the folder and tossed it back towards Ryeznya. He turned back to face Jessíca, and she wrapped her arms around him, burying her face into his shoulder. Crying softly, she clung to him tightly, and he wrapped her in his arms supportively.

Kiyle had been here just last night. Darzíel was clearly watching him closely as this had just happened. He needed to call Oníx as soon as possible and warn her to shroud herself. Sin'ka could not afford to be pulled into a mess of this magnitude either. Kaiźer opened his mouth to ask who he was after, but the Hunter was already walking away, saying over his shoulder. "I will leave you to your own. My source link is now written in your codex. I shall return eventually. For now, I am going to find the Fore-Lorne Looking Glass. I suggest you tell me if you hear anything relevant. Oh, and I almost forgot." Ryeznya paused at the double archway and said ominously, "I hope you have not spent too much time in front of a mirror this week...."

As Ryeznya walked out, he repaired the door, removing all traces of his intrusion with the deep pool of magic he possessed. The one thing he had running for him was his near-endless magic reservoirs.

Kaiźer thought to himself that at least he wouldn't have to clean up the mess when all at once, every mirror in the club shattered into trillions of shards. Jessíca screamed, and in a blur, Kaiźer covered her. The shards pelted his back before hitting the ground with a tinkling sound that made him think of sand. Looking around, he watched as the shining sea around them began to sizzle, effectively turning to ash.

"Damn it, you bastard," Kaiźer grumbled. Checking Jessíca for scrapes, he cursed the man for being alive still; he had hoped the man would have shriveled up with age by now. Jessíca had a couple minor cuts on her arms, but overall, she was okay. Nothing a good night's sleep would cure. He openly cursed when he took in the chaos around them once more.

Sniffing, Jessíca wiped a hand over her cheeks. "I guess we won't be opening for a while," she looked up at him. "Do you want me to let Sin'ka know?"

Kaiźer shook his head. Jessíca just wanted to help, he knew, but she didn't need to be involved. She would need time to adjust to what had just happened; he knew he would if he was in her position. But before he could, Kaiźer had to do something he knew he'd regret. He heaved a heavy sigh. "Don't you worry, I'll find her?"

Sin'ka

chapter 7: Demons' calling

Daemons call me in my sleep; they whisper to me, tell me things I wish not to hear. I wake cold in sweat and hot of skin only to find myself alone with but a lone mirror that throws its grinning replication back at me, taunting me.

Lucifer
Before the Breaking

Sin'ka woke slowly, feeling the sun kiss her cold skin. Opening her eyes, she watched the creamy shadows dance against the glow of the morning light as she listened to the breeze blow through the curtains. Sitting up, she stretched her arms high and arched her back. As she did, the blankets fell, revealing her glistening skin to the glow of the rising sun, the sensation sending small quakes down her spine.

Rising, she stood and moved to the bureau that was a part of her wall. Picked out a silk gown that matched her mood, she clad herself in its soft layers with ease and left her room, heading to the living room, the green and gold trim of her skirts trailing behind her.

She had been packing for the last couple of weeks, so the halls and rooms were full of boxes. Weaving through the cluster, she reached the center of her house.

The living room was huge. A large fireplace burned with a small fire along one wall, and furniture was scattered all around. Catching sight of the black dress, Oníx had worn the night before, Sin'ka went and held it up in the light of the hearth.

She had been convinced that Oníx had gotten drunk on the Red Fountain's ale, but she could recall Oníx shrugging off her drunkenness at the last moment before she'd passed out. Had she been faking the whole time? Sin'ka had no idea why Oníx would have done such a thing? And to think she had used sex magic on her?

It didn't come as much of a surprise, really; she knew Oníx was into girls. What really came as a surprise was she had used her tricks on her!

Sitting down on the couch, Sin'ka took a deep breath as she buried her nose in the dress's soft material. It had been painful at first, but after a few years, she'd found in Julian's journal a multitude of ways to control it and use it.

A ShadowWalker's nose was built like an animal's; the anatomy held a similarity to a Lianica's, a mountain being similar to a lion but held the abilities and a few characteristics of a dragon. Her sense of smell had become overly complicated after becoming a ShadoWalker. Her sensitivity had been heightened with her change, and she could even trace colors when she focused.

It had only been recently that she'd figured out how to find someone by their scent. So, when she took in the spicy scent that was Oníx, she searched. She wasn't close, that was for sure, and from the range, she had to guess somewhere on the coast within the... now that was odd? Based on the distance, Oníx's placement put her within the Kingdom of Light.

Sitting down on one of the many crates that held her paintings, Sin'ka stared into the hearth and cradled the dress in her arms. Oníx had left, and for a good reason, she was sure. Sin'ka had tried to reach for Oníx as she stood but had been too exhausted to lift a finger. She hadn't been touched in ages, so to feel Oníx's touch had been like fire against her skin.

The hard part was it made her yearn for another's embrace. And for some odd reason, the person that came to mind was Kaiźer. She barely knew him, but she felt a strange sense of familiarity that only confused her every time she had been around him.

She felt a heat in her belly that she'd never felt before. She burned with it, even craved its warmth while wanting it to fade once more. She wished things would go back to the way they were before her change. If she had not been on the east road on her way to the castle that night, she would be dead and with her ancestors long before today. Even so, she would have taken that life any day if it meant not living forever as she was.

Standing back up, she let one of her maids take the black dress from her arms, and as the young lady swept out of the room, she tied her hair back in a loose ponytail and rolled her sleeves up to her elbows.

If any man saw her as she was now, they would question her modesty. She had none when showing her body, but she knew when it was okay and not okay to wear specific attire.

Her dress had long sleeves that flared at the ends, and as the rest of the morning passed, she busied herself by helping the maids pack up the majority of stuff she wouldn't need in the days to come before the move. If she were in the castle of her origin, she would be doing her singing lessons instead of helping the maids work around her home.

As she moved through the bare halls and empty rooms, Sin'ka realized that the house had grown gloomy now that all of the art and decor had been removed, so she helped her staff place flowers around the place. She had always asked them to do so to brighten the rooms, and right now, she knew her home needed them more than ever.

Besides, the fluorescent colors made her feel better. By now, what she'd come to call home was just another place she was leaving, and with her furniture covered, the only place she wished to be was outside. Looking through the windows, she noticed the sun sinking low in the sky, marking mid-day.

She headed for the garden, and moving through the tall hedges, passed through the simple maze of shrubbery to where her garden sat. With tender care, she began to pick out a small assortment of different fruits and vegetables that had been planted at the beginning of the season and placed them in the apron she had dawned before entering the gardens.

Years before, she had decided it best to grow her own food. Of course, she couldn't get everything from the garden. She still had to visit the market once a month, but her days had meaning in the flower beds. It kept her rooted, so to say. Her plants were her babies.

Her own staff had told her she seemed happier after the garden was planted, and as the years had passed, she'd built upon what remained the year before and let her garden grow.

Now, as she moved through what she'd come to call the Elemental Orchard, she remembered the day Oníx had planted it.

Broken into four sections, the area was at the heart of her garden. Its four parts represented the four seasons. The first quarter was made of dark blues and creamy yellows for summer; the second section consisted of bright pinks and purples for spring, while the one for winter had white and black roses.

The last quarter was for fall and had a wide assortment of light browns, rich reds, and vibrant greens. Each section was planted with whatever survived during that season and each glowing bioluminescent. Secured and preserved—to an extent—with her maña, the flowers never wilted or died of age unless she died. If she plucked one, it would fade like any typical flower, but it would grow and stay in a mature state if she left the bud alone.

On top of her trick, she also never had to worry about the weather affecting her flowers. Her head of staff, James, had placed a spell over the entirety of the garden, and as she looked around, she took in the stark difference between her garden's limit and the land surrounding it.

Right now, outside the barrier, the cold snow of winter shone under the mid-day sun. It was still odd to look at, even after ten years. She'd never been good with wards herself; she'd always been more suited towards body magic.

Not wanting the garden being ravaged every year by the elements, James had placed his spells. It wasn't till after the first sprouts that Sin'ka had begun to notice the weather change every year.

The garden wasn't the first ward he had put up either. When James had become her head of staff, he'd started warding her homes, guarding it against magical intrusion. Nothing happened, but he had told her later that it was better to be safe than sorry.

Sin'ka had only six staff, but they were all family, and she trusted them. She stood in the heart of her garden and looked up at the back of her house, thinking about Kaiźer. She'd been telling the truth when she'd told him about how it was time for her to move on, find a new home. She had been thinking about going across the sea, but now she wasn't so sure. After their last meeting, she felt she had to make things right with Kaiźer.

At the club, Oníx had noticed how she'd been tense around the man. Sin'ka had thought things were fine, but clearly, what had happened was still bothering her.

And with the mention of Kurai Aka Hoshi, Kaiźer had gotten really gloomy. She didn't like that. He was one with the blade and pen, a Hunter! She cringed at the memory of his eyes when he had left. He had looked to be in such pain, such sadness. She had wanted to take him into her arms, to comfort him and love him, but feared doing so. Gods, his very words had been laced with poison, burning her senses. I would have tried to save her. That had been what he'd said. And with those words, he'd seemed to wilt.

A warrior has wounds he doesn't want to admit, but you had to first face danger to have such injuries. No one, not even someone such as Kaiźer, should have to bear the weight of such for too long.

Sin'ka had felt his very soul cry out, and her heart had wept. He'd made her soul break and shatter, piercing any doubts she had had about how she felt about him.

She couldn't quite say she loved him. She was sure she had deep feelings for him as a person, although she didn't know if they were good or bad yet. And what if he fell into another trance as Oníx called it and attacked her again? What would she do if there was no one there to stop him from killing her? She couldn't very well kill him.

In the ancient language, a ruin had burned against his chest, and she recalled the truth's rough translation. At the thought, she recalled how his sword had lit with ethereal magic right before he'd returned from wherever he'd been. Plus, it had blazed incandescent, matching the glow of the black blade. And to top it off, what she had thought to be genuine—but could have easily been her imagination—was the spirit of a man framed by a light that had appeared beside Kaiźer; he had had a wild mane of thick silver hair framing dragon-like eyes.

He'd gripped Kaiźer tightly, speaking to him urgently, but she had been unable to hear his words. Besides, he'd looked to be only partly there. She knew it wasn't impossible; she was a ShadoWalker, after all. But still, what she had seen had seemed mystical, not physical.

Leaving the garden, she headed inside. The day was ticking away, and she was restless. Those around her approached many times, but she waved them out, ignoring their worried questions. Stepping into her studio, she considered the concept of Guardian Angels. Or better yet, daemons; the man hadn't seemed very heavenly. In fact, she was sure she'd seen scales under his eyes and on his ears. Did angels and daemons have pointed ears because his ears had been pointed... that was for sure!

Picking up her paints, she grabbed the collection of brushes she used for her oils. Moving to one of her smaller canvases, she began to paint what had happened that night with Kaiźer. Her hand shadowed over the cloth, drawing on her memories to guide her. Combining blues with blacks, she recreated her vision of the reptilian fellow she had seen at Kaiźer's shoulder. He had had such a severe expression of his eyes as she drew her brush along the canvas; she felt a smile grow upon her lips at the image she saw before her once more. Lips set in a determined line, eyes focused, nose pointed; the man was dragonish in stature for sure. She could see the signs of long-lost heritage that had been thought to be long lost to the ages. Dragons were supposed to be extinct, killed off in the Five Kingdoms' battle during the Second Age. The man that was emerging before her was not human, but neither was he angelic or demonic. He was something else, something older.

So lost was she in the creation before her; Sin'ka didn't know how long she'd stood there, but turning towards the window, she saw that the sun sat low in the sky, its rays peeking from just under the shadow of the mountain face. Its light painted the clouds above in a myriad of red and gold starbursts, and she drank of its magnificence. The beauty of it was enough to break through the cloud that surrounded her mind, and she realized how long she had been standing with her paints in hand.

Sin'ka put her brush down and, with a sigh, staring at the canvas before her for a second. She was not the best artist by far, but she wouldn't consider herself the worst either. She had met many artisans through the last two generations, and many had built their skills atop what she knew already, saying that a true artist should carry on the craft that their old fingers could not over time. They had all begged, really, thanks to her immortality.

Focusing once more on the painting, she realized it was incomplete. With regret, she forced herself to step back. She would finish the memory later and store it with the others, but her hunger burned now, and she needed to hunt. She had forgotten entirely about the man at the Lover' Bite who had been waiting for her upstairs. She would need to apologize when she got the chance. Besides, she hadn't taken much from the young man in the ally, which meant she was still in need of blood. Going back to her courters, she casually clothed herself so she'd be more suited for the hunt ahead. She dawned her blackened jerkin, which consisted of hardened leather across the chest and back, leaving the arms and sides pliable for movement. With it, she wrapped her legs in thick cotton and covered them in matching leather breeches. Each leg had many straps and silver buckles and, within each, hung a silver dagger. Across her lower back, she strapped her throwing daggers, and once secured, she wrapped her winter cape around her shoulders. It consisted of a Lianica pelt, which produced its own heat and was a rare commodity even on the black market. Sin'ka had been lucky to find it during her stay within the Market City of Traiathica ten years back.

Once ready, she walked down the hall and entered the front lobby. "I'm going out for a bit," she called out. "Hold the place down for me?"

James was walking down the stairs, a rag in his hands. "We've got the place covered, Lady Sin'ka, don't worry," he said, running his free hand through his long black hair.

Smiling up at James, she remembered the day he'd arrived. Even after twelve years now, he seemed to never age. She had no idea what race he was... he looked human to her. His aura was a mystery and held no positive identification for her to identify, but he was loyal to her, and that was all that mattered.

"I won't," she said with a smile.

Sin'ka knew he would keep things in order while she was gone. Hiking up her fur-lined hood, she stepped out into the chilly winter night. The solstice had passed, and the very land hummed with its energy. Fresh snow covered the grass, sparkling like pure white sugar as it layered itself upon the ground in bright sheets. Frost dusted the trees making their branches droop in the wind.

Passing into the greyish-green embrace of the forest's grip, she summoned her wings. Smoke curled around her, bringing with it the familiar scent of thick leather that clashed with the natural fragrance of winter. She crouched then, flinging her wings wide, their black expanse gleaming in the setting sun. The thick muscles bunched, rippling along with her wings, and in a blur of motion, she launched herself into the air.

She burst from the trees just as the sun dipped behind the horizon, her body streamlined. The wild winds of the sky touched her skin, and a wash of strength sang through her, warming her body, preparing it for the hunt. Not second after her launch from the earth, she banked above the clouds and caught the headwinds to float above the fluffy White Sea. The wind rippled the surface of them, making her think of water, and she smiled peacefully at the thought. Up here, she didn't have to deal with the constant hum of the people around her; for a change, her mind was quiet.

She opened her eyes with a sigh when her belly grumbled. If only she could stay up here for eternity. Gathering herself, she slowly descended, letting the moisture around her sink into her, wetting her skin and her hair till she broke through to gaze once more upon the land below. Training her eyes on the forest below, she searched. She could see elk grazing, wolves hunting, and bears hibernating. Soaring lower, she let her eyes sharpen till each tree branch was prominent in her sight. Still high above, she stared into the forest till she caught sight of her prey, clothed in shadow, a lone mountain cat stalking a wounded deer, a young doe by the looks of it. The youngling had a slight limp and was trailing behind the herd. If the cat pounced, there would be no escape.

Folding her wings, Sin'ka dropped. Rocketing down from above, she moved faster and faster, then faster still, till she was a mere blur to the naked eye. The cat was readying to strike. She could see it in the way the cat's tail twitched and in the way its muscles bunched as it readied itself. Summoning her claws, she dropped from the sky like a wraith.

The great cat shot up, launching towards the frail doe. Ears folded back. Legs stiff, the doe stood, eyes dilated in fright. Claws extended, fangs bared, the cat snarled, unsuspecting.

Only to be smashed into the ground as Sin'ka struck.

With a tight roll, she extended her feet down, smashing into the cat's spine, snapping it. Absorbing the impact in her knees, she bent her legs and, thrusting her sharpened fingers down through muscle and bone alike, pushed past the cat's ribs to grab its beating heart within. With a mighty pull, she ripped the bloody organ from its home and tossed it away.

Looking up, she watched the doe flash through the trees. Licking her hand clean, she savored the sweet metallic taste of the blood. Lying dead, the cat looked almost shocked. She felt sudden shame in her abilities at the sight. Being able to take the life of such a mighty animal so quickly was not correct. All the same, she needed to feed. Lifting the corpse, she bit into it, drinking deeply, drained it of blood. She didn't need to consume such, but she'd found that draining a body fully allowed her to go for weeks without feeding, and that's why she chose to hunt beasts of the wild. Killing humans was not good for morality, plus she didn't want someone to find the bodies. Better to hunt a deer or a bear deep in the woods and use its body after. Fur for warmth, meat for food... bones for, she hadn't a clue.

Slowly she rose, wiping her mouth as she did. She'd made a mess in her need to feast. The blood of others was something she hated most about her life. It was one of the effects of her change, and she had always thought of it as a curse. The uncontrollable urge made it impossible to find someone she could live with and love as an equal.

Looking down at the corpse before her, she was reminded of the Hunter she had become. A predator hunting under the light of the moon, bathed in its glow, captured, and unable to escape its haunting light. Her mind fell back to when she had stumbled into her house, bleeding and barely conscious. Her fiancée had found her a few hours later, and at the thought, a sob wracked her throat. She had sensed his arrival, and it hadn't been until he had laid his hands on her that her eyes had snapped open. She had latched onto his neck then and had been unable to stop till the rich, succulent flow stopped.

Her emotions tumbled into turmoil, and with a shuddering cry, she fell to her knees, tears carving bloody paths along her cheeks. Dropping into her hair, they cascaded down over her leather that adorned her chest.

Just the thought of losing someone she called a friend was too much. How could Oníx think Kaiźer and her to be a match? He was the complete opposite of William. How could Oníx think such when she was what he was sworn to kill; a fucking OtherWorlder. The un-forbidden nature was exciting to think about, but she was still a ShadoWalker while he was a Hunter. They were two sides of the same coin, yet too far apart to be with each other. Julian had told her that for years the Hunter's had captured and killed what they'd deemed dangerous to mankind, whether it was angelic or demonic. And she was sure that Kaiźer was just like those he'd trained under. That kind of childhood grooming didn't just vanish!

Turning her gaze heavenward, she took in a stuttering breath in an attempt to calm her mind. Her emotions were getting the best of her, and with Kaiźer being the main focus, she felt like she was losing control. Why did he have to be so... ravishing, so masculine? It is like he'd been bred for war, and the idea of him as a mate? Both were too much for her. She knew she shouldn't think such things, but the idea was so tempting. Fantasies of intense and wild pleasure filled her mind. She cried out in despair as they ran rampant; Kaiźer kneeling before her, his mouth capturing hers, Kaiźer under her as she pleased him, Kaiźer above her with their roles reversed, Kaiźer... Kaiźer... Kaiźer...

He took up her thoughts to the point of her losing them. He was not the one; he couldn't be. Julian had dedicated a whole page of his journal to the idea of a second soul for every ShadoWalker. If Kaiźer was her second half, she didn't want him. A roar escaped past clenched lips, and clenching her fists, Sin'ka shattered her arms into the rocks beneath her. She snarled as pain raced up her arms.

Looking at the damage, she saw that her hands were embedded with shards of crystallized stone. Her forearms had shattered, causing the bone to protrude from under her skin, the white texture gleaming against the red shade of her blood.

As she watched, the bones sank back into her arms, and as the skin knitted together, each scar faded away till nothing remained. Small pops and snaps sounded as her mangled hands reset, the muscles webbed back together once more to knit together. What was left of the shattered stone was pushed free, and the tiny protrusions that remained vanished, becoming whole.

Within seconds, not a trace of evidence remained that would have marked the deadly wounds that she'd inflicted not seconds ago; her skin wasn't even different in color.

Lifting the beast's corpse onto her shoulder, she stood up and breathed in the incredible scent of a winter's promise, a promise of chilled adventures and frosty regrets. Thoughts of Kaiźer were once more under control, and she lifted the cat, letting smoke envelop her once more as she launched into the dark night, trailing the scent of bloodied leather.

Arriving at her house, Sin'ka gave the animal to James. He would handle the bloody tasks that she didn't want to do. She had killed it, sure, but she wasn't up for the job of skinning, curing, and what not when it came to the dismantling of the carcass.

Some may think it weird how, as one of the ShadowFolks, she could hate the sight of blood. However, Sin'ka found it typical that she was the black sheep, and it wasn't like she panicked every time someone got a paper cut; she wasn't like that. Blood itself didn't affect her in that way. She just didn't like having to drink it. If someone was hurt and she was able to help, she did. In fact, she kept a stopper of her saliva mixed with oils and herbs on her person at all times. It wasn't much, but in all her years, she'd had the chance to learn a lot when it came to herbs. She knew of about two thousand different plants, as well as hundreds of ways to use each for both their healing and poisoning properties. It had become her calling, actually. She'd opened her first herb shop in the year 3726 A.B. and had found that she genuinely enjoyed it. Knowing she held a person's life in her hands was scary at first but seeing the look on her regulars' faces had been heartwarming, and it had made the negative side of being a healer worth it.

Walking into her private courters, she remembered how even Onix had praised her for her skills. Her friend was always getting hurt, and she'd patched her up a couple of those times. She still remembered the first time Onix had come to her for help. She'd just come back from a dig that she had procured just outside Sha'arda. With a long gash running across her back, she'd literally collapsed onto Sin'ka's front porch one day; she'd had to drag her inside her hut so that her neighbors didn't call the city guard. The cuts had been deep and had bled copiously, so Sin'ka hadn't been able to start with her normal salves. If her heart had beaten, it would have been racing as she'd stitched Onix up. After numbing the surrounding area, she'd cauterizing the wound and stitched her up. Applying her healing salves, she'd bandaged her up and waited for her to wake. Oníx still told her how great a job she'd done, but she always felt like an amateur at times. She'd only sold tea and cookies up to that point. So yeah, she'd been scared.

She quickly shed her thick leathers out of her bathroom, switching them for a black blouse and breeches before heading down to the pantry. It sat at the back of the kitchens, and out of it, she grabbed a bag of dried fruits that she'd cured some weeks prior. With it, she snatched a bottle of milk from her icebox. She still got the munchies whenever she went hunting. She guessed it was something from her time as a human that would never leave her. The idea that food tasted like dust to the ShadowFolk was totally bogus. She could still eat human food; the only difference being it didn't affect her; no calories, no protein, and no weight. It was like a dream come true actually; she could eat whatever she wanted and not worry about the consequences.

Her arms were loaded with the food as she stepped out into the kitchens once more, and when she looked up at the full ceiling mirror, she grinned. Her image rippled in the polished silver, and she realized she looked funny with her arms loaded with food. The silver metal above covered the whole room, and she was sure she would have laughed at how she looked if its reflective surface if hadn't been moving on its own. With a start, she froze upon realization. She lost the grin as she saw something other than herself on its surface.

As if something was pushing against it, she watched with growing horror as a handprint moved up against the surface. It looked wrong; the joints were too long, the all-over shape of it not familiar. She gasped as she saw two glowing orbs light with demonic fire beyond the surface.

She barely had time to jump back when the food she'd placed on the center island vanished as a grotesque beast pushed from the mirror, dropping into the center of her kitchen, smashing the island to splinters. Damn! That island was carved from the purest marble! The thought only lasted a second, as the thing before her bared long jagged teeth. Its skin was slimy and shone a reddish-brown. Its skull was reptilian, the eyes within, empty and oozing, and their depths burning with a blue flame.

Frozen with fear, all she could do was watch as it extended razor-sharp claws from the ends of bony fingers. Rippling with muscle, its bulk had cracked the marble flooring on impact. It now stepped from the rubble to face her, reptilian-like scales writhing in a red wave along its arms and legs, and with each step, its clawed toes crushed the stone floor. She noticed then, a long-spiked tail extending up to connect to the mirror, its end sinking into the reflective surface.

She flinched suddenly, for a voice filled her mind then. She looked at the monster. Did it just speak?

~*Where Is Oníx?*~ The voice said again, more demanding this time.

"I don't know." She said. It wants Oníx? Damn it, Oníx, what did you do now! Looking now, she noticed the creature's chest and palms were reflective, polished even. Thinking back, she tried to remember Oníx's description of the people she'd been tracking. Mirror lords, she'd called them. This guy had just come from a mirror, were the two one and the same? If so, she didn't look forward to what came next. If they were as powerful as her friend had made them out to be, she was in for a world of hurt.

"You're quite the ugly fucker, aren't you?" she said quickly. She needed to find a way out of the kitchen. Its confined space was not ideal for combat. She needed to distract it.

Slowly, ever so slowly, she crept sideways, moving to the door. Leading outside was her only option. "I thought you guys were long gone."

~*Still trapped, weak, too weak to escape*~ the beast turned its head to follow her movements.

She stopped. "So, you didn't come here of your own free will?"

The thing laughed, its deep chuckle rumbling through her mind. *~Why does the pretty lady want to know? Does she think we had help?~* The big guy crouched onto all fours, its empty eyes flashing green. *~Does she think James helped us?~*

Shit, did it just read her thoughts? It couldn't have, no, she'd been thinking of James, but it could've only been a coincidence. Onix had said once that her mind was blocked from magical sight. She was pondering if it could read her mind when the demon spoke up

~Pretty lady takes too long!~ it shouted. *~Where Is Oníx?~* She cringed at the mental whiplash. If it wanted Oníx so severely, she wasn't going to let it find her. Besides, she had no idea where Oníx was herself. She'd left last night and had yet to contact her. Of all that was holy, a whole day had passed.

Observing the beast, she took in its form. Strength radiated from it, and she would have to stay clear of those claws. But its skin looked to be soft and slimy; it could be a weakness.

Dropping to one knee, she hid a hand behind her back and extended her own claws.

"You are all the same, you beasts! I will never give up my friend even if it costs me my life," she snapped, readying herself.

~Foolish Human!~ the beast barked. *~You cannot keep us from our goal; we will destroy the seal, and Darzíel will reign free once more!~*

"Oh yeah, well, I got three words for you"—her eyes flashed red, and she loosened her body, relaxing her limbs while readying her claws—"Go, fuck, yourselves!"

Green fire spewing from its nose and eyes, it launched itself towards her with a blood-curdling roar. Claws extended, it swiped at her head; its goal was clearly to decapitate her, but she wasn't there.

Smashing into the wall, the beast scrambled to its feet. Looking around, it became confused. The lady was not where she'd been. She'd vanished just seconds before its claws had passed through her neck. The beast became angry; no one had ever escaped its wrath before. It would not let this human be the first. A soft whisper of movement caught the beast's eye, and it threw an arm out, shooting scales in a wide ark, riddling the walls with holes.

But again, no one was there.

She had been faster, and as it had thrown its arm wide, she'd dropped with a twist, kicking a leg out to sweep the beast off its feet. With an angry scream, it came crashing down.

"You dare to come into my home." She shouted, swinging her arm down at lightning speed, claws gleaming.

Seeing her attack, the beast rolled away, so her claws passed him by to enter the marble below. Slashing into the floor, her nails passed through the stone like butter. With a snarl, she looked at the beast.

It was jumping to its feet. Only a few seconds were available before the demon attacked again. And it did, but as its kick flew towards Sin'ka, she moved.

Blasting through his defense, she came at him with a jump, using her claws—that had become lodged into the floor—to propel her body forward, smashing into his chest. But to her surprise, what she'd thought to be soft was as hard as a stone.

Shit! Pain lanced through her shoulder as it fractured on impact. She groaned, but even as she began to heal, the beast gripped her hair and yanked her into the air. She felt herself become weightless as she was swung in a wide arch.

She stopped just as quickly, meeting the floor with a crunch. She could only gasp as her ribs cracked in multiple spots.

~You surprise me, human. I should have known that as a friend of Onix, you would be substantial.~ As it spoke, a bony spike extended from its forearm. *~A valiant effort, but you are still no match for us Mirror Demons~*

She watched through blurry eyes as the beast raised its spike high, aiming for her heart. She struggled to move, but her spine was cracked. Even as she realized it, she felt her ribs snapping back into place. One of her ribs slid free to snap into place. She felt one of her lungs empty of blood, the Vampiri Enzyme in her blood draining it as she healed.

~I am legion! Remember the name as you burn in the fires of purgatory~ With a low growl, the demon thrust the spike downwards towards her heart. It was moving as a blur and was inches away when her spine snapped back into place.

Throwing her arms up, she knocked the spike to the side and pulled herself up along its length till she was able to grab the demon's face. The beasts' inner fire burned her skin, but she tightened her grip all the more. With a savage intensity, she thrust a hand through the beast's bony exoskeleton, pushing through ribs and organs alike to grip the demon's spine.

"You threaten my friends," she whispered next to its head. Its jaw cracked as she tightened her grip with her words. Gods, the demon's blood burned against her skin.

A low whimper escaped through its teeth. *~Such strength... such power... How can a human have such?~*

Baring her fangs, she let her eyes shine red, showing her bloodlust. She tightened her grip on the creature's spine as she said softly, "I am no such thing."

Pulling the demon's head to the side, she watched as his eyes burned purple.

Moving in a blur, she sank her fangs into his neck and pulled at the bitter blood. It stank of sulfur, and it burned its way down her throat. She convulsed in pain as it hit her stomach. It seared her from the inside out. She'd never felt such pain before, it racked her body, and she pulled away after only a brief span of feasting. All the same, as she went, she pulled the demon's spine free, letting it drop from limp fingers as she staggered back—vision flashing white in pain—to collapse against the wall.

Falling to her knees, she collapsed and lay on the floor, her body shivering uncontrollably. She was there for what felt like hours.

The pain that passed through her was quick to vanish, but when she opened her eyes to watch the demon stagger back, she realized only seconds had passed. Its blood streamed to the floor, sizzling on contact. She groaned as the demon's blood melted into the floor while she listened to its crazed screams. All at once, the creature was pulled up into the air to get sucked up by the mirror. The house was silent then, with her and her kitchen in ruins.

Pushing to her knees, she had to struggle for air before laboring to her feet. The metallic taint of blood lingering in her mouth and what blood she'd drank boiled in her stomach. She was recovering—if slowly—but as she looked up at the mirror once more, she blanched.

The reflective glass was writhing with motion. There was more than one source of demonic light this time, and as Sin'ka stood under the writhing mass, the three pairs of glowing eyes lit within the chaos above as they landed on her.

Calling for backup! That son of a bitch; even in death, the thing hunted.

By the gods! Today was just getting worse and worse.

Sin'ka

chapter 8: Recreation

Hunting, tracking, trapping, with skins of molten gold, they howl behind me, their kin not long in reply. How long I wonder, will I last?

The Magician
The Age of Heroes

Walls rush past, a myriad of colors, all painted to complement one another. Sin'ka rounded a corner, flying through rooms and halls alike, but every nook and cranny could hold one of those things. After killing the demon that had fallen from the mirror, more had arrived at its disappearance. All were identical and just as grotesque. What did she do?

She ran!

Blurring through the house, she looked for a way to escape. She couldn't use the exits; it was just her luck that she had a mirror at every door. She'd always found it odd how they weren't visible in mirrors in most myths about the ShadowFolk. She wasn't a ghost; she had a reflection. For years now, she had had thousands of different people tell her that she was beautiful, but she'd never thought so. It did, however, make her fill her house with mirrors. She'd always had a fear of all her years coming back onto her at once, but so far, she'd only aged a few years. She'd stopped aging once she'd reached her prime. She had once been young and petite, a tiny little mouse of sixteen that had been afraid of every little thing. That fear was now returning; she felt once again like the little girl she'd been, the little girl who'd been afraid of the shadows. Truth be told, what she feared now was only a few deadly demons, no big deal, right?

She wished that were true.

Every single room had at least one small mirror, all of them rippling with malevolence as she passed, but once she got far enough away, they stopped moving. If that had been her only worry, she could have easily escaped, but at every exit, a demon stood guard. She had soon realized that she was a hostage in her own home. The irony was damning. Usually, the dice rolled in her favor when it came to dangerous situations, but she was now the one trapped for a change.

Once she had left the kitchen, she had been shocked to find that the demons hadn't followed her. She'd doubled back and found that they had, in fact, vanished, or at least she'd thought so, till she stepped out of the shadows into the light of the kitchen. Like clockwork, she'd watched the mirror ripple at her arrival.

Right now, her mind raced as she trying to make sense of what was transpiring. She'd left the kitchen, running through her house in agitation. She had ordered her staff to secure themselves in the basement, and they had all done so without question. She could see neither heads nor tails of James, and that worried her more than the demon presence did. If he was nowhere to be found, that was not good. Running to the front of her house, she barely escaped the grasp of a flailing claw that shot out of the silvery banister that circled the stairway. Avoiding the railing, Sin'ka raced upstairs. So far, the demons had not chased after her, and as she reached the second landing, a crazy idea came to mind. So far, the only daemons that hadn't gone back into the mirrors were the ones near the doors, and she had noticed that each one had a tail connected to a mirror-like an umbilical cord. It seemed the mirror demons could use anything reflective as a passageway, and that was the fact that she memorized for later.

There was only one way to test her theory and only one place worthy of such a test of courage.

Reaching the top of the stairs, she ran into the massive center room. Configured like a dance studio, most of its four walls were one huge, polished mirror of copper metal. Taking up a good 70% of the second floor, the room was huge, and it was here she stopped, standing in the center of the polished wood floor to wait.

Her gaze caught the sight of three demonic pairs of eyes, and she watched as their owners stepped through—the glass rippling along with their bodies, clinging to their limbs like liquid mercury—till they pulled free, eyes lighting with a blue flame.

Side by side, the three demons stood; claws extended, their teeth bared.

She eyed the demons warily, waiting to see if she was right, and if she was, they should only be able to get so far from the mirrors. She widened her stance and, extending her own claws, lifted them up into a defensive posture. Stepping forward, the middle one let loose a roar, fire glowing white-hot within its mouth.

In response, they shot into motion, the two on each side whipping to the left and right while the middle one shot towards her.

Any second now, the demons would reach their limit. Sin'ka prayed she was right, but she got the feeling her plan was going to backfire, and sure enough, the daemons kept coming.

She was on her feet once more about to retaliate when a second demon smashed her to the floor. With a yelp, she zipped with pre-natural speed through the demon's legs—passing just under it—as it rushed past. It jumped away before she could retaliate, but all the same, she hadn't seen its attack in time.

Damn it! She should have kept an eye on the other two. Tapping into her own inner-demon, time slowed around her. Running in wide circles, the demons lost speed—to her sight—and she knew then, the two who'd followed the wall were back up. She saw it in how they held themselves, with their heads low and movements balanced, ready.

Turning, she watched them circle around, eyeing her with those empty sockets of theirs. The middle one was digging its claws into the polished wood floor. Its muscles were bunched, and she knew; it was going to pounce.

And it did, with speed too fast to track. If not for her enhanced sight, she wouldn't have been able to get clear in time.

Jumping side to side, the demon moved closer, its movements quick and sure. Sin'ka scrutinized its path, and just as it reached her, she moved with a speed that matched the demon, and as the thing's mouth opened wide to take her head, she dropped into a low crouch. Grabbing its arm, she used the muscles of her legs to propel her forward and thrust a fist into its jaw, punching through to exit the top of its skull.

Turning at the last second, she barely had time to retaliate as the second demon jumped forward. She gripped the writhing daemon, crushed its arm in a death grip, and swung it in a tight ark to thrust its shattered skill into the chest of its ally.

Both burst into flames, their bodies disintegrating to dust almost instantaneously. Sin'ka stumbled forward as the fire parted around her as if too afraid to touch her. She watched them get sucked back into the mirror and stood in shock, her fingers tingling. Her skin was slightly pink from the sudden combustion, but it quickly faded.

Burns usually took longer to heal, but as she watched, they vanished in a matter of seconds. She could only assume the enhanced healing was an effect of the demon blood she'd consumed. Looking back at the mirror, she glanced at her hands again. It was possible. She'd just done what had been hard before with ease.

Clenching her hands, she looked up at the third demon as it circled her warily.

~Pretty lady says she not human; we see the truth in her strength~ it said coldly.

With a shiver that rippled its scales, the demon bulged suddenly, its body growing more prominent and uglier.

~Pretty Lady Will Still Die!~

With a blur, it flickered and vanished, reappearing before her. It had traveled the length of twelve meters in less than a second. She couldn't have stopped it even if she'd wanted to.

She was slammed into the floor, her limbs pinned down by eight arms that extended from the things back as it knelt over her, its regular arms bent slightly, claws extended above her chest.

~Pretty lady is very pretty~ the demon said as it tilted its head. *~Should I kill her?~*

As if listening to something, its eyes flared orange, and with a sound like steel on steel, its claws lengthened.

~Pretty~ The demon took a deep hollow breath, *~Legion want, but master says Legion don't get~* She blanched and watched, horrified as the daemon raised its arm high. She tried to escape, but she couldn't move. She was trapped. She was overcome with fear at what the thing had in mind, but she kept hope that an opening would present itself, she would escape! Shit. Shit. Shit. Bucking, she fought against her bonds but like before, she couldn't move.

The demon growled, claws gleaming, when she caught a flicker of movement out of the corner of her eye. She despaired, had another arrived? Why did this have to happen?

Throwing its arm down, the demon aimed for her heart, and she waited for it to end but knew her prayer was but a fantasy. At the last second, she flinched, and just as quickly, the demon jerked to a stop, narrowly missing her skin as its claws severed her clothes down the middle. She looked up and saw its empty sockets blaze white, its scales turning grey.

A black blade had punched through its groin, slicing right down the middle of its genitalia.

Looking down in shock, the two of them stared at the black metal as it gleamed. Liquid fire pooled free, and when the black blade moved up its body—the tip blazing incandescent—the demon screeched, its jaw seeming to come unhinged with the ferocity of its cry. It was being severed in half. Like a knife through butter, the sword cleaved through groin and skull alike to exit with a flash. Upon the blades exit, she was splattered with sizzling goop, and she could only stare up in terror—and wonder—as she followed the path of the blade and beyond to where the demon's flames were getting sucked into the dark metal of what she saw now was a dragon-metal blade.

Standing behind the blade was Kaiźer, his chest adorned with black scales, which made him gleam before her like a dark prince. With a quick flick of the wrist, his sword vanished into its sheath—but not before he knelt before her—his gaze wild as he took in her nubile body. His eyes gleamed, but not with lust. It was more like he was inspecting her, and when he reached her face, his gaze caught hers. His eyes were bright with battle rage, but they suddenly darkened to a smoky blue, becoming rich with worry.

Blushing, she slid her arms across her chest in an attempt to cover her nakedness. "Kaiźer..." she whispered as tears threatened. "How did you...."

His eyes became cold, but she barely saw it as she stared up into them. "I tried to contact you, but I didn't sense your energy, so I came to find you." His hands fisted, the knuckles going white. "When I saw the demon trap you, I lost all reason. I don't even know how I got inside."

Looking away, she tried to keep herself from breaking down in front of him. He had been looking for her. She'd been sure he wouldn't take her up on her offer to talk. Right now, more than anything, she wanted to be taken into his arms, but she knew if he did, she wouldn't last. She would succumb to the tears she was fighting to hold at bay, and she would wet his shoulder with their red stain. He was here now, but what if he hadn't come. What would she have done?

She had let the demon get the upper hand! She'd been helpless, trapped, and she would not have survived; this she knew. It was embarrassing; she would have most likely been killed. Why though? She needed to understand why it had chosen her and why it had attacked her. She shivered, curling up, so her knees pressed into her chest. It had been like it was being told what to do. Who was so cruel that they'd do such a thing? Damn it! She was dwelling. She needed to think of something else.

Something else...

As if reading her thoughts, Kaiźer placed a warm hand against her back. Barely inches away, he towered around her like a protective shield, his body heat soaking into her, warming her, and at his touch, she barely held back a moan as the comforting touch of his hand sent tingled down her spine.

"Are you hurt? I have a feeling I should be apologizing...?"

Something else... she needed to...

Her breath caught as her core clenched with need. Why did she feel so... hot? With just a simple touch, he made her hot with desire. How was this man any different than those she worked with?

She gazed up at him through thick lashes and took in his worried expression. He looked so cute with that frown of his; it made his lips pout slightly. And with his eyes being so dark, she felt like she was drowning in their gleaming depths. She was about to show him just how he affected her when a woman's voice froze her in place.

"I should have known they'd come after her but not to worry, anything with a reflection has been warded."

Kaiźer's hand dropped from her shoulder, even as he stood up swiftly. The sudden absence of his warmth left her feeling cold.

"Oníx, don't beat yourself up over one simple mistake. I had thought the thing was sealed away, unable to escape. We both did." Kaiźer looked down at her. "We are both to blame here."

Sin'ka watched him through her hair as Oníx stepped into the room, her arms raised high. She looked like she always did, but something odd caught her eye, a few things, actually.

Emblazed upon her skin, erratic patterns and designs writhed as if of their own accord. Glowing white, they crawled like snakes along her skin. They hadn't been there before, had they? She would have known if her oldest friend had tattoos.

Even as the *tattoos* faded, she took a few seconds to find her bearing. She still had yet to close her mouth when Oníx rushed to her side, pulling her into a tight hug. She looked up at Kaiźer with a scowl. "Turn around, will yah; a little privacy would be nice!"

Kaiźer opened his mouth as if to argue but decided against it. He turned, and with long strides, stalked from the room.

As soon as he left, Oníx pulled her to her feet and stepped back. She waved her arms, and light bloomed, trailing along with her fingers like liquid. Chanting in the ancient language, Oníx spoke as she used her magic. She noticed that her spells were consistently more potent, her results continuously improving when she did so. The only time she didn't speak was for simple things or when there was little time.

Right now, for instance, Onix was striving for perfection. A slight tingling sensation took over as she felt her body being covered. Looking down, she watched as what remained of her original clothes peeled away, getting replaced with new layers. She raised an eyebrow, and Oníx smirked as she worked her magic.

A loose sleeved blouse unraveled into existence around her and was quickly wrapped in a tight black corset embroidered with satin designs. With a grin, she watched as her legs were swathed in black leather. Covering her in ribbons, the cloth fibers melded together to cling to her like a second skin.

To finish it off, Oníx gave her a pair of black boots that rose till they just barely touched her knees, coming to a stop and curving up into an armored guard at the front. Dressed in a traveling mage's attire, she looked at Oníx with wide eyes.

Oníx let her magic go and dropped her arms in sudden exhaustion. She considered her work and gave a curt nod before catching her eye and giving a wink. She waved a hand, and Sin'ka felt something happening to her hair. Raising a hand, she ran her fingers over her head and found her thick red locks tied back. She raised an eyebrow, but when Oníx blushed, she giggled and wriggled her eyebrows comically.

"Do you think short is a good look with this much hair?" she laughed.

Oníx shrugged. "You look beautiful, no matter what you do?"

Sin'ka smiled at that. She hugged Oníx, and her friend embraced her back just passionately.

"I didn't know what to pick; there wasn't much else to choose from, so I...." Kaiżer walked into the room then and trailed off when he saw them.

"Why did I even bother? I should have known you'd do something like this!"

Stepping away from Sin'ka, Oníx grabbed what he held and fell into a fit of laughter. "I didn't tell you to do anything; you did that on your own."

Going through what he'd found, she gasped. "Oh! What do we have here, soft black leather, for both shirt and slacks? I don't see any undergarments here, though I admit these do look rather comfortable."

A deep blush overtook Kaiźer's cheeks—even reaching his ears—as he looked down at the wood floor.

"I couldn't find anything that was... casual... for undergarments, I mean."

Sin'ka couldn't hold back her laugh. If he had looked through her closet, she wasn't surprised that he hadn't found anything he would have considered casual. Oníx looked at her like she was mad, but her expression only made her laugh all the more. Like an infection, it spread till both she and Oníx were hunched over, laughter running free. Kaiźer joined in and everything that had happened over the last couple of days vanished. Sin'ka felt like she was once again among family. The house finally felt like home with them, and with laughter filling its halls, things finally felt right.

Kaizer

chapter 9: confusion of past and present

From the land of twilight they come, skin as black as coal, eyes as white as ice. And among them march the changelings, the half breeds, the ones not born of the shadow. How, I wonder, do such beings exist?

Unknown traveler of the Five Kingdoms
The Age of Knowledge

Sitting on the plush carpet covering the hardwood floor of Sin'ka's living room, Kaiźer went over what had happened. Going over the rage he'd succumbed to, he readied his mind and body, rearranging his maña and his magic till both were in alignment. He eased his mind and calmed his heart, so both were in perfect synchronization with each other. Slowly, he let each part merge as one till he descended into what was called the *Jackals Rumination*. He sat with his back straight, breathing relaxed, deep breath in, slow breath out, then a repeat. During his training, he had found many ways to enter his psyche. Overall, he had found that the easiest had been using his more in-depth cognizance to enter into *Rumination*. Since then, he had used his inner sentience to reach complete unification of mind and body.

As soon as he sat down, it took only seconds before the sounds around him faded, their disturbance vanishing to a slight buzz till even that vanished. He was now fully submerged within his mind, and with that, he began to descend into the stillness that was his consciousness, and it was there he rested at the center of the quiet storm.

Thinking back on what had happened, he watched the memory flash by; the arrival at her house; him jumping to the second-floor balcony where the sounds of battle raged; Sin'ka taking down the daemons; then finally, his killing of the third demon. Slowing the rush of memory as best he could, he focused on what was happening. It was here that he had lost consciousness and where his answers lay exposed. Easing himself into the memory, he took physical form within the room above where he sat. The room took on the illumination that had been, and with it, the shadows of the three demons emerged. Unable to be completely free of the mirror dimension, the puppets' tails were connected to the mirror in what could have been a spiny umbilical cord.

Watching the memory, Kaiźer gazed down with a bird's eye view—he'd never figured out why it was this way—but for him, it gave a better story than the first-person perspective of things. He watched himself draw Kaín and jump into the room, but he didn't attack; he vanished. In the blink of an eye, he was simply gone. Quickly rewinding the memory, he slowed down the frames until he watched himself move an inch each second. Floating down to stand before himself, he watched in confusion as he flickered and became incorporeal. With a start, he jumped to the side as his body took on a demonic form. Jumping back a good ten feet, he checked his surroundings to make sure he was still in control of his maña flow. Watching the mirage that was his figure move along with the polished copper mirror that circled around the room, he blinked when he drew his sword and thrust it into the reflective surface. The reason for his surprise was not the act itself but what happened when he did such. Without a sound or change in texture, the mirror simply folded around the sword like smoke and let the blade pass through without breaking. No cut was made, and no trace of its passing was left to mark its entry, and yet, he plunged Kaín into the mirror—no, not the mirror, the mirror dimension.

Still watching in slow motion, Kaiźer stood rooted in place, unable to look away from what was happening. He watched as his form solidified, only to vanish completely, again and again, reappearing each time in a different place than he couldn't have reached if he had just walked or even ran, for that matter. He seemed to be vanishing in and out of sight at first glance, but after closer inspection, he noticed he was actually passing back and forth between the spirit realm and the physical realm. Perplexed, he watched—unblinking—as he came upon the demon and thrust Kaín into its pelvis, plunging deep to slice through skin, bone, and genitalia alike to rip up, passing the blade clean through its chest, neck, and skull. Finishing in a defensive posture just behind where the demon had been, he held Kaín before himself, ready to strike if something else came upon him.

Ending the memory, he closed his eyes and took a deep breath. He was more confused now than before. This had happened three times already. This time, however, was different, and the thing with the mirrors? How had he done that? He questioned the concept. Why had he exhibited the characteristics of a shadow-daemon? The things he'd watched himself do; weren't normal. Only a celestial or daemon could have done such. It was impossible for him, a mere mortal, to take on a dragonic form; such powers had been lost to myth centuries before he had been born. His mind couldn't lie to him in this state, though, so he knew he didn't imagine anything. He was more surprised by the fact that he'd never thought of trying this until now with all the other blackouts.

With that in mind, he cast the thought aside and focused on his spirit, falling deeper into his meditation. There were other matters to be attended to. Coming to his senses, he opened his eyes to the darkness of his mind and took in its warmth, letting it calm his racing heart.

He thought of Sin'ka and of how she had held her own against the demon's puppets. Her grace, her speed... her rage, it had been awe-inspiring to know such power dwelled in such a tiny being. Her beauty gave a serene feel to that power, and it, combined with the control she had had, made her in his eyes one of the deadliest beings on the planet during those few short seconds. Even as the final puppet demon had attacked, he'd watched her respond. Her speed was even faster than his own. But his surprise had quickly turned to red-hot rage when the demon had gained the upper hand. Oníx herself had been unable to stop him, apparently.

He thought about how his body had seemed to hum with satisfaction once he had gained consciousness once more. The feeling of battle rage as it raced through his muscles, making them thrum with anticipation and need, a need to kill more of what he had. Most of that feeling had come from Kaín, but he had never found out how to bring Kaín into the *Rumination*. The dragon never answered his questions about the blackouts when he tried to ask.

And sitting here now, memories restored, Kaiźer knew why. He was sure he had known why since the beginning. He had unconsciously fought the idea even if he recalled. Had someone erased his memories of the blackouts? He was sure he would have thought to do this before now. Would the memories he'd recovered vanish once he returned to his physical form? He couldn't know for sure, and he had no way to secure the new information now that he had it.

Thinking back once more to what had occurred after the blackout, he smiled as he remembered how flushed

Sin'ka had become. Her aura had turned to shades of pink and purple as her mind had taken in the fact of his presence and the predicament she had been in. if Oníx hadn't walked in as she did, he was sure Sin'ka would have acted on those feelings.

In his meditative state, he could still feel Sin'ka in the next room over with Oníx. The two of them were talking girl stuff, and he smiled at the conversation. They seemed to have forgotten about the horrible things that had just occurred, no thanks to Oníx, of course. He swore if the woman wanted to, she could charm the wings off a fly.

He focused on Sin'ka, letting his spirit pass over her and through her. He wasn't surprised to find her mind blocked but to discover her aura was obstructed as well. When he tried to reaccess her spirit, all he got was a mental backlash.

Flinching, Sin'ka looked up and towards him. He froze but just as quickly relaxed when she looked through him and not at him. His spirit hummed with energy, its corporeal essence flickering from what had obviously been a magical ward placed by a powerful mage or sorcerer.

Usually, he could read a person just by touching their aura, but for her, he saw nothing. She was a black void to his eyes where others were full to overflowing.

It disturbed him. Did Sin'ka know of the ward? Did Oníx? More questions, he knew. No one's spirit had been hidden from him before. For her to be hidden from even his sight meant much.

But most importantly, the one who had put the ward over her was powerful. The question now was, why? What could it be that was so important, it required magic to hide? Did she know something?

Returning from the other room, he scoped the room he sat in, sensing a tension of betrayal; Sin'ka was torn with the idea of leaving...? Looking around, he realized that it showed in the many boxes that lay scattered about. But despite it all, there was a mix of another tension, a tension he didn't expect.

Sexual energies flowed through the room, their phantom lights glowing blue and pink before his inner eye. In a mixture of pleasure and pain, the pain was Oníx's, its nature telling him... oh! It sat throughout the entire house but originated in this room, and boy was it intense.

Wait; Sin'ka and Oníx? Wow.

...It explained the sexual tension coming from Sin'ka. Oníx hadn't changed.

Returning to his physical form, he slumped. He now knew why Oníx had been so tense when she'd come to meet him. It was apparent now.

~Wow, it's sort of disturbing that I can't read your thoughts whenever you meditate?~ Kaín said almost immediately upon his return.

Jumping to his feet, he ignored Kaín. His mind was in a funk. Oníx and Sin'ka, a thing, or were they just letting off steam? If so, he was most likely to blame. He'd been the one who'd awoken the heat he felt now. Its energy burned all around him, just as it had the night before.

Knowing Oníx, she must have picked up on the fact as well. One of the ways she replenished her magic was through sex, but she and Sin'ka? He'd never have thought she'd go for Sin'ka, being all uptight and worrisome all the time. Here though, swirling around him at such high levels? Something had definitely gone down.

~I told you!~

"Come on, man! I don't think I'll ever get that image out of my mind." *though it is pretty appealing to think about.* Gods above, he needed to get his shit straight. He couldn't be contemplating like this. In the hopes of finding something to distract himself with, he analyzed the room. However, in his efforts, he picked up on a hot spot where the energy seemed thicker. Despite it all, he moved to investigate. He was curious; what else was he going to do? Odd, it was the couch. Crouching down, he looked under it. In the shadows, he caught a hint of red, and reaching out, he gripped what felt to be a small bundle of cloth. It was slightly warm to the touch, as soft as silk, and when he pulled it out, he froze. Eyes going wide, he looked down at what he held.

Clutched in his hand was a pair of silk undergarments, their rich color still glowing with Sin'ka's maña. Damn it all to hell. Was there no end to his torment?

Climbing to his feet, he held them out and eyed the material as it pulsed with energy. It was unreal. He'd be caught red-handed literally if they arrived with him holding such a personal article of clothing. He had to find a place to hide them.

Kaín snickered, *~and... three... two... one...~*

At Kaín's last word, voices sounded behind him, causing him to freeze in mid-stride as he headed back to the couch.

"—all your mirrors have been blackened, and I also took the liberty of upgrading your wards so no demons or creature similar will be able to see or enter into this house again."

Onix walked into the room, Sin'ka in tow behind her. Crap, those clothes were not helping any. Think of something else.

~Yes, think of Sin'ka without them. I bet she has a rocking body!~

~Shut up!~

Kaín wasn't helping. He had grown used to Onix and her attire but only out of necessity. She wore it because she needed her skin bared to the elements when she fought to refill herself with magic. He remembered how she used to go to battle nude back in the day. For Sin'ka, though, her bare skin was perfection in of itself. Just like Abika, its alabaster hue shone under the low lights of the room; it left his heart pounding. Right now, that was something he could do without.

Sliding up to him, the lady who had taken his heart smiled brightly as she cheerfully looked up at him. He noticed then that all the minor cuts and scrapes that had covered her arms and legs had faded, leaving her skin flawless once more, its pale hue glowing in the dim light of the hearth that circled the room.

"Who are you talking to?"

"No one!"

"Okay then..." she paused. "What are you looking at?"

He was staring, he realized, but he didn't care. He had to take in every shadow and curve; Sin'ka looked so much like his Abika. It was uncanny. He swore to himself that if things settled down, he would claim her heart once more.

"You," he caught her eye, and she blushed. Damn, he'd said that out loud. "I mean, I was just checking your injuries; they've healed nicely." Fuck! He was... ugh, had he just said that?

Cheeks, still flushed, she shook her head and grinned as if he'd just shared a joke. "I doubt that but yes, they have healed nicely, but they always do."

Looking down, she didn't notice him let out a low, struggled breath. "I bet they do—"

"Hey, what are you holding?" Sin'ka, he realized, was eyeing his hand, and at her sudden question, his first response was the wrong one.

"Nothing!" shifting his hand, he put it behind his back.

Sin'ka's eyes gleamed with mischief. "Uh-huh, sure"—she pounced for his hand—"if it's nothing, then you won't mind if I take a peek."

He quickly shot his hand high, free of her reach, but she followed its movement like a cat, snapping her hands out in an attempt to grab his arm. She jumped higher when he lifted his hand higher, even using his left side as a ladder.

"What do you think you're doing?" he chuckled as she gripped his arm.

Swinging a leg across his shoulder, she huffed. "I want to see what you're holding; it smells funny."

With a foot on his belt, she had her leg draped over his shoulder casually. It put her right in front of his face, and he swore her pants were going to give him a heart attack and as she pulled at his closed fist, he fought the fantasies running through his mind. He couldn't let her distract him.

She was strong—nearly prying his fingers wide—but he was stronger, keeping those fingers tightly wrapped around the silk bundle. Still, she didn't give up. He gripped her thigh, and she shifted at his touch but didn't pull away like he expected.

"Watch where you put those hands buddy, you might lose them."

"I think I'll risk it; besides, I quite like the view down here."

That got him a knee in the face. He blinked in surprise. Did Sin'ka just...?

He pushed her off his shoulder, and as she fell, he twisted to catch her in his arms. With his hands around her shoulders and thighs, he stood looking down at her with a smug smile. She looked up at him in return, her eyes wide, cheeks flushed. Hmm, he could be imagining it, but he was sure he caught a hint of arousal.

"Do you still want to know what I found?"

"Yes. Is that a bad thing?"

"No."

She raised an eyebrow. "Then why won't you let me see?"

"I'm not keeping anything from you. I'm waiting," Kaiźer said finally.

"Waiting for what?" She wasn't clueless; she knew what he was doing. If he wanted to play hardball, so be it. "Are you waiting for me to beg? Not a chance, buddy."

"Oh, it's nothing like that. I want to know what's in it for me."

She gasped.

"But if you won't tell me, then I can't let you see."

"Why you!" she raised her legs and swung them up and around his neck to sit atop his shoulders, the speed of her movements swinging her around him.

Shocked, he stumbled forward as she flashed around him. She was using pure strength and momentum to bring him down. Clever, but he was more elegant. As she moved, he moved, stopping her with an upraised arm just as she came back around. He held his breath as he did so—ignoring how it put her right in front of him again—and pulled her away. As she fell, he flipped her around and lowered her to the floor. Towering over her, he lifted her hands—which he'd captured as she'd dropped—above her head.

"You're trained well," he whispered beside her ear. "But so am I."

"Let me go this instant!" She snapped.

He only smiled. Sin'ka wasn't uncomfortable; he'd know if she were. What gave her away was how she blushed at his closeness, in the way she tightened her thighs together, and in the way her breath quickened. Her actions betrayed her true feelings.

"Oh, I will but don't you want to know what I have first?"

"No!"

He grinned. "Don't be like that; I can give you a hint?"

Her eyebrows knitted together, but she slowly turned her anger into a wide grin. Kaiźer frowned at her sudden change.

"What?"

Her grin widened, "I hint? Oh, I don't think that's necessary?"

Sin'ka opened one of her hands and in it sat what he was, had been holding. When did she? He looked at her with wide eyes.

"How did you?"

"I have my ways." Sin'ka grinned as he laughed, the sound rich and deep, vibrating out from within his chest. She gasped as it touched her skin, the sound humming slightly.

So, she had snuck past his defenses unawares all while playing the helpless 'I can't do a thing act,' huh, just like Abika. He was impressed. He had been oblivious to the fact they'd been missing. The only thing to do now was to take them back.

And he did so with a quick flick of his wrist.

"Hey!"

Sin'ka didn't hesitate in trying to get them back. With her hands trapped high, she'd been unable to get a good look. She'd have reacted, and he would have seen it. Undergarments were something you didn't respond to! In fact, as the thought crossed his mind, she moved. Suddenly he was looking up at her, and she down at him.

"Give them back!" Straddling him, she held his hands up beside his head, eyes determined. He simply looked up at her, matching her stare with his own.

"I'd give them to her if I were you," Oníx stated, her presence becoming known to him suddenly.

He looked up and found her sitting on the sheet-covered couch. How long had she been there? Her eyes told him to obey or be humiliated, and he knew he'd instead follow.

Letting his fingers uncurl, he revealed the silk cloth. They were gone just as quickly as they appeared. Sin'ka didn't hesitate in snatching them up.

"Where did you find them?" she asked him. He shouldn't have been surprised when he'd scented Sin'ka on the silk. Most of the selection in her closet had been the same. A lot of choices had even been a bit more provocative. Oníx thought him a pervert when he'd, in fact, been unable to find anything... normal.

"Under the couch."

"Hey, aren't those the ones you wore last night?" Oníx still sat on the couch and couldn't see what Sin'ka held, but she didn't need to; she felt what he felt.

Sin'ka jumped, letting out a cute little squeak in surprise. She quickly shoved the red bundle into her shirt. She was blushing. Oníx smiled, and he got a bad feeling. Standing up, she walked forward and came to stand before Sin'ka. She slowly took the bundle out of Sin'ka's shirt and turned towards him; yep, definitely a bad feeling. Those eyes of hers made him want to grab Kaín and kill something. Doing so would be better than what she had in mind; her gaze was heart-rendering, almost deadly; he barely held her gaze for as long as he did.

Turning to Sin'ka, he broke the spell she'd been working on him. He'd almost cracked, but everything she did was a test of power, and he remembered how hard those tests could be at Sin'ka's following words.

"How did you find them?" He went still, not knowing how to respond.

"Yah Kaiźer, tell her how you found them," Onix said, and he could see the gleam in her eyes. She was barely holding her own composure; she knew full well how he had found them.

He'd felt her pushing against his block as he'd meditated. One of the first things they'd unlocked as Jackals had been their minds, opening the psychic channels of their brains. In doing so, they had become Hunter's. Maliki had taught them to block their mind from mental attacks while at the same time making Onix and him learn how to get into their attacker's minds in turn. And after running into Onix and Sin'ka at the club? He'd been reminded of how powerful Onix's mind was compared to his.

Back when she'd been a child, Onix had been a small, timid flower that would get knocked over in a strong wind, afraid to fight, afraid to change. But when pushed into a corner, her true nature had come out. She had been uncontrollable, destroying anything and everything in her path; even his master had been shocked.

Her first master had forced her through her training, pushing for perfection, pushing for the perfect Jackal, but he'd never been satisfied.

Partway through her training, he'd abandoned her, thrown her out, and disowned her. She'd been forced to live on the streets, fighting for scraps. For three years, she'd moved from town to town, never staying in one place for very long, till—at the age of sixteen; she'd found him.

Upon hearing who her previous master had been, his own master, Maliki, had insisted they send her on her way, but he had forced him to see her potential, and soon enough, she became a part of their family.

Too soon, however, Onix grew to be a pain in his ass as well. Even under his masters' tutelage, she teased, taunted, and harassed him at all hours of the day.

Now, after years of separation, he found himself relaxing under her familiar teasing. He looked at her smoldering gaze and saw how similar it was to Maliki's. She saw this and spoke up.

"Or should I tell her for you? Because you seem a little shy."

He couldn't jump forward fast enough at her words. In less than two seconds, he crossed the distance between them and slapped a hand over her mouth. She jumped, and he heard a muffled cry escape from beneath his hand. Her eyes didn't lose his, though, becoming lasers of triumphant surprise. As if he'd let her embarrass him any more than she already had.

Gods! He needed to end his self-imposed celibacy, and soon. He could very easily accept one or more of the constant offers from the ladies who bugged him at the club, and now that he thought about it, most of the women he had debated taking to his bed had found his dark mood to be a thrill, but looking at Sin'ka now, he was frozen, unable to speak. He was losing his edge against the intense pressure in his chest he had every time he was with her. It was keeping him in a state of mind that wasn't good. He couldn't stop thinking about sex. He was gathering that courage to tell her how he'd found the bundle when she saved him the trouble.

"Oh, forget it! It doesn't matter; at least you found them."

"Uh..." was all he said.

"What I do want to know, though, is how you arrived at the time you did? A few seconds later, and it would have been too... too late." She wrapped an arm around herself and gripped her elbow, trailing off into a whisper.

Seeing her fall into what had happened, he moved to stand before her. He cupped her cheek and drew her gaze to his. "Hey, focus." Looking into her eyes, he took in their platinum shine. He noticed that the rims of her irises were painted black, and seeing it up close, it was... exotic despite it being a cause of her fear.

As she looked at him, he saw a shadow of red igniting her pupils, its dark shade bleeding into the silver of her gaze. "Hey, forget about what happened. You're with us... you're with me." He caressed her chin, and the red tint in her eyes faded as if wilting; she relaxed, her hands unclenching from around his shirt to rest on his chest, her fingers slim and elegant. She tilted her head into his hand, eyes half-lidded as a smile grew upon her lips. He slid a lock of hair behind her ear, and she opened her eyes and glanced up, then away just as quickly.

Biting her lip, she fiddled with his shirt as she spoke in a soft voice.

"How can love be so unknown? I don't know what to feel around you." She swallowed past the lump that was building in her throat. "I don't... I don't know what to do with these feelings. It's as if I'm drowning." She ran her hands up his arms, barely touching the skin. The slight tickle of her skin on his made him shiver inside. He felt it travel down his spine and the hair upon his arms stood on end. Her hands reached his shoulders, and she grasped his neck softly. Stepping forward, she stood just a hair's breadth away. "I don't know why, but the feeling of your arms around me is comforting, almost familiar."

She was so close he could smell the peppermint of her breath, the incredible scent sinking into him, enveloping him in its overwhelming texture. Placing his hands on her arms, he struggled between kissing her and stepping away, and oh how he wanted to kiss her. His heart raced faster and faster till it ached, but he couldn't. Not yet.

Stepping back, he cursed himself. It hurt to do so, but they had things to do before anything could happen between them. "Sin'ka...I—"

His words were cut short as she closed the distance he'd just opened up, placing her lips to his in a soft kiss that spoke of need and desire so intense it sang. He felt the warmth of her breath enter him, and as their lips locked, he didn't pull away. He couldn't! Her mouth was scorching hot in its demands, bringing with it a misty rush of spice and heat. His strength clashed with her supple curves, and he lost all sense of awareness. All that mattered was her, her hair as it caressed his face, her scent as it wafted over him, her skin as it slid against his, the pale texture smooth against the dark bronze of his, cooling the fire inside him.

Sin'ka deepened the kiss, and he felt a slight poke of one of her fangs against the delicate flesh of his bottom lip. Drawing blood, Sin'ka groaned as its metallic taste interrupted their kiss. She tangled her hands in his hair and licked at the succulent red flow of it.

He felt a sudden lull of weakness and growled. This woman affected him the same if not more than Abika had. It was as if he was possessed, unable to stop the flood of lust and desire that flowed from her to him. She felt like Sin itself. The only other time he had felt like he did now, he had been with Abika after they had become newlyweds. Even Kurai Aka Hoshi...

He froze.

How could he have become so complacent? He was currently kissing and wanting to take this woman before him to bed while his closest friend was most likely fighting for her life as a prisoner of war. Her disappearance was still fresh in his memory, and he had no right to get caught up in the heat of the moment when there were still things to be done. He didn't want to let Sin'ka go now that he held her in his arms once more. The thought of losing her because he hadn't done what he needed to do was enough to clear his mind, though.

Standing before him, she looked at him, her face flushed, eyes shining with confusion. She looked at him through her thick red hair, the color of each lock burning red around her face.

"I need... we need to leave." He turned to Oníx. "There are still things to be done, Oníx?"

Oníx had been silent so far, but at her name, her gaze refocused, and her eyes burned with disapproval. At what, he didn't know, but it was there all the same. Speaking slowly, she turned and looked at Sin'ka.

"Something had come up, and we're going to need to stick together from now on. Sin'ka, despite it all, you are now involved; then again, you are not some normal human girl."

The last part was for him, and he frowned as she turned and plucked her keys from around her wrist. She tossed them at him and smiled knowingly.

Snatching them out of the air, he gave his best; I hate your smile in return. He never knew what Oníx had up her sleeves most of the time, but he did know that she did everything for a reason.

Turning to Sin'ka, he thought about his past. With a silent prayer, he asked for things to work out, if only just this once.

"You ready?" he asked.

Sin'ka didn't say anything, but she nodded, a small smile on her lips.

It was time for answers.

Ryeznya

chapter 10: searching

Blades bathed in blood, a crow flies high yet never settles.
Witnessing such I wonder does the battle really ever end?

Unknown
The Enchanted Age

Ryeznya was well pleased with himself. He had walked just slowly enough down the alley to hear the explosion of glass and what a superb sound it had been. Add that to the fact he'd blown up the mirrors in the brothel, probably ruined what was left of Kaiźer's night, and Ryeznya was in a good mood indeed.

As much fun as that had been, though, he had work to do. Ryeznya had assumed Kaiźer would have the ancient artifact, so he had only searched for his aura alone, but since the boy didn't have it, Ryeznya had to look for another artifact, and for that; Kaiźer's night had had to go to shit. He had caused the Slayer extra work, never mind the idea that a keeper of artifacts should have looked for the mirror of retribution first... well, either way, he resolved to himself. He could find the Fore-Lorne Looking Glass quickly enough. He'd still have to pinpoint it, but at the moment, he had other things to process.

Ryeznya made his way to the highest part of the city. He needed a place to meditate, and with a grin, he reached a clause and jumped to the tallest tower of the royal castle that stretched up into the sky; it was the perfect spot.

While he had paid Kaiźer a visit, he had entered the kid's mind—relatively quickly—the poor lad was most likely pushing his limits. That was good for the kid and better for him. He was confident that Kaiźer hadn't noticed or even cared about his intrusion. He may not have even seen. Besides, Ryeznya had gleaned several names from his dive into the boy's mind. All of them having several interesting emotions attached to them—the kind he wanted to look at.

Moving around the north end of the open balcony that circled at the top of the tower, he took his time finding a spot that was well hidden and free of moonlight. He settled into the generic lotus position—one leg crossed over the other—and let the familiar sensation of falling flow through him till he was relaxed, mind and body merged as one. He cast a cloaking spell over himself and went to work.

~*All these feelings, my old nemesis*~ Ryeznya thought to himself after entering the memories. They flashed by him at speeds too fast to comprehend. He could only slow them down so much, but he got enough from those quick flashes alone.

~*Such useless things to dwell on, tsk, tsk; you Hunter of old, let me see. I will ignore Abika; I know who she is or was, heh, heh. Kaldär as well; he has my Looking Glass. Though it's odd, he is hidden from your sight. That leaves me with Sin'ka, Oníx, and Darzíel*~

He chuckled. ~*You hold nearly as much hate for this, Darzíel, as you do for me. I care not about what enemies you have unless they interfere with my work~* That made him frown. If a Fallen did decide to interfere, he'd find out how bad of an idea it would be real swiftly.

~Now Kurai Aka Hoshi... seriously intense passion and guilt, HA, did you dump her just in time to realize she was the one? Next time, I should bring her up just to see how many shades of red your face can come up with. I do find it odd how I am unable to sense her aura. Perhaps you fed her to Kaín like I did Abika to my Repidar. That is far more hilarious in sheer tragedy~

He smiled inwardly at the thought but quickly shifted his inner eye over the flashes of stolen memory. He focused as they flew by on a continuous loop till something caught his eye. He let the memories slow, and he watched it play. It was of Oníx. So that crazy bitch was back. How curious. *~For her, you have a strange mix of pride and envy. The satisfaction I can see with all the help and training you gave her in Ascaria. But envy? That I cannot see. That bitch wasn't very powerful when I knew her. What changed? Could it be because of this Sin'ka? Towards the end, a strong sense of worry attached itself to your thoughts of her and Oníx. Oníx must have pulled her lesbian act on your friend. I can sense you and Oníx converging in the southwest... but I do not feel a third~*

Time was flying by, and as his mind raced over the land, he looked at the rising sun. He needed to get what he needed.

~ Sin'ka, where are you, my dear? Kaiźer has respect for you, guilt as well, and even love. My, my, that is quite the tirade of women you've got yourself, Kaiźer. Now, if I just concentrate on her name...~

A sudden flash hit his mind, and like cold water, it shocked his senses. Sin'ka's scent had been very dominant at The Lover' Bite, he realized, and it was... familiar and tinted. It couldn't be! But if history were to teach anything, it was that nothing was impossible. She was an OtherWorlder then, but what kind? If Sin'ka was who he now thought she was, he was going to be very upset. For he had assumed that deal finished.

Following her scent through the city and out into the surrounding mountains, he let his psyche pass over the trees till eventually, he reached the end of the trail. It mirrored the direction that Oníx had come from while going towards Kaiźer's aura. He had what he was looking for.

"Over the hills and far away, how romantic," Ryeznya said to himself as he ended his musings and cut his shroud. It was time to investigate the faraway scent. Just a single look at her would confirm his suspicions. Plus, if she were indeed a supernatural, he could very quickly kill her and ruin Kaiźer's day further. His smile was perhaps a bit murderous at the thought as he rose to his feet. Opening his eyes, he let their red glow pass over the city beneath him.

Ryeznya had begun his meditations just before dawn, and now it was mid-afternoon. Even with the short hours of winter's daylight, he'd spent too much time on the trivial things. That didn't suit him at all. He resolved to kill something even as he stepped off of the snow-covered walkway of the tower and fell to the courtyard far below. Landing with a light tap, he flashed over the wall and headed into the city. He weaved over the roofs in the direction of Sin'ka's scent, and as he passed over the main gate, he began to realize the daunting distance that lay before him. He felt the urge to take to the skies to reach his destination but knew he would leave a magic trail if he did that, and he didn't want to announce his arrival so blatantly. It would be like blowing a bugle while dancing in a clown outfit and shouting, "Here I Am!" to anything capable of detecting him. For certain prey, that could be entertaining, but for an utterly unknown target, it could be dangerous indeed. No, it would be much more prudent to conceal as much of his presence as possible.

The sun was setting by the time he reached the mountains, and with a slow breath, he let his magic go and slowed to a run that soon became a brisk walk. Continuing to keep himself shrouded, he crept through the trees. He was in for a hike without magic, but the cold made his body hum with anticipation, so he didn't care. Finally, after an hour, he saw lights through the trees and, with a grin, viewed the house as it showed itself to him

As he drew closer, though, he saw the light of a Rakariage arriving and watched as if flashed back into the night sky. With a growl, he sensed three people, Kaiźer, Oníx, and what had to be Sin'ka; because all he perceived was a black void where there should have been at least something unnatural.

Well, at least he wouldn't have to deal with them. All he wanted to do was find out what Sin'ka looked like. At this distance, it was apparent she was not the usual supernatural. No, she was very much more indeed.

And with them gone, it left the driveway quite empty.

Onix

chapter 11: Arrival

All is revealed when one steps over the veil

The Eternal Seer
The Age of Heroes

Throughout the whole time they had zipped through the skies, Onix watched Kaiźer as he sat beside her, keen eyes on the surrounding forest. When they had left the house, a sudden downpour of rain had started as they crossed over the mountains, its thick sheets covering the windows of the carriage as they went. Despite this block, in his vision, Kaiźer didn't stop looking down at the ground as it flashed past them.

The three of them wound over the forest like a wraith, the soft purr of the gremlin as he sat out front as he took them towards the city. She sat beside Kaiźer while Sin'ka was opposite them in the shadows of the corner, hidden from prying eyes. She knew her friend was full of questions. It was inevitable after what had just transpired. Moreover, for her to be so quiet made her worry. She was still thinking about Sin'ka's reaction to what had happened when they reached the mountain pass. She hadn't changed much after learning that angels and demons shared the world she lived in. Oníx herself had been only ten when she'd learned about the fact, and the fears she'd felt had made her feel like she was crazy. If she had known that her friend would come face to face with the things she had been fighting against for the last hundred years, she wouldn't have hesitated in training Sin'ka in the ways of the Hunter's Coven.

Breaking through her thoughts, Sin'ka finally spoke up. "What do the demons want? How did they find me? Where do I fit into all this? And who the fuck is Ryeznya? Pausing, Sin'ka's breath came in great gulps as she blurred through her questions. Oníx opened her mouth to calm her down but could not get the words out in time as she started up again.

"And how did your sword devour that fire? Is it magic, or is it a mystic ward? Is it magic? Wait, I already asked that."

"Sin'ka!"

Oníx looked at Kaiźer in surprise. She rarely saw him lose his cool, but as she jumped at his outburst, he looked calm. The only thing that showed his restraint was a golden glow in his eyes. The skin around them was even crackling with energy, and despite his relaxed posture, he was gripping his knees in a death grip, the skin of his knuckles standing white. Still, his following words came out slow and controlled.

"I know a lot is happening, but if you wish to know the facts, you need to calm down. Can you do that for me?"

Physically she didn't react, but the red in her eyes died. It was incredible; Kaiźer had stopped the beast buried inside Sin'ka with just a few words. If things went well, she promised herself she'd make sure Kaiźer pulled his head out of his ass. She would make him see the truth in his feelings.

Sin'ka as well, she clearly had feelings for Kaiźer and seemed ready to accept those feelings, but with his distance, Sin'ka didn't see his true feelings. Oníx could literally smell the conflict going on inside their heads.

Kaiźer, you're such an ass! Can't you see the pain you're causing by trying to keep her free of pain in the first place? As these thoughts ran through her brain, Kaiźer himself, as if sensing Sin'ka's calm demeanor, cooled down, the light vanishing from his eyes as he unclenched his hands from his thighs. Oníx felt the carriage entered the mountain pass and speed around the bottleneck turns with ease.

Rakariage's have a few tricks up their sleeves, and one of them was in the form of a second being that resided in the carriage itself. Once awakened, the carriage gained a more commit-like shape. A *Rakariage* usually has a max speed of 236 mph, but the speed limiter jumped to a max of 261 mph once awakened. It was rumored that *Rakariage's* moved at a rate of at least 280 mph when not carrying anyone, and she wanted so badly to know if the rumors were true.

As he hit the next corner, the *Rakariage* dipped, and she felt gravity lessen as they edged out of alignment and drifted slightly around the bend. They were washed back in their seats as the torque picked up, and it made Sin'ka squeal. Which made Oníx smirk, but she didn't let that stop her from speaking up as they leveled off.

"You had questions that need answering?"

Sin'ka leaned forward in her seat and nodded. "Yeah, all I want is to do is understand."

"Okay, so what do you want to know first?" Oníx had a good idea of what she was going to ask.

"Why did the demons attack me?"

To that question, Oníx hadn't a clue, but she had an idea of what might be the reason. "Well, to start, the demons want all of us dead. It's not just you."

"What did you guys do?"

Sin'ka's question was unexpected, and she had to think before answering. "It's a long story, but in a nutshell, we killed their boss and imprisoned them alongside his spirit, so you can guess, they didn't like that very much."

Oníx didn't like thinking about the past for multiple reasons, one of them being their enemy—the boss she'd mentioned—had roamed free for years before they'd been able to stop him. She hated the fact that she had had to bury thousands of graves in his wake.

"This boss of theirs, who is he?" Sin'ka asked.

"Darzíel ..." she answered.

Sin'ka gasped, and she continued. "He craves power and will do anything to gain it. Thankfully, we were able to stand against him—"

"Wait, you told her about him?" Kaiźer had turned from his daydreaming-like state at the mention—or lack of—Darzíel, and he looked ready to throttle her.

"Yes, I told her!" She filled him in with a quick breakdown of their talk, making sure he got the point.

Sin'ka spoke up, and with another question, made her forget Kaiźer for a moment. "So, I see how this angel, Darzíel has some kind of grudge against you guys for imprisoning him and of how he's connected to the demons, but I don't understand why they came after me?"

"The demons came out of the mirrors, rights?" Kaiźer asked. She nodded, and he continued. "Okay, well, those demons are actually just puppets or extensions of a bigger demon. Behind every mirror or reflective surface is the Mirror Dimension. Mostly they watch on the other side and take what they see to their puppeteer. I suspect, once it saw you with Oníx, it added you to its list of targets."

"Wait, list of targets!" Sin'ka butted in. "What does that mean?"

Kaiźer cursed. "You can say it's a list of all the people it can use to get to me."

Oníx looked at Sin'ka. "That's enough about Darzíel and the Mirror Demons. I think it's about time we told you about Ryeznya."

Kaiźer let out a breath, and she noted it. They were both on edge, apparently. "You want to know who he is," she asked, and Sin'ka nodded. "Well, to start, he's an old frenemy of ours. We just learned he's in town. He even paid Kaiźer here a visit; apparently, he's been tracking the Mirror Demons as well. Unlike us, he knew they were free."

Taking a deep breath, she let Sin'ka take it in. She watched her digest the information, her eyes changing from silver to red to black, then back to silver in the space of a second. Her face twisted through an assortment of different expressions. She didn't look to be in a lousy mood per se, but she wasn't happy; that was obvious. She looked more pained than anything else. It was moments like these that Onír wished she could read Sin'ka's thoughts, but she had always been a black void where others overflowed with thoughts and emotions.

Sin'ka had yet to speak a word as they passed out of the mountains. Her eyes showed little, and her face was blank, revealing nothing. She hadn't shown anything close to fear or realization on the outside. However, she got the feeling that inwardly, both were tearing at her. There was no way someone could be as calm as she was after hearing what she had just heard

"So, we're basically facing the 'end of days like before when you first put Darzíel away," Sin'ka finally said.

"Yep."

Sin'ka bit her lip as Onír imagined the gears turning in her brain. They had just spilled the whole story to her, and she couldn't help but feel a twinge of fear despite knowing what Sin'ka was going to say next.

"Sounds like you need all the help you can get."

Onír let her breath go and turned back to face the road. "You'll be needing our help just as much as we'll be needing yours, I'm sure."

Sin'ka was not one to back down from a challenge, never had been, but was she ready for such a challenge as this?

They were quiet as they crossed into the city. Focusing on the buildings that passed by in a blur, he soon ordered the gremlin to pull into a side ally that was just a few blocks away from where The Lover' Bite sat hidden.

"Why are we stopping here?" Sin'ka asked as she leaned forward and stared out at the dark alley before them, the silver of her eyes glowing slightly.

Oníx didn't dare voice her thoughts as she got out of the carriage to stand in the rain.

Sin'ka soon joined her, and they stood side by side as the sweet smell of fresh rain cleansed the air. Sin'ka's skin shines bright against the brick beside her, the silver of her eyes gleaming against the rain. When they all stood on the cobbled stone of the alley, the Rakariage flashed up into the sky.

"Promise me you'll keep your temper in check," Kaiźer said. "Ryeznya did leave the place in quite a bit of chaos."

"Even if the place was leveled! As long as no one was hurt, he won't have anything to worry about."

Her words confirmed her calm demeanor but inside, Oníx knew she was most likely boiling with emotion while keeping a calm and collected mask in place, just like a Hunter, which in her mind was another fact that she was meant for Kaiźer.

"Time to go," Kaiźer stepped past them, moving from the shadows of the ally. For a few seconds, he seemed to vanish into the darkness itself only to reappear in the light of the streetlamp above, and Oníx paused.

Was that... did he just ShadowStep?

Ryeznya

Chapter 12: Fire & Brimstone

First of the Fire elementals; the angel of old thou came down and laid with of thy mortal femininity.

Forgotten Folkweaver
The Age of Heroes

James looks young, but his Psychic defenses are strong, Ryeznya silently said to himself as a murderous smile appeared on his pale face. James walked towards the sinister cowboy but stopped with about thirty feet between them.

Knowing full well that the woman was not home, Ryeznya rolled out in his gravelly voice, "*Γεια σου αγόρι*—hello, boy. I am thinking Sin'ka requires a little redecorating."

"Hmmm, and what does the *Slayer* want with the Lady Sin'ka?" James demanded, sounding quite confident indeed.

To Ryeznya's oddly red-tinted eyes, James was hardly a man, barely in his twenties if the Hunter were to guess, but in the magical spectrum, he glowed with years of magic.

Ryeznya knew the boy who was not a boy could feel his aura too, but an odd look upon the boy's face bade Ryeznya press his luck despite being recognized as a Hunter. Perhaps today would be entertaining, after all.

"Well, James, I find it odd that you possess such aura but think only one hell exists."

Okay, this guy's not normal. James thought to himself. Out loud, he said, "Fine then, please tell me who in the 'hells' you are?"

"That is better, thank you. There are nine circles, after all. Now, do forgive my intrusion upon this plot of land. I am Ryeznya Bon Rykiel, the Hunter who you already know as the Slayer. I am here to speak to Lady Sin'ka."

Ryeznya noticed the boy bristle and had to give him credit when he replied calmly.

"Sorry to say, but lady Sin'ka is out. I will have to ask you to leave. I'm also quite certain the lady won't want to speak to you, so you need not return."

Ryeznya smiled, visibly fraying the boy's nerves all the more.

"Oh, I will not be going so soon. I beg my leave to stay. The conversation I must have with the Lady Sin'ka is indeed a necessity."

"Leave to stay?" James asked through clenched teeth, entirely done with Ryeznya's attitude, it would seem.

"It means permission."

"I have none to give... sir...."

"Then that is a problem." Ryeznya could feel the boy's aura swirling and gained strength as he spoke. Ryeznya slowly took off his black trench coat of very odd-looking leather, folded it, and tossed it aside. It glided a few feet to set down smoothly upon the ground. He then threw his Stetson aside, which flew to gently land upon the folded bundle. All the while, James watched and seethed.

The Slayer then allowed some of his aura to build and swirl at his feet. Not too much, though. *We don't want*

Kaiżer to sense the looming battle and come with that infernal weapon of his.

Ryeznya mused, then said to James. "I know nothing of who you are, but I am very sure you will fail."

"Oh, Yah?" James shouted, immediately throwing an orange fireball at Ryeznya's face.

That caught him off guard, though he'd never admit it; Ryeznya was surprised. Either way, his superior eyes allowed him to summon his purple and blue flames, surround his index finger in said flames and then catch the little ball on the said flaming finger.

With a quick flick of a wrist, Ryeznya shot the orange ball, now swirling blue and orange in kaleidoscope fashion and at ludicrous speeds, right back at the boy to explode on impact.

However, it didn't explode. The explosion ruffled the branches of the surrounding trees, and with a loud whoosh, the flames... simply stopped moving. Turning in a swirl, Ryeznya watched with a growing frown as the fires of the impact shrank. They turned around and around, finally vanishing with a soft hiss. The boy had eaten the flames...

"Oh my..." Ryeznya mumbled.

Only immortals learned to eat magic; fire users learning only after their hundredth year of immortality. This kid!

"Nice try, *Slayer*, but I'm still alive." James boasted, with the word Slayer dripping scorn. Again, James had a fireball in his, well, both of his hands now. Ryeznya saw this and quickly spread the flames on his finger to both hands, enveloping them in the purple/blue flames. They crackled slightly as he moved.

James widened his stance a bit...

Ryeznya prepared a counterspell...

James slammed his hands together, collapsing the orange fireballs into one, subsequently using the force of the impact to send a small beam of concentrated yellow flames at Ryeznya. It shot at lightning speed and grew in size as it rushed to its target, roaring like a giant hell-spawn.

His counter spell was not quite adequate for this level of a modified flame blast technique. Ideally, fire magic needs more room. James's fire was quick indeed but still not fast enough.

Ryeznya clapped his hands together.

The clap caused his purple and blue flames to collapse into themselves, creating a six-foot-tall vertical flame blade, it too a crackling purple/blue fire. The sinister crescent of angry flames stood proud; its edge pointed at James.

James's yellow flame blast—hell-spawn roar and all—slammed into the purple/blue razor-edged flame blade with a vicious collision, creating a concussive sound wave that shook the mansion's windows. Ryeznya's flame blade spit the beam with ease, sending two separate beams well wide of the Hunter. Rushing past its target, the two yellow flame lines hit the ground way behind Ryeznya, gouging the soil with deep ruts. James halted the attack when he saw such.

Ryeznya banished his flame blade.

"Why don't you try something other than counterspells, *Slayer*?" James taunted, once more filling the word Slayer with as much scorn as he could.

Ryeznya eyes changed to a violent green.

Six wisps of ethereal black smoke began to emanate from his back. The epicenters of which stood at about the middle of his shoulder blades. Said ghostly wisps came in three sets, three wisps on each side. The upper group was in an upright delta; the middle ones primarily horizontal, and the lower set falling in a downward omega. Ryeznya chose to fully summon only the upper group of his Wings of the Azure.

As the chosen wings solidified, James shifted his stance. His new perspective suggested hand-to-hand combat. James then made his hands into fists and ignited them in yellow flames.

Ryeznya stared, his eyes pulsing green. They sparked with green lightning as he stretched out his newly formed wings to their total thirty feet. Layer upon layer of flaming feathers gleamed iridescent, black fire near the edge, fading into layers of purple, purple-blue, blue, then white at the tips of the lower layer of flame feathers. If one saw it, like James was now, they would think of the wings of a phoenix and be afraid.

James wasn't. He looked on without wavering, but Ryeznya knew all hell was about to break loose and shit was about to hit the fan. James was tense, and he could see the boy contemplating counters... sadly, for him, only one thing would save him, and Ryeznya got the feeling this boy didn't have it.

He soon decided on his favorite spell, a modified flame lance. Such a low-level shot would show the boy something to look forward to if he survived.

With his wings still stretched out, Ryeznya summoned ten green orbs in the middle row of flame feathers on each branch. The spheres compressed into pyramidal diamonds of jade.

James wasn't sure what was about to happen, but he officially nixed any idea of a counter strike and just got himself ready to dodge what came his way. He un-tensed his muscles and relaxed his breathing.

Knowing the boy's inner turmoil, Ryeznya's smile was perhaps a bit murderous when he gave the final verbal component to his attack.

"*ADVENT BARRAGE!*" he barked in his gravelly voice, and immediately all twenty of the green pyramidal diamond spheres shot at the boy in sequence from the outside of each wing, instantly spawning new spears and reversing sequence with each volley.

Ryeznya fired ten volleys in less than a second.

James dodged most of them. He had jumped at the last second but came back down as he shot more. James then jumped about like a ninja who'd been given a shot of epinephrine, leaping, rolling, jumping, cartwheeling, and flipping all over the place. He was passing through the volleys like a leaf on the wind, and Ryeznya watched as he tried to grab one of the lances, succeeding only in tearing the skin on his palm. Doing so caused three lances to rip through him. On the plus side, it caused him to stumble for just a second.

When the attack ended and the shots ceased, James stood panting in fatigue, a gash on his left thigh and another outside his right arm. He didn't see the third but soon saw blood leak past the boy's black hair fall over his eye, marking the third location.

"Is that"—James took a heavy breath—"all you got?

It was a challenge... this boy was playing a game that he knew he had already lost.

"Oh, I have plenty left," Ryeznya called out. "You, on the other hand, are nearly spent. The Divinejump uses too much magic for you to handle, apparently." As he spoke, he banished the green orbs.

James didn't reply. He was pretty sure he would die. But this pompous jackass was going to go down with him. James gathered his breath, calming his aura until he found his center. He then began to build upon his inner fire.

"Well, boy, the aura you emanate is impressive. I can see it, and it is quite angry. I wonder what... what is it you think will work against me." Ryeznya was careful to add mockery and condescension into each word. Helping the boy collect his power, he kept his upper wings ready, his eyes glowed green, the violent light sparking as he added to his mockery. "I wager you will faint after the next offensive you take. Then what, boy?"

James shot his hands out to the sides, igniting them in his yellow fire. He swung his arms in a wide arch, one rising up while the other fell to his waistline. His arms still stretched straight, met with a tiny spark as they came to cross together before his chest. The resulting sweep of his arms left a ring of energy floating in the air before him. It glowed an angry incandescent as James, sliding arm against arm, brought his hands to meet at his chest. He pressed his thumbs and forefingers together and arched them into a spade.

"Dance of Flames," James whispered. Ryeznya watched as a pentagram formed within the circle before James and grinned. *This kid! He has got to have a good three hundred years on him I didn't know about. That's a masters' technique!*

When the pentagram appeared, Ryeznya ignited his fists and his fire. He could punch through it regardless. He was a master to boot. Granted, he still had years before he reached Magician levels, but this kid would be easy money.

James continued his spell. "Art of the Dragons Breath," the magic circle began to spin, growing faster and faster as an orb of yellow fire appeared within the pentagram. It was like a circular tornado as it sat between the circle and his fingers. Growing in size and power until it was the size of a softball.

He then grasped it with both hands and pulled it back like it was a slingshot.

Ryeznya prepared his counterspell.

"FLAME PILLAR!" James shouted. The orb flashed as it jumped out of the circle. Once released, it shot forward at lightning speed, starting small only to explode into a twenty-foot wide sphere of yellow fire that swirled like the barrel of a rifle as it shot at Ryeznya.

Ryeznya noticed tiny sparks of green mixed in and, with a mental grin, put his arms forward in a triumphant manner, intending to simply catch the yellow fire, hold it and overpower the spell by letting his own purple and blue flames consume it, causing the boy's fire to essentially frizzle out. That was the plan anyway.

What actually happened was, right as the yellow pillar of death was about to contact his outstretched hand, James pulled his hands apart? The yellow fire shot apart like a five-pointed star to swirl past his outstretched hand. Caught completely by surprise at this turn of events, Ryeznya didn't know what had happened for a second.

Within those few short seconds, James brought his fingers back together in a double hammerhead fist, which in turn caused the five pillars of fire to reunite just behind him.

James finished the move by dropping his locked fists down to one hip as he fell into a crouch, one leg out for balance while the other bent to slow his descent. The now single pillar of magic slammed into Ryeznya's back, the force of which put him to one knee.

That didn't please him in the slightest...

The flames crackled and hissed as they died in power, leaving Ryeznya's back smoking with tendrils of smoke.

"Looks like you lost your bet, old man," James said with a huff. "I'm still standing. *That should have at least knocked the Slayer unconscious,* he thought as he took a heaving breath.

"Still standing, eh?" Ryeznya sneered as he stood up. "Well Congrat-fucking-lations, boy."

James had about enough time to blink before the Slayer had moved. In a flash, he crossed the entire distance between them to stand before James with a finger on the boy's chest, almost as fast again, before James could even tense a muscle to jump back, he was shot backward by Ryeznya's poke. James smashed through the huge fountain then into the front door, going right through it, destroying the surrounding wall with his passage. James came to a stop just behind the couch in the living room, very unconscious indeed.

Ryeznya heard the squeals of the housemaids and the boy's skin sliding on polished marble alike. He banished his wings, fetched his hat and coat, and entered Sin'ka's home with his oddly red-tinted eyes.

Ryeznya

chapter 13: Mysteries Revealed

When thy angel came down thou was followed by one of ring and vow. Thy feminine charm turned to rage and chaos which turned upon thy angel.

Forgotten Folkweaver
The Age of Heroes

Moving into the house, Ryeznya passed through the remains of the doorway and let his steps echo through the massive lobby; James had collided with the door and passed through it quickly from the force of his passage.

Passing the boy, he grabbed his collar and lifted him up onto the couch. He was out cold, skin red from sliding on the marble. Ryeznya was okay with such; he would wake him once he was done. He gave a quick glance around and made a mental note of all the boxes and sheets covering a few of the tables and shelves in the room. A soft scuffle sounded behind him, and turning, he was faced with a group of two men and three women who were clearly the house's staff.

He only had a second of hesitated, "Where does the lady of the house slumber?"

A young maid was pushed forward. She looked at him with fear, and he gestured for her to speak.

"Uh, her chambers are in the back room, down the hall on the left when you enter the lobby. There's no missing it...."

His smile was a bit murderous as he turned back to the foyer, time to find out if he was right.

He passed back into the lobby and headed down the hall. It was softly lit, and there were flowers along the walls, each complementing the next batch as he traversed the distance. Finally, he reached a slightly different door. It was engraved and was made of oak. He could see the wards preventing unwanted entry and read the weaves. Clearly designed to give those who activated it a slight shock, it had several levels of defense. The first level was for mortal protection, the next for immortal protection, and finally, the last for angelic and demonic protection. Apparently, if he tried to open the door, he'd be turned to dust. This was Oníx; the weaves were her work.

Clever girl, but he simply raised a hand and cut the complex in half. His fire burned the weaves, and he shielded himself as the door was blown off its hinges. The staff had most likely heard that, and he quickly sealed off the hallway. He didn't want them interfering; there was little they could do anyway.

Stepping through the gap that remained, he entered a room clearly being used by a woman. It was well decorated, and each color accentuated its compatriots. The lady was an artist. He admired the picture on her wall and, fondling the frame, inspected the depiction of Revelations. It was an oil painting and an original to boot. Wrapped, it was just like the real thing. Not a shred of another's inspiration could be seen. The picture was a direct image of Heaven in all its glory. Even the bottom half was correct in showing the landscape of the Underworld. This, in itself, made him wonder. Did Sin'ka know a seer, or was she prophetic? It didn't matter any; she was an OtherWorlder, and if he was right, someone he had vowed to kill.

Giving the painting one more glance, he looked around the room. He took in the bed, with its tall posts and drapes, then the wardrobe alongside it. Walking into the closet, he inspected the clothes and grinned at the lady's diversity. She was a woman of many ages, for sure. But he was not finding what he was looking for. He went back out into the bedroom and looked around again, this time in the magical spectrum. What he saw was once more nothing. He was passing over the bed when he did a double-take.

He came and placed his hand on the bedpost and found a small dial. At the top of one of the posts, a tiny flicker of magic pulsed, weak enough that he had almost missed it. However, when he touched it, he pulled his hand away with a hiss. The skin of his palm was singed.

Looking at the magic again, he inspected the single weave. It was demonic in power, and he grew confused. No one here used dark magic, but here he looked at evidence of such. He shattered the single weave with a finger and destroyed the magic. He twisted the dial, but nothing happened. Frustrated, he inspected the gears within. Made of iron, he was able to sense them. By the time he figured out the required positions for each spring to unlock it, he was not in the mood to smile.

He turned the knob and soon heard a combination of clicks. He stepped back as the bed swiveled. Nothing could be seen to show its path, but he could listen to the gears beneath his feet, working as the bed swiveled to reveal a hidden passage within the floor. Steps led down, and he fisted his hands in anticipation.

He descended into the dark passageway.

Ryeznya lit his magic and let it glow white-hot. It was his most potent magic, but he liked the light. He didn't need it, but still, it was comforting. The stone of the channel was dry, and he traveled down till he sensed the land surround him. This was definitely the place. No one had something like this unless they had something to hide. It reminded him of when he had gotten his powers; that day had been one of the causes for his claustrophobia.

In next to no time, he reached the end of the road and stepped out into a large chamber. It was dark, but he caught sight of a traditional light switch. Light flooded the section with a flick of a finger, and he squinted at the sudden brightness. Letting his magic go, he moved to the center of the room and let his sight adjust. His smile was a bit murderous when it did, for on the wall before he was an old portrait of a beautiful lady. Looking to be from early-3700 A.B., the painting was old, and the lady's face was an exact representation of his nephew's long-dead wife. Dear Abika looks like you were given the gift of the gods.

The gift of 'Direct Reincarnation' was a rare thing indeed. Clearly, someone in the higher-ups hadn't been happy with the outcome of her life. He had the angels to thank for such, but he still wasn't pleased to learn of it. He hated it when someone interfered with his work, even if it had been complete, to begin with.

Forget the boy; he had to find the mirror to finish what he was being paid for. After, he planned to finish the job he had thought done. Activating his magic, he passed from the chamber. He then shot out of the channel to blast through the roof and out into the night.

He was late for a date with a magician.

-Part 2-

Kaldär

chapter 14: shifting façades

Six eternals, six mortals, six evils. Six were chosen for each. Six pure, six innocent, six tainted.

The Eternal Seer
The Age of Heroes

112 B.B. the High Kingdom

Bright and ever going is the expanse of the sea. Its turquoise waters fill the gaze of the virile eyes that look upon its beauty. A gust of wind flows along the cliffs, bringing with it the sounds of silence and the scent of death.

Stained red with blood, a cloak flows in the wind. Covered in silver, the owner closes his eyes of pure gold to the horror that surrounds him, but even he cannot escape reality. Even in death, old enemies torment the peace he strives for. The sound of the wind, the flap of his cloak, everything fades as Kaldär looks back...

Love, one of the most potent forces in the known universe. Capable of creation... as well as destruction. A hearth burns orange with warmth in a small house as it does its job in striving off the cold grip of winter. Lost within the flames, his eyes glazed in pain, Kaldär is trapped, and all he sees is past sins.

"Honey?"

Out of the obscurity, a hand breaks through to wipe a tear from his face. After six months of non-stop battle, he had come home victorious. Fighting for the High King, he had watched as men killed for power, again and again, never able to satisfy their need for more.

He'd finally had enough. After the battle, he'd snuck into his King's bed chambers and stolen one of the objects they had taken.

Unbeknownst to him, he carried a divine artifact. Warping it in cloth, he'd fled, leaving no trace of his thievery. When dawn broke, illumination the morning sky, the King's fury was heard throughout the five Kingdoms. Oblivious to who had taken what he cherished, the King blamed those who had surrendered in the previous battle and had had them slaughtered. Yet, he'd found no man who knew where his mirror was and soon realized he would never again see its beauty before him or hold its power in hand.

Upon arrival at his home in Genesteria, Kaldär had hidden the mirror within the stones of his house, its power and beauty wrapped in showy silk.

Not three hours later, his wife had arrived, jumping into his arms with joy, unaware of his betrayal and theft. Now, after the day was at its end, her words broke the black void that clouded his mind.

"Don't worry, I'm here; everything is going to be alright, your home now."

For as long as he could remember, Sara had been the only person who was able to pull him from his dark pain. After Sara had come into his life, it was never the same. She was the one who was there, ready to embrace him, love him, and cherish him. As a Death Dealer, those around him had never accepted his skills. Blood was his life, death his only friend, and who could love a man who knew nothing but such.

That had been his crucible until Sara, and as he looked up into her eyes, he once more felt the warmth of her love fill him and couldn't help but smile. She had accepted him as hers.

Many years had passed since he had lost the love that Sara had offered freely and openly.

It had been on that fateful day that he, after a long day in the fields, was on his way back from town with a surprise. He had finally found a vendor who sold what he had been looking for.

After leaving the war, he had embraced the simple life of a farmer. It took a lot of strength and endurance to teal a field by hand. It was grueling, but it kept him fit.

At his side, a silver wolf moved, yellow eyes bright and alert. Looking up at him, Ba'ile waged his tail, pink tongue hanging free as he trotted beside him. The day was at its peak, and he was sweating. The wolf had found him during the war and ever since had never left his side. Young in age, the pup had shown a humanlike understanding since the first day, but he'd never found out why. He patted Ba'ile on the head as he stopped, but as he did, Ba'ile looked behind them. Ears alert, the great wolf growled, letting a low rumble escape from his lips. Seeing the anger in his companion's eyes, he looked ahead to see what had caught his attention?

Dust... and lots of it clogged the distant road.

"Ba'ile, we need to get off the road," he called.

Jumping into the thick underbrush, with Ba'ile on his heels, he sprinted for the trees. Merging with the trunks, he jumped and scaled one of them before turning and looking at the road from high in the branches. As the dust cloud grew closer, it revealed at least twelve riders, led by a thirteenth. Surprised, he watched as the leader's face was exposed. It was his old company, he realized. And the man leading was his old apprentice, now infamous general Kusko!

Gritting his teeth, he tried to think of why such a man would come to such a back-alley country. Could it be because they had found him? No, that couldn't be it, and the only other thing would be that they were here on orders from the King. It looked like they had just finished and were heading home...

Once they passed, Kaldär dropped amid the scattered dust. He watched the man solemnly—who had taken his spot as the chooser of the slain—as he vanished on the horizon.

Gripping Sara's gift tightly, he started for home once more, where he knew she would be waiting, her arms held complete, and a smile on her face.

Hearing Ba'ile bark, he looked up as he reached the break in the road and faced his home. The sight that met his eyes, though, was one he would never forget. At the end of the driveway, flames rose high, licking at the remains of what had been his cottage.

The chocolates he'd bought fell from limp fingers, and with a cry, he started running. He reached the end of the road and rushed into the flames. Not feeling the blaze as it bit at his clothes, he searched the debris, lifting beam and wall alike in a desperate attempt of hope, all the while praying he wasn't too late.

His hands ran red by the time he found his beloved. Lifting the shattered stone from his wife's limp form, he found she had been left untouched by the flames. With tears streaming down his face, he turned her over and saw her holding a purple bundle of cloth in her arms.

Sara's eyes fluttered, and she reached up to touch his cheek.

"Kaldär, my love," she whispered.

Crying openly now, he clutched his beloved, his eyes locked onto the bundle in her arms. "How long have you known about the mirror?" he asked.

The skin around Sara's eyes crinkled as she smiled. "You always thought you were so sneaky," she chuckled. "I'm your wife; I've known since the beginning."

Sara struggled to breathe, and he sat, unable to move as her eyes lost their shine.

"Don't... don't let Markilios get... get the mirror," she struggled to say. "It belongs to the gods, you ... you must protect it at all c... at all costs...."

Lifting the bundle, Sara pushed the mirror into his hands, but he threw it aside. "Don't say such things, my angel," he sobbed. "What will I do without you?"

Sara smiled and gripped his hand. "You have a long road to follow, this, I know."

Her words faded, and her eyes lost focus, her hand going limp against his as her eyes glazed over.

Throwing his head back, he cried to the heavens, letting his anger and sorrow echo into the sky. Ba'ile approached his ears flat and his tail low as he sniffed at Sara's hand, licking it before letting out a quiet whimper, showing his own sorrow.

He sat unaware when a warm light caught his eye. The bundle that held the mirror he'd stolen was glowing with a soft golden light. The cloth moved as if in a slow breeze, picking up speed till it whipped in a wild frenzy, coming free of the hand mirror.

Blazing bright, the artifact lit with divine fire that shot up in a spiral, splitting the clouds above. Kaldär watched as the flames moved in a slow dance, sparking and sizzling. The glass itself shone gold; its image a pool of celestial stars that shone bright,

The ground rumbled, and with a roar, the flames exploded out. Whipping Kaldär's hair back, the very air was sucked out of his and Ba'ile's lungs as that fire shot high.

A strong streak of light shot free of the artifact, rocketing into the sky on great wings. The light flaked free of the being, revealing a bronze-skinned muscular form. Clothed in gold armor, the being floated in the sky before them on wings of white light. Feathers dropped to the burnt soil, glowing softly amid the still-burning house. With eyes of bright blue, he stared down at him, his hair curling long and golden blond. Upon appearing, the man spoke, and his words were laced with power, echoing on the wind like faraway music.

"Kaldär Morningstar, you have protected *The Fore-Lorne Looking Glass* and kept it from those who wished to use its power for great evil," the man bowed his head in thanks. "But still, they come to claim what is not theirs to wield. It is for this reason we, the divine beings, charge you with the protection of the heavenly artifacts and gift you with the power to carry out our request."

Raising his hand, the angel summoned a mighty sword that hummed with energy and pointed it at Kaldär's chest. Tensing, he listened as the man spoke once more.

"Thus, we grant you true immortality, opening both the divine and the demonic within you."

A beam of searing white light shot from the blade to strike his chest. He cried out as he felt liquid fire run into his veins, his skin crackling with gold and blue energy. His clothes burned away as the power traveled to his eyes. All at once, his vision flashed incandescently. His hair began to smolder, and with a flash, his hair's roots lost all their color.

"And for Ba'ile, we grant the spirit of the wild to run free once more within his blood. Giving everlasting life and the strength to stand as he had once before."

Overcome by the energy that filled him, he barely heard the words as he watched the wolf get struck by a bolt of light similar to his own. Growing more prominent, his muscles denser, Ba'ile's form rippling from his sudden growth. Kaldär heard him howl and watched as the wolf bared canines that lengthened, growing sharper. Finally, the wolf opened eyes that shone golden yellow, the pupils glowing bright white. In a rush of fur and rippling muscle, the wolf shifted quickly and smoothly, taking on a humanoid shape only to return back to normal then back to stay human. Ears pointed; the wolf was a shifter, Kaldär realized. Tribal designs wrapped around the man's body, and as the fire in his own veins faded, his companion sat up slowly, his chest rising and falling heavily.

Lowering his blade, his task complete, the angel shot into the sky, trailing light. Vanishing among the heavens, the only evidence of his visit was a light trail in the sky, marking his flight.

Sitting with Ba'ile at his side, he looked at himself. He was covered in soot, and Ba'ile was no better off. However, both of them were thrumming with energy and looked down at Sara once more. He felt his tears fall free once again.

Gathering her into his arms, he stood. Ba'ile rose as well, and they walked from the house, ignoring the flames licking at their legs as they moved into the clean air. Kaldär stopped and turned back to face what he had hoped would be his home for years to come.

Weeping softly, he kissed his wife's forehead. "Take her to stand by your side," he whispered. "Your heavenly grace holds no bounds, but her love surely surpasses it still. Cherish her as I did."

He pulled back with a start and watched in growing wonder as Sara's skin began to glow. He had spoken, thinking nothing would happen and that he would bury her at sundown, but ever so slowly, his wife turned into light, her figure flowing up to the heavens to join the stars. He stood still till he saw the last traces of her light vanish into the sky and only then turned and strode back onto the road.

"Come one, Ba'ile, we have a king to slay."

Ba'ile moved up beside him, and he saw that they stood eye to eye. The wolf met his gaze and nodded with a knowing glance, and Kaldär wandered what the angel had done to the wolf. *We grant the spirit of the wild to run free once more.* Once more? That was what he had said. As a shifter, he wondered what their newfound power had done to his friend.

"So, you kept your heritage a secret. Why?"

Ba'ile looked ahead. He didn't answer for a long moment, and Kaldär waited as they walked. Dressed in the remains of their clothes, the two of them walked side by side.

"I am an outcast and could not let my true face be seen," Ba'ile said after they had walked a reasonable distance down the road.

"Why is that?"

"I was a disappointment to my family, but my mother smuggled my sister and me away. I left when I came of age to keep them safe."

Kaldär nodded in understanding. It wasn't much, but it was a start. A disappointed family, he understood that full-heartedly being raised by a father that was never happy with his achievements and a mother that cleaned his wounds after each sparring match at his hand. Having grown up as a warrior, it had been no surprise when the King took him away. If he had taken the path that Ba'ile had, he and the shifter would have been one and the same.

"So, you found me after all that happened. Why me?" Kaldär asked.

Ba'ile took a deep breath before answering. "I saw the same light in your eyes that I saw in the mirror every day while with my mother. You wanted a better life, and I wanted to help you achieve that. And now, with this... power, I believe I can do just that."

Kaldär picked at his ruined shirt. "Well, let's at least get a change of clothes beforehand."

Ba'ile smiled. "Yes, let's. And then, what was it you said back at the house, oh yes, we have a king to slay."

Grinning, Kaldär ripped the ruined shirt from his shoulders. Yeah, nothing would stand between him and vengeance.

Present Day: Five Years Previous ~

If only Paris would notice her. Floating somewhere off the coast of Londinium, Eźmeralda Starlight moved her arms through the crystal-clear waters of the Nirvana sea, its smooth texture cooling her skin as it flowed around her, singing a silent symphony.

She was miles from the shore, its outline barely visible atop the waves. Most would panic from being this far out, even more so if they were alone with no one in sight like her. She did this a lot, so... she didn't panic; most of the time, she came out here to escape. She enjoyed the peace and tranquility that came with being out at sea. The waves flowed with a dancer's grace, and when they grazed her skin with a lover's touch, it felt almost sensual.

As she looked at the clear blue sky, its great expanse reaching from horizon to horizon, she took in the slight salting of white clouds and their peppered shades within. Gazing at the beauty above her, she tried to clear her mind of the man that filled its entirety. His face was always a contrast of both light and dark and good and evil. She remembered the sinful bronze of his skin as his muscles bunched and rippled while he worked. It had caused her heart to jump with infatuation. With a hammer, he was a god, and during his training, she had tried not to watch but failed as he gleamed with sweat, his face a mask of determination, the green of his eyes focused.

She had often built up the courage to approach him, but every time she'd turned away like a scared little girl. With her unnatural green hair, you'd think she'd stand out but nope!

What really made her stand out was the furry cat ears and soft tail she sported.

She was a shifter and, like most shifters, held a resemblance to her animal form while human. The townsfolk looked at her as an oddity, but this was a time of change after all. So far, she was the only one of her kind that she knew of, and it was hard to hide her features. A lot of magical creatures have it easy, being able to look fully human when they choose. Her ears were her biggest problem. They sat where her ears usually would have. They were pointed as well and stuck out of her thick hair, making it obvious she was different. They were soft and quite sensitive to the touch too. It was one of her weak spots, actually alongside her tail. Both were covered in silky red fur and were easily noticeable when exposed. She usually tucked them in her clothes to seem normal, but the locals knew her and had accepted her, if only partly.

Her eyes were the reason behind the reluctance from the townsfolk. Framed by thick lashes, their bright color stood stark against her tanned skin. What made it hard for most were her pupils; they were long and pointed like a cat. She may look like a cat, yes, but she loved the water.

So, she came out here to escape the people and the noise. It was where she could be herself. Good portions of the people in Londinium were travelers passing through, which was hard for her despite the locals. She didn't care, but the stress grew to be too much at times. However, like a lover, the sea always accepted her.

Still....

She wished Paris would notice her. He had never looked at her, never even teased or picked on her like all the other boys did. Hell, she bet he didn't even know she existed.

Watching the sun fall to its home within the sea, she started to swim back to shore, taking her time, thoroughly enjoying the salty caress of the waves. After a time, the white sands of the beach appeared, glittering brightly.

She soon touched her feet to its gritty texture, the soft granules shifting around her feet, slowly oozing between her toes. Emerging from the water, she pulled her shirt over her head and rang it out before slipping it back on. Shaking her head, she let her hair pool as it dried in the cool breeze.

Moving up the beach, she heard a small splash behind her and, turning, found herself looking into a pair of pure... black... eyes.

Yanked off her feet, she was lifted into the air and dangled high above the creature that held her. She found herself staring into a mouth filled with rows upon rows of sharp teeth. Caught by its gaze, she could only stare for a second, and by then, it was too late to escape the tentacle that had wrapped around her leg. Cut off from the land, she did the only thing she could think of.

She screamed.

Paris stood just off the edge of the beach with his cronies. They'd come here to train today and had been doing so since noon. The sun was now dipping in the sky, and looking up, he was about to call it a day when a young man came up to him.

"Yo, Paris. Whatcha doin?"

Looking at the guy standing there, waiting, he turned away without responding.

"Dude, why da cold shoulda?"

"If you're asking to hang, I'm busy," he said.

"What's so important ya'd ditch yo friends?" the kid asked.

Wanting to get away, he turned his back to the boy. "You're not a friend; you are not even a local, so get lost. I have my training to do."

That wasn't the truth, though. Paris was actually going to go catch a glimpse of the young lady with the green hair. It was around this time that she would be coming back to shore. Something about her fascinated him.

She had been in Londinium when he had arrived a while ago and had felt different from everyone else. Besides, her other features gave it away. Shifters rarely left their clans and even those who did never stayed in the mortal cities of man, at least not in this realm.

He was about to tell everyone to wrap things up when a loud shriek pierced the air. Looking around, he realized it had come from where he knew the green-haired lady was! *No, no, no! It can't be!"*

As soon as the thought ran through his mind, he was running in the direction of the screaming.

It was too soon.

Screams echoed across the beach. The sounds filled with terror and anguish. The Kraken looked up at her as it lowered her to its gaping mouth. Oh, gods, I'm going to die! She was still a freaking virgin, for Christ's sake! She hadn't even done anything yet with her life.

Her throat constricted in terror, cutting off her screams at the thought, well damn, life's a bitch. She thought of Paris and wondered what he'd think if he saw her now. Would he save her, or would he run like everyone else and let her die to save his own skin?

No sooner did the thought cross her mind than she heard flesh slice and felt herself falling. She screamed as she plummeted towards the beast's gaping mouth, only to have the wind knocked out of her when something hard collided with her.

Landing on the sand, she heaved in an attempt to breathe, rolling about like a fish out of water. Her chest felt like it had been used as a boxing bag. She took great gulps, and as she began to regain feeling, she heard a familiar voice.

"Holy Shit!"

Looking up, she squinted into the setting sun and watched as a figure ran up. He was sweaty and looked to have been running. His breath came in great heaves.

"Stop where you are," a second person said.

She jumped at the voice. The object that had hit her hadn't been an object at all. It had been a man. And a handsome one at that, she realized as she stood up. Looking at Paris, she watched him stop a short distance away with the sun on his back. He stood before her, but he looked off somehow like the sun was eating at his figure.

"I don't know who the fuck you are, but that's my girl!"

She had to pause for a second when she heard it. *His girl?* Had she just heard him, right? He thought she was his girl. No way. Her jaw dropped, and she felt her cheeks grow hot.

She sat up and began to smile when Paris stepped out of the light but lost it when she saw his face.

With eyes as black as coal, the skin around them was bleached and cracked like clay. He smiled at her, and she blanched when she saw his teeth. They were pointed, and she realized then what she had thought to be the sun was actually his body flickering like smoke. This couldn't be her Paris... could it?

Paris knew his plan was fucked. He had called the Kraken but hadn't expected it to show up so soon. Instead of him being there to save her and gain her trust. He had shown up to find her on the beach, already saved, and by a mountain of a man. Looking at him standing there, he got the feeling he should stay back. But he wasn't like that. As a prince, he listened to no one and always got what he wanted.

The green-haired lady looked at him in wonder and recognition as if she had seen him before. Had she noticed him at one point? There was no way! His own friends had been oblivious to his straying eyes, and with his own mission on this plane of reality being to destroy, he usually blended in with the locals, infusing them with false memories of him. Every time it had been the same.

Death, death, blood, and carnage, all blending into the symphony that had filled his ears for centuries, its verses dripping with crimson when his blade swung, killing both enemy and friend alike. The very fires of purgatory burned within his veins, its power bringing cleansing to the mortal realm in the name of the unseen one.

This city was to be the same; every man, woman, and child would be slaughtered by his hand.

But this woman, the woman who had the power within to give him what he desired, was looking at him... in horror. He had let his true face come out after seeing the man above her, and now, he had fucked everything up.

He roared at the heavens.

Eźmeralda sat frozen on the sand, her eyes locked on Paris as he stood before her. His smile was no longer bright, and she shivered as he looked back at her, his eyes cold and his grin deadly.

As he stood there, he let loose a cry, and she watched as thirteen holes opened in the sand. Blazing bright, they spewed fire, letting out a wide assortment of... of demons! Her eyes went wide as they settled on their feet.

With eyes a mixture of blacks and reds, they snarled and grinned, their lips framing sharp teeth that gleamed; canines standing prominent.

Three females crouched, their beauty lighting the air around them. They all sported black wings with leathery skin stretched tight against thick muscle.

Ten men and three ladies, all looking like they wanted to eat her alive; it was too much. And it only got worse as Paris stepped forward, a pair of his own wings flinging wide. Their generous length was covered in black feathers. As if sucking the very light from the area, the wings crackled with black flames. As he shifted, her eyes were drawn to his lips as they moved in a sensual sweep. He was smiling at her.

"My dear," he said. "How I have longed for a pet of such beauty as yours. Rise so you may join me. I can give you what you desire. I can please you like no other. I will make you a queen."

His words echoed with power, and she moaned as heat suddenly flooded through her body. At his words, she felt an odd urge overtake her, and her vision flashed white. She suddenly saw herself writhing on a bed of silk, skin hot as Paris knelt above her. He pleased her, and she ached evermore. It felt so real, but under it all, a dark image bloomed. Swimming beneath Paris's spoken words, a sinister reality was painted before her.

Where she stood happy, a hand on her swollen belly as Paris, and she laughed in joy at her upcoming pregnancy; underneath it, she saw herself chained with demons swarmed her, their bodies burning. They ran on cloven hooves, their chests carved with bloody glyphs, all of them watching as she rocked back and forth, her eyes glazed in confusion.

She stood transfixed in horror as she slumped. Paris came to stand before her, and the demons closed in, their eyes filled with rage.

The images became distorted, and suddenly she was sitting in a different room. Paris held her hand as doctors helped her give birth to a baby boy but once more, the images muddied, becoming replaced by a vision of Paris standing over her once more, his eyes glowing with Greed.

"You are mine!" he said coldly.

Once more, the image shifted, but it wasn't a happy change. Eźmeralda was holding two babes, their tiny hands grasping. Biting at her with sharp teeth, their clawed hands gripping at her as she nursed them.

Paris filled the image suddenly, standing behind her, his voice chilling her very soul.

"You have given your body to me, you have built my army, and now you will behold the ones you gave life to." Thrusting his arms wide, a door opened, and she saw the multitude of monsters, both beautiful and ugly, fill the image.

She cried out, and the horror before her shattered. She stumbled back, her skin clammy, her heart racing in fear. Paris frowned, and the demons behind him growled.

"She resists you, my lord; she sees the truth," one of them said. She gasped as she saw that the demons before her were the same as the vision.

"Shall we kill her?" another asked, this time a female.

"NO! She can't resist forever," Paris snapped. "Kill that man and bring her to me!"

She stumbled back as the demons advanced, weapons drawn. One of the males spoke, its voice rumbling with darkness.

"I look forward to when our master is done with you," it licked its lips with a forked tongue. "We haven't had a wench like you for centuries."

She came to a stop against something soft yet immobile. She tried to scream, but a lump had formed in her throat. Rushing forward, the demon that had spoken jumped towards her, claws extended. She fell back as the daemon's hands closed around her neck, but as she fell, a streak of silver flashed, and the demon vanished.

Having forgotten all about him, Eźmeralda Collided with the blond man from before. She froze against him, searching for the demon she'd seen vanish. When she found him, though, she cried out in fear. Hands gripped her shoulder, and she froze. She found herself looking upon the demon and what had ripped it away from her.

Standing on all fours to her left was a wolf. Its eyes stood bright gold, and within its jaws, the demon hung, neck shattered. Blood dripped, its color staining the wolf's jaw crimson.

The wolf severed the demon's head from its shoulders with a quick shake, and she watched as the guy burst into flames. The fire licked at the wolf's fur, and she stared in shock as it coated the hair, its angry hue dissipating into the thick coat. Glowing white, the wolf shook its head and turned to her. It seemed to grin at her.

Moving forward on huge paws, its eyes lit with energy, sparking with power. Eźmeralda scooted closer to the blond man who held her, and the beast tilted its head.

"Easy there, don't go scaring the poor lass."

She looked up at the man behind her. He looked at her, but she realized he hadn't spoken. He crumbled into light fragments, and she stumbled into the arms of the same man. He was a reliable handhold in a sea of raging confusion, and she clung to him as her mind tried to comprehend what had just happened. Had the first man been an illusion? If so, it had kept the demons at bay until he had arrived.

"Eźmeralda Starlight," the man said. "I apologize for any discomfort my friend may have caused."

The wolf was a friend? From the smile on the man's face, she had to guess it was. His voice was rich with an accent unknown to her, and as she looked at him, his smile grew warmer. She was lost in his eyes and didn't notice when Paris approached.

Looking up, the blond mountain of a man shifted till he had her behind him. She watched as he faced Paris and was surprised when Paris paled, his eyes becoming wary.

"Haven't these guys caused enough trouble?" He whispered.

"You didn't answer our master's question," a demon called out. "Who the fuck do you think you are, messing with his prize?"

Paris raised a hand and closed it into a fist. As he did, he whirled around to face the one who had spoken and the demon clutching at its neck. It fell to its knees.

"Master, I..." it struggled to speak, and Paris lowered his arm. The demon collapsed, gasping for air. Turning to face them again, he looked at them in disdain.

"Kaldär..." he said with a snarl.

Looking up at the big man before her, she watched as his golden blond hair moved in the wind, the long locks framing icy blue eyes that stared back at Paris with a calm intensity. He spoke suddenly and ran a hand through his hair as he did, fully revealing startling blue eyes that stood out against a dark outline of thick lashes.

"We both know your name's, not Paris, Greed."

"So, you know of what I am?" Paris snarled. "Yes, I am called Greed, and if you don't move, I will show you the true might of a Dark Lord. Get him, boys."

The demons shot forward; their faces twisted in glee. Kaldär simply sighed. With a casual wave of his hand, ten bolts of lightning shot down from the heavens, the blasts causing the breath to be sucked from Eźmeralda's lungs as her hair whipped in the aftershock.

Kaldär showed no sign of having moved, and once the light faded, ten circles of charred grass were revealed where each demon had stood.

Paris or Greed—she didn't know who he was anymore—stood, his face painted red with fury. Kaldär watched him with a hooded gaze.

"Y-y-y-y-you, You Dare Mock Me!" Greed stammered in barely contained rage. Eźmeralda cowered behind Kaldär as the man dropped his gaze and looked at her with unadulterated hatred. When he smiled suddenly, she nearly peed herself. How had she thought this man to be beautiful? All she saw now was the demon he had tried to hide. Not a trace of the Paris she'd known was visible.

"How about a taste of what every man craves," Greed raised his chin, "Ladies?"

Moving forward, the three female demons swarmed them. Eźmeralda fell away as they cooed, letting out soft moans as they pressed their bodies against Kaldär, brushing their bare breasts against him.

She knelt, transfixed by their beauty, unable to look away. There was no way any man could resist such overwhelming temptation.

"Enough!"

She jumped as Kaldär spoke, breaking the magic being weaved around him. He took a step forward, disappearing in a flash. She jumped in surprise.

He'd... vanished. Looking around, Eźmeralda realized he was behind Greed? Looked between where he'd been and where he now stood, she watched as Kaldär gripped the black wings on Greed's back suddenly and pulled. Greed cried out as muscle and skin ripped free, bones breaking in a bloody arch.

Standing with wings in hand, Kaldär's eyes glowed with energy. As he did, Greed looked at his three remaining demons.

"Help me, you worthless sluts!" he cried.

Kaldär looked at them, standing beside her. They had not moved, but at his gaze, they turned and vanished with a flash, their cries of trepidation slowly fading on the wind.

Her ears rippled with tiny shivers as the wind whispered through her hair, causing the short green locks to block her view of Kaldär as he looked back down at Greed. By the time she moved her hair aside, Kaldär had Greed by the throat and was holding him aloft.

She gasped, jumping to her feet. Her eyes locked with Paris's as Kaldär held him high. His eyes were no longer pure black, and they now had heart-rending fear. She stumbled in the sand, her heart racing from the need to save this thing before her. It tore at her very soul. She couldn't watch him die. He was her love... love? She barely knew him...

She paused, but like a wave, she felt the need to save him wash through her once again. She was running now, stumbling, then crawling, then running again across the sand, her face still warm from the setting sun as she was encased in shadows. Her mind grew fuzzy, all thoughts flying free till nothing remained. She could only feel the fine granules of sand as they slid underfoot, their rough texture slipping around her feet, as well as an intense need to save Paris.

"Eźmeralda! Look at me!"

She slowed to a walk as the warm words broke through the fog that was enveloping her. Its heat bringing with it a quick flash, the image that had filled her sights changed till she felt like she was looking through a kaleidoscope till the image fractured into a million pieces of light. She had been watching Kaldär step away, letting go of Paris. She had seen a knife appear in his hand as he turned to her and raise his arm high in a throwing thrust, aiming for her heart and as his arm was coming down, she called upon the land, intent on stopping Kaldär's arm, but as that power rushed into her veins, it all vanished. Kaldär, the knife, Paris, it all disappeared in a flash. She found herself standing back where she had been. She looked around in a daze as the colors from the land and sky clashed in a blend of surprisingly vivid textures. She stumbled and fell to the ground. She rose up into a low crouch and looked up at Kaldär but once more, the land rolled, causing her belly to flip-flop.

Trying to keep the contents of her stomach from taking a stroll down memory lane, she looked at Kaldär again, this time more slowly.

Standing over Paris, he pulled a sword from what looked like a pocket of light that hung in the air beside him. He held it high, its tip hovering between Greed's eyes. He began to speak, but she couldn't hear the words through the ringing in her own ears. Gods! She hated illusions. Each one now had left her feeling sick. Looking up once more, she finally caught a hint of their words.

"Your tricks won't work on her Greed," Kaldär said. "Shifter Druids are immune to demon magic, and you just picked the wrong day to show up."

Wait, he thinks I'm a druid? Why would he believe that? He seemed like the type to catch onto things like that, but she couldn't know if he was just guessing or making shit up. As far as she knew, she wasn't a druid, so why would he say she was? She didn't have any tattoos that she knew of.

Greed frowned but didn't look at her as he said, "what a shame. I had hoped to add her to my collection. Such a prize would have looked good upon my mantle."

If she hadn't been dealing with such a bad case of motion sickness, she'd have slapped the smug look off his face. Laced with scorn and ignorance, his words continued.

"But that matters not. The big thing now is how you're going to deal with the big man, the Archangel Gabriel himself?"

Kaldär banished the sword with a huff. "You have no place to speak, snake."

She watched a smile grow on Greed's face. "What a shame," he said.

Looking away, she glanced at Kaldär, standing silent, his expression blank. He crossed his arms over his chest, and his thin black t-shirt was stretched over his bulk. She couldn't help but stare.

"Have you heard of an artifact by the name of the Fore-Lorne Looking Glass?" Kaldär said suddenly.

Greed's face blanched, and she wondered what he could be talking about.

Kaldär grinned. "Ah! So, you have. Good." His grin faded till it was barely visible as he summoned a leather satchel. Appearing beside him, it hung in the air as he reached inside and pulled free a small handheld mirror.

Greed squirmed, crying out as his open wounds spurted blood. "No, no! You can't."

Why was he afraid? He raised the mirror before Greed, and all her theories faded from her mind. It was only a mirror as far as she could see, but as she watched, Kaldär began to chant.

The mirror was glowing, and it wasn't a soft glow either. It was an angry red that swirled with magic. She could feel it in the air, a thick soup that spread in an ever-expanding ring of raw energy. She watched it mix with the colors of the land, whitening the soil, enriching the grass, and scenting the air. Everything it touched it made new.

Except for a small ring that became old, the area withering and smoldering as she watched. The land surrounding Greed became a dull grey as its very color draining till only dust remained. Greed's body began to spasm, his limbs shaking, and she watched as the same skin upon his body turned to ash, painting the air in a swirling of black and grey.

She didn't notice it till it touched her, but the ever-expanding energy hit her with a flash and didn't touch her.

A shimmering wall of liquid blue light had surrounded her, blocking her from the magic of the mirror. Kaldär looked at her, a question in his eyes, but she didn't have an answer. She had no idea what was creating a wall of blue energy. She was shaking her head in bewilderment when a sudden heat burned against her chest. Wincing, she pulled her necklace out from under her shirt.

Glowing hot within her palm sat the blue diamond scarab that her mother had given to her as a child. Unable to hold it, she let it dangle between her fingers by the thin chain she used to keep it around her neck.

"I don't believe it...." Kaldär breathed. She looked up and saw his face was a mask of awe. Greed, too, was looking at her, but his eyes showed shock. He looked back at Kaldär and grinned in triumph. Too late, she saw the magic flicker.

She reached out, a silent cry on her lips as Greed gripped Kaldär and pulled him close. His body began to vibrate, his skin cracking and letting loose slow-moving bolts of red lightning. Kaldär cried out, and she despaired. He wasn't protected.

She barely registered it when he vanished, his body fraying for a second before disappearing entirely, only to reappear before her.

She jumped as he wrapped his arms around her, covering her with his body. She blushed at the contact, her mind going blank. She had half a mind to scold him when the world exploded.

When the light cleared, Eźmeralda stood up as Kaldär released her. She looked around, turning in a slow circle to take in the surrounding area. What had once been beautiful white sand and green grass had become a charred corpse of dust and cracked soil.

Covering her mouth is anguish, she stood beside Kaldär and looked at the scene around her with a solemn serenity. They had been left untouched by the blast, and as Kaldär moved towards the source of the explosion, she lifted the blue scarab that hung around her neck and looked at it. It was warm to the touch, and she knew.

"Thank you," she whispered, placing a soft kiss upon the jewel.

Tucking it under her shirt, she drew comfort from its warmth as it settled against her skin. With a deep breath, she raised her gaze to look at the crumbling form of the once deadly beauty that had twisted her reality.

Moving to stand beside Kaldär, she cried inside as the feel of the empty land, devoid of life, wept beneath her bare toes.

"How can such things happen?" she said to no one in particular.

"Such beings bring only death and destruction in their wake. We have you to thank for our survival." Kaldär gestured to her chest. "If not for that artifact around your neck, I'd have had a slow night, trying to heal your body, and only after I had recovered from the blast myself."

"Recovered?" She looked at him like he was crazy. "We'd be dead if not for the scarab's protection."

He looked at her and raised an eyebrow.

"What?" she snapped. "Are you like an immortal or something?"

He just stood there.

"Ugh," she choked. "Y-y-you're i-i-immortal?" she stuttered.

Nodding slightly, he looked at her with gold eyes that crackled with yellow lightning. How could she have been so blind? The incredible speed, the absurd strength he'd showed, plus his immunity to the siren's song... she wondered if he even bled?

"Well, that explains a few things," she said softly, turning to the corpse before them. Lined with cracks, the crusty form glowed molten hot, "but what about this guy?"

Summoning his odd leather bag again, Kaldär pulled out an odd-looking vial of black liquid. Kneeling in front of the corpse, he uncapped it. "First, we must seal the land so the Sin cannot escape."

"The Sin is still in that thing?" she said softly.

Turning his head, Kaldär looked at her, but loud cracks lit the air before he could speak. A low laughing rose on the wind as sulfur began to curl around them.

Whipping his head back to look at the corpse, Kaldär jumped to his feet and gripped her arm, pulling her away.

The corpse raised its head and let loose a crackling laugh as huge cracks on its body glowed brightly. As Kaldär pulled her away, she looked back at the crippled body's molten stone and watched as it began to flake. Where the eyes should have been, red-hot lava leaked free. The corpse let loose a roar that echoed with an angry rumble.

Stopping just shy of the charred ring of soil, they watched as the blackened being crumbled in on itself, starting from the chest in a swirl till nothing remained but a vortex of circling dust.

In a sudden concussion of air, the vortex imploded only to expand, letting loose a blast of air that rippled through the very fabric of reality. The shockwave knocked Eźmeralda back into the arms of Kaldär. He locked those arms around her, and despite it all, she was filled with a sense of safety. She nestled into his embrace and prayed that everything would stop shaking.

It did, if slowly. Eźmeralda soon gathered the courage to look back at the vortex. What she saw made her shake. In the storm's center, a pitch-black orb of negative light hung like a miniature black hole.

"You will not send me to serve judgment under the divine beings this day."

The voice came from the orb, and its dark echo caused cold shivers to travel down her spine. She looked up at Kaldär, but his gaze was focused on the dark sphere.

Looking back at the orb, she watched it as the voice spoke again, sending out cold quakes that froze her very soul. Moving in sync with the words, the sphere strobed and morphed with liquid fluidity.

"Damn you, Kaldär, damn your mirror, damn your power, we will meet again," it said, the words berating her mind in a shout.

With a boom, the orb shot up into the sky, blasting down at them only to swerve at the last second, rocketing across the sand. It hit the waves, splitting them in an arch as it sped into the setting sun.

Slowly the silence fell into place, her mind questioning if it indeed was over. The dust soon settled, and the land seemed to gain her spirit again. The damage didn't vanish, but life began to grow within her grasp, letting loose tiny sprouts across her burnt soil. It was as if Mother Nature was stepping in at a personal level in repairing the land.

Stepping away, Kaldär moved from behind her. Trailing a hand along her shoulders till he stood beside her, his hand alighted upon her arm. He was the support she needed, and looking up at him, she wondered what he was thinking?

"Kaldär..." she whispered.

Dropping his hand from her arm, he moved away, not saying a word. She felt awkward without his warmth, and as he moved away, she wrapped her arms around herself in a tight embrace. Afraid of the feelings running through her blood, she watched Kaldär move to stand, looking down where Greed had shown his true face. He looked so... lost, almost to the point of heartbreak. She took in his hair, memorizing its golden glow as the sun hit its shiny texture. Moving along his broad shoulders, she watched the muscles ripple with tension. Trialing her gaze along his back, she absorbed the smooth flow of it till she reached his waist. She let out a silent gasp at how the denim of his jeans hugged him; her heart did the samba at the concept of his muscular rear. Cheeks flaming, she moved her gaze along his legs, taking in their lean length, his calves stretching the fabric in an upside-down teardrop. His physic was masculine, and yet he... was elegant.

With a deep breath, she moved to stand beside him, but she stopped just shy, standing behind him instead. She lifted a hand, not knowing what to say to comfort him when he spoke suddenly.

"I did it again... I failed."

Warmth bloomed in her chest at his words, and she stepped up, placing her head against his back, following it up with a hand, spraying her finger as she put it softly in the small of his back.

"You didn't fail," she whispered. "You saved me, right?"

She felt his back tighten and loosen beneath her hand. "I did, but I still let him escape," he said, turning to face her. "I did not expect such an outcome."

Placing his thumb and forefinger against her chin, he lifted her gaze to meet his. Trapped within those now icy blue's, she noticed again how thick his lashes were. It gave him the most intense smolder. She had thought he'd been wearing kohl around his eyes, but he wore no such thing. So absorbed was she in the beauty of his gaze, she didn't hear him speak at first.

"Eźmeralda?"

"Hmm?" she said, trying to hide her embarrassment

Kaldär smiled knowingly. "I think it best you come with me."

She stood there, confused for a second. Was Kaldär asking or telling? "You know, I barely just met you." Stuttering, she placed her hand against his chest for balance.

"I heard of a prophecy about a year ago. It talked about a blue scarab swimming in a sea of green. Accompanying the scarab was a beautiful maiden clothed in a rich red coat. Nothing was said about my involvement but at the mention of an intense maw in the form of corruption that would arrive upon white sands in the glow of the setting sun I knew."

Kaldär was looking out at the sea as he said, "little did I know I'd find such a beautiful creature in a place of the maiden?"

A lump grew within her throat as he looked back into her eyes. An intense passion filled them, and not knowing how to respond, she jabbered like a hummingbird on speed, fast and incomprehensible.

Placing a finger against her lips, he silenced the flood she was trying to wash him away with.

"I need... an apprentice if you'd be willing? No longer will you fear those in the dark, no longer will you face death... no longer will you be alone."

No longer alone... how she longed for such a life... looking at Kaldär, her mind flashed through a future she'd thought would never come to pass.

She saw herself standing firm, with her eyes bright. She was armored in leather and silk, her hair hanging rich and long. At her side, Kaldär stood, the same as ever except for a slight twinkle in his eye. She looked proud, and Kaldär looked happy. No longer did thunderclouds surround his aura. She didn't even think before she answered.

"If it will make you happy..." she paused as he tucked her hair behind her ear. "Then, my answer is yes."

She wished to see that twinkle become a reality.

[illegible] confused for a second, was much [illegible] feelings, you know? Anyway, look at me [illegible] placed her hand against his [illegible].

[illegible] they [illegible] ago, alone. I [illegible] something [illegible]. According to [illegible] couldn't [illegible] could [illegible] was something [illegible] comparison, that would arrive upon whiteness in the [illegible] I know?"

"[illegible] looking at [illegible]," he said. "How did [illegible] he had such [illegible] of the [illegible]?"

A [illegible] grew within her. [illegible] into her [illegible]. An [illegible] possession filled [illegible] and [illegible] how [illegible] he jabbered like [illegible] on [illegible], lost, and incomprehensible.

[illegible] a finger against her [illegible] the silence [illegible] to wash him away with.

"[illegible] an apprentice [illegible] you [illegible], no longer will you fear those in the dark, no longer will [illegible] no longer will you be alone."

"No [illegible] alone," how she [illegible] for [illegible] looking at Kaldur, her mind flashed through [illegible] to peace.

She saw herself standing there, with her eyes [illegible]. He was [illegible] and she her [illegible] and [illegible]. At her side, Kaldur stood, the same as ever, except for a slight twinkle in his eye. She looked at him, and Kaldur looked [illegible]. "No longer" did [illegible] [illegible] his [illegible]. She didn't even [illegible], or she answered.

"If it will make you happy," he [illegible] as he tucked her hair behind her ear. "Then my answer is yes."

She wished to see that twinkle become a reality.

Kaldär

Chapter 15: True Nature

Time will draw one to gain the power of the gods yet will be cursed to live a mortal life of extended years.

The Unseen One
Before the First Age

5 Years Later, Present Day

Damn it, Damn it, damn it, damn it! Everything was going to shit, and to make matters worse, he'd started it. Now he was literally running for his life, or maybe he was fleeing the inevitable... you know what, how bout both.

Besides, running was an understatement. If Kaldär were to get technical right now, flying would be a better term. When your surroundings are stretched to a blur, reality itself means nothing. Its weaves are torn at the slightest ripple from anything abnormal or supernatural, and every time Kaldär's foot touched against the soil, their pressure caused small puffs of flame. It may only last a millisecond, but it still shocked the quartz reminiscent of a phantom meteor strike. It was this that had allowed her to track him so far.

Beauty had always been a weakness of his, and her beauty had captivated him from day one. She reminded him so much of Sara. The way she spoke, the way she moved, even her mind, it all made him ache inside. The last five years had been filled with his training of Eźmeralda. Most of it had been easy, if only thanks to how hard it had been. The magnitude of it nearly tearing his heart to shreds, and he knew that if he were to listen to his heart, everything would change, knowing that Eźmeralda was his soul mate only made things harder. *I swear that woman is going to be the death of me.*

For such a scared little bird, she was incredibly resilient. It had made for a challenge when it came to breaking her down. For the first year, she'd fought against Kaldär's lessons, doing things that he'd thought impossible to overcome the mental and physical struggles he put her through. With every fall, she had gotten back up, and with each broken bone, she had grown stronger. However, throughout her time with him, something had been missing.

However, that missing piece had shown itself not hours ago.

"I have to learn at some time, right?" Eźmeralda had said.

He'd looked at her then and considered if she were truly ready.

"How about this; a contest, if I win, I get what I want, but if you win, I will let it go." she'd petitioned.

It had made sense at the time, but he had pushed her away till this moment. He was sure that if he hadn't, this wouldn't have happened.

Jumping the small distance across a lone lake, he entered the forest surrounding it. Weaving through the trees, he felt the ground respond to his passing. He knew it wasn't him causing the soil to grip his bare feet. Leaves swirled around him with every pause, and even with his keen sight, he couldn't spot the cause.

Falling into a crouch, he scanned his surroundings, waiting, waiting...

Now!

With a rush of power, he added speed to his jump. One thing you need to know about aerial attacks; you can't change direction once you start, especially when you're moving at pre-natural speeds. It's a bitch to stop; at least that's what he used to think.

With her back to him, Eźmeralda balanced herself in the upper limbs of a tree that towered over the rest. Emerging from the thick canopy, he rushed through the air towards his target. Arching through the sky, he called upon the heavens.

Not looking away from the lady before him, he sensed the pressure drop as the temperature chilled around him. He had grown to enjoy the thrill of the hunt, knowing that the more challenging the challenge was, the greater the triumph would be.

Right before he reached her perch, she turned at the last second, and moving quickly to avoid his outstretched hand, dropped back off the giant branch. Passing over her, he watched as, with great agility, she gripped a lower limb, causing herself to fly wide in the direction he'd just come.

Upside down, he watched her merge with the bark of another tree. Damn it. Having overshot, he twisted his body so that it was feet first when he landed back to the ground a reasonable distance away.

Touching lightly, he took off, moving fast; no need to get caught out in the open. He needed to keep his guard up with her being able to jump from tree to tree, no matter the distance between. He was kind of regretting training her now.

There! Shooting to the left, he rocketed through the trees, moving in an ever-shrinking circle. Using the shadows for cover, he watched as Eźmeralda emerged. In a flash, she stumbled into the small clearing. To the naked eye, it would have looked like she'd simply appeared, but to him, he saw it all.

Blooming within the heart of the tree, her aura grew till it filled the entirety of the bark. It then shrank to a small orb that pushed free. At first, it looked like the bark itself was peeling free in the form of a female figure when, in fact, that was only half true. It was bark, but that bark began to crumble away, becoming soil. It sloshed free to reveal soft sun-kissed skin that gleamed in the morning light. He moved transfixed as she ran her hands through her hair to unravel the last of the soil from it.

Stopping in the shadows of a tree at the edge of the clearing, he began to feel uncomfortable. His face grew hot, but he was unable to look away as Eźmeralda ran her hands over her figure, moving along the curve of her hips. His breath caught as she ran her delicate fingers along with her smooth calves. Standing back up, she closed her eyes and began to chant.

Speaking silently, she stood nude before him. Thinking quickly, he studied the area. Only Eźmeralda and he were in the area, along with a small fox, a gathering of insects, and a lone owl which perched high in the branches above.

Everything seemed familiar, but still, something felt off. No one else would have felt it, but a slight ripple in the sound around him alerted him of the illusion. *Back to your old tricks, are you?*

Concentrating, he clapped his hands once, causing an orb of invisible energy to expand out. It effectively shattered the illusion around him and not a moment too soon.

Jumping to the side, he turned, deflecting a foot directed at his kidney. It was followed up by five quick jabs to his core, each one quick and as fast as a mountain breeze, designed to make him miss the next. Moving with skill and precision, Eźmeralda jumped high, swinging a leg in a lightning-fast twist that seemed to warp the air. He blocked it quickly—though the force behind it blew his sleeve to shreds—he then maneuvered, twisting his wrist and grabbing her ankle as he slid forward to grasp her thigh. Landing in a wide stance, he twirled her around in the air and slammed her to the ground—one thing he didn't do. Go easy on his student!

Kneeling over her, he smiled slightly. "Looks like I win."

He reached out and placed his index finger on her temple, but it cracked when he contacted her skin. He watched as she crumbled to fine soil at his touch. Neat trick! Standing up, Kaldär looked around. He quickly stepped out into the clearing. Assuming Eźmeralda had watched the fight through the clone's eyes, he grinned. As soon as he had contacted her clone, he had become a slave to her sight.

After five years of training by his side, Eźmeralda had become quite the formidable foe. She knew most of his tricks and had come up with a few of her own behind his back. Her skills as a druid had multiplied as she had picked up on things bit by bit. It took a while, but by the time the first year had passed, her feelings toward him cooled, and she had become a dedicated student, taking in every word, accepting every failure as a lesson, and above all, she had stopped flirting.

By the gods! The audacity of the woman was out of this world. After he had shown her the hidden tattoos she had, she had grown close to him. She had always had this smile she gave him when she was up to something, and as he emerged into the clearing and looked at her, he knew. She had come out of the lone tree that stood in the center, and she had that smile amped up to eleven. She stood before him now, clothed in a black sash that wrapped around her chest and a pair of silk pants that hung loose and baggy around her legs. He saw again the gleam within her eyes that said, "Your mine!"

Moving along the edge of the sunny clearing, he watched her as she watched him in turn. She smiled wide and called on the land to fill her with its energy. With a quick wink, he smiled back just before he shot forward like a bullet from a gun. Eźmeralda lost her grin and dropped into a low stance, too low for defense, though. Something was off. He was about to question her intent when the soil shifted, becoming like a liquid while holding its solid form. Clever girl, no wonder the low stance.

Channeling energy through his feet, he stepped into the air. If the land had become his enemy, he would become allies with the sky. He would use DivineStep to its fullest, if only for a second. With a whisper of wind, his magic activated.

Jumping through the air, he moved side to side as if on solid ground. Eźmeralda abandoned Elemental Voodoo just as he reached her. Raising her arms in a block, she didn't expect a ground attack. He dropped low to the ground as she blocked her own sight and swept her legs out from under her. Continuing the motion, he rose with a twirl and placed a palm flat against her chest.

She hit the ground, only to burst into a swarm of butterflies. Kaldär froze, awed by her speed. She'd adopted in just milliseconds, choosing the best course of action for Kaldär's attack.

Glittering in the sunlight, the butterflies moved in a myriad of colors, floating through the air to come back together, forming a liquid-like figure that solidified instantly behind him. Twisting around, he caught Eźmeralda's fist in a big hand and thrust his other hand into her abdomen. She gasped as the wind rushed out of her, leaving her breathless. She dropped to her knees, her arms wrapping around herself. He sighed as he looked down at her.

"Eźmeralda, how many times have I told you to only use that move for surprise attacks."

Looking up, Eźmeralda smiled, her eyes suddenly turning to the soil. He stood shocked as the clone crumbled. He looked around, his mind whirling. He couldn't believe she had fooled him so easily. When had she switched out for a clone? He'd punched it with enough force to scramble her connection to it! She had clearly grown strong indeed if that hadn't fazed her.

Suddenly a jolt shot through his veins. Behind him! He twirled, moved away from the lone tree. Eźmeralda was emerging once more, the bark still falling as she gripped his shirt. Tumbling back, he fell, and time seemed to slow. He saw her hand move, index finger extended, but it was too late. The game had ended.

Hitting the ground, he lay defeated. Eźmeralda sat atop him, her legs straddling him as she looked into his eyes, not yet believing what had just happened. With her finger pressed to his forehead, she was flush against him, her thighs hugging him.

Breathing hard, he spoke softly, trying to hide the hoarse sound in his voice. "It looks like you win...."

She shifted, unaware of the fact that she sat atop him, her figure still nude

"I, I did it... I Did It!"

Lifting her finger, Eźmeralda pumped the air in victory, he blushed when she moved, and her look of triumph changed to curiosity. *Oh shit! I'm a dead man!* How could he have let his body get the best of him? Her bare chest was right there, and she was acting like everything was normal?

"Do you like what you see?" she asked in a coy voice. She met Kaldär's gaze and smiled like the cat that had just caught the canary.

"Uh... I don't... um...." He sputtered

"Oh, looky here, is itsy bitsy Kaldär embarrassed?" Eźmeralda cooed as she placed her hands on his chest. His face grew hot, and he stuttered.

"Ah!" Eźmeralda gasped at his reaction. "Quite the eager one, aren't ya?" Her words grew sensual as the scent of her arousal filled his nose. His nostrils flared at the strong scent. "Is little ol Kaldär wanting to go back on his word?"

She moved her hips a little, and he sat up like a bat out of hell. She fell back in surprise, all traces of her teasing manner gone. He looped a hand around her lower back and pulled her up to grasp the back of her neck lightly.

"Do you know how hard it's been," he said. "Having to deal with your teasing for the last five years?" as he spoke, he feathered his lips against hers.

For years he had wanted to do this, but always his fears of its outcome stopped him. However, with Eźmeralda now in his arms, he didn't care about the end result. She was the only thing on his mind at this moment.

"Do you know the pain I was in?" he said softly. "I fought my feeling, tortured my very soul, and all because I was afraid of you."

Gripping her tightly, he lifted her slightly as he stood up and pressed her against the tree that sat in the middle of the clearing. He buried his face against her neck, placing soft kisses along her neck as he followed her vein as it beat faster with her arousal. Her breath caught as he trailed his lips back down, leaving a shadow that grew cold in the wind. He shivered as she began to nibble on his shoulder.

"I don't know if I can control myself," he whispered. He grew still as he thought about the outcome. If he chose Eźmeralda as his own, he would no longer be alone, but at what cost? He didn't want to feel the pain of losing someone he loved once more.

A soft hand touched his cheek, and he opened his eyes to see Eźmeralda looking at him, compassion and trust in her gaze.

"Then don't," she said with a warm smile.

Gods! How could such a woman exist? She touched his mind lightly, sending her strength and assurance to him. His chest grew tight once more, and he glanced at her lips.

Leaning forward, he kissed her lightly, merely savoring the fresh rainy scent of her. She gasped as he pressed his body against hers. The warmth of her skin was like a furnace in the cold morning air, and as he ran his hands along her sides, that warmth grew hot. Tightening her legs, Eźmeralda ran her hands through his hair and pulled him closer as she deepened the kiss, claiming him as her own.

"Kaldär..." she whispered between breaths. "I think... you should lose the clothes."

He grinned against her mouth. "Is that so..."—reaching behind him, he unhooked her legs and lowered her to the ground—"well, I do feel a bit overdressed."

Stepping back, he waited as Eźmeralda slowly lifted his shirt, revealing the body he had honed through battle and training alike. He never lost what he gained thanks to Gabriel's gift, and as the cloth blocked his vision, Kaldär couldn't help but grin as he heard her gasp. Finally, he threw the shirt aside, feeling the sun hit his chest with its warmth.

Eźmeralda stood before him, her skin gleaming in the morning light. He watched her eyes move, taking in the contours of his stomach, then widen at the sight of his chest, slowly moving her gaze over the strength of his shoulders till her eyes met his, trapping him in their scorching heat. The green of those eyes seemed to grow, and as a slight blush appeared on her cheeks, she crept forward, placing a hand over her mouth. He smiled at the sight of her shy composure as she took a deep breath. Reaching out, she spoke under her breath.

"Oh gods..." she groaned. "Even after five years, I've never tried.... you look absolutely... ravishing." She hummed the last word as she dropped her hand from her mouth.

He reached out and took that hand and placed it over his heart. He struggled to speak but couldn't get the words past the lump in his throat. Instead, he put his hand over Eźmeralda's and moved till he stood just shy of her. He took a deep breath, pulling the rich aroma of her into him. He pushed against her mind, speaking the words he struggled to say aloud.

~You give me a lifetime of solace. I wonder about destiny and yearn of love. But if the gods have chosen you, I fear for losing you. This life is no wonderland; it is filled

with dangers, and death awaits every corner we take. It is not what I want for you~

Eźmeralda smiled, placing a finger against his lips as she spoke in turn. *~Shhh, there is no reason to think such. You have tried to protect me from both the world and you. You have trained me, honed me, and made me into who I am today~*

Quick as lightning, he captured her lips; marked her as his own. The mental link between them flashed, flooding them with each other's emotions. He felt her need to prove herself; she wished to show that she could handle her own. All of her feelings flooded him in a rush of happiness, sadness, and anger. He saw her for who she indeed was for the first time. Never had he seen her in such clarity.

He knew she was feeling a similar experience by the depth of her kiss. Emotions rolled along with her tongue, filling him with their energy. He opened his eyes as she glanced at him through her lashes.

Speaking suddenly, her words swam through his mind. *~Things are never what they seem. I guess you didn't know me as well as you thought you did, did you?~* She nipped at him in a teasing manner.

Grinning, he wrapped his arms around her waist and spun her around. She squealed, laughing as he set her back down, tears filling her eyes till she wiped them away.

"What are we going to do now, mister?" she said aloud.

He pretended to think, but he couldn't get her out of his mind; the golden bronze of her sun-kissed skin, the green of her hair as it made the black of her lashes stand out, all of her was something new to explore. He breathed through his nose and took in the scent of her. She smelled of fresh rain and rich soil.

"I can think of a few things," he said.

"Oh?" she breathed. Kaldär smiled at her innocent act. "I'd love to see where you're going, but...."

"But what?" he asked.

Looking up at him, Eźmeralda's eyes gleamed as she spoke slyly.

"I require this first," she said, swiftly pulling the red silk sash free of his waist. Turning away, she whipped it behind her, looping the smooth silk over the full swell of her breasts.

His pants pooled around him, and she turned back to face him. She'd tied the sash in a tight knot in the front, and as he stood there in shock, she smiled.

"I'm actually quite famished after our... battle." She said with a downward glance. She bit her lip, and looking back up, she nibbled on her thumb, her eyes dilated. She looked ready to pounce

Instead, she turned around, drawing his eyes to the sway of her hips. "How does the slaughtered Lamb sound?" she said, mentioning the pub that they frequented in Londinium as she looked over her shoulder. She summoned a pair of silk pants that hung loose and baggy around her legs.

Oh, ho, ho, you little vixen! Pulling his pants up, he rushed after her. It was going to be a long day indeed.

Eźmeralda's heart was racing. Just hours ago, she and Kaldär had finished her training in Acreage Magic. It had taken her three years to finally master her control over the element. Kaldär was a great teacher, if not a bit demanding.

Nevertheless, she couldn't help but think he'd let her beat him. It hadn't been easy, but it hadn't been tough either, and what had happened after the fact? Gods! She is still throbbed with need after seeing Kaldär in his prime. She had nearly jumped him then and there. But even after years of being celibate, she didn't want to ruin her first time.

She'd gained her immortality six months after she'd met Kaldär thanks to her ancestry, but it was with his help that she had been able to reach her prime.

"Eźmeralda?" she heard Kaldär say.

"Hmm?" she looked up from her food.

Smiling, Kaldär looked at her from across the table. At five past noon, they had arrived at the Slaughtered Lamb. Known for its cheeses, the place... was usually busy. Right now, she wasn't hungry, though. She'd told Kaldär that to escape. She'd wanted more than anything to do what they'd teased each other about, but it hadn't felt right. Looking at Kaldär now, clothed in loose slacks and a grey sweater, he seemed almost normal.

"Are you going to eat that?" he asked, pointing at her untouched plate.

Shaking her head, she saw that he'd already devoured the food he'd ordered for himself. When he wanted to, he could eat!

Looking over at Kaldär, Eźmeralda saw that he'd stopped eating. She was about to ask him if he'd like to order another plate when a shockwave of energy rushed through her, passing along like a wave of magic. Even the other patrons seemed to sense it. They looked around in confusion, even got up and hurrying outside. The big man behind the bar just went back to what he'd been doing. His gaze was focused on the window, looking out and into the distance.

"What is it?" she asked.

Getting up, Kaldär slid a generous pile of silver onto the table. She stood up as he turned to the bar and thanked the owner for the meal.

"Kaldär?"

"We need to go!" he stated. He then rushed outside.

Kaldär!" she snapped, following after him. She grabbed his arm and tried to steer him around when he faced her suddenly and wrapped his arm around her tightly. He called upon the heavens. He was using Golden Blaze now?

They vanished into the sky with a flash, becoming pure energy. After a few seconds, they struck down with a bang in front of their home. Turning, Kaldär let her go and faced the mountainside. He seemed to be waiting. She looked but saw nothing. When she saw his face, she knew they weren't going to be going anywhere anytime soon.

She could only wait by his side.

Kaldär

Chapter 16: True Immortal

Thou will be charged with thy protection of thou mother; Gaia. Love her, cherish her and never forget thou life that come from her bosom.

The god of nature, Pan
The First Age

Eźmeralda looked at Kaldär. He moved through the tall grass like he expected an attack to come from any angle. She couldn't see anything, and her senses were almost as good as his with the aid of Gaia. She watched him as the wind flowed across the field, making the grass ripple like water. It felt serene, but she knew something was up; she could feel it. She followed after Kaldär and came up beside him only to freeze when he drew on the divine magic's and looked up.

Unmoving by Kaldär's side, she felt the air heat. She followed Kaldär's gaze and looked up. As she did, the sky rumbled. It felt like a meteor strike. Looking higher, she saw the streak of light heading their way.

"Kaldär?"

She gripped his arm as her senses when haywire. Looking at him, she saw only tension. It wasn't fear she sensed; it felt more like he was anxious. What could cause such, she wondered? Why weren't the two of them moving? They were about to be crushed by a fucking ball of fire!

Kaldär!" she yelled. "What's happening?" She had to shout over the screaming wind, but he didn't answer. She could only watch as the streak of light impacted the middle of the field. Not ten feet away, it crashed into the hilltop.

The shock wave rippled the air, and she had to plant her feet to keep her footing. Kaldär didn't budge. She envied him for his ability to stay rooted to the ground like a rock due to his size. He had to use some kind of magic to remain unmoving in that way.

Looking past him, she gazed through the dust and debris. She felt the crater in the land through her contact with Gaia and felt what sat in the middle of it and knew it wasn't a meteor, but neither could she distinguish what it actually was.

Yet even as she started to see its outline, it vanished. She saw the air ripple from its passage and barely leaped back in time as the person who appeared before her... appeared. If not for Kaldär, she would have been toast.

He, at the last minute, had grabbed the man by the throat and stopped him. She looked up from the ground and took in the trench coat and cowboy hat. He had oddly red-tinted eyes, and as she watched, they flashed green. When they did, his body emitted a shock wave that pushed Kaldär and her away from him.

Kaldär vanished only to appear behind her, his hands on her shoulders. They slid across the grass and came to a stop just inches from the Cliffside. She took deep gulps of air and looked at Kaldär, only to lose what oxygen she had gained.

He had stopped her from tumbling off the cliff, but he hung in the air. She turned to look back at the man in the trench coat to see him looking at them with his head cocked to the side in curiosity. Kaldär had been forced to use DivineStep to stop them from falling to the rocky reef below, and to her, it looked like that had been their visitor's intention. He had just forced them to show one of their cards.

"So," the man called out to them. "You're the one I've been looking for."

She sat up, and Kaldär helped her to her feet. He had a ball of white flame in his hand, and she quickly filled her tattoos with her own magic. She didn't know who this guy was, but Kaldär clearly did. He had shown recognition as his magic had passed over them at the pizza parlor.

Kaldär quenched his fire. "And why would you be looking for me?"

The man with the oddly red-tinted eyes grinned. She shivered as he looked at her for a second, then back at Kaldär. His magic felt tainted and dark. Like it had once been pure but was now corrupted by the deeds they'd been used for. It was unnerving.

"First, I must confess, I thought a true immortal had no need to take apprentices."

"Well, you should know personally that we non-mortals crave companionship in our long lives." Kaldär placed an arm around her.

She looked at him and smiled. He had that twinkle in his eyes that she had thought she'd never see. She saw it now in the pride he showed towards her. Looking back at the man before them, she grew cold inside. He was just standing there.

"Is that so? Hmm... you should know that I hate people."

"I know."

"Then, you also know that I am not here for pleasure but for business."

Kaldär took a step forward. "You can't have it."

Eźmeralda grew confused. That didn't make any sense. What couldn't this man have? They had plenty of artifacts and trinkets from lost eras, but she still had no idea what they were referring to.

"Kaldär," she asked. "What does he want?" Looking between the two of them, she was at a loss. They both had their magic on high, but neither was on the verge of unleashing it. Kaldär was calm now, like the eye of a tornado. His magic ululated in soft waves while the man in the odd leather coat, his magic pulsed like an angry nest of hornets. "Kaldär?" she asked again.

He turned and looked at her, but just as he did, his eyes went wide, and he flickered. He pushed her away as two solid blades of magic flashed by. One phased through his head, passing through him like he was smoke to go flying off the hillside. The other zipped in front of her face where she had been standing.

She gasped as she stumbled back. Kaldär crouched down, and she felt the land rumble at his touch. His eyes were now locked on the odd man before them. She felt Kaldär's magic rushing through the ground, but just as it reached their guest, he vanished.

Kaldär saw it and rushed forward. She watched as he threw a fist forward and met the air with a shockwave of energy.

Rippling like water, the air congealed, and the odd man flickered into existence as layers, his form appearing from afar like he was being pushed towards Kaldär.

When he was fully visible, she watched as Kaldär and the old man struck at each other. Their attacks rocked the very air, and she grew afraid. Such power! She would be torn apart if she stayed here.

~Gaia! Help me! Please, grant me sanctuary!~ she called to the land and felt it ripple around her in response. - Druid scared - death nearby - grant passage -

She kept up the call till the land enveloped her into its dark embrace. She was carried down and was lowered into a small underground chamber that sat below her home. She could feel the stone above. She sat up slowly and took a deep breath. The cave had a breeze, and she knew they were close to the surface but far enough away from the battle to not get in the way.

Kaldär, be careful. That man wants something you clearly can't give. She couldn't do anything. She'd frozen up, and it had nearly cost her her life.

Sitting on the hard dirt, she listened to the rumbling above. She kept her anxiety in check. However, she couldn't help the shivers that rocked her every once in a while.

Kaldär was smiling. He hadn't had a good fight in a while, and this Hunter was mighty. His magic was tainted, which came as a shock upon recognizing the type of magic it was.

The seraphim were heavenly creatures, so to see one of them in an infected state was surprising. In most ancient texts, they were portrayed as fiery six-winged beings. Within the Nypherian Kingdom's angelic hierarchy, they were often placed in the fifth rank, and in the Kingdom of light's celestial hierarchy, they were considered the highest class.

Looking at the man before him, he saw a coupling. This man was one with the seraphim, and that was not at all good news. The two of them were fused in spirit, and in the magical spectrum, their joining could be seen through the three sets of wings that flared out from the man's back. It was quite a sight, but it gave him a bad mojo. A Hunter with this much power would wreak havoc on the world if taken by Darkness. This man could only summon three of the six wings, and that was good for him because if the guy had been able to call upon all six, nothing would be able to stop him. He was just a man and knew he couldn't defeat an angel, no matter how hard he tried.

With each impact of fists, Kaldär learned more and more about the man's fighting style. It seemed chaotic at first, but he was soon able to distinguish a pattern, and it was a familiar one to boot. All of the Seraphim was taught to fight by the Archangel Gabriel. The man had trained Kaldär himself back in the day. This fighting style was one of the oldest in the book and hadn't been used in centuries. No wonder this guy had such a reputation. His fighting style was so unorthodox and outdated it was comical. But even when old-fashioned, the angels were the best fighters in the cosmos.

What the ancient texts didn't talk about when it came to the Seraphim were their daily lives. Yes, the Angel's protected their lord's throne, but they were ordinary immortals on the side. Each Angel had its own personality and lived like regular people, just without the worry of Wickedness. He lived a mortal life and had human concerns, but he could travel to Heaven and Hell whenever he chose.

This man, who wished for what he couldn't have, was his uncle but had been gone by when he was born and hadn't found out till his aunt had told him on her deathbed. She had been immortal and had lived a long life but wasn't immune to death when it came knocking on her door. She had been wounded during the burning of Ascaria. He had only seen his uncle from afar and had never met him till now. Clearly, his dear old aunt hadn't thought to tell her hubby that he had another nephew.

Rushing forward, Kaldär changed his attack at the last second and flipped Ryeznya on his ass before kicked him away. He flew off the cliff and disappeared for a second. Picking up the Stetson, his uncle cherished so much he placed it on his head and waited. His breath had yet to grow heavy, and he was a little disappointed. He'd hoped for more of a fight once he'd figured out whom it was, he had sensed during his lunch.

Standing silent, he glanced behind himself and looked at where Eźmeralda had taken refuge. She had had yet to see him in an actual battle, and you could say this had kind of counted. As he made a note to take Eźmeralda to see the famous arena battles hosted by Gabriel, he felt Ryeznya's magic flare up and didn't have to wait long before he saw him rise up on his wings. Three wings were child's play to him. All three were visible, and as he settled back down to the ground, the wings darkened. He watched as they bloomed with light but didn't move from where he was.

As soon as the magic solidified, he moved, body flickering as he jumped forward and grabbed Ryeznya by the throat. Devine Jump for him could be done without thinking, and even his uncle couldn't match his speed. His brother might, but he doubted it. He was still young. Looking at his uncle, he frowned

"You need to speed up your reaction time, old man," he said as he cut the seraphim off from its divine connection with heaven. Like a candle, his uncle's magic went out, and he fell limp as his body regained its actual age. The funny thing about magic, when misused, makes the body feel younger, and after such, if you lose it, your body ages tenfold. Talk about consequences.

Face now weathered, Ryeznya looked at him with pure hatred. It was unnerving, knowing that his own flesh and blood could hate him with such a passion and yet not even know anything about him to cause such loathing.

"Will you comply," he said. "Or am I going to have to teach you some manners?"

All Kaldär got in response was a growl. Well, if Ryeznya wasn't going to comply, then so be it. The game was simple, and he had grown used it with Eźmeralda for the last five years. He had grown to know patience as a close friend. Calling on the Divine within him, he locked away the man's magic and let him go before stepping back.

As if sprung from a trap, Ryeznya leaped back. When he tried to use his magic, though, he became confused. He looked at his hands and then at himself before looking up at him.

"What have you done?" he shouted.

"Nothing permanent," Kaldär assured him. "We need to talk." Turning, Kaldär began to walk away. He let his body relax, for he knew Ryeznya wouldn't attack again; they both knew it wouldn't do any good.

He soon heard his uncle following grudgingly and grinned. The family had always been thickheaded, and his uncle proved that fact now. Time to see why the old man had taken the trip here for the Fore-Lorne Looking Glass; after all, it was the *only thing* on the geezer's mind.

Once the shaking stopped, Eźmeralda opened her eyes and asked the land to let her out. It complied, and she emerged inside the large living room within the mountain. Carved from the very rock, the place she had come to call home for the last five years sat dark. The rich furniture around her loomed like shadowy creatures, and she jumped when she bumped against the couch. She rushed to find the light switch in a hurry, and after gaining a few bumps and bruises, she found it. She lifted the small lever and watched the lights above grow bright.

Kaldär had kept up with the newest technology, so despite being a massive fortress that had been carved from the very mountain, the place was top-notch. He had installed the best security gold could buy and had spared no expense when it came to entertainment. The torches she had ignited hung high above like stalactites, and as she moved through the assortment of couches and chairs, she looked up at them. They glowed softly, but their light easily lit the entirety of the room.

Consisting of six sections, the mountain was basically hollow. Kaldär had infused the rock with support magic, and she had questioned the stability of the place at first, but she had soon realized her fear was misplaced. She had quickly learned the structure was made up of five wings, and Kaldär had placed her in the north wing. She headed there now, trekking up the stairs. She soon reached her bedroom and found it bare. Looking around, she gaped. Where had all her stuff gone? No one could have taken it, so where did it all go? Opening her closet, she found her clothes gone too. Freaking out now, she rushed back down to where she had emerged. Running through the room, she passed into the studio and then into the hall. The hall circled the whole mountain, and she ran along its length until she reached the east wing.

Consisting mainly of a training room, Kaldär used the area for storage. Any artifact he found or picked up, he placed here. She didn't go into the room where he kept them, but she could feel the magic through the wards; she would need to tell Kaldär he needed to strengthen the wards that kept magic in. He probably hasn't replaced his wards for years. The man's rhythm was ever-changing, but still, he was sort of conservative.

After a few more turns, she reached the maglev-elevator that led up to the top of the mountain. It had initially been a ladder, but Kaldär had taken her advice early on to switch it out for the elevator. She stepped into the blue light and rose up on the empty air. She pushed magic from her hands and picked up speed. She soon stepped out into Kaldär's bedroom and took a beeline straight for the side room.

She stepped into it and threw magic towards the torch in the corner to light it and almost fainted as the one thing she had thought would never happen was revealed. She leaned against the doorframe in shock and looked around the large closet. Kaldär had moved her stuff; that was for sure. Stepping lightly, she moved up to the shelves that held her shoes and shirts. She opened the drawers and found her undergarments inside, sorted by color. He had always been a little OCD, and she smiled when she saw how he had laid her clothes out in an orderly fashion.

She was just picking up one of her shirts when she felt a proximity ward go off. She dropped the shirt and fell into a low crouch. Had Kaldär been defeated? No, he was the strongest person she knew; he hadn't been defeated, so why the alarm? Had he brought that man inside? If so, why? He had tried to kill them, right?

Sliding out of the closet, she went up to the large panel that sank into the wall beside Kaldär's bed and clicked on the furnished silver. It lit up, and she looked at the assortment of security torches that surveyed the entirety of the place. The only rooms without the torches were the bedrooms and bathrooms. Though Kaldär had threatened to install some when she had acted out and pretended to go the restroom to escape her training. She grinned at the memory. She had hated her new life initially, but now that she had gained her first Element, she couldn't wait for what came next.

Looking at the panel again, she looked for Kaldär and soon found him in the south wing with the man from before. They were sitting at the large table that he had placed in the center of the room, and she gasped when she saw that their guest was not restrained. He looked to be free. She quickly turned off the link and rushed back towards the elevator. She reversed the polarity and dropped down the chute until she reached the bottom floor. When she hit the floor, she came out running. If she didn't hurry, she could be too late to warn Kaldär. Why would he let the enemy into their home without detaining him? It was stupid, but as she reached the entrance to the south wing, she slowed.

He must have a reason, right? Kaldär wasn't injudicious. He was a strategist and thought everything out before he did anything. She paused at the door that led to the room they were in but hesitated. She had pulled a rookie move by rushing here. She hadn't thought everything out; instead, she'd let her emotions rule her actions.

She was at a loss within her sudden despair. Kaldär was just on the other side of this door, and she was afraid to face him, knowing she had rushed in her actions to get here.

Raising her hands, she gripped the handles but didn't pull on them; she listened to Kaldär's muffled words. It sounded like he was explaining something.

"—I swear on my life I don't know you!" That was the stranger. Eźmeralda wondered why he sounded so out of sorts, like someone had just killed his dog.

"—and I swear, it's the truth!"—that was Kaldär—the universe works in mysterious ways and... one sec."

She heard steps and jumped back as they grew louder. The door opened, and she looked at Kaldär in embarrassment. He just grinned and gave her a wink. She smiled but couldn't stop her cheeks from growing hot.

She walked into the room after him and followed until they reached the table. In the corner, on his bed, lay Ba'ile. His eyes were open, and he seemed to be watching Ryeznya closely. Turning to the guy, she was struck with a loss of words when she came face to face with the man in the odd trench coat. He looked older, she realized, like he'd aged ten years in the last hour.

She realized now why he wasn't chained to a chair; his magic had been severed. She looked at Kaldär then back at the creepy man. The guy's eyes glowed red even without his magic, and she wondered if he was totally human. He seemed off, and she was getting the shivers just being near him.

"So," she said as she looked at the floor. "What do we owe this pleasure?"

She couldn't look him in the eye; with his unblinking stare, she felt like he was studying her, trying to assess her weaknesses. She crept back but tried not to make it obvious. She reached the far side of the table and sat down beside Kaldär. He seemed calm, even at ease, which she drew upon now.

"Eźmeralda, meet my uncle Ryeznya," Kaldär said as she sat down beside him. "Ryeznya, meet Eźmeralda, my apprentice in training."

Sitting down opposite them, Ryeznya smiled, "In training? She seems to already be a master."

Kaldär grinned. "Yes, but she still has four elements to learn.

Ryeznya's eyes went wide, and she felt his mind go blank. He was at a loss, she realized.

"You know the fifth?" he barked in shock. His voice was a rough baritone that held a scratchy undertone. It was pretty creepy.

His face was a mask, but his mind was open to her, and she saw his thoughts scrambling for clarity. She had always thought everyone could reach Kaldär's level but apparently not. She looked at Kaldär and frowned. "Uh, what's different between us and everyone else?"

Ryeznya stood up and gestured to Kaldär. "Each person can wield one Element but is limited by their aura's capabilities. Only a magician like Kaldär can unlock each pathway of the Divine and the Demonic energies within the mind and body." He paused, but only for a second as he took off his coat. "Normally, one or two pathways are unlockable, which is where a single element comes in. Acreage unlocks the physical channels, Wind the spiritual channels, Fire the Demonic and Water the Divine." He sat back down, and she listened to him describe the different types of magic and their limits. It was not news; she had heard it all from Kaldär, but she'd never grown bored of it. For her, it was like listening to a history lecture.

Ryeznya eventually stopped talking and looked between the two of them, set his sights on Kaldär. "I still want that mirror."

She and Kaldär shared a look. After such a lengthy lecture on magic, she was surprised Ryeznya still had a mind to ask for such. She wondered if Kaldär would comment on it, but he just looked at their guest with a frown.

"No," was all he said. Eźmeralda mentally did a fist bump. There was no moving him once he made up his mind; she'd learned that the hard way, and when Ryeznya scowled, she covered her mouth with a hand to hide her grin. This was fun to watch. She had thought him scary, but he was just a grumpy old man with an attitude without his magic.

"I need it!"

Kaldär raised an eyebrow, and Eźmeralda looked between the two of them in anticipation. She wondered what the Hunter would need a Divine Artifact for. Had he lost his car keys? She leaned forward and placed her chin in her hands. "Why do you need this... artifact? Is that what you're looking for?" she asked.

Ryeznya looked at her and seemed to consider answering. She looked back at him and waited. If he were going to answer, he would; if not, she wasn't going to complain. The ball was in his court.

Ryeznya looked at Kaldär but didn't hold his eye, choosing to look at the table as he spoke.

"I'm tracking a demon that is plaguing the living realm. It steals its victims' souls by trapping them in their own reflections, so they are helpless to stop their own murder. It's left a trail of bodies. And from what I have gathered, it's been residing in Nypheriam for the past two days.

That perked Kaldär's interest. He had sat up at the mention of the capital of the Nypherian Kingdom.

"Nypheriam, you say?"

"Yes..."

Kaldär laced his fingers together before himself and leaned his elbows on the table. He was a cipher, unreadable as he looked at the man across from them.

"You're tracking a Mirror Demon?"

"Yes."

"Okay, now let me guess, it's heading straight towards Kaiźer."

Ryeznya looked at him in surprise but smiled not a second later. "Yes, it is."

Kaldär looked at her suddenly. His face was tight, and she wondered if he was alright? He looked pained.

"Pack your bags," he said to her, his voice constricted. "We're going on a little trip."

She nodded. She wondered why Kaldär was choosing to help the creepy man after he had tried to kill them. At the mention of Nypheriam, he had clearly made his decision almost immediately, and that made her wonder. Did he have something he had to do there? She could only get ready to go and hope to find out when they got there. Moving from the room, she gestured for Ba'ile to follow and headed to her new bedroom, smiling once more when she walked through the doorway. It was a nice change from her single room in the north wing. It was more prominent for sure, and as she gathered a few things and threw them into her dimensional locker, she grinned at Ba'ile. *Did you move my stuff here, big brother?* Eźmeralda could quickly grab what she needed by reopening the space with a metal command, and as she spoke to Ba'ile, she locked the passageway.

Rippling with light, Ba'ile's form melted away, becoming that of a man. Covered with tribal patterns, the shifter's fur was silver and hid his parts from view. She had thought it odd that he chose not to wear clothes, but after learning it was because of an old tradition, she'd dropped the topic. Looking at her with a lopsided smile, Ba'ile's face crinkled pleasantly despite his scars. The x-shaped scar on his left cheek caused his lips to curve up more on the left when he grinned, and so even when he smiled, it looked lopsided.

"Kaldär told me to do so after you were done training. Good job on that, by the way." He said as she went to look for a new outfit for the trip. Standing in the doorway to the closet, he watched as he shifted through the selection of shirts lined up on the wall. "How about the grey one; Yes, that one." Pointing at a cloud-gray shirt of smooth cloth, he guided her to his choice. She picked it up and slipping it on over the wrappings that held her chest tight; she looked at herself in the polished mirror of sliver that sat against the wall. He had made the right choice; it went well with the pants she wore and even matched with the boots she wore as well.

"How's your task from Kaldär going?" she asked Ba'ile. She didn't know what Kaldär had tasked her brother with, but any sort of slip-up she could cause was more than anything she could get out of Kaldär himself.

"Oh, the lady is doing fine. She"—Ba'ile scowled at her suddenly—"hey! You know I can't talk about this, so why do you keep trying?"

Eźmeralda shrugged indifferently. "No reason... I'm just curious why he needs you to keep an eye on; a lady is it, who he doesn't even know?"

Scowling, Ba'ile crossed his arms over his chest and fell silent. His eyes flashed with anger, and she pouted at him.

"Don't be like that," she said sadly. "I don't mean any harm, you know that?" *He acts like I'm going to do something to ruin his mission.* She moved past him with a shrug of her own and turned to the door, but just as she was starting to turn the nob, it swung open, and Kaldär walked in. She jumped out of the way as he brushed past and took a breath as he threw off his shirt. Stepping into the adjoined bathroom, he shut the door with a snap, and glancing at Ba'ile, Eźmeralda inquired if he knew what was up. Shaking his head Ba'ile looked just as confused as she felt. She heard the faucet run high, and she felt his energy through the door as it pulsed. He was angry, but about what? She moved and listened for a second before opening the door.

She found Kaldär sitting down on the edge of the giant clawfoot tub, tears running down his face. He looked at her in surprise, and she stood there for a second in shock. He...was crying? She rushed to his side once she could move and, grabbing a towel, brushed his tears away as she knelt down beside him.

"Kaldär..." she whispered. "What's wrong?"

"I worry for my brother..." he hummed. "H-he's the reason for my unease."

"Why? If he's your brother, he's got to be the same age as you, right? I'm sure he's fine."

Kaldär shook his head. "No. He's half as old as I am and still has much to learn about who he is. I hid his true name from himself, and he still has no idea of his heritage."

She looked at Kaldär, sitting before her, his eyes red with tears, and felt her chest tighten. She gripped his chin and pulled his gaze up. She met her lips with his and let her understanding pass to him. He kissed her back, and she spoke against his lips. "I'm sure you had your reasons. You've never done anything without thinking of every outcome beforehand, right? Don't worry; I'm sure he's okay."

"Yes," Kaldär gave her a thin smile. "It's just that he's my brother, and the Mirror Demon was sealed away by him and his friends, so when it got free, I should have known. I worry because I didn't sense its release."

She pursed her lips. That would mean a celestial had interfered. If Kaldär had failed to sense such a significant change in the magical realm, something big prevented it. They had their work cut out for them.

She stood up and held out a hand. Kaldär took it, and she pulled him to his feet. She loved how she could match him in strength now and couldn't help but think about all the times she had bragged about it. She led him out into the bedroom and pushed him onto the bed. Looking at Ba'ile, she stared at him till he blanched. Walking backward till he bumped against the door, he fumbled with the handle.

"I think I will leave you two alone for now. I should... I should go keep our guest company till we leave then." Ba'ile rushed out of the room without a second glance and let the door shut with a bang. She locked it with a click of her wrist and looked at Kaldär then.

He met her gaze with confusion, and in a slow crawl, she crawled up beside him and ran her hands through his hair. "Let's not worry about what we have to do till we do it, hmm? Just relax and let me take care of you; Ryeznya can wait for a bit, right?"

Kaldär nodded reluctantly, and she grinned.

"Okay. Now relax. We have plenty of time before we have to get going."

She pushed him back and, leaning down once more, merged her lips with his.

Sin'ka

Chapter 17: Demon Trails

I thought if funny to frizzy the wifes skirts with my experiments but her fury was second to none. Still, it only doubled the funny.

Forgotten mortal
The Enchanted Age

Filled Filled with confusion, Sin'ka walked beside Oníx as they followed Kaiźer into the Lover' Bite. She noticed that the safeguard she'd had Hex put up was no longer protecting the entrance. With the knowledge that both he and James had worked together to put it up and that it was their strongest ward, she steeled herself as they entered the building.

"Oh," Oníx breathed, "looks like we missed quite the party."

Looking at her, Sin'ka scoffed. How could Oníx joke at a time like this? The place was in shambles. She barely recognized the site where the mirrors had been; only red brick remained. She moved to stand beside Kaiźer as he surveyed the place. What had once been intricate glass had now become a sea of black shards covering the floor, tables, and chairs in a thick dusting.

"Ryeznya did all this?" she asked Kaiźer. He nodded as he moved to the bar, his face stony. Turning back to face her, his expression changed only slightly, becoming more serious.

"Yes, and if I know him, he went off in search of someone he had thought long dead," Kaiźer said softly. She thought for a second that he looked at her for a second as he spoke, but he looked away just as quickly. Still... his hesitation in saying who Ryeznya was looking for worried her. If she had to guess, she was the man's target. But why was the question at hand?

"So... why destroy the place?" she asked him.

"For the fun of it, of course," Oníx put in. "If he can ruin another person's day, he will." Her face was grim, and Sin'ka got the feeling Oníx was speaking from experience. Kaiźer pushed off of the bar, and she looked at him as he spoke up suddenly.

"To start off, I am not one to let another OtherWorlder stand alone, and you are young. You can choose still to stay with us or forget any of this ever happened."

Confused, Sin'ka looked at Kaiźer as if he'd grown horns and a tail. His attitude now was completely different a moment ago.

She could understand why he would act this way, but she'd thought she had already proven herself to be on his side.

Like, come on, he was working like he didn't want her by his side. That, combined with the way he had been pushing her away, showed just that, but she wasn't stupid, and she could see the way he looked at her. He clearly cared for her, and that was what confused her the most.

"Kaiźer, she's not going anywhere." Oníx snapped.

"I don't want her in this life. It's no way to live." Kaiźer snapped back.

"It may not be what you want, but the only way she'll be safe is if she's with us," Oníx reasoned, "and I want her safe, not dead."

Looking between the two of them, Sin'ka began to see why Kaiźer had been avoiding her, and it hadn't been because he wanted her gone. It had been because he cared too much to see her become like him, to become broken.

"But what about this afternoon, you said—"

"I know what I said," Oníx snapped at Kaiźer, "and I still think it is the safest path for her."

Kaiźer's eyes grew stern. "But the risks—"

"Are well worth it as long as she'd safe," Oníx finished.

Kaiźer's eyes flashed as he jumped to his feet in anger. "I will not let you erase who she is!"

That caught Sin'ka's attention. Taking a step forward, she cut Oníx off just as her friend opened her mouth to speak. "Wait, how can Oníx erase who I am?"

Both Kaiźer and Oníx turned to face her, their expressions painted with unease. Kaiźer looked to be in actual pain as he began to look around at everything except her.

With a considering glance, Oníx pursed her lips. Sin'ka waited as Oníx stood silent, glancing at Kaiźer. Regarding them again, Sin'ka saw an agreement come to a close.

"Sin'ka," Oníx spoke up. "After you and I got home the last time, Kaiźer contacted me. We agreed to meet at a secret location within the Kingdom of Light, the Enchanted Lagoon, in fact. It was uh..."—whipping around to face Kaiźer Oníx grimaced—"Kaiźer! ...I think it would be better if you tell her."

Kaiźer crossed his arms and scowled at Oníx but slowly, that scowl faded, and he let out a heavy sigh. "After Ryeznya left, I didn't wait. The club was in ruins, and I needed to let Oníx know about Ryeznya and why he was back."

24 hours earlier~

Oníx had cut the source link, filling Kaiźer's mind with a slight ringing. Damn it, Oníx, you know what happens to me when you do that. Ugh, he missed her, but it still hadn't been long enough.

After Jessíca left the Lover' Bite, he spent the next couple of hours trying to clean the place up. Using a little magic, he was able to pick up most of the glass remains, but after one look at what remained of the front door's magical ward, he knew that nothing could fix the damage to it. Abandoning the effort, he quickly closed up and made sure that no one would try to enter the establishment until he could fix the place up. He did so with a simple dissuasion spell that would make someone who came to close face the other direction with the thought that they had forgotten to do something elsewhere.

Heading out into the alley, he passed through the door that Ryeznya had had the courtesy to repair, but when he looked at the magical shards that remained of Hex, he cursed. Damn Ryeznya and his magic. The little fucker needed a lesson or two in common courtesy. After a quick check of the surrounding area, he headed out into the night's dawning light.

Moving through the buildings, Kaiźer crept through the shadows till he neared the center of the city and, with a gathering of his magic, activated the Eternal Pool that lay directly under the central courtyard and let the magic boost fuel his Shadow jump.

Traveling into the enchanted lagoon required massive energy thanks to the place being protected by a strong deterrent towards all mortals and immortals alike. The lagoon creatures were very protective of their territory, but any who could reach the water's edge were treated with honor, showing the appreciation of the person's abilities in bypassing the wards.

Only the elves and those he knew personally had reached the place with a sane mind.

He was teleported through the null void to pop back out onto soft white sand with a grunt. Keeling, he took deep breaths to steady his stomach.

Why, of all the secure places, did she have to choose the lagoon? The place was quiet even during the morning hours, the turquoise waters shifting slowly to a slight breeze. He could sense the mermaids just offshore, and with a bow elegant enough to make the Queen blush, he winked at the closest lady in the water. Her eyes went complete and, after tittering with the others, dove into the depths.

Grinning, Kaiźer looked at the high black rocks the rose into the sky on both sides of the bluffs that surrounded the inlet. Curving around in a teardrop shape, the high cliffs veered around on both sides to shut off the area peacefully, leaving only one way in or out.

Nestled at where the two cliffs met, a tiny sliver of a gap ran up the wall. Near incomprehensible to the physical eye, it was surrounded by strong elemental magic. Kaiźer quickly scouted the area, moving down the sands to where the wall met with water and back to the opposite side. Once he was positive, the place was still secure, he settled down by the water's edge.

Sitting comfortably, he erected a thin proximity ward that would alert him of when Onix arrived. When alerted, the mental noise was loud, and he was sure to get a kick out of her reaction when it filled her head with its ringing screams. He had to have some fun once in a while. Now he had only to wait.

Noon was in full swing, and Kaiźer had yet to even move a muscle. Deep within his meditation, he was aware of all that was around him. With this, Onix didn't have a chance to sneak up on him. Besides, she had yet to see his surprise.

Hidden from sight, a firecracker had been tuned to her aura's signature. After much consideration, he had decided to erect the bomb for laughs. He smiled as the alarms were tripped suddenly. Oníx had arrived. Keeping his face straight, he waited as she walked past the firecracker. It activated as soon as she got near, going off with a whistle and letting off a loud bang as the gunpowder inside was sparked. He opened his eyes to her tiny yelp pf surprise and chuckled; it wasn't every day he got the jump on her.

~Looks like we have a visitor~ Kaín said smugly

Sitting in the lotus position, he looked out at the water, watching as the sun painted patterns across its surface.

As the light flashed along with the watery gleam of the Enchanted Lagoon, he relaxed. The cold sensation of the shadows that flowed with the warmth of the sun calmed him.

Patiently he waited for Oníx to find him. Nevertheless, he didn't have to wait long; she was at his side within seconds.

"You're still up to your old tricks, I see," she said, trying to sound calm.

Kaiźer smiled smugly. He knew full well that his tricks, no matter how dangerous or coy, made for a satisfying feeling, and he knew Oníx didn't care for it, but why else would he do it but to tease her. Besides, she looked like she needed the distraction. He wondered if something had happened last night between her and Sin'ka.

~I bet they had sex~

Kaín, I doubt anything like that happened; he shot at the dragon. At least he hoped nothing had happened.

~You know I'm in your head numb nuts; you aren't getting anything past me~

He growled at Kaín's smug attitude.

"Ryeznya's back!" he stated suddenly in frustration.

With a sigh, Oníx dropped down beside him as if exhausted. She said nothing, but when he looked at her, he didn't see what he expected. Instead, he saw relief. Odd, he would have thought upon hearing that Ryeznya was back in town; she would be more... well, not relieved, that was for sure.

Dropping his head, he chuckled.

"What's so funny?" she snapped.

Looking back at the water, he contemplated his following words.

"I thought you'd be more...."

"Afraid?" she finished

He opened his mouth, but all that came out was a gurgle as he struggled to find the words.

~Oh, oh! Tell her I think she's doing a good job~ Kaín said.

With a scowl, he turned to Oníx. "That's not what I—"

Oníx cut him off. "I no longer fear Ryeznya!" she said as she squared her shoulders.

With fire in her words, she had spoken with both her voice and her mind. The words echoed in Kaiźer's head, and he heard and even felt the truth in them and knew that she would be by his side no matter what he said. So, with his own fire, he told her everything, from the escape of Darzíel to how the mirror lords were hunting them. As he told her about Ryeznya warning him that Darzíel was using the mirror lords to gather power, she didn't look surprised, though. But he'd figured she'd already guessed as much.

He finished with the mess at the club, telling her about how the mirrors were destroyed. She said she could fix them but suddenly looked at him in shock and jumped to her feet.

"Sin'ka!"

He looked up at her. "What about her?"

"I went to her house yesterday."

Dread filled him as he saw where she was going. If the mirror lords had been watching her, they had likely added her to their list of targets.

"Then I ran into you two at the club," he said.

"Yeah, and if the mirror lords saw her with either of us, they may think she'd be involved."

Oníx sprung into motion like a cannon, her stride hasty. He rose to follow her, rushing to catch up. Moving along the sands, they passed through the crevice in the cliff without any difficulty and, moving through the gap, soon emerged in the thick forest of Ascaria.

"Oníx," he called as he followed through the trees. "Do you think Sin'ka's in trouble?"

Turning to him, she spoke, but she transferred her thoughts to him telepathically instead of talking. "Sin'ka has a man called James, who runs her staff. He mainly keeps the place clean, but his main duty is to protect Sin'ka, and he does through wards; some for defense and others for an offense."

~Oh, pish posh!~ Kaín butted in, *~Offensive, defensive my ass; sounds more like a tasty treat. I bet he's an air elemental~*

"Okay," Kaiźer said. "So, this James is good with magic, which means the house is safe. Why are you worried?"

In answer, Oníx spoke aloud, her voice dripping with regret. "James didn't take into account Demon magic when he placed the wards."

Now that Kaiźer thought about it, demons could bypass elemental magic when astral magic wasn't involved.

"That means..." he trailed off in dismay.

The trees parted into a clearing, and Oníx rushed towards the center of the glade. She flickered with a flash of light, and tracking her path, he merged with the shadows, following her into the busy streets of Nypheriam. Landing in an alleyway, he rushed out into the crowd that milled about the city's market area. Oníx was weaving her way through the public, and he struggled to keep up with her as he thought of a way to get to Sin'ka's house. He didn't know how to find a place he'd never been to.

~ There's always you know what~

~No, it's too dangerous~

~But I know her scent~ Kaín insisted.

~I said no, and that's final!~

The last time Kaiźer had used that, he'd ended up losing his memory of the next five days. He had made a promise to never use it again.

Passing into the city's industrial section, he spoke telepathically as he pushed through the crowds after Oníx.

"Hey!" he called out. "The only way I know of that's fast enough is *DivineJump*, and I can't use it yet with three people." He racked his brain for ideas, but everything he thought of was beyond his power level. He couldn't use magic to go to a place he hadn't been to, and he hadn't felt Sin'ka's aura all day. Struggling past people and animals alike, he didn't see Oníx move till he was falling. In a flash, she appeared behind him and pulled him into one of the dark backstreets.

Her grip on his shirt tightened, and with a whisper, reality warped around them.

Going black, the surrounding area vanished, giving way to a pool of swirling magic. He felt like he was being spun around in circles while, at the same time, not moving at all. Oníx had meshed herself against him, and he blinked to make sure he didn't imagine things.

Skin glowing slightly, she clung to his shirt. She caught his eye and, with a quirky grin, gave a wink. He blushed as her clothes unraveled into small ribbons of fabric. Floating before him, she became wreathed in light, glowing brighter the longer he looked. He noticed that it clashed with a dark figure, or he should say half a dark figure. His body shimmered with the same light that covered Oníx but mixed in with it was a crimson red that glowed with an angry luminosity. Before he could question why his vision blurred. His body stretched into a long spiral, but no pain assailed his senses. A loud roaring filled his ears, and the black void around them split apart with a tearing sound, and he watched in shock as they materialized in the sky and came hurling towards the ground at light speed. He didn't have time to see where they were when they hit the ground all too quickly.

Oníx twisted them at the last second, absorbing the impact with her legs. He crashed down beside her, swerving at the last second to land on his side instead of his neck. Oníx let go of him and placed her hands on her knees. She caught his eyes as he looked up at her in anger and confusion.

She stood and held out a hand. Kaiźer took it, and she helped him up.

"Interesting..." she mumbled as she pulled his arm towards her. "Your aura..."

"Yeah, you think that's interesting. How about telling me what the fuck all that was just now?"

He pulled his arm back, but the motion sent ripples of unease to his stomach. He suddenly felt like throwing up. What Oníx had just done was something he could live without. He swore she'd had wings in those short couple seconds of travel, and clearly, they'd traveled quite the distance because they stood in the middle of a thick forest that was beyond the mountains outside the city limits. Once again, though, as he turned around, he felt his belly quiver in discomfort and tried but failed to keep his last meal from taking a trip down memory lane.

Falling to his knees, he heaved the contents of his stomach into the snow. Gods below! He'd never had such an adverse reaction from magic before. He was dry heaving still, and even Kaín commented on the effect.

~Tell her to never do that again~ he said with a growl, *~I think I'm going to be sick as well~*

Oníx came and knelt beside him and placed a hand on his back. He felt tiny tendrils of magic ease past her hands, moving through him, finally settling his core, giving off a cool sensation that warmed and settled his troubled stomach.

"I apologize. Angelic travel can be...." Oníx paused, thoughtful. "Unsettling your first time."

~ANGELIC TRAVEL!!!~ Kaín blurted, clearly uneasy. Kaiźer felt him shiver against his back.

Afraid of another flash of vertigo, he spoke slowly. "What do you mean, angelic travel?" Raising his head, he waited for his body to settle before he rose into a kneeling position. Placing his hands on his knees, he looked at Oníx. She looked at him in turn, lips pursed. He tried not to fidget under her gaze. His worry for Sin'ka was burning away his patience. After a few seconds, Oníx stood gradually. He watched as she turned away and stopped a few feet away.

In a quick flurry, white wings sprang free from her back. They started as icy tattoos upon her skin that crackled and pulsed. They slowly peeled away with a fairy dust effect till a pair of bright white wings sat between her shoulder blades. Covered in thousands of feathers that sparkled with divine light, they stretched to a good thirty feet. Layered with thick muscle, Kaiźer had no doubts that they could carry her through the heavens with ease. They moved about effortlessly and yet caused the wind to whip about with each mighty sweep. Their strength was evident.

~I hate when she does that~ Kaín said

~What? You knew she could do that?~ he asked, *~and you didn't think to tell me?~*

~Well, it's not like I could since I thought you already knew~

~When did her...uh...~

~How should I know; I'm just surprised you don't remember?~

Stepping lightly, Oníx turned and, with an elegant saunter, came to stand before him. He couldn't believe his eyes—but when she held out her hand—he took it without a second thought.

"How long?" he asked.

Focusing her gaze on him, she lifted him to his feet without a sound. He could feel the strength in her grip that he knew hadn't been there moments before.

"Since Darzíel first fell," she said as she turned and began to hike up into the trees. "Now, we need to hurry. Our destination is just through these trees."

Moving swiftly, the two of them passed through the forest's icy embrace, and using Divine jump, they both crossed the mountain, soon coming across a small mansion that glowed with a warm light. Built at the top of the hill, the house had many wards stretched around its entirety. So, James was a fire elemental then? And when he looked at them in the magical spectrum, they glowed in a myriad of reds and oranges. Made sense; they were the most common.

~You lose~ he said to Kaín.

~I still think he should have been an air elemental; fire is so overrated~

~ Aren't you a fire-breathing dragon?~ he asked.

~Humans aren't the only ones who wish they could be different at times~

He didn't argue with the guy. They exited the tree line, and with a shiver, he felt them pass through a thin barrier that tickled his senses. Clearly designed to alert the caster of their arrival, the magic pulsed.

Stopping beside the elegant fountain that sat in the center of the paved pathway, they only had to wait a few seconds before the massive front doors swung open. Unmoving, the two of them looked on as a young man came out. Dressed in a middle-class man's evening attire, he strode towards them.

"Oníx," he called in greeting, stopping to stand before her, clasping her forearm. *"Arwä-arvo olen isäntä, ekäm—honor keep you, my sister."*

"Oníx responded in kind, tightening her grip. "*Arwä-arvo pile sívadet*—may honor light your heart."

Stepping back, the boy turned to him with a kind smile. "And who is this?"

Looking at him, Kaiźer could see the magic of many years in his eyes. Yellow in color, the magic was a level three, but a hint of higher power sparked under it all. The boy was powerful for his age, and Kaiźer could see his potential, but the question was, would he be like his predecessors.

"This is Kaiźer, my step-brother," Oníx stated, "and Kaiźer?' "This is James, my blood brother." She turned away from the boy.

He and James looked at each other in shock, each at a loss for words. He looked at Oníx in surprise. She had a brother. Like a real brother? That meant... this boy was a Hunter! Stepping forward, he held out this arm. "*Bur tulé ekämet kuntämak*—well-met brother kin."

James grasped his forearm tightly, his face a mask of shock. "You know of my culture?"

Oníx grinned. "Kaiźer grew up with our people before he was taken into the Jackal's coven."

"You're a *Paznicii de tdaté*—Guardian of all!" It wasn't a question.

"Not for years now, but yes, your ancestors used that term."

His master had started his training in Ascaria, and they had spent the majority of it there. That had been during the Enchanted Age. At the mention of his ancestors, James's eyes flared. It happened so quickly Kaiźer almost missed it.

"Well, Sin'ka isn't here, but she should be back soon. Would you like to come inside? I just finished cleaning up the place."

Looking back at the forest, Kaiźer surveyed its bare skeleton, searching for Sin'ka's aura, but for some reason, he couldn't focus the magic.

Breathing through his nose, he concentrated the energy, pushing till he saw a flicker of her aura, but that was all. Frustrated by the lack of energy, he realized her scent, which should have covered the area, was non-existent. It was nowhere to be found.

"James," Oníx said. "Could you add Kaiźer to your codex?"

"Oh sure,"

Still struggling to gain control of his magic, he only grunted to James's request to enter his mind. Once he did, he realized his mistake too late, and his magic came to him in a rush. It was like a nuclear blast in his head. One second, nothing was there; the next, both his physical and magical senses were overloaded. His vision flared, and he winced as the colors around him brightened in texture. He gasped as a multitude of wards appeared before him, no longer veiled.

"Ugh..." he groaned. "What kind of wards do you use, gods!"

"Oh, don't be such a baby. You would have seen the outcome if you hadn't been so fixated on locating Sin'ka."

He glared at her through his fingers as he cradled his head. She had a point, and he knew it. His worry for Sin'ka was clouding his judgment, causing years of training to fly out the window. Never did he have to deal with such strong emotions. Remembering what the lady in the garden had said, he couldn't help but think about fate. Had she known this would happen?

Had she known he'd lose his edge? Had she been warning him by telling him what she had? He hadn't thought so at the time. Even now, he had his doubts. Maybe it would be best if he kept his distance. He didn't care what Maliki had told him. Love was a noose. It had been his crucible since the beginning, and he wasn't going to think it would change because some goddess said it would.

"Oníx," he called. "We should check the grounds."

She gave a quick nod and turned to James. "Kaiźer had a point; we'll come in once we finish out here."

"No problem, I'll warm some tea for when you come back."

With a bow, James turned and jogged away. Instead of using the door, he leaped for the second-story balcony. He cleared the stone railing in a smooth flip and landed on his feet, not missing a step.

"Did he just..."

"Yep,"

Shaking his head, he led the way, moving silently around the side of the house, using the shadow of the walls to hide their progress. If any of the demon lords were around, he'd sense them before they did him. He hated them, but he hated the idea of them hurting Sin'ka more, and that hate strengthened his resolve.

"Oníx, I've been thinking."

"Oh, yeah?" she teased. "We both know nothing good can come from that."

He glanced back at her and raised an eyebrow. She was looking at him, but her expression was light, always the tease. Looking away, he gave a brief look at the moon.

"It's said that Horus was able to wipe the minds of his enemies with a single look but could never bring them back once he did."

"An old legend, half-true at best," Oníx stated.

She was friendly, he knew, for memory control was something she was good at. He didn't want her to use it one Sin'ka, and he would order that she don't.

"Do you want me..."—she paused—" to wipe Sin'ka?"

"No, I want you to take my memories of Abika."

She gasped, "What! I can't do that!"

"Yes, you can, and I need you to so you can give them to Sin'ka when it's time."

"..."

"Oníx?"

Damn him for even asking. He had been hoping that Oníx would be okay with the idea.

"If I need to, I will," Oníx said. "But first, you need to tell her everything, even if you have to break it to her slowly."

He stopped and stared up at the moon, "How? She would think me crazy."

"You don't know that! If you keep pushing her away, she will begin to hate you, not love you. I can see the connection between you two. She loves you even if she doesn't know it yet, and you love her too! I think she'd understand if you tell her the truth."

"I... I don't want to lose Sin'ka like I lost Abika," he mumbled.

Oníx looked away with a huff. Her eyes were hooded, and when she spoke, her words were sharp if still soft. She pinched the bridge of her nose as she stepped up to him, leaving only inches between them. "I can see that, but she wants to be with you! Sin'ka can handle her own, and if you truly love her, then prove it! If not, I will have to clear her of all memories about us and everything connecting her to us."

"You won't need to. I promise." He stated as he squared his shoulders.

~You with me?~ he thought

~ Don't ask me. I'm along for the ride even when I don't want to be~ Kaín responded.

Not surprised, Kaiźer smiled. Turning, he scanned the forest, using a mix of the magical and the physical spectrums to pick out any demon rot from the surrounding area. As he passed over the lake, he found what he was looking for.

"Oníx!" he urged, "the lake."

"I see it," she whispered. "I think it best if you...."

With a single thought, his clothes melted away to be replaced with black armor made of thousands of scales. The armor came hand in hand with heavens Bane. The scales were of Kaín's devising, and they glittered like obsidian. Hardened with magic and dragon fire, the armor was nearly indestructible. Finishing it up was Kaín himself, strapped securely to his back in a sheath that was one with the scales.

~Ah!~ Kaín hummed, *~finally, some action. What do you think is down there?~*

Kaín thrummed against him and lit incandescent as he spoke. He could quickly think of a few things, but they were about to find out for sure.

They soon stood at the water's edge, looking down at what had clearly been a ritual circle. A small ring of half-melted candles smoked slightly but what really caught their eye was the tiny corpse that sat in the center. It was headless and seemed to be drained to blood.

"Is that a bunny?"

His words were strangled, and he was surprised to find his voice hoarse. In a perfect circle around the body, the ground was rotted and black. The scent of sulfur stained the area, and when he kicked a pebble into the blood-stained waters, it was joined with hints of brimstone.

"Damn it!" he cursed. "Look at the symbols. This was a binding!"

~Clearly, whoever did this wanted something specific~ Kaín added, *~and it looks fresh~*

"Yeah, and I bet they got what they wanted."

Turning to him, Oníx gave him a look that screamed, Yah Think? He would have laughed if not for the potential demon risk that could still be brewing. Oníx opened her mouth, and he knew what would follow, but in shock and a tiny bit of relief, a voice behind them stopped her from speaking.

"Oníx! Kaiźer!"

Oníx's mouth snapped shut as she turned, shrugging her shoulders as she went. In a wave of blue light, her black sweater and jeans melted away, leaving her with her normal chest wrappings and tight leather pants with her high black boots that went all the way up to her knees.

On her right forearm, a white silk sleeve adorned her skin. It hung loosely, glittering with magic. Even as her attire shifted, two icy blue fireballs sparked to life before her, floating at the ready. He drew Kaín from his sheath.

James no longer wore the simple clothes he'd had on before. In fact, his clothes were not of this realm. Red in color, they shimmered slightly as if they were covered in flames, but those flames flickered, and he saw that the clothes beneath were torn and bloody. Their shock soon vanished when it was a friend and not an enemy that emerged from the trees.

In a flash of shadow, Kaiźer covered the remaining distance between James and himself, catching the boy just as he stumbled. Despite his injures, most of the blood wasn't his.

"What happened?"

Coming up beside him, Oníx knelt and cradled the boy's head in her lap. He stirred at her touch, groaning slightly as he reached up and pointed at the house.

"I was in the shop when it happened," he stated.

Moving back, Kaiźer spoke to Kaín as James told them about how the house had come alive.

~Kaín, can you search the house for activity?~

Nothing but silence greeted him.

~Kaín!~

~I can't ~

~Why not?~

Kaín seemed to shrug. *~You have to be more specific. Are we talking about alien activity, paranormal activity? I gotta know what kinda action we're talking about?~*

"Search the damn house!" he shouted, "and do it for demon activity, you prick!"

Oníx and James both looked at him in shock. He shook his head at their confusion, trying to hide his frustration. He gripped the blade tightly and waited, but it wasn't Kaín that spoke.

"You can't," James said. "The house is—"

~Blocked~ Kaín finished.

Looking at the water, Kaiźer despaired as the blue depths filled his vision. He watched as black blood slowly spread into his sight, clouding the water in dark swirls of red. Demon wards were hard to crack, and he doubted they would be able to get through them.

~ I'm hungry~ Kaín said suddenly.

"How can you be hungry?"

"Kaiźer, what I think Kaín is trying to say is, he can get past the demon wards."

Frowning, he looked at Oníx then at the black blade. Damn Kaín and his arrogant ass. If he weren't so damn helpful, he'd have sold him for a fresh bowl of Raman.

~Oh! I've always wondered what that would taste like. Is it as good as people say?~

Kaiźer tried to stay angry, but he couldn't stop the smile that grew on his face. Kaín had the moments he had to give him that. Sliding past Oníx and James, he strode towards the house. Surrounding the exterior of the home, the demon ward swirled like a glowing mirage. He quickly examined the swirling display before him and grinned. I hope you're starving because these weaves look really thick. Kaín glowed brightly and literally thrummed with energy.

At the edge of the grass, he stopped. "You ready?"

Hefting Kaín, so his tip pointed towards the gyrating magic, he waited.

~Once I'm touching the ward, place your thumb upon the blue jewel on my crest, and hold on~

Following Kaín's instructions, he thrust the black blade into the barrier. Nothing happened for a second, but when he started to wonder, he felt it; a slight tug, barely there at first, then stronger. Tightening his grip, he began to feel the blade heat and start to vibrate. His fingers went numb as a loud, sucking sound filled the air. Fine cracks appeared, and Kaín grew brighter as the magic was sucked into the black blade.

All at once, the wards shattered, falling around him in a shower of grey dust. Completely void of energy, what remained of the demon magic lay at his feet. Suddenly he stumbled back as power rushed through him. He felt it in his veins, burning as pure, clean magic. It held no form and was new, almost arcane. Kaín had just done a cleansing.

"How did you do that?" he asked in shock.

~I don't know; it just happened~

From behind him, James whistled in appreciation. "Never in all my years have I seen anything like that." Beside him, Oníx stared, her eyes twinkling. He smiled sheepishly. Do you always have to show off? I bet you love being the center of attention.

~Hey! I do not!~

~Oh, finally, he speaks. I was wondering where you were. Did you keep any of the magic for yourself?~

~Yeah, I split it fifty / fifty~

~Oh...~ slightly disappointed he had been expecting Kaín to be more selfish, but before he could shoot another jab at him, the scent of sulfur and fear filled his nose. Looking up at the second story, his vision flashed red. Sulfur meant demons, and the fear was from Sin'ka.

~Kaiźer, don't!~

"Shut up," he growled at Kaín.

Flashing up to the top balcony, he stood before the window and looked inside. He watched the battle between Sin'ka and one of the demon puppets till one of them took her down. At that moment, he rushed forward, and as he did, his vision went black.

Sin'ka stood in shock as Kaiźer finished his story. She had had no idea all that had been going on. She remembered the smell of sulfur and brimstone being everywhere, but after Oníx and he had arrived, she'd questioned its existence. Their appearance had seemed to purge the stench of Hell from her halls. She'd wondered if Oníx had done so, but she'd been with her the whole time and hadn't seen her do any type of cleansing. Besides, Kaiźer had been too busy fretting over her wellbeing, so he couldn't have had the time. That left this, Kaín person, and from how Kaiźer talked about him, he seemed to be an egotistical prick. She wondered how a sword could have a personality, though it did prove the man she'd seen that night at Kaiźer's place had been confirmed.

They'd moved over to the tables as Kaiźer talked. Oníx had cleaned the place up. It now gleamed, but instead of replacing the mirrors, she put smooth glass in their home. Oníx had totally remodeled the area. Behind the glass, the wall's red brick had been replaced for polished marble, and trickling down the stone was water; blue water lit by purple fire encased in glass orbs. The main area had been expanded slightly, one wall was totally gone, and she saw that the upper floor had been decorated with silks and flowers. The rooms each had a theme on the door, and with a gasp, she read the titles; Goddess sweet, Shifter sweet, Royal sweet, Servitude sweet, and more, some being too suggestive to read aloud. Still, she marveled at the detail.

"Who's the pervert now?" Kaiźer blurted out.

Sin'ka smiled as Oníx blushed. She could see the reason behind his words; the new editions screamed perv material.

"I thought the place needed it," Oníx said sheepishly.

Embracing Oníx, she gave her a kiss on the cheek. "It looks great, all the same."

"I'm glad, unlike some people, you try to rub things in," Oníx said as she shot a look over her shoulder. Kaiźer's scowl was priceless. It was so unlike him Sin'ka giggled at how flustered he looked.

"At least I don't dress like a fucking prostitute every hour of the day."

Her jaw dropped, and Oníx gasped. Kaiźer grinned in triumph when they became the ones scowling. He then vanished with a poof of white smoke replaced by another Oníx that spun around in a circle.

"Look at me; I'm sexy. You just stand there and drool as I kill you," the new Oníx said.

After a brief lapse of shock, Sin'ka collapsed into stitches at what was obviously Kaiźer pretending to stab an invisible enemy?

Oníx looked mortified as he mimicked her. "I do not talk like that!" she said in a rush.

Kaiźer or was it Oníx, whipped his hair and, with a quirky smile, ran his hands down the swell of his chest, continuing along the curve of his hips. "Should I take off a few layers? It is hot in here... oh wait, what layers?"

Sin'ka's face began to hurt. She couldn't stop laughing, and she felt tears appear in her eyes as Kaiźer did a slow shimmy with his hips. Oníx grew red, and with a gasp of anger, rushed forward. "I'm going to kill you!"

Kaiźer's image of Oníx flickered suddenly, and he vanished just as Oníx reached him. Sin'ka hiccuped in surprise as he reappeared behind Oníx. She gave a start as he tapped her on the shoulder and stifling a giggle; Sin'ka watched as she vanished right after twisting to face Kaiźer. She then appeared above him, landing on his shoulders. She grabbed at his hair as she landed, and they both vanished with a flicker. They reappeared again in the center of the main floor, and moving with the pre-natural speed, they threw kicks and jabs, tackling and wrestling each other to the floor again and again. It became hard to tell the two of them apart. They both fought in similar styles and were matched in strength, speed, and endurance. The fight was even, but they never stopped, and they never slowed. Kaiźer was ignoring Oníx's demands to change back and was simply smiling as she struggled to trap him. Sin'ka soon resigned to letting them do their thing and moved over to the bar.

The shelves were fully stocked with a mix of colored glass with a mirror behind them that rippled like liquid. Watching the fight from the mirror, Sin'ka grabbed her usual bottle of Commandaria wine. Looking for a mug, she found with a gasp a new assortment of Pearl Sea-folk cups. Grabbing one, she filled the tall glass with wine and, leaning against the polished counter, proceeded to watch the show.

"Kaiźer, I swear, if you don't stop, I'll—"

"You'll what? Fry me? I bet you can't even burn me with those puny flames of yours."

Enraged, Oníx captured Kaiźer in an armbar and lifted him into the air to smash him into the floor. She heard his ribs crack, but he didn't show it as he swept Oníx off her feet with a leg, knocking her onto her ass.

Lying on their backs, the two of them were breathing slowly despite throwing each other around like rag dolls. Walking out from behind the bar, she headed out onto the floor. She knelt between Oníx and Kaiźer, glass in hand.

"I can see quite the resemblance between you two," she said while trying to keep a straight face. "You could very well be sisters, twins even."

"Oh, we are not twins!" Oníx shot at her.

"Sisters?" Kaiźer said. "Yeah, no, but I think I make a better Oníx."

Sin'ka laughed. "Yeah, I don't think so; I have to agree with Oníx on this one. You're not her twin in any way." Kaiźer was turning out to be quite the tease, and she found that she actually liked this side of him. It was so different from the quiet, brooding side of him yet so similar it made him seem complete to her, and now that she was up close, she noticed his eyes. They were still the same glacier-blue in color. It was the only thing that gave him away physically. "I wonder if you could pull off an impersonation of me?" she wondered aloud.

Sitting up, Kaiźer grew serious as he looked at her. "I could never match your beauty," he stated. "I'd shame you if I tried."

She swallowed at the emotion in his words. Placing her hand upon his, she dropped her gaze. "If so, then why do you still insist on pushing me away?"

Gripping her chin lightly, Kaiźer lifted her gaze back to his. She saw tears in his eyes and couldn't help but reach up to catch them.

"I don't want you to get hurt," he said.

"You hurt me more by pushing me away," she said. Kaiźer was looking at her with such passion she could literally smell its depths. A red tear slid down her cheek only to be wiped away as Kaiźer slowly lifted her to her feet.

"Then I won't push you away," he said softly. They stood with not a breath between them, but Sin'ka couldn't help but notice they were eye to eye. She wasn't looking up at him for once.

"I don't think I can handle all this, though," she said as she looked him up and down with a giggle.

Grinning, Kaiźer looked down at himself, "too much for ya?"

"No... it's just that I prefer Mr. Muscles is all."

As she spoke, a tearing sound erupted behind her and instantly had Kaiźer standing over her. Eyes intent, he looked past her, a hand on the hilt that adorned his back. Looking back, she saw a thin trail of light suddenly appear in the middle of the room. Looking like a tear in the air itself, the hole widened slightly, and from it poked odd phantom protrusions. Slowing they grew, becoming... fingers? Confused, she watched alongside Kaiźer and Oníx as huge hands pushed into reality. Looking like the night sky that shone with a thousand stars on its black canopy, they were hazy and yet clear as if not entirely there.

All too quickly, they stopped and held steady, pausing with an air of hesitation. The back of the palms pressed together, the digits beginning to shake as if under strain. All at once, with the sound of fabric tearing, the air before them ripped asunder. Suddenly, a shining Cliffside was revealed. Sin'ka could see a far-off shoreline, but as she recognized the outline of it, a figure filled the light of the day beyond the portal and shadowed the room they stood within. Blurred and incoherent to the eye, he was walking towards them quickly. Clearly, the man seemed cautious, like he didn't want anyone to know he was doing what he was doing.

"Who could that be?" Oníx, now dressed in an odd exotic outfit, glanced at the portal with open curiosity and befuddlement. Kaiźer had a similar expression as well, which made Sin'ka curious as to what was happening.

"I don't know, but this is magician-level magic. Even I can't do this. Besides, this aura feels... pure, like that of an elemental." Kaiźer stroked his chin thoughtfully. Sin'ka noticed that his attire was that of black scales once more. When had he had the time to change clothes? Hadn't he just been dressed as a civilian?

"I can... feel that too," Oníx stated. Sin'ka saw her look at Kaiźer's back warily and wondered what her friend was hiding. Her actions said she recognized the aura. So why hide the fact? Something fishy was going on here. Looking back over to the portal, she let her claws extend fully. Her vision washed red despite her efforts, but she held control as the man they were watching emerged from the other side. With a flash of vivid colors, the area became vibrant with the rush of energy that was suddenly unleashed. Even she felt it, her skin tingling slightly.

Wow, enough to make any woman mushy. Even as the thought went through her head, she looked up slowly, taking in the designer jeans that clung to the man's legs like a second skin; she could literally see every line and couture of his calves and thighs, continuing up she saw that he wore a grey sweater that stretched across his broad chest and massive arms. She gave a huge gasp as her eyes alighted on the man's face, though. Now clear and un-muddled by the portal, he was blond in hair and blue of eye, his skin fair if not tanned slight. The man was a mirror image of Kaiźer in every way. All the way down to the way he held himself while standing still. The only difference was... nothing actually.... maybe a tad taller? The portal behind him closed up, but she didn't react to its ephemeral. She was staring at their guest with wide eyes. She was sure that Kaiźer was doing the same unless he knew the guy? He must, right? They did look *exactly* alike.

Tearing her gaze away from the stranger, she looked at Oníx and Kaiźer and saw their expressions. Kaiźer was not in a state of recognition but in shock. With his lack of acknowledgment, it was as expected, but Oníx, she was *playing* surprise; she knew their guest. Sin'ka saw as much in the blush of her cheeks. Not quite reaching her ears, it only covered her upper cheeks. Oníx only blushed so openly when she had something to hide. If she were genuinely shocked by a sharp blush, it would have covered her entire face and made her ears beet red. Even with her olive skin, her blushes showed in all their glory. Sin'ka found it to be quite becoming of her friend, made it easy to read her.

Standing before them, the man gave a bow, the flourish so elegant it was like a dance in of itself. Grace sang in his every movement, even when standing tall once more. Sin'ka felt her heart flutter despite herself. In an attempt to control her anxiety, she moved to stand beside Kaiźer. Taking his hand, she drew his gaze from the stranger. He seemed at a loss at her being by his side, but it quickly changed to a warming smile that had her chest glowing ardently. Looking back up at the man before them, Kaiźer gave a bow that was just as smooth.

"What me we offer for this visit, my lord," he said with a hint of bewilderment. He was trying to hide his own discomfort Sin'ka realized. Smiling, she looked up at their guest and saw that he was looking at Kaiźer with a mixture of mirth and confusion. Had Kaiźer done something wrong? Tapping him on the shoulder, she made Kaiźer look up, but the stranger masked his face too soon for him to see what she'd seen.

"Please, I am not a celestial in demand for worship. I am a man just like you." Facing them now, he looked between her and Kaiźer before looking off to the side at Oníx. Sin'ka saw a flicker of recognition flash through his eyes as he looked at Oníx, but it faded just as fast, becoming replaced with the look of mild disconcert. She couldn't tell if it was an act to hide his true feelings or that he really was uncomfortable. But all the same, he was hiding the small spurts of emotion that flashed new in each new moment that was evident.

"What's your name if I may be so bold?" she asked tentatively, unsure if it was her place to ask him anything."

The big man smiled knowingly as if reading her thoughts, and she blushed deeply at the familiarity that flashed through his eyes. It too quickly vanished, though he smiled wide as he turned to her personally. Giving a deep bow, he held an arm out all gentlemen like as he spoke.

"You may call be Kaldär"—he paused for a second, seeming to hesitate, but Sin'ka felt power in the word; power that seemed ancient—"Kaldär Corinika." He stood and gestured to where he had appeared. "I do apologize for the abruptness of my arrival, but I am not the only one to be coming here."

Oníx spoke up then, and Sin'ka turned to her expectantly. Was she going to keep up the act or say what was on her mind?

"And who would come here with you, the last of the Magicians?" Oníx asked Kaldär. So, *sticking to the mystery of what is happening, huh? Okay then.* Facing Kaldär, Sin'ka waited for his answer. It was quick in coming.

"My apprentice and someone I believe to be an old ally of yours?"

Oníx and Kaiźer looked at each other in bewilderment. Sin'ka hated it when they did that. They were clearly speaking to each other and making conversation, which left her out. Oh, how she would have words with Kaiźer on the topic; she wondered if she could learn how to do it herself? Maybe then she could be included in their mental conversations. Looking at Kaldär, she smiled shyly and mouthed sorry. He only shook his head in meek understanding and waited till Kaiźer and Oníx turned back to him.

"When will they be arriving?" Kaiźer asked.

Kaldär moved to the side and gestured to where he had appeared. "Any moment now, the doorway should still be connected; all that my apprentice needs to do is find it and reconnect it."

Oníx shook her head as if that explained everything. Kaiźer just looked on grumpily as he had lost an argument with Oníx, which he probably had. She smiled slightly at the thought.

Looking on, the three of them waited till Kaldär alerted them. Kaiźer and Oníx looked on with keen eyes as a small ball of light appeared and began to stretch down to the floor in the middle of the air.

It seemed to be fighting reality, coming in small stretches of light till they all began to see; pair of smaller, almost feminine hands began to push into reality. Sin'ka looked at Kaldär from the corner of her eye. *His apprentice is a lady; I wonder if they're mated.*

She looked at Kaiźer, and he met her gaze and gave a wink. She looked back at the doorway in a rush and watched as it struggled to open fully. She felt her cheeks heat as she blushed. She couldn't help but picture him in royal attire, standing at the altar as she walked towards him in the tradition of matrimony.

"Hey, is it just me, or is something wrong with the portal?" she said suddenly. She snatched her opportunity to say something, but she mainly wanted to distract herself from what was roaming through her head.

Kaldär, following her finger, looked at the portal. "I think you may be right. She may not have been ready..." the last part trailed off as he moved towards the tear in reality.

"What will you do?" Kaiźer asked, his words wary.

Kaldär shooed them back, and they all shuffled to the other side of the room and watched as he took a deep breath. He seemed to draw the very light from the lanterns into his lungs, dimming the room with his draw. Raising his hands up before himself, he cocked his elbows back and, with a grunt, thrust them forward into the small bowl that floated before himself. Veins popped up along his neck, and with a mighty shove, he pushed his arms out wide, practically ripping the doorway open fully before diving to the side. His sudden flail had them all gasping in surprise but what came after had them all in a state of silence.

Popping out of the center of light, a female figure flew out onto the floor, her skin crackling with light, to land with a soft thud.

She scrambled to her feet in a rush and turned to face the portal just as a second figure stepped out with an air of nonchalance. They all looked on in bewilderment as the two figures came into focus; the magic about them faded from their forms as wisps of smoky light.

Standing before them, the two strangers were complete opposites in stature. Sin'ka looked at the tiny man to the left as he flung his odd coat wide and put his hands in his pockets.

He wore a black Stetson, and his eyes had a creepy red tint to them. She shivered as he caught her eye. Looking away quickly, she took in the sight of the lady that stood to the right. Surprisingly voluptuous, she was quite beautiful. The first thing that caught Sin'ka's eye was the fiery red tail and matching cat ears that stuck out of her startling green hair.

The lady wore a red sash across her bust and had a pair of baggy grey training pants that hung loosely around her legs. Sin'ka noticed that her eyes were bright green as well, shining like Eźmeralda's.

When the lady saw her, though, she let out a little squeak and jumped behind the small man beside her. She looked at Kaiźer to know if he recognized the two people, but what she saw was not recognition; it was rage. Stepping in front of her, he spoke with authority, "what is he doing here?"

Sin'ka looked at Kaiźer's doppelgänger, and when it wasn't him that spoke, she jumped. Instead, it was the creepy bloke in the cowboy hat and coat that spoke up.

"Would it please you if I told you I came here to aid your sorry ass?"—*god's below even his voice was creepy*—"and from the looks of it, you need as much help as you can get."

She watched Kaiźer as his face was washed red with rage. He was pissed, she realized! She peeked out from behind him and saw that the sinister cowboy was smirking as he tore at Kaiźer's nerves.

She didn't even see the Kaldär move till he struck. Swinging his leg wide, he kicked the odd cowboy in the center of the chest.

Still, the stranger got his arms up to block despite the speed of the kick. He didn't keep his footing, however, and the force of the attack blew him backward. Sin'ka let out a small squeak, but as she watched, the cowboy turned his flight into a smooth flip, landing on his feet to slide across the floor.

"Ryeznya, if you say something else like that again, you'll have to deal with me again, and I don't think you want to brush your teeth through your ass," Kaldär said, his voice calm.

Oh my god! That's Ryeznya? He looked so fragile. In fact, now he looked a bit pale. He had managed to keep his hat on somehow, but he kept quiet, silently creeping over to the bar, his face hooded.

Kaldär turned back to face them. His hair had fallen about his face, and he swept it around with a hand as he spoke. "Now that we're all here, I believe I should say the reason for our visit." He went and stood beside the green-haired lady. "We came to help. We understand you are having a bit of trouble with a Demon and a Fallen Prince of the Heavens?"

They all looked between themselves at that. Oníx had the courtesy to act surprised, and Sin'ka began to feel jaded at her continuous acts of ignorance. She faced Kaldär as Oníx looked at him. Kaiźer had taken a step towards Kaldär when she hadn't been looking. Skipping forward, she came to stand beside him.

"You... came to help?"

Kaldär nodded. "Yes, as hard as it may be for you to accept it, we are here to stay, and nothing you say will deter us."

Kaiźer nodded. "Okay, then." He looked over at Ryeznya. "Will you at least tell me why he is here?"

"Yes, but if I am to do that, you should know our names. For we go hand in hand with each other, and none of us will be leaving until this is done and done."

Kaiźer scowled, "of course." Sin'ka saw a slight twinge at the edge of Kaldär's eye and wondered if the man had realized he had said the wrong thing if he wished to get on Kaiźer's friendly side.

"Okay..." Gesturing to the lady who and been behind Ryeznya, Kaldär smiled as he continued. "This here is my apprentice, Eźmeralda." His words were warm, and Sin'ka saw how the young lady returned his smile. They were definitely more than teacher and student. She wondered about how they'd met because they looked perfect for each other.

After introducing Eźmeralda, Kaldär looked over at Ryeznya and scowled. "And you've, of course, have met Ryeznya already." Turning back to face them, he grinned, but Sin'ka noticed it didn't reach his eyes. She got the feeling there was more to be discovered between him and Ryeznya being together.

As Kaldär had introduced them, Sin'ka had thought their names sounded of far-off lands undiscovered, and as she had greeted them individually, she had noticed that both Kaldär and Eźmeralda had a tattoo on their necks in the shape of a scarab.

If her folklore was correct, it was the mark of a demigod. Once they were all acquainted, she smiled warmly at Kaldär and held out her hand. He took it in his palm facing the ceiling, her palm cradled down, and she realized it was very formal, if weird.

"Why do you wish to help us?" she asked him after she shook the cobwebs from her head.

"Thank Ryeznya; he's the one who came to me."

Ryeznya glowered from the bar but said nothing; he seemed content with staying out of the conversation.

"Doesn't seem like him to be helpful. I'm guessing he didn't arrive at your place asking you to help?"

Kaldär grinned. "You are quite right."

Kaiźer scowled. "He clearly had something to gain out of this then, or he wouldn't have come?"

Kaldär smiled knowingly, and his eyes flashed suddenly. The golden light crackling as he took a step back, his clothes rippling in a hidden wind. The output was tremendous but barely left a trace as he moved. Sin'ka was usually able to smell the traces left each time Kaiźer used powerful magic, but this was like a twister of power that left no destruction in its wake.

Reaching the center of the floor, Kaldär closed the breach that Eźmeralda had opened and, in its place, drew a collection of glyphs that morphed into a multitude of transmutation circles. Appearing in the air at his finger, they shaped the outline of a doorway, and space appeared, showing another room. "If you would join us," he said as he stepped through the new breach. "We have a lot to talk about."

Onix stared with hidden wonder at the towering spires that made up the rocky Cliffside. After first stepping through the portal behind Kaldär, she'd thought they'd been in a castle of old, not a mountain!

It was true, he had brought them to a castle, yes, but instead of it being a building, it was built into the very rock of the land. Kaldär told them of how he'd constructed it from the inside out. He'd told of how at first, it had been a small natural cavern within the mountain that he had eventually chiseled out over time.

Extending from the top of the mountain into the ground, the massive home could fit a whole country within its walls. They had gotten a tour of the entire interior, but by the time the sun had risen, more than half of the castle's secrets were still a mystery.

It was now late afternoon, yet she couldn't wrap her mind around the concept of such a geographical feat.

Most of the rooms had been huge, the great hall itself taking up two hundred percent of the mountain's central section.

With four side wings, there was so much open space beneath so much rock she knew only magic could be holding it together.

That and the architectural design confirmed her suspicions; it was a creation from the Age of Heroes. *The public would have a field day if they found this place.*

With the sun sitting high in the sky, she bathed in its warmth, taking in its energy while she watched the clouds pass over the land.

They were somewhere off the coast within the Nirvana Sea. She watched the waves as they crashed on the rocks down below. She wondered how Kaldär could've lived in such solitary all these years.

At least, his home had a woman's touch, probably thanks to Eźmeralda, but still, he had no neighbors, the nearest one being a town that was miles away. His only help was from his daemon butler.

Onix undid the wrap around her chest and lay down, her bare back facing the sun. Her skin had a soft tan and glowed with a bronze hue.

She took pride in her looks, but she felt a bit self-conscious after Kaiźer's joke at the club. She wondered if Kaldär had the same dry sense of humor. They did look like twins; she just wished she didn't have to know as much about the two of them.

Being family and all, Kaiźer had kept very few secrets, and she very few from him as well. She fought the urge to tell him of his true bloodline every day, but she knew that the prophecy would come true if she did.

Rage is its key, while love is its curse

Seek the mist and find what's lost for a gem will break
and darkness will shine; giving way to a star reborn

The words kept running through her head, and the more she tried to understand them, the more confusing they got. Their meaning had eluded her since the day she'd heard them. The only clear thing about the prophecy was its origin; the words were given to none other than Kaldär by the archangel Gabriel.

When she stumbled upon Kaldär in the year 372 B.C., he'd been posing as a scribe. After learning of who she was, he'd told her of his brother. Afterward, he had charged her with his protection, telling her to keep his seal from breaking. Still, to this day, she didn't know what he'd meant by protecting Kaiźer's seal? Did he have some kind of inner demon? Or worse, was he a demon prince and didn't know it? She sat up in shock at the thought. The dark energy she'd seen; could it be? Picking up her top, she stood and began to slip it back on as she turned to face the countryside.

"Oníx?"

Kaldär! No. Not now.

She fumbled, dropping her wrappings just as he came into view. She summoned a shirt to cover herself, but when she glanced down, she cursed. The shirt hid nothing! It was white and entirely too thin—besides, the darkness of her skin shown through the cloth.

Turning slowly, she watched as Kaldär came closer. He had a huge smile plastered on his face, and he held a small box engraved with a gold star. She stood there unsure of how to cover up, but as he got closer, she dropped the thought. It would be fun to see his reaction; the poor man had always had a weakness for beauty; time to see if Eźmeralda had changed that?

Kaldär reached the rise and caught her eye. He raised his arm in greeting and dropped his gaze with a wide grin, where it froze in shock upon her décolletage.

Slowing to a stop before her, he gaped like a fish out of water. "You—you—your, umm I uh, this..." struggling to speak, he held out the small box. Made of lead, the star was made of magic, not gold like she'd initially thought.

"For me?"

A quick nod was all he gave as he tore his eyes away from her breasts. She smiled and took the box. It was lighter than she'd expected. She felt it humming with power, and her curiosity took hold, for she knew that lead was too brittle to hold any magical properties. It was a valuable mineral for seals through, as its dense structure was perfect for blocking out magic.

She opened it up slowly, enjoying the anticipation of what she'd find inside. Her excitement turned to amazement as she saw it.

The black scarab, nestled in white silk, gleamed like obsidian and was just as beautiful as the last time she'd seen it.

"You found it?"

Kaldär nodded as he caught her eye. He grinned sheepishly.

Onix

chapter 18: Destiny's Gift

At one time a mortal decided to test the boundaries of the mortal realm and the afterlife. He succeeded, entering the underworld and exiting after, but in doing so marked his skin as a traveler. When it was time to collect his soul he was taken to the unseen one and presented with a choice; to face him or to face the true death.

Unfinished document
The Age of Echelons

Oníx had been sure that damn thing had been lost, but here it was, in her hands once again, the beauty and power of it overflowing. She'd thought she'd never see or even hold it after she'd lost it in Peru sixty years ago. Given to her by Kaldär, the black scarab had fed on her magic as she fed it. It had spoken to her, helped her. The power over reality had been its last gift to her. She wouldn't be where she was today without it, and now Kaldär had returned it to her.

"I didn't know how to give it to you until now. Maybe I thought it wasn't time yet," Kaldär was looking towards the sea as he spoke, his eyes misty. All the traces of the awkwardness he'd had before was gone; he was all business. "But with all the chaos that's around you, I think it's the right time."

"I thought I'd never see it again."

"Well, I guess it's your lucky day."

She reached into the box and pulled the scarab from its silk confines. Upon contact, her body heated as magic coursed into her. Like a tidal wave, the energy washed through her in warm waves. She met Kaldär's gaze as she clenched her fist around the black jewel.

"Don't lose it again; I'm not going to find it for you a second time. Once was enough," Kaldär said, his tone serious. Still, despite his serious tone, his eyes held the twinkle they always did.

Onix knew he was honest, but she couldn't help but smile at his hidden joke. "Don't worry; I won't be going near any snake-infested waters anytime soon."

"Sorry, but we're dealing with an infestation of snakes already, so I don't expect you to keep that promise."

She laughed. Kaldär had a point. They were dealing with snakes; these just have a deadlier bite. She looped the gold chain connected to the scarab around her neck. The black beetle nestled between her breasts as she dropped it under her shirt. Kaldär was watching her do and blushed suddenly at the sight of her nipples as they grew hard against the tingle of the jewel.

"I, uh, I think it best if we um...."

"I agree."

Kaldär nodded as he hid his noticeable relief. Turning, he headed back down to the base of the mountain.

"It's good to see you too!" She called after him.

I guess you and Eźmeralda have yet to get into the bedroom; it serves you right for holding out. Some things didn't change. Eźmeralda had clearly learned to control Acreage magic based on her power level, and that meant she'd been with Kaldär for five years now. He was quite the package, and she looked forward to when Eźmeralda made him submit, and from the looks of things, she had already started.

No...

He was not budging, and Oníx needed Kaiźer to do so if they were to have a chance of survival.

"We'll need her, and you know it!" she insisted.

"Sin'ka can't handle——"

"Can't handle what?"

Kaiźer turned to face Sin'ka as she spoke. His face showed his displeasure, and Oníx knew that Sin'ka didn't like it.

"Say what you were about to say. What can't I handle?"

"I uh, it's just that I know Darzíel, and he's not one of those people who hold back. You would get hurt, and I can't risk him using you to get to me?"

"Then all the more reason to take me with you. If I stay here, Darzíel could get to be a lot easier than if I was at your side"——Sin'ka placed her hands on her hips——"you may not have the balls to let me go, but I do ad I say fuck you, I'm going!"

"But you——"

"And there's nothing you can do that will change that."

Kaiźer frowned, but he seemed to wilt under Sin'ka's cold stare. Oníx looked at Kaldär and rolled her eyes. Kaldär was with Eźmeralda, and they both had grins plastered in place, and at her eye role, Eźmeralda lost her composure.

"What's so funny?" Sin'ka snapped.

"Oh, uh, nothing...."

Kaldär stood up and moved to the window. Their unique feature gave the room its rocky structure, and as Kaldär had told them upon arrival, they formed to the mountain's exterior. It was probably one of the many reasons no human had found the place.

"She was probably thinking about how cute you two look. You know I am ordained if you two decide to get serious."

"Kaldär!" Sin'ka squeaked. "I don't think...."

Looking at it, all Oníx sighed. They weren't getting anywhere. Here they were arguing about marriage when they needed to figure out how to stop Darzíel. If he broke out and tried to gain control of this realm, they needed to hurry.

"Yeah, we're not...." Kaiźer trailed off. "You're certified?"

Dropping her head into her hands, Oníx cursed the day she'd met Kaldär. He wasn't ordained! So, to begin with, he wouldn't be able to perform the vows of matrimony even if he wanted to. The asshole always loved to play around.

"Well yeah, I am immortal. I've gained many skills in my many years."

"Give me a break! I bet you don't even know how to scratch your own ass!"

That was Ryeznya. He was here? Looking up, Oníx groaned as he walked into the room. Not him; how could she deal with his annoying attitude alongside everything else?

"Ah, you've arrived! And just so you know, I can scratch my ass quite fine unless you're offering your services, then, by all means, I would love to make you my personal ass scratcher."

"I'll pass."

Standing in the shadows, Ryeznya's eyes glowed eerily. If only he'd wear something less creepy all the time, people would be less inclined to hate him.

"Now, about that marriage—"

"Enough!" she shouted. She'd had it with all of them. Things were getting out of hand, and if they kept going like this, they'd never find an end. "We need to stop Darzíel, and we can't do that while you're all goofing around. Grow up and get your heads in the game."

"Yes, ma'am."

Everyone looked at Kaldär and Kaiźer in shock. Both had spoken in sync, and both hadn't hesitated in their reply. The two of them looked at each other but looked away just as quickly.

"Oh, I'm surprised you have such command over those two, all the same though, I don't regret throwing you out—"

"Shut up, Ryeznya, or you'll have to deal with me as well," she snapped.

All she got was a smirk in response. *You prick; I hope Kaldär wipes that smug look off your face one of these days.* Looking at Kaiźer, she glowered. "Now, as for Sin'ka, she will be coming with us."

"But—"

"Kaiźer, you've seen her fight; she'll be fine. She's not like Abi—"

She stopped herself before she finished. She had almost compared her to Abika. She recovered and winked at Sin'ka, making her smile. She knew Sin'ka was not your traditional vampire; she just wished Kaiźer would see it too. A movement caught her eye, and she turned to watch Kaldär's butler walk in with a plate of refreshments.

There was an arrangement of fruits, sweets, and meats, as well as other odd-looking confectionaries she didn't recognize. In the center, a bottle of wine sat nestled in a bowl of ice. The cart they sat on was wheeled to the center of the room, where José spread the treats out on the low table that took up a good portion of the lower floor. As soon as every tiny detail was in place, he lifted a thick stack of rolled-up papers and what looked to be maps and blueprints.

"As requested, I have your dimensional records, sire."

"Thank you, José. That will be all."

Kaldär turned then and, with a dismissive wave, passed down the stairs with a gesture for everyone to follow. Moving down from the upper balcony floor, they all soon stood around the massive round table. She stood beside Kaldär, and Eźmeralda sat on his other side. Kaiźer and

Sin'ka mirrored them while Ryeznya sat alone between the two groups.

"As you wish, master, call if you need anything else."

With his last word, José vanished in a flicker of red smoke. Ba'ile lifted his head and cocked it slightly at the scent, but after a second, he settled back down, eyes closed.

Kaldär rolled the papers out, and using the plates of food, pinned them open.

"Do you think it's wise to share this knowledge?" Eźmeralda said warily. They all looked at Kaldär and waited for him to reply. He looked at Eźmeralda then at all of them in turn, ending with Ryeznya.

"I believe everyone can be trusted; I'm sure it's safe." He replied. Onix noticed that Kaldär stared at Ryeznya as he said it, and she was glad he had because it took Ryeznya's eyes off her for a bit.

"Ba'ile, if you would."

Sin'ka looked up in shock as he spoke. She had recognized the name, it seemed.

Standing slowly, the giant wolf shook himself as it opened its jaws in a huge yawn, showing off sharp canines. As all eyes were drawn to him, he looked at Kaldär with a knowing look. Onix leaned forward and studied them both closely. She was witnessing a transaction that shouldn't be possible. She saw strands of magic move between Kaldär and Ba'ile in the form of deep thought. They were using magic as a psychic link. It wasn't a source link; such would have been impossible to weave. They were merging their cognizance at a cellular level.

It was a sight to behold, and she knew she wasn't the only witness to what was transpiring.

Ryeznya was also watching with keen curiosity. His eyes flashing green as he concentrated. Kaiźer as well as Sin'ka looked confused by something, and after following their gaze, Onix herself became confused.

Ba'ile had vanished and in his place was a silver-haired man. He had nothing on, but he wasn't nude, at least not entirely. Thick trails of fur moved along his abs to plunge into the junction between his legs, forming a V-shape. It was exceptionally provocative, and she found it to be quite sexy. *Damn it, you're a lesbian! Don't get turned on by a man, no matter how ravishing he may be...* However, despite her thoughts, she still found herself disappointed when she saw he seemed to be sexless. How could such a robust man not have any genitalia? She took in the width of his chest and the strength of his legs. She saw that on the back of his forearms and calves, thick tufts of fur stood up like spikes, and she noticed with growing frustration that they only added to his sex appeal. That, along with his wild mane of hair and bright gold eyes, made for a very beastly aura that made her very uncomfortable and hot, incredibly hot. His face was covered in scars, but still, his appearance was making her sex ache, and to her growing horror, he noticed it.

Ba'ile's nose flared as he turned to her, his eyes gleaming with apparent interest.

"It looks to me like I have an admirer," he said.

Oh shit. Even Ba'ile's voice was sexy. Its deep baritone radiating through her, and her sex gushed almost instantly.

Ba'ile noticed and, with a grin that revealed prominent canines, turned to Kaldär.

"I like her."

"Hmm..."

Oníx despaired. Kaldär's response confirmed her thoughts. They were linked together, and she knew it. Everything Ba'ile knew Kaldär learned, and right now, she was clearly Ba'ile's first thought.

"Anyway!" she blurted. "Why are you now a, uh, a man?" Her question was answered by Eźmeralda and quite thoroughly.

"Ba'ile here is a shifter like me. He's usually in wolf form, but occasionally, he likes to feel human. Kaldär sends him on missions, and he's gone for days, but he always comes back. I think it allows him to experience things he can't normally experience as a wolf. Like sex, and he's told me all about how—"

Eźmeralda had moved to stand by Ba'ile, but he clasped his hand over her mouth as she spoke.

"I... told her about how my interest in the matter of sex is private. Isn't that right, sister?"

Eźmeralda nodded quickly, her eyes wide. Once she did, he dropped his hand slowly as if expecting her to continue.

She grinned at his reaction. That was for sure not what he had told Eźmeralda. Oníx decided then that she would find out the truth behind this sexy man standing before her.

At that moment, Kaldär stepped up to the table. Instantly, the mood changed in a heartbeat because his face was all business.

"You gonna keep flirting, or are you going to help us find Darzíel?"

Still looking at her, Ba'ile only shrugged. He had her frozen, unable to look away, but when Kaldär said Darzíel's name, she tore her eyes off him—and with no small amount of willpower—tried to find something to distract herself.

She ended up looking at the blueprints Kaldär had set up. They depicted the different layers of the Underworld and seemed to keep changing as she watched. On top of that, the language it was written in was not one she recognized, and she knew a good two hundred different languages. But for some reason, she couldn't read the words before her.

"Kaldär..." she asked after a few seconds. "What are these?"

Coming up beside her, Kaiźer glanced at the papers, his jaw opening slightly as his eyes moved over the foreign letters.

"Kaiźer, can you read this?" she asked.

Glancing at her, he gave a quick nod, looking back at the papers again.

"Interesting... what does it say?" Kaldär spoke up, appearing behind them as if from nowhere. Eźmeralda and Ba'ile were to his left. They looked at Kaiźer expectantly, and at Kaldär's request, Kaiźer took a deep breath and started reading aloud.

"The words speak of the nine circles of the Underworld. It describes the patterns each floor takes for each shift." Shifting the documents, he picked out a page that looked different from the others. "This one, though, it's different."

"How so?" Kaldär asked.

"*Igalma Satonis*. It means—"

"Satan's soul!"

They all looked at Kaldär when he spoke. Oníx looked at the table, her mind racing. Satan's Soul was the name for Lucifer's resting place. It was supposed to be somewhere in the first and lowest level of the Underworld.

"There's more," Kaiźer blurted. "It's some kinda poem or spell."

Lifting the papers, he moved closer to the light. He was squinting, but it wasn't because of the lighting. He was sorting through the magic weaves of the paper.

"Okay, I think I figured out the pattern."

"Well, don't keep us in suspense," she said in annoyance when he didn't continue right off the bat.

"Alright, alright," Kaiźer gave her a stern look before looking down at the papers intently. "Here goes..." he cleared his throat, and they listened as he read the ever-changing script.

Nine circles, nine kings, combine them you die; separate them you die.

Find the door but don't open the key, through loves dark cry, twelve hells will die—

"There's a second part," Kaiźer started. "But it's in the old language. Uh, let's see, Rage is its key, while love is its curse. Seek the mist and find what's lost, for a gem——"

"——will break, and darkness will shine, giving way to a star reborn," Kaldär finished for him. "Damn that seer and her riddles of prophecy, for once she gave me something real, and what did I do? I ignore her."

Kaldär's outburst caused them all to jump. It was so out of place they almost missed the fact that he'd finished the second part of the poem. It was Ryeznya that spoke up.

"How long?" he barked.

Directed at Kaldär, the question held no meaning to the rest of the group.

"Centuries," Kaldär stated.

"And you didn't think to stop them!"

"Don't you think I've tried?" Kaldär shouted. "They just keep coming back!"

She stepped in front of Kaldär and looked him in the eye. He stared back, unflinching. "What is going on?" she asked him quietly. Sin'ka was still on the other side of the table, trying not to stand out, but Oníx saw her glance up at them and, with a start, look over at Ba'ile before staring back down at the table. Looking at the shifter, Oníx stared at him for a second. She hadn't looked away from him since he had shifted till now.

Turning back to Kaldär, Oníx pushed him from her mind. "Is it Darzíel?" she asked this time.

"No, it's the thing controlling Darzíel."

His statement hit her like a wall. Of course, it had been there this whole time! The first time she'd faced Darzíel, she'd thought she'd imagined it. His energy had felt tainted like it was being poisoned. Everything made sense now! The reason Darzíel was using Kurai Aka Hoshi, his constant need for more power, even the reason Kaldär had joined the picture. It was all because of a Deadly Sin, one of the Seven Dark Lords! How had she never once noticed? Suddenly a question came to mind.

"Which one is it?"

"Envy,"

Bingo! Just as she'd thought, only he would go to such lengths.

"I'm guessing you have a plan?" she asked him.

"Yes." He didn't hesitate, but his gaze was wary.

Kaiźer had had no idea he could read anything other than the languages he already knew. He hadn't recognized the odd lettering, but he'd learned how to read them for some reason. He'd felt them speak to him, call to him, almost like they had sensed him.

But riddles? They only brought more confusion, more questions, and he didn't need any more of the two. He sat in silence after handing the maps to Kaldär, pondering over the two riddles, trying to figure their hidden meanings. The thing that bugged him the most was the last part. *A gem will break, and darkness will shine,* it said. Was Kira in danger? He was sure Darzíel would have treated her well, with her helping him and all... even though she'd been forced into it, he couldn't imagine Darzíel hurting what he saw as a reliable asset to his goals.

So deep was he into his musings, he didn't see Ba'ile come up till he sat beside him. He gave only a quick glance to see that Ba'ile was still rocking the commando.

"Dude, put some clothes on."

Ba'ile looked down at himself, then back at him with a wide smile. "Why? You can't handle what I'm sellin, too much for ya?"

~I wonder where he stores his junk~ Kaín contemplated, *~in another dimension, maybe?~*

Kaiźer tried not to laugh as he ignored Kaín. He looked back at Ba'ile. "No, I just don't want to see your naked ass every time you're not facing me."

Ba'ile chuckled. He didn't seem insulted in the slightest. On the contrary, he seemed not to care.

"Just so you know, I do have a dick. It's just—"

"I'd rather not... hear about your little guy's hiding spot. Now, why are you bothering me?"

"Oh! I caught the scent of fear, and I was shocked to find it coming from you. I'd have thought with you being one of the Morningstars, you'd have been afraid of nothing."

"One of the Morningstars?"

He was an orphan. He didn't have any brothers or sisters, and his parents had died when he'd been a child. Did Ba'ile know something about his past he didn't? The only blood family he'd had were dead, and his uncle's surname was not Morningstar, though Maliki had kept his surname a secret; had it been Morningstar? He looked at Ba'ile with a questioning gaze, and the man smiled self-consciously.

"Did I say one of? I meant one of the last surviving heirs to the Morningstar family, yah, that's it."

Ba'ile was clearly flustered. There was something Ba'ile wasn't telling him, and Kaiźer would find out what it was he was hiding, or he should say, whom he was hiding.

~Hmm, he might be a shifter, but he's the first with kangaroo traits; you think he stores it in his pocket?~

Kaiźer grinned but cast the idea aside. Right now, he had more pressing matters to attend to that involved saving Kira and stopping Darzíel.

Kaizer

chapter 19: warfare

Wreak havoc and let loose the screams of the unseen one or thy will be crushed by the hand of death.

Unknown mortal
The Age of Heroes

They'd sat at the table, eating the snacks that had been set out by José. The conversation was light at first and only lasted for a short while. Kaiźer barely heard any of it; he only started listening when Sin'ka's phone rang.

Looking up, he saw her take it out of her pocket in confusion and, with a glance at Oníx, answer it.

"Hello?"

The voice on the other end was muffled, but he could hear the speaker's frantic tone.

"James!" Sin'ka said. "Calm down. What do you mean, an intruder?"

Intruder? If so, James must have taken care of them. That didn't explain the frantic tone. Did something happen to him?

"Wait, slow down; did he find it?

More muffled words followed, and he struggled to hear what was said. He caught only snippets, but part of it involved a creepy man with six wings, and only one man met such a description, and he was looking directly at him.

Jumping to his feet, he stalked towards the one man who kept causing trouble to those he loved. Ryeznya watched him approach, his face showing nothing. Infuriated by the man's calm demeanor, he grabbed Ryeznya by the collar and ribbed him out of his chair.

"Kaiźer!" Oníx warned.

Ignoring her, he tightened his grip. "I should kill you here and now," he growled between clenched teeth. The one thing he hated the most was a man who killed for pleasure. And that was precisely what Ryeznya was. Kaín thrummed with anticipation upon his back.

~Yes, let's kill this prick and avenge Abika. She was nice to me, and this dirtbag took her from us~

Ryeznya smirked and, too quick to see, grabbed his hand and squeezed. "Ah, but I doubt you can."

Bones popped, and Ryeznya lifted his hand from around his neck. With a groan, Kaiźer felt the bones in his hand start to break. Only twice now had someone been able to break his very bones. He would not let Ryeznya become the third. His eyes flashed gold / black, letting off sparks of black lightning.

"You dared to hurt Sin'ka?"

"I'd dare to do more to her if I got the chance." Ryeznya said with a sneer, "just like I did to your precious Abika."

"Kaiźer!" Sin'ka snapped.

With his vision bleeding red, he glanced at Sin'ka, but his rage dissipated when he saw her. She stood tall, her eyes on Ryeznya. He could see the crimson shine of tears, but her face didn't show fear; it showed anger, and with eyes of blood, she stared at the man who'd disrespected her privacy.

"Let him go," she stated. Her voice was steady, but her hands shook at her sides, betraying her control.

"Slayer... I'd listen to the lady."

Kaldär hadn't moved from where he sat, but they all knew that didn't matter. If the man chose, the distance wouldn't matter. Looking back at his uncle, Kaiźer watched him, and Ryeznya watched in turn. Slowly, a smile appeared at the corners of Ryeznya's mouth, and with a snort of contempt, let go of his hand.

Kaiźer let out a breath he hadn't known he'd been holding and stepped back, his eyes no longer glowing but still just as deadly as he glared at Ryeznya.

"Now," Kaldär stated. "What did Ryeznya do to permit such a violent reaction, hmm?"

"I'll tell you later. First, we need to get back to the club. James needs my help, along with Oníx's.

As Sin'ka moved to stand by his side, his hand tingled while the bones reset. It tickled slightly, but he ignored it. He let Sin'ka inspect him, which involved her running her fingers through his hair and along his neck with a slight touch. He felt shivers run down his spine as her musings made him tremble. No one noticed as far as he knew, but hey, he didn't care either way. Let them see how much she affected him. Still, he could do with some looser pants.

"I'm fine," he said to her. "But if what he said is true, we must go now. James is at the club, I assume?"

Sin'ka nodded. "Yes, a few of my staff dropped him off, thinking we'd be there."

"Kaldär, can you open a breach—oh!"

Already, a doorway stood open behind Kaldär, its edges pulsing. Sin'ka hesitated for only a second before heading towards the portal, but she paused just before passing through to thank Kaldär with a peck on the cheek.

Oníx followed her, Ba'ile two steps behind, his eyes locked on her rear. Eźmeralda skipped through, giving a kiss to Kaldär as she passed. Kaiźer let Ryeznya pass and went to follow, but Kaldär stopped him. He didn't want to leave everyone alone with his uncle, especially Sin'ka, but Kaldär looked like he had something important to say without the prying ears of others.

"What is it, Kaldär?"

"I saw the way you reacted back there. It felt off."

"I was pissed!"

"I know," Kaldär said. "He has that effect on people. What I'm worried about is the black magic you were letting off. Does that happen a lot?"

"Nope, first time, why?"

Kaldär pursed his lips but didn't say anything. Kaín was silent, but as he pulled from Kaldär's grasp, he sent a question his way. Not wanting to stay any longer than he had, Kaiźer stepped through the breach and joined the others. The portal shut behind him, leaving a slight seam of energy that faded.

"Kaín, what do you mean?" he asked.

~Well, we both know that black magic is the dark side of the elements. Do you think it was related to what happened back at Sin'ka's house with the demon?~

That could be it, but he couldn't know for sure. Pondering, he looked towards the bar, where he saw Sin'ka as she stood with Oníx. They were hunched, their figures hiding the focus of their attention, but he didn't need to see to know what it was.

James didn't look to be in good shape. Burns covered his body, and he was bruised as if he'd been dragged behind a car. Sin'ka held a greenish/blue paste-filled vial and smeared it over the worst of the boy's wounds. It sizzled on contact, giving off the scent of mint and fresh soil. After doing so, Oníx passed her hands over the area. Her skin glowed with magic, and her mage tattoos rippled and writhed.

Ba'ile came and stood behind Sin'ka, putting a hand on her shoulder, while Eźmeralda held James's hand and stroked his forehead. Both looked pained at the sight of the young man's physical state; soon enough, though,

James's breathing slowed and his body un-tensed as he succumbed to sleep.

Kaiźer looked around at what had been his nightly sanctuary for the last three years. It had only been four days since he'd met Sin'ka, but it felt like an eternity after all that had happened. Looking at Sin'ka, now he saw what he'd ignored out of respect. Her hair fell over her shoulders, its bright color made brighter by the black of her clothes. He watched as she reached to move a lock of hair from James's face. Doing so caused her shirt to drop, revealing a fair amount of her cleavage, and he blushed. She was so intent on her work that she didn't even pause as she adjusted.

His gaze traveled lower, and he took a deep breath as he passed over her bare belly. Her pants cupped her like a second skin, the texture showing every couture and curve, hiding nothing. As Onı́x and her lifted James off the floor and onto the bar, her shirt got trapped. However, as she reached back to free it, her eyes met with his. They stared at each other for what felt like an eternity till a deep blush spread into Sin'ka's face, and she looked away quickly. She faced Onı́x and started discussing James's wellbeing.

He had been caught red-handed looking at her, and he knew it. Still, he couldn't help but keep looking, and every time he realized he was watching the small movements she made; a sweep of the hair behind her ear, the biting of her lip when she concentrated, even the tapping of her foot when she was inpatient, it all had him searching for the rest of them with a piercing gaze. Even with Kaldär by his side, he kept watching Sin'ka as she worked. Her actions were the same as Abika's, and he recognized each like the back of his hand.

"Quite the beauty isn't she, your Sin'ka," Kaiźer said.

"Yeah...wait, what? No, she's not my—"

"Oh, don't try to deny it. I saw the way you were looking at her just now like you were trying to undress her with your eyes alone."

"I wasn't..." his words died as he saw the twinkle in Kaldär's eye. The man was enjoying his embarrassment, the jerk. Looking back at Sin'ka, Kaiźer lets a smile grow as he watched her. There was definitely something between them. Call it chemistry or love; it could very well be both.

"Okay, yes. Sin'ka's quite the beauty. I just don't want to lose her to my way of life, this life, our life. She's not ready for it."

"Were you?"

"Huh?"

Kaldär turned to him, "Ready for it?"

Kaiźer thought about that for a minute. Had he been ready? Ready to face demons and walk beside angels at the age of eight... if he was honest with himself, the answer was simple. No, he hadn't been ready. Not for any of it. He'd grown up as an orphan within the Jackals' Court after his home had been taken away by fire and ash. He'd been thrust into this life by no fault of his own.

"Honestly," he said to Kaldär. "I wasn't in any way ready."

"Yeah? Then you know what it's like. Besides, she has all of us. Who did you have?"

"No one..."

After a second, Kaldär raised his hand as if to say Ya See, she'll be fine! It was almost comical; Almost.

"Fine, I see your point," he mumbled.

When Kaiźer compared his past to Sin'ka's future, he saw how lucky she was. She had become an entity able to hold her own and had had people to stand with. She had them now, and he saw no way to counter the truth. She was not the same as his Abika; she was better in every way.

Sin'ka had a better chance than he did, and she was already able to handle her own. He looked at her again and saw her in a new light. The fear of losing her wasn't going to leave, and he knew that now. He knew more now than he did back then and had no concerns about not protecting her when needed.

~No way will I let you botch this~ Kaín said. *Sin'ka could be like Abika and have a thing for dragons too!~*

He grinned and was about to tell Kaín to shut it when James awoke with a start, letting out a low groan.

"James, we've healed most of the damage to your body," Oníx stated, "but your mind has yet to adjust to the rapid recovery."

Ba'ile held out a bowl of green goop that James eyed warily. "What is that? It smells rancid," he questioned warily.

With a soft chuckle, Ba'ile gestured to the bar counter. "I made it, old family recipe. I promise."

Eźmeralda held out a glass of brandy, and after draining the drought—trying not to gag as he did—James washed out his mouth with the water. Kaiźer saw that the boy's eyes were glassy. He was concussed but seemed to be okay.

"James?" he asked as he came to stand beside Sin'ka. "Try to use your magic."

Raising a hand, James focused, but Kaiźer felt it, a hollow hum. James didn't have any magic, and sure enough, after a few seconds, James's hand dropped to his side.

"I don't even know what's wrong," James whispered. "Even at my weakest, I can produce a spark at most...." He looked at Sin'ka, but his face dropped as he saw her worried expression. "I don't have any magic," he stated, making it sound like it was the end of the world.

Sin'ka nodded. "Your connections have been severed as if from the extreme force, most likely to the chest or back. Your heart skipped, causing a temporary loss of magic."

"So, it's not permanent?"

"We can't be sure."

"Gods..." James sagging in despair, "why?"

Walking up to James, Kaiźer put a hand on his chest. James flinched, but when nothing happened, he settled back down. Drawing on his magic, Kaiźer pushed tiny tendrils of warm energy into the boy. James let out a soft sigh as he felt the magic. What he saw, though, didn't match what Oníx said. The boy's chakra chain wasn't just severed; it had been sabotaged. Where it'd shattered small punctures as if from shrapnel was visible, hidden in the destruction of the magical and physical separation.

"When the demons arrived, do you remember if anything happened to you from behind? Did they blindside you?" If he was right, his fight with Ryeznya hadn't been the origin of such a wound.

"Actually, yes, I was tackled, and I felt like I got shot in the back by a shotgun, but when I inspected the area, only my clothes held the proof of the attack. My skin was okay."

So... that's what happened. Just as Kaiźer had thought, Ryeznya's attack must have shattered what remained of the connections. If this were to be healed, it would have to be soon. It might even be too late, but they at least had to try.

"Oníx, you got any juice left?"

"A little,"

"A little is better than nothing right now," he stated. He held out his hand, and Oníx took it. Her grip was firm, and he was filled with new hope. They might just pull this off. He looked at James reassuringly and, with care, eased his other hand under James's neck. "On my count, empty your magic into me. I'm going to try to channel it through the damaged area.

~ I'll help!~

~Great, just help in any way you can~ He linked his connections thoroughly with the dragon's and squeezed Oníx's hand as he did.

"Have you done this before?" Oníx asked.

"No."

Oníx said nothing, but she focused her magic all the same. She knew him, and he was relying on that. He trusted her to know what to do.

"On three,"

Magic pooled between their hands, growing bright as it condensed under their concentration. Ryeznya knelt with them and placed his hands on their shoulders. His face was like stone, showing nothing, but as he knelt forward, a green jewel dangled free of his shirt. It was in the shape of a scarab, and upon contact with his hand, it began to glow with a warm light.

The result was instantaneous. Kaiźer lost control of their magic, as it took on a life of its own. They were all trapped, unable to move, and unable to speak. The three of them could only watch as the animated magic sank into James. It washed through him in waves, back and forth, its path causing all the anomalies in the boy's body to vanish. A small scar on the boy's thumb faded from sight; even the bruises that were left began to fade.

They watched in amazement as James was healed to such a degree, it didn't seem real. Soon the magic began to diminish as it got absorbed into James's body. They all un-tensed as it ended and fell back as one, looking at one other in confusion. Kaiźer eyed Ryeznya, but the jewel was hidden once more. The man acted like it hadn't just been there. Looking back at James, they all waited for him to move, but nothing seemed to be happening. Oníx sat up slightly and edged towards the boy when he shot up into a sitting position like a spring. Oníx squeaked in fright and covered her mouth in surprise. They chuckled as she did, and she glared at them; they shut up quickly.

Looking better than he had even before his injuries, James looked around at them in confusion. Slightly disoriented, he cradled his head with a groan.

"How?" he blurted.

Kaiźer was speechless himself. He'd never see such magic. He'd lost control as soon as Ryeznya had touched him. The energy both Oníx and himself had gathered had seemed to come alive.

Looking at his uncle, he caught a hint of the green jewel that had glowed so warmly a minute ago. It vanished under Ryeznya's coat as she shifted, and Kaiźer wondered why he'd hid it so quickly. Had the scarab been the cause of what had just happened?

~Kaín?~

~Not me, I was just as trapped as you...~ Kaín said at the thought. Kaiźer looked at Ryeznya in shock, but the man gave nothing away. He was already walking away as if he hadn't just pulled off the impossible. Maybe he wasn't such a prick as he made himself to be...

"I guess that's three," he said, turning to look at Sin'ka with a grin.

"PFFT! No kidding, a little warning next time," Oníx snapped at Ryeznya's back. She was trying to contain a grin, and her lips kept twitching as she struggled. It was so funny to watch. He felt a huge smile grow till he succumbed to himself. He fell over as he burst, and it came out so loud, Oníx jumped. She soon started laughing herself until they both had tears in their eyes and hiccups in their chests.

"Gosh. I totally didn't see that happening," Oníx said between gulps of air. "Ryeznya, the healer... I thought I'd never see the day."

Kaiźer stood and helped Oníx and James to their feet. If he hadn't seen it, he wouldn't have believed it either, but he had, and it had surprised him.

~I don't actually think it was him doing the act,~ Kaín said.

The comment was so out of the blue Kaiźer was confused at first. Want did Kaín mean by that?

~What I mean is something was puppeteering Ryeznya~

What! No, that wasn't possible. How? Kaín sent back that he didn't know, and more questions filled his head. What could have that control? It would have to be powerful, right? What could it even be? Had it been the odd jewel he'd seen or something else?

Or someone else... he looked around but didn't feel anything out of the ordinary. He could only file it out of his mind for the moment. James probably had his own questions, after all.

But no questions were going to be asked because Oníx had her signature look in her eyes that said forget it; now was not the time for questions. They needed to stop Darzíel, and he needed to save Kira to do so.

"Kaldär," he said slowly.

Looking away from James, the big man perked up at his name. Kaiźer noticed that Eźmeralda was at his side, but when he said Kaldär's name, she looked at him and then at Sin'ka and scowled. Kaldär saw as well and whispered something in her ear. He wondered what it was when she blanched only to turn red in embarrassment.

Kaldär walked over, and he raised an eyebrow in question.

"She's not a fan of vampires. She doesn't understand how you can stand to be around Sin'ka.

"So, what did you tell her?"

Kaldär grinned, "Oh, just that a vampire's life can be extremely... wild at times."

His jaw dropped. He's said that. Did he know that because...?

"Did you..."

"Date a vampire?"—He nodded—"I did, actually."

Wow. Kaiźer was genuinely surprised. He had been with Kurai Aka Hoshi, but he'd never known her as more than a casual friend but... still. "How was it?" he asked.

"It was like any other normal relationship. The only difference was the sharing of blood."

"Sharing of blood?"

"Vampire couples share blood, it's said to deepen their connection, and it's partly true, I admit."

"How did Eźmeralda feel about that?" he asked.

Kaldär's grin fell a bit. "You know, I have yet to find out. We don't talk about what happened in our lives before we met. In fact, it was only just today she busted the move on me."

"Oh? And how long did it take her?"

"Truth is, I have actually been keeping my distance for the last five years. I told her no relationships during her training. She didn't take it very well at first."

"I bet," he looked at Sin'ka. She stood with the others, mainly Oníx and James. Oníx was with Ba'ile through, so Sin'ka was talking to James, and by the way, she kept checking his forehead as if he had a fever; he had to guess she was still a bit worried. She'd be a great mother, he thought. Could she become with child? Even more important, would she accept him the way he did her? He'd only know when he told her the truth, but he wasn't going to do that until after Darzíel was taken out of the picture.

"So, it would be awesome to hear about yours and Eźmeralda's personal lives, but I need to know, what's your plan for Darzíel?"

"The plan is actually just to go with the flow, mainly because no plan ever works out," Kaldär explained. "I have thought about all the different scenarios, so I'm not unprepared. There are always times that call for improvement."

That made sense, and coming from him, it sounded simple when it wasn't in any way simple. It would require quick thinking. They would need to stay on their toes 24/7 till everything was done.

"Okay," he said. "So, how are we going to get into the Underworld?"

"Simple. We use a mirror."

Kaizer

chapter 20: the Mirror Dimension

Mirrors are a way into a mans soul, they show us our true face, and those who have something to hide lose their mask in the sight of the spirit of the Mirror.

Unknown scribe
The Age of Heroes

Okay, Okay, so when Kaldär had said all they needed was a mirror, Kaiźer hadn't believed it was going to be so simple. Even with how easy the guy made everything look, he didn't think Kaldär would have a plan that would let them just walk into the Underworld.

After their talk, the two of them had slipped up. He'd gone to talk with Sin'ka, and Kaldär had gone to stand with Oníx. Still trying to figure out what Kaldär had in mind, he smiled as Sin'ka fiddled with James's collar. She was all over the boy, trying to keep him from leaving, but James said he had to get things back in order after all the chaos of what had happened at her house. His mind was set, and Sin'ka saw it. She let him go—with no small amount of reluctance—giving him a long hug before watching him leave, stepping out into the night's dark embrace.

"It's weird to think, we were just off the coast of the Kingdom of Sand where the sun marked high noon," Sin'ka said at last.

He no longer considered the concept, but most of what the humans found weird was familiar to him, so he found it odd that she thought such.

"I thought you traveled for a living?" he asked her.

"Yeah, but I never went very far most of the time. I always came back; even after 200 years, this is my home. I grew up here?"

The idea of Sin'ka living in Nypheriam was almost hard to imagine. She just seemed so worldly, like she could live anywhere and still fit in. unlike him, a person who always seemed to mess things up, she had adapted with the times.

"I've lived long enough to say that not a lot can surprise me."

"How old are you anyway?" she asked.

"I, uh, you know I don't actually know... I do know that I began my training under the Jackals in the year of 720 A.D., but I can't... remember when I...."

"You're a good 1,500 years old if I recall."

He looked up as the person spoke. He'd felt the man approach and had recognized Kaldär's aura, although he hadn't thought he'd say anything, with Oníx, Eźmeralda, and Ba'ile being alongside him. Wait, had Kaldär just told his age like it was common knowledge. Kaiźer got the feeling there should be something he should know, something important about that, but... there was nothing.

"And how would you know that?" he asked, his mind foggy with confusion upon the sense of something forgotten.

Kaldär shrugged and met his steady gaze with his own and stated simply.

"Your aura,"

He could tell from his aura. Made sense; the question he had now, though, was could he do the same?

"My aura, so if I was to look at your aura, I'd know how old you are as well?"

"Try and find out."

He was and what he saw had him shivering. Inside Kaldär, power burned strong enough to match the sun. It started at his core and radiated out to the rest of him. It was that of a celestial being. Oníx said once, only those who live past a couple thousand years or more can gain such power, earning them the title of Magician. So far, only one such being was said to be alive today, and he couldn't help but think that this man before him was that being.

He let go of the magic and looked at Kaldär with normal eyes. "Your age holds no meaning," his voice quaked but was steady. "Only a god has such power."

"Wrong!" Kaldär stated softly. "Only the Seraphim and high daemons have such power, and I am nowhere near as strong as them."

Kaldär raised his hand, revealing something he held. It was a small hand mirror, and he faced them as he spoke.

"This is a divine artifact, and it is a celestial gate of sorts." Kaldär moved past them and walked towards the last remaining available mirror in the club. "It can be used to ferry whatever you desire to any place of your choosing. In 104 B.B., a King tried to use its power within what is now known as the Forgotten Realms, but it didn't end well. He nearly unleashed the powers of the Underworld on the living with the use of its gifts. I commandeered it before he did too much damage, and with the help of the Seraphim, stopped what legions were unleashed."

Hanging behind the bar, the full-wall mirror reflected the room from behind the wide assortment of drinks. Kaldär flicked his free hand, and rows of bottles lifted free of their shelves. Settling on the floor in a half-circle, their caps lit with tiny flames at a snap of his finger.

Turning to face them, Kaldär slid into a crouch and placed the hand mirror in the middle of the half-circle. Chanting softly, he locked his hands and sat in the lotus position. He faced the mirror and focused his energy through the seven points of his life force. It became centered, growing upon his skin till he looked to be made of gold.

His chanting stopped, and opening his eyes looked at the wall. No longer blue, his irises shone pure white, pupils and all. In a firm voice, he spoke.

"Igälimä Ingordä Mesä Intunyä!"

They were words of power, and they all watched as the glass shelves detached from the mirror in response. They began to circulate around Kaldär until only a blur remained. The next thing they knew, all was calm. Kaldär sat motionlessly, eyes unblinking, all movement stopped.

Only to explode! All the magic churned, trapped within the circle of liquor. Kaldär's figure was pulsed with potent magic as all the external energies collected into his outstretched hand to form a ball. He brought it up to his lips as if to swallow it, but all he did was blow on it, which caused it to fly into the mirror before him as a stream of white light.

Hitting the mirror, the divine magic sank into it, causing the room's reflection to bend and warp as the mirror's surface liquefied. Falling to the floor, it seeped over the bar to collect around Kaldär as he sat Motionlessly.

In the center of the liquid was the hand mirror. The two rose together like a tornado, and Kaldär stood then to place a hand on the small hand mirror's reflective surface. In a soft voice, he began to speak. To Kaiźer, it was like hearing two voices as one, the first unrecognizable and the second as modern English. It was a tracker spell, targeted to Darzíel. However, Kaldär seemed to grow frustrated as he searched. Finally, with a huff of satisfaction, he let his hand sink into the mirror. The two mirrors merged, and taking two steps back, Kaldär exited the circle of gyrating magic. Facing them all, he spoke in a tired but steady voice.

"I found the closest portal to our destination. However, we'll still have a way to go once we're through."

They were going now. It was unexpected. Kaiźer had thought Kaldär would tell them beforehand... and Oníx had had the same thought as well based on her outburst.

"What! What's the plan, then? We can't just go unprepared!"

Looking at her, Kaiźer frowned. "You said it yourself; time is of the essence, did you not?"

Oníx looked to be trapped, and he knew she agreed with him. Time was something they needed, and they couldn't be more ready than they were now.

"Yeah, but—"

"—You need to believe we will get through this."

Oníx was frozen. She opened her mouth to argue, but he put his hand on her shoulder and spoke for her.

"—We're ready. We've been ready for a while now, and it's best not to waste any more time here."

He looked at her and cocked an eyebrow. "We've got this!" he said softly. Besides, Kira's with him, I'm sure of it. The last part, he said to her mentally, for her ears only.

Eźmeralda had joined Kaldär, and as she did, Kaiźer went to Sin'ka. She had been quiet for a while now. However, when he reached her, she smiled, taking her hands in his, but that was all.

"You alright?" he asked

She didn't respond at first as she watched Eźmeralda drag Ba'ile through the portal. He resisted but with a massive grin as she pulled on his arm.

Sin'ka's face was pained when she finally faced him. He took her face in his hands and touched his lips to hers. He kissed her lightly, moving his mouth to capture her groan as she kissed him back. She was ravishing, her mouth scorching, its heat passing to him in a wave of passion. Surprised, he let up to look into her eyes. The sudden hunger of her kiss had been reeling in its intensity.

Sin'ka dropped her gaze, letting her head fall against his chest. In a slightly husky whisper, she spoke softly, "I'm fine. It's just... I have a bad feeling, and I need to say one thing before we go." She fisted her hands in his shirt, her body meshed to his. She clung to him tightly and looked back up at him. "I want you to know that I... I like you and, and I...."

He smiled as she struggled to speak. He saw the deep blush in her cheeks and couldn't help but feel happy; he liked her as well, certainly more than liked her. He took her arms in his hands and pulled her away without breaking eye contact. Her mouth shut, and he smiled once more as her blush grew.

"I do, too, and I'm sure everything will be fine." He reassured.

"Sin'ka?"

Oníx had come over and stood beside them, her posture almost shy. "You okay?" she asked.

Sin'ka looked at him and smiled. Glancing back at Oníx, she nodded.

Oníx smiled in relief. "Okay, then I was wondering if you'd like to go through with me." She was looking between the two of them, and when Sin'ka looked at him, he nodded. Oníx would take care of her.

Beaming, she took Oníx's hand and let her lead the way as they passed through the shimmering liquid of the mirror.

Only Kaldär, himself, and Ryeznya remained, but as he watched, his uncle slunk past, his Stetson pulled low over his eyes as he passed through the portal without hesitation.

Just himself and Kaldär then... "Just you and me," he said. They both faced the liquid gate to the Underworld. Standing shoulder to shoulder, the two of them were quiet, "...so, somewhere around 5,000 years, huh?"

Kaldär looked at him for a second, then grinned. "Yep, glad to know you figured it out."

It had taken him a little while to figure it out, but he wasn't going to admit it. The number was immense and put the man's birth in the first age before the breaking. And to think, he had thought of *himself* as old. He made a note to sit down with the man and question what happened to the world. But right now, he had to put it out of his mind. He squared his shoulders, summoning his armor with a whisper of his magic. Kaín sat on his back, and Kaiźer felt him purr with excitement.

~About time~ the dragon hummed. *~ Let's do this!~*

Let's do this!" he said in sync with Kaín. He and Kaldär strode forward, entering the portal simultaneously, and as one passed into the Underworld.

The first thing Kaiźer felt was the sensation of being underwater. It left his skin tingling after he stopped, however. But the next thing he knew, a war waged around him. A fireball blew past to smash into a cloaked figure focused on driving Sin'ka away from the portal.

"Eźmeralda!" someone shouted. The speaker sounded frantic, and he looked towards the source.

Ba'ile stood, his eyes wild as he fought against a group of cloaked figures. The man's fists crackled with blue lightning, and he was virtually using it to burn the enemy to a crisp, but the cloaks kept replacing the ones Ba'ile felled. He followed his gaze and saw the reason behind Ba'ile's fear.

Eźmeralda stood, surrounded by cloaked beings. They were slowly crowding her in. she let a tiny bolt of energy shoot from her hand with a panicked gesture. It hit one of them, but his place quickly vanished before she could think of escaping. He glanced at Sin'ka then back at Eźmeralda. He could only be in one place at a time, but just as he was tensing up, a flicker of motion caught his eye.

Vanishing from his side, Kaldär had jumped first, reappearing before Eźmeralda to gather her into his arms. As he did, those surrounding the two of them crumbled to dust as their energy drained from their very cells.

Mirror lords! They were mirror lords. Human, but injected with demon blood, the lords could walk in the Underworld without death. However, right now, the question was, how were there so many? How had he not noticed their rotten auras? Last he knew, only three remained.

He pushed the question from his mind and added it to the pile of things he had to figure out. He had to reach Sin'ka before she got too far away. The mirror lords were slowly gaining ground, and he ran faster. He let three bolts fly as he went. They came out blackish red, and he frowned at the color. They flew wide, but the last passed through the lord's cloak. It gave Sin'ka an opening as he looked down. He saw him shiver, then hunch over, a fist through his back.

Sin'ka had punched her hand into his chest, and the force was too much for him. She dropped the mirror lord's spine and lowered him to the ground, her mouth latched to his neck.

He arrived at her side just as she finished feeding. She dropped the guy and knelt back on her legs, a small trail of crimson trailing along her chin from the corner of her mouth. It was a little unnerving to see.

"Ugh..." she gagged. "I hate demon blood!" She was wiping her hands on the dead guy's cloak as she spoke. Her face twisted in disgust, and not only that. She was wounded, although he couldn't tell if she noticed her injury.

"Hey uh, Sin'ka—" he said, gesturing to her side where a dagger protruded. She followed his finger and, with a curse, grasped the handle gingerly.

He watched in awe as she pulled the blade free without even a second thought. She tossed it aside, and putting pressure on the wound, stuck two fingers in her mouth. Within seconds the deadly wound had stopped bleeding, and he stared as she pulled her now wet fingers from her mouth and slid them along the skin of her injury.

Within seconds the puncture vanished before his very eyes leaving her skin flawless. He looked at her with a questioning glance, and she gave a tiny smile as she stood up. Her grin didn't reach her eyes, though, and he knew she was nervous. He saw it as she bent and picked up the dagger.

"That blades rusted," he said, taking it from her. "Use this one."

He pulled one of his red firestone daggers free of his belt and brought it out from behind his back. He held it out to her sheath and all. She took it without comment. Pulling it apart, she watched as the red metal glowed with an inner fire, lighting the black stone around them.

"Better?" he asked.

"Yeah, much better,"

"Good," he said. "Then I'll get rid of this."

He chucked the jagged blade, and Sin'ka watched it sink into the back of the final mirror lord, severing his spine.

Oníx looked up in shock, her hand still lit with icy fire. He gave a short laugh as he drew Kaín.

"Did I steal your thunder?" he called. Oníx frowned and dropped her ball of fire on top of the dead mirror lord.

"Nope!" she called back.

"Are you guys always like this?" Sin'ka asked.

"Only on Tuesdays,"

They had arrived back at the gate to stand with Oníx and the others. Eźmeralda had a few minor cuts on her feet, but Kaldär was treating them. Ba'ile knelt beside her, his jaw tense with worry. Kaiźer didn't see Ryeznya, though. Hadn't he gone through before him?

"How'd they know we'd be here?" he asked to no one in particular.

"Even we didn't know we'd be here," Eźmeralda said. "We'd planned to pop directly into Darzíel palace, but I don't know why we didn't...."

Kaldär stood silent before them, his eyes hooded. "They must have cloaked their presence, for I did not sense them," he said, turning to face the long tunnel before them. "Beyond this cave is the first layer of the Underworld. We only have a short way to go, thankfully."

Kaldär led the way and crossed the black sands, passing sulfur pits to reach the Underworld's mouth. A towering ceiling sat covered in stalactites, each of them dripping mercury, which fell into rivers of the shiny liquid. Following it past the deep pits and molten landscape, he saw their destination.

It towered above them, dark and menacing, yet beautiful with elegant spires and black gardens along its base. Kaiźer knew Kurai was near. He could sense her aura.

She was with Darzíel within his black castle.

Darziel

chapter 21: Visitors?

Pleasure me my lord, and know that I will wait for the time when I can take what I too desire, and it will be quite heart stopping indeed.

Katie, The Jackals Court lead Assassin
The Enchanted Age

Darziel stood outside the doors to what had become Kurai Aka Hoshi's private chambers. He'd kept her under lock and key since giving her his minions. He knew how a woman's hormones got when they were pregnant. She'd done a fine job in building his army, and even though she'd fought it every day, he knew there had been times she'd enjoyed the emotional overload. She'd hated him after, but still, his work had paid off.

Standing here now after four years, he couldn't wait to give her the happy news. Oh, how he shivered in anticipation.

Unable to stand it any longer, he pushed from the antechamber and stepped into the adjoining room. Red candles lit with his passing, the dark shadows pulling away to reveal phantom chains stretching from all four corners of the room. They were connected to a large cage suspended several feet above the floor.

He gazed through the obsidian bars and took in the shapely form within. Kurai Aka Hoshi lay upon a mountain of pillows, which he had designed to heighten the user's sense of physical pleasure. Even in sleep, he could see their effect on Kurai Aka Hoshi's skin as her breath came steady and robust. He'd had some crazy nights in this cage, but they weren't for him; they'd been for Kurai Aka Hoshi. Little had she known; she wasn't merely his sow to breed as he pleased? He'd found out her bloodline was known to give birth to powerful offspring, and oh how he'd enjoyed the fact. He had been wounded when she had fled the first time, but his frustration had turned into a red hot rage after learning of her heritage. He now felt only a gnawing sensation in his core that made it hard to think of anything but her naked figure.

As he stood there, wrapped in candlelight, he watched Kurai Aka Hoshi's sleeping form. Her chest rose with each breath, and its mesmerizing motion drew his eye. Her figure had filled out quite nicely after her long pregnancy.

Stepping up to the bars, he passed through them, their shapes fraying like smoke as he moved past them. Stepping over the pillows, he felt the tingly effect of them enter his feet, filling him with their sexual rush.

He ignored the feeling as he knelt beside Kurai Aka Hoshi. He ran his hand along her thigh, trailing his fingers over the curve of her hip, and grazed her breast as she shifted. Slowly she awoke to look at him with hazy eyes.

"Hmmm... Darzíel..." she whispered in a thick voice. "What are you doing here?"

She lifted her arms over her head, stretching deeply. Her chest rose as she arched her back, her thighs clenching together, and he grew drunk on the sight. His body ached, but Kurai Aka Hoshi had always affected the angel so, it was a shame things weren't as they were before. No longer was he the angel he'd been. He was Fallen, and as his core heated with sexual need at the sight of Kurai Aka Hoshi before him, naked and aroused, he had no second thoughts.

"I came with a gift," he said softly as he ran a thumb over the plump flesh of her lips.

Kurai Aka Hoshi bit her lip and sat up on one arm, her skin growing dark with arousal. Its hue becoming flushed, "I doubt that" —she hummed as she stretched— "I think you needed to release a little pent-up stress." She wet her lips and rose to her knees, whispering in his ear, "and I'm in the mood for a little excitement."

He stood, his mouth opening to tell her what he'd come to say but froze; she gripped him. His manhood complained, but he cast away what he had come here to say to her. He looped his arms under her legs and lifted her into the air. She let out a squeal that turned into a moan as he merged with her. Too soon, he lost all train of thought as he listened to her breath stutter with his movement. She clung to him; her eyes glazed with pleasure, and with a groan, it ended. Their climax was intense and short-lived, and they both let out labored breaths as their sexual stupors faded. Kurai Aka Hoshi still clung to him, and she had left deep nail marks across his back. The pain cleared his mind, and he regained his focus.

"My gift..." he had to pause. "My gift wasn't sex..." he said finally, his chest heaving.

Kurai Aka Hoshi looked at him quizzically. She unwrapped her legs from around him, and he let her fall back onto the enchanted pillows. "Then what did you come here to do?" she asked in a breathy voice.

He smiled wickedly. Kurai would love what he was about to tell her. If only Kaiźer were here now.

"We have visitors," he said

"Who?"

"Oh, if I'm correct, you know one of them already." Hope painted Kurai Aka Hoshi's eyes, and he bathed in its light. He looked forward to snuffing that light. "Get ready. I need you to look *presentable* for our guests." He gestured to the wall and, turning, walked out of the cage. He let the obsidian bars melt, crumbling in his passing, leaving a gap in the bars.

He turned and let the doors shut behind him. His eyes glowed red as he strode down the hall. He was looking forward to what came next.

Kaiźer looked up at the towering wall before them. They had crossed the rocky terrain and now stood before the black castle's front gate. All of them had been trying to find a way inside but to no avail. Kaldär had said they couldn't use magic, or Darzíel would know they were here, and so far, no luck; the obsidian walls seemed to hold no weak spots. The gate itself was impenetrable, and the more they searched, the more it seemed impossible to get in.

"Shit!" Oníx barked as she kicked the gate in frustration. "Ugh! Gods, how long are we going to stand here?"

Kaiźer looked up at the towering black barrier once more but had no answer. Even though Kaldär had said no magic, it seemed like the only way, and with Oníx on the ground, her back to the wall, he didn't see how anything he said would help.

"How's your foot?" he asked.

Oníx stuck her tongue out at him, and he grinned, but it was short-lived. Everything reeked of sulfur and stole any good feelings that came to be. He felt the effects too. The Underworld was not a place he'd put on his top spots to visit twice.

"Kaldär," he asked, "any brighter ideas?"

Kaldär came into view, Eźmeralda, at his side. He didn't respond to the question, but Kaiźer knew it wasn't going unanswered. Kaldär eyed the gate with a keen eye, his arms crossed over his chest, lips pursed in a frown.

"The only way to open this gate is from the inside," he stated.

"Then how are we going to get in?" Ba'ile asked. He sat with Oníx against the wall, his shoulder just inches from hers. The two of them looked at Kaldär expectantly. They didn't get the answer they were waiting for, however.

"We don't," as Kaldär said it magic bloomed within his chest, spreading to his arms.

"Kaldär! Eźmeralda snapped. "What about—"

"Doesn't matter now!"

Stepping up to the gate, he placed his hands against the black stone. The magic that covered his chest and arms shot down to protect his fingers, and as it grew in strength, Kaldär's eyes sparked with gold lightning.

"I call upon the old gods," he chanted. "Anubis, grant me your guidance, for I need your power."

Kaiźer felt the pendent of death grow hot around his neck. He looked down to see its red glow against his chest. As a part of his armor, Anubis's amulet had been a gift from Maliki, his master. Looking back at Kaldär, he watched as the man used his master's technique. Same stance, same weaves, and style, but as he watched, Kaldär's power level surpassed his masters' limitations. It sank into the obsidian and gathered into a seam within the wall, marking a gate's outline.

"Open thy gate of Arcadian!" Kaldär called out in the ancient language, but just as Kaiźer thought the gate would burst from within, the energy backfired, kicking them all back a few steps.

"What the!"

On its own accord, the gate groaned as it slid apart, its bottom edge gliding just inches above the ground. Kaldär gazed inside, and everyone stepped forward to follow his example, soon moving though as he stepped inside.

"Was that supposed to happen?" Kaldär asked him in a whisper.

"No..." Kaldär pulled a golden blade out of thin air, its metal materializing from pure light. "He knows."

It was all he said, but Kaiźer didn't need an explanation. He could sense Darzíel's aura from here and, with it, Aka's. The time was near; no longer would the Fallen Angel use his friend. No longer!

Passing through the black garden, their party of six looked around at the tall plants surrounding them. Kaiźer watched a team of small monkeys with red fur swing through the trees, jumping from branch to branch, weaving in and out of the black leaves. One of them stopped and plucked a strange purple fruit from the branches of one of the trees and studied it, but it seemed to sense his gaze and looked up directly into his eyes. Lit with red fire, the monkey's eyes shone like firestone.

It was a daemon lemur. Thought to be extinct, the creature had been forgotten to myth. It didn't stay interested in Kaiźer for long, soon popping the fruit into its mouth and disappearing into the trees. He realized he had fallen behind and rushed to catch up with everyone, passing a multitude of daemon breeds thought long dead.

Approaching Oníx, he spoke quietly. "This place must be a safe haven for those nearing extinction."

"Also," she said back. "Most of these plants are born of demon magic. You won't find them anywhere else in the nine circles."

"Even the Unseen One's palace?"

"Even there," she said.

He looked around at the dark plants. Some were red and others purple, while some were deep blue, but all had the same black exoskeleton and seemed to glow with a dim light. He felt like he was passing through a hostile world. He saw white snakes, green-furred deer with extremely wide antlers, and white-blue birds with their feathers tipped with what looked to be ice. Alongside the weird animals, demons walked, most likely the caretakers of the black garden.

Just as they neared the entrance to the castle, he noticed something odd. The garden held a mirror resemblance to the Garden Eternal, only this version felt sinister and seemed to be warped.

They stood at the bottom of the steps leading up to the open doors of the castle. Just as Kaldär had said, Darzíel was expecting them. Why else would he leave the way clear to them?

"What's the plan now?" he asked.

Kaldär stopped on the first set of steps and spoke in a firm voice.

"We hold steady, I'd planned to surprise the Fallen and force him to the mortal realm, but we lost that chance. He'll be waiting for us in the throne room, and I believe he had a prisoner. She speaks your name Kaiźer."

Kaiźer tightened his grip on Kaín. He'd kept the blade in hand since stepping into this realm. He held hope that Kaín would be ready when the time came.

~Oh, I'll be ready~ Kaín said. *~Demons taste delicious, the Sins even more so~*

Kaldär looked at him and, in a calm voice, stated. "If she is one of us, we will free her, but the Fallen's demise comes first."

"What if Darzíel tries to kill her first?" Oníx asked.

"Then you and Kaiźer will attack first. The innocent come first if that happens. Leave the Fallen to me."

He could work with that. He'd been planning on saving Kurai Aka Hoshi, to begin with. "Then let's go!" he said. He didn't want to wait any longer, and he led the way into the mouth of the dragon.

Darzíel had had this coming for a while now.

Stepping into the throne room, Darzíel settled himself into the oversized chair that sat at the end of the room. This was his home, his castle, and his realm. Settling back on the rich leather of the throne, he let out a satisfied sigh. His inner eye watched as the small party of six circled the outer wall of his castle. He recognized Oníx and Kaiźer, but the other four, not so much.

A redhead and a lean-muscled man looked to be a wolf-shifter, but he couldn't place the other two for some unknown reason. They seemed familiar as if he knew them, but as an angel, his memory never failed him, and he knew he'd never met them. He'd remember if he had once known a giant of a man and a lady with green hair.

He knew why they were here. Kaiźer of course, for Kurai Aka Hoshi, and since he'd brought friends, Kaiźer was also here to kill him. Darzíel was looking forward to how that was about to turn out.

Still watching the group outside, his attention was drawn to the side hall where Kurai Aka Hoshi approached, her hips gliding along in a sensual sweep. He'd left a small gift for her upon the pillows when he'd left, and he was happy to see it decorating her figure. In the light of the many candles, its gold chains glistened like liquid metal.

Kurai Aka Hoshi arrived to stand to his left, unabashed in her new attire. Starting at her neck as a multitude of ropes and chains, the outfit fell over her chest. It then trailed down along her abdomen to slip between her legs. The two chains then merged into a cluster of gold ropes interlinking to cover her sex. Finishing the outfit, a sheer cape of smooth silk fell from her shoulders to flow in a phantom breeze as she approached. Under the golden trails of sensual pathways, a thin sheet of cloth covered her skin like mist, its color making her skin shine like water.

As he admired her, he summoned a collar and chain and connected it to the arm of his throne. Kurai Aka Hoshi knelt upon the steps before him, her face showing nothing in response to her bondage. He ignored her then, turning back to watch the scene outside. A spike in magic drew his eye to the giant of a man. He saw then what had passed him by. His aura was that of a magician, one of the six celestials, or beings of old! And as he watched the immortal try to gain command over his gatekeeper, he smiled. He'd had his fun; it was time to get things rolling.

He blocked the magician's magic and opened the gate along with the front door, leaving the way clear to them.

"Kurai Aka Hoshi, our guests have arrived. Sit up!"

She did so with a scowl, her back becoming ramrod straight at a yank of her chain. He saw her expression but was too busy watching their guests pass through his gardens to scold her properly. His guests soon followed Kaiźer up the steps. Darzíel waited, and when the doors burst open, he stood arms held wide in greeting.

"Welcome!" he called out. "I happily invite you into my humble abode. I pray your travels weren't long?"

Everyone looked at him, and then amongst themselves except for one, who had eyes for Kurai Aka Hoshi alone. His eyes didn't stray once, glued as they were to her. Darzíel watched as Kaiźer opened his mouth, silently wording Kurai Aka Hoshi's name. The two of them seemed to be lost in the sight of each other. It wasn't a surprise the two of them would stand in disbelief before each other after so long. If only he could wipe those hopeful expressions from their faces.

He moved his attention away from them and let his gaze pass over the others, stopping on the magician. He was the only one he found dangerous. His aura radiated well past his figure, encasing the group around him in a bubble. Even to him—angel that he was—the man's magic burned greater than his own if not just beside it. Throughout the age's only one being of mortal heritage had held such magic. Yet here before him stood an immortal with such.

It transcended what even his own previous superiors had thought possible. This man should not even exist; he and his... brother? Kaiźer and this man, related? They were of the same blood! He could see it, not just in their physical similarities but in their aura's as well. Although, as he looked between the two of them, he came to see a single difference. Even with their identical aura, one was tainted while the other was pure. He became sure he would not have noticed this if the two had been separate.

"The *μισός φυλή* returns and with its friends to boot, all in the hopes of stopping me," he called out. "However, I must disappoint." He got up and grinned. He flooded the room with magic and, in doing so, let all his wards show in the visible light spectrum

"As you can see, this place is rigged to activate if either of you takes one more step." moving to stand at the edge of the steps that lead to the throne, he swept an arm wide, gesturing to the room. "Nonetheless, I wouldn't worry about those. The real threat is here around my neck."

He picked up the neckless that hung against his chest. He noticed how both the eyes of Kaiźer and Kaldär went wide upon seeing it. No ordinary piece of metal, the neckless had been one of the first artifacts he'd gotten his hands on. It now stood as his box of tricks, so to say. Right now, though, he was using it as a trigger that he'd attached to his heart. The reason the brothers were wary was because of what that trigger led to.

He had created a string of condensed maña that he'd linked with his heartbeat, as well as the heartbeat of Kurai Aka Hoshi.

"Oh, yes, that's right. If I die, Kurai dies! And don't think I won't do it. I've already activated it, and only I can deactivate it."

"Wait, what?" Kurai Aka Hoshi looked at him in shock as she shouted. She groped at her chest and pulled away from the chains from her chest. The skin was red and irritated underneath them, but there was a thin string of maña protruding from between her breasts in the magical spectrum. Once she'd put on his gift, the magic had gone active. If things worked out as planned, he'd kill six birds with one stone: all without lifting a finger.

"Yes, if either of us dies, so does the other."

Looking at her, he grinned. Kaiźer wouldn't risk this woman's life. He was a piece knocked off the board, now to take care of the bishop.

As he had been observing them outside, the silver-haired shifter had caught his interest. Tailing Kaldär, he'd come off as a support piece; a pawn, but once they'd entered the garden, he'd realized him to be the third strongest of the group and had done what he could on short notice, growing wolfbane and unleashing Kama Gansha into the air around the shifter, thereby eliminating his magic. He wouldn't be shifting for a good eight hours.

Now the redhead, he recognized her as one of the ShadowFolk, though not by birth sadly. She wouldn't be any trouble. The only one near that she could drink from were her friends, himself and Kurai Aka Hoshi. Demon blood was like acid to the Vampiri, so she wouldn't gain anything from them besides a stomachache. Though now that he thought about it, something seemed off about her, he couldn't put his finger on it. He was sure it wasn't a threat. What was a threat though, was the big guy in the middle? He had been the hardest to figure out. Clearly, the strongest, gauging his power level had been difficult. There was no telling what he could do. For all he knew, it could have been a trick, but to contain such magic and hold it steady showed training. This guy was the real deal.

Turning back to Kurai Aka Hoshi, he beckoned her to him. She had been trying to break his trigger weave after hearing what it would do, but once he called on the secondary weave he'd placed on her, the chains activated.

Looking up, she stopped and stood without a second's hesitation. She was under Darzíel's control now and would do whatever he asked.

She stopped at his side, and he smiled. "Lose thy gift of mine." He commanded in the ancient language.

Eyes glazed over, she did as he said, pulling the chains from her shoulder and letting them fall around her waist. She let the chains free from her hips and pool to the floor around her feet. Under the chains, she wore a sheer chemise that covered her figure sensually, barely hiding her sexuality in its entirety.

"Do you see, she's all mine!" He looked at the group below. Kaiźer was grinding his teeth, and Kaldär looked at him with contempt. The rest looked on in horror.

Moving behind Kurai Aka Hoshi, he cupped her in his hands. "Come on! Try to stop me, I bet you can't, for I am in control."

Turning away, he faced his back to the group and drew his dark blade as Kurai Aka Hoshi succumbed to his magic in slow gasps of heavy breathing. All the pieces were falling into place. All that was left was to—

"NOW, Eźmeralda!"

Looking up in surprise and irritation to Kaldär's shout, Darzíel watched with icy eyes as the green-haired chick stepped forward. He'd forgotten all about her. Now that she had stepped out from behind Kaldär, he realized why.

She was a druid!

Too late! He tried to draw on his magic but was too slow, as Eźmeralda activated her tattoos and blocked all connection to magic in the castle. He watched as his beloved weaves crumbled around him, the sword he had summoned vanished from his hand, and all the ties to his creation around him snapped. He was too late to save them, but he kept the weave connecting him and Kurai Aka Hoshi stable through his pendent. It was his only card left that he could play, and he was for sure not going to lose it.

Kaldär

Chapter 22: Greeting of Fists

War is the gods playground, bloodshed their wine, and any who cross their path, will become that of their throne; decorating a hall of thou own making in their name.

The First General to the Unseen One
The Age of Heroes

Kaldär watched Darzíel as he drew all his magic in and put it into the death chain between him and Kurai Aka Hoshi. He knew then what to do.

"Eźmeralda, take Sin'ka and flank the throne on the right. Oníx, Ba'ile, the left. Kaiźer and I will go in from the front."

Everyone jumped into motion, and he summoned Excalibur while Kaiźer drew Kaín. The plan was simple; unleash the Dark General inside Darzíel and trap it. It sounded simple enough, but in all actuality was going to be extremely difficult. He and everyone else would need to do everything perfectly if they were to have the slightest chance of success. Darzíel had a vast supply of stored maña in the pendant around his neck, and they needed it to run bone dry before they did anything.

"Kaiźer, you ready?" he asked.

"Long overdue, let's go!"

Shooting forward, they ran through the crumbling weaves that had wrapped the hall not moments before. Excalibur morphed to cover his arm in a gold and silver gauntlet, and he punched through the cracked barrier to reach the bottom of the steps.

Darzíel met them there, clashing fist against fist. The ore of Excalibur rang from the impact, and he growled at the guy's smug attitude. He'd just blocked with his bare fist.

Darzíel grinned. After securing Kurai Aka Hoshi, he'd met Kaldär at the base of the stairs, infusing his body with magic to make his muscles more prominent and his bones denser. Trading blows, the two of them duked it out. With each hit or block, the air whipped about in a flurry of power. Looking at the man before him, Darzíel thought he saw something in his eyes, something familiar. When he finally placed it, he grinned.

Blocking a kick, he caught Kaldär's eye. "You were trained by Gabriel. I thought I recognized your fighting style."

"I may have trained under him, yes, but I've got more up my sleeve." Kaldär pulled his leg back and abruptly changed fighting styles. It was so sudden it caught Darzíel off guard. Now on the offense, he was pushed back one step at a time. Using a range of kicks and flips, Kaldär moved through every attack he threw at him. It was impossible to touch him, and every time he discovered a rhythm, it would change again.

"You," Kaldär said between strikes to the ribs that Darzíel barely avoided, "you used to be a guardian, but all

I see is a Fallen," he was slowly pushing him to the top of the stairs. "I expected to see a fight, but you've been consumed by hatred."

Darzíel wasn't going to listen to this nonsense. He quickly drew on the pendant in a last-ditch effort. The hall bloomed with light, and he let loose a roar as he sent out a magical shockwave from his whole body. That should disrupt them for a while.

Kaldär was on the last few steps, having been blown back. He was breathing hard from the effort he'd put in the blast, but with the king in check, all he had left was to pick off the rest.

Kaiźer had gone straight for Kurai Aka Hoshi instead of him, but when he started back up the stairs, he was attacked from both sides; Eźmeralda and the redhead from the right Oníx and the shifter came from the left. Ducking a swing from the redhead, he kicked out, and she went flying even as he knocked one of Oníx's fireballs away and backhanded her. She collided with Eźmeralda, but as he grinned at their failure, the male shifter blindsided him with a sweep of the legs.

He lost sight of him as he did and tried to find him but had to deal with Eźmeralda once again as she appeared behind him. *Did she just use shadow magic?* Blocking three consecutive punches, he caught the last and crushed her hand, snapping her fingers like twigs before throwing her past Kaiźer. She sailed through the air to smash into the wall and didn't get up.

Facing the other four, he watched them as they tried to flank him. Oníx summoned two daggers and charged. He expected her to stab at him but had to dodge when she threw them at him. They sailed past, and he knocked all of them off their feet with another magical burst, draining the last of his magic. He stood in the center of the stairs and watched them get up. Even Kaldär was rising.

"This is pointless. You can't win," Darzíel snarled. "Go home, and I might decide to let you live."

"Oh, we're not going anywhere," Kaldär called. "Kaiźer, do it now!"

Darzíel started to turn when he felt a sharp pain in his back. It felt like a needle had just punched through his heart to be pulled out just as fast. Turning, he looked up, and his eyes went wide in shock.

Kaiźer had stabbed Kaín through Kurai Aka Hoshi's back. When Oníx had drawn the firestone daggers and thrown them, he'd assumed she'd been aiming for him, when she'd been aiming for Kurai Aka Hoshi! The blades had buried themselves into her belly, and at Kaldär's command, Kaiźer had punched Kaín between them, shattering the three orbs of immortality that resided in all celestials.

Groping at his chest, his hands came away bloody. He'd been so sure! Damn that man and his cold heart. *I guess it's true that a Jackal always stays a Jackal...*

Turning back to face Kaldär, he swayed on his feet. "You didn't plan on saving Kurai Aka Hoshi at all, did you?"

Kaldär's face didn't show anything.

"The only reason you came here was to kill me," Darzíel said as he spat blood out of his mouth. "You got me, so finish it!"

Kaldär didn't say anything, but reaching into a hidden pocket of his pants, he pulled something out. Wrapped in a silk cloth, Darzíel watched as he opened the bundle, revealing what was inside.

It was a black scarab.

Kaldär held his hand out, and Darzíel fell back in fear. Sitting in his palm, the black scarab came to life.

"No," he cried. "It can't end like this!" He scrambled up the steps, trying to get away but only made his wounds tear open further, which made him sprawl to the floor in pain. The scarab jumped into the air and flew towards him. He tried to swat at it, but it just weaved past his attack to attach itself to his chest. Sinking into the skin, it burned against his heart, and he cried out. His sight flickered, and he fell back, his back arching in pain. He felt like his mind was being torn asunder, and as the scorching agony enveloped him, he began to see double.

A scream ripped from his throat. And with one final cry, he was torn in two, the last echoes of his death outlasting him.

Kaizer

chapter 23: Awakening

The end is always the same for gods and mortals, a light shines bright and the song of beckoning rings true.

Unknown mortal
The Age of Echelons

Kaiźer pulled the dagger out and watched as the death chain disconnected. He quickly sealed the wound, knitting together the internal organs and the muscles around them, finishing with the skin till only a thin scar remained. Kira would feel every move she made, but she'd be fine.

Holding her up, he watched as Darzíel stumbled away from Kaldär. Pulling the black scarab from his pants pocket, Kaldär let it activate. Lowering Kira to the floor Kaiźer covered her with a blanket and watched the scarab fuse with the Fallen's heart. He watched as the black feathers burned away from his wings. Once each one was gone, the very skin upon his body began to glow red hot, burning to ash.

Darzíel fell to the floor, his limbs locked as his very bones turned to stone. Screaming, he writhed as his body was torn apart by the scarab. Light and dark clashed as the dark lord was pulled into the heart of the black jewel. It fought its bonds but was no match for the same artifact designed to trap it.

Like paper, its essence was ripped from Darzíel. To the naked eye, only a clash of light and darkness could be seen, the two separating with a roar to tear apart in a blast of magic.

Covering Kira's unconscious form, he waited for the storm to subside. Tendrils of pure arcane magic rippled throughout the air, each strand growing smaller till only thin wisps flowed past.

Sitting up, he watched the remaining magic merge with the castle's stone. Where Darzíel had been, the black scarab circled, its black depths pulsing crimson. Draped, along with the steps Darzíel laid, his skin bleached white. His hair was now black, the long locks spread out in erratic tangles. Kaldär slowly took the scarab in hand and stepped back.

"Is Kurai Aka Hoshi alright?" Kaldär called up to him.

Slipping his daggers into their sheaths, Kaiźer gave a thumbs up and knelt beside Kira. She was still breathing; that was a good sign. She'd always been strong-willed. It had been what had drawn him to her. Her fire had burned strong, still burned strong. But right now, they had to get back to the mortal realm before the cavalry arrived. Darzíel had goons to do his dirty work in his absence.

"Oníx!" he called. "Give me a hand?"

Kira wasn't very heavy, but there was no way he would carry her in the nude. The blanket wasn't enough; it barely covered her, which was why he needed Oníx and her spatial magic. Clothing was a specialty of hers, despite her lack thereof. During the fight, she had ditched the boots and silk wrappings for fire, choosing to cover her figure in white / black flames.

As she came up the steps, he saw that her flames had died to a rich red. They licked at her and crowned her head like a wreath. He'd always found flame elementals to be boring, but he didn't think that with Oníx. At first, she's been an average mage, but right after she'd stayed in Londinium a hundred years back, she'd changed. She'd gained a heightened control over her magic, gaining abilities only other elementals could use. He'd never figured out how and he was sure he'd be in the dark until she decided to let him in on her tricks. He stepped back as she reached his side. The heat of her flames warmed him, and he let out a breath when their comforting embrace touched him.

"Is she okay?"

"I healed her like Kaldär said"—he paused for a second—"but she's still going to feel sore for a bit." The mission had been to save Kira—who was a succubus—to take down Darzíel. The plan hadn't been ideal, but it had worked. Envy was captured, and Kira was safe. Thanks to Eźmeralda, they had been able to get past the castle's safeguards, and once she'd blocked the magical flow of the area, it had been down to him to get to Kira. Kaldär had called the outcome on a dime, everything Darzíel had done he'd anticipated. Looking at Kira, he wondered why such a person had chosen to help them. He had to question the man's motive.

"Hey, Oníx, do you think the capture of Envy was Kaldär's only reason for helping?"

Oníx froze, and he almost missed it as she spoke to cover it. "How should I know? Why don't you ask him?" she said as she pulled the blanket from Kira and began to chant. In a flow of fabric, Kira was covered in a loose robe. It looked like she was covered in a thin layer of paint that hid the fine contoured of her figure. It would do.

Oníx helped him lift Kira up, but he heard a low groan just as the rest of their group arrived. Eźmeralda gasped, and turning, he saw what had drawn her eye.

Darzíel had rolled over onto his back.

"We need to get out of here!" he urged.

"No..." Kira mumbled. He looked at her when she grasped his shoulder. She was awake!

"Kira..." he was worried for her, but he was more concerned about the Fallen. If the man was still alive, they weren't done yet. He glanced at Kaldär. "I thought you killed him."

"I did. Upon extraction, the separation should have torn Darźiel's body apart."

The Angel looked acceptable to him. He lay on his back, but his groans were enough to prove he was in pain.

"We need to go," he urged once more, "Kaldär."

"No..." Kaldär said. "Something's different. His aura is... pure."

Moving forward, Kaldär took the steps two at a time to kneel beside Darzíel. He placed a hand on his chest, and they waited.

"Darzíel, hey, what's the last thing you remember?" Kaldär asked.

The Fallen sat up—with great care—to look around. He looked like he had just woken up, and with his response, Kaiźer's breath caught.

"High noon, I was out at sea when everything went black."

Kaldär helped the Angel to his feet and held him steady. The man stood on unsteady feet, and Kaiźer watched as Kaldär looped his arm over his shoulder.

"Kaldär," he called. "Are you sure he's back to his normal guardian ways?"

Kaldär looked at him, and he dropped his gaze. He didn't want to question the immortal. If the man thought Darzíel was okay, then he might as well just go with the flow. He looked at Kira, but she was all eyes for Darzíel. She was watching with keen eyes, and he sighed. He wondered what she was thinking. She clearly had a lot of worry for him now that the Sin was free of him, and he sensed a deep longing to feel his arms around her? Had they been lovers at a time? An angel and a demon... no, a guardian wouldn't risk such. There was more to the story of their past that had yet to be revealed.

"Well, you may be able to convince Kaiźer, but I'm not so easily convinced," Oníx snapped. She stepped up to the fallen and gripped him under the chin and stared into his eye. They all waited, and after a few seconds, Kaiźer watched the tension leak out of her shoulders. Slowly Oníx's fingers slipped from the Angel's chin and fell to her side. She turned and looked at them. "He... he's lost his memory, but his soul is no longer corrupted."

Kaiźer stood still, Kira at his side, and watched as Kaldär held the Angel steady. His wings were gone,' and in their place, white skin sat half-healed. He seemed not to notice, though, as he had other things to worry about.

As the Angel looked around himself, all he saw were guarded gazes. Eźmeralda was the only one who didn't seem worried. She knew more than they about what had just happened.

Darzíel stood before them, his head held high despite the obvious pain he was in. His face was scarred with remorse, but he kept his shoulders back all the same. Clear as day, the man saw where he was, paired it with their injuries, and compared them with his own.

It was evident when he guessed the truth of what had happened. All without any recollection of what had really happened.

Kaldär had moved back once Darzíel had gained what balance he could, though he favored a leg and seemed unable to breathe steadily. All the same, he took a stuttering breath as he spoke.

"I know not what I did, but I feel my chest burn and know I have wronged you. I stand here now, confused yet knowing, for I see the truth within where we stand. As a guardian, I feel—"

"Uh, Darzíel," Kaldär interrupted, "if I may?"

The fallen leveled his gaze with a nod and placed his hands behind his back. Kaldär took a step towards him and stood once more at his side.

"Your wings are gone, old friend. Envy took your power with him when we severed him from your aura. He was paired with you for too long.

Darzíel looked at Kaldär in disbelief. When he saw the truth in Kaldär's eyes, he turned and grasped at his back. He and Oníx took a step forward, but Kaldär raised a hand to stop them. Doing so caused him to stumble into Kaldär.

Darzíel was grasping at his back in desperation as he sank to his knees before them. Kaldär had his hand on the Angel's shoulder, and as the realization dawned on him, they all looked on in sorrow as the man cried out in anguish.

Kira slipped from his grasp and stumbled towards the Angel, and he went to stop her when Kaldär shook his head at him. He stopped as the man took Aka's hand and led her to the Fallen's side.

Kaiźer let out a slow breath and struggled to get the knot out of his throat. Raw emotion was pouring free of a man who had just minutes ago been as cold and heartless as a winter storm. He wasn't the only one who felt the truth in what was transpiring, though. Both Oníx and Eźmeralda had tears in their eyes. He saw Sin'ka hiding behind her hair and watched as Ba'ile scrubbed a hand across his face to hide his own emotion. They all felt the weight of what had been lost. They had known a price would be paid but knowing such had been taken was still hard even with it being the enemy who had lost such.

He moved towards Darzíel and dropped to one knee beside him. Looking up at him, the man who had been trying to take everything from him for the last hundred years met his gaze. His eyes shone white and compared to the firestone of his eyes before, it was a night and day difference. He saw what Oníx had seen and saw what had once been and was again.

"Kaldär asked you about the last thing you remember, and you answered the sea. Do you remember why you were out at sea?"

Darzíel looked between him and Kira but ended up looking at the floor.

"I went in search of a sword."

"A sword?"

"Yes."

Kaldär leaned forward. "Was this sword made of gold?"

"It was," Darzíel said with a sideways glance. No longer were there tears, but he still hadn't forgotten the fact that his wings were gone. "Do you think my loss is the price I paid for my theft?"

"No!" Kira snapped, "It's not."

Kaldär looked dubious, though. His eyebrows were knit together in concentration, and Darzíel noticed.

"What is it, Magician?"

"What year is it?" Kaldär asked.

Darzíel smiled slightly. "1921 A.B. Gabriel just gave me my tenth star. I couldn't wait to tell Starli—" he paused and shot a quick glance at Kira. "Uh, I mean Kurai Aka Hoshi that we had been given such."

Kaiźer goggled. 1921, that meant two thousand years had passed since Envy had taken control. What had he done since then, and that slipup with her name? Star-something? Things weren't adding up. If Kira had had a different name before he'd known her, it was likely that she hadn't always been the same person. One out of every ten demons was Fallen. The rest came from the mortal realms. So, it could very quickly be possible that Kira wasn't a succubus by birth.

Kaldär must know it too, but he didn't comment on Darzíel's slip.

"You've been paired with one of the Dark Lords for over a hundred years; the day is December 23rd, in the year 3921 A.B."

Slowly it dawned on the Angel, the gap in his memory, and how great it really was. His eyes went wide, and he looked between them in shock and despair. He had just heard that one of the dark lords had been controlling his every move since the day he'd found the sword. His memory ended there, and he knew nothing after, till waking up in this room.

"What did I do?" he asked.

"Much," Kaldär answered.

Darzíel's head dropped slightly. He looked between them all again, moving to each of them in turn till he reached Aka. He met her eye and seemed to reach a mental decision. He raised his arm and held it out to Kaldär. "Help me up?"

As Kaldär clasped his hand, Kaiźer looped a hand under the Angel's other arm. They lifted Darzíel to his feet and let him find his center.

Settling onto his heels, he looked at his hands. "How many did I hurt?"

Kaiźer met the man's eyes. "Mainly, you used Kira to get to us after we tried to protect her."

Darzíel's eyes went wide, and he looked at Kira in horror. The block he had held steady until now broke, and Kaiźer caught a hint of the man's inner thoughts before it reformed. The Angel had kept his training. All the same, the man's memories had been leaked. It had revealed what truth had still been hidden. What doubts Kaiźer had held onto flew from his mind. His memory was not there; the last thing representing visual sight was of bubbles rising. The Angel's last memory was of drowning. He would have assumed since he could go fifteen minutes without breath that as an angel, he could hold his breath much longer, if not indefinitely.

When Darzíel learned of his use of Kurai, his thoughts had been of anxiety and... envy. Directed towards Kurai, it explained why the Dark Lord had attached itself to the Angel but didn't solve the question of how it had happened. Kaiźer spoke with command as he looked at Darzíel and caught his eye.

"Why did you envy her?" he asked.

The Angel drew his eyebrows together and looked at him closely. He met the questioning gaze with his own and waited. Kira looked between the two of them, and Kaiźer noticed her inner confusion at his question. So, she doesn't remember? Now that he thought about it, Kira had looked human, like she did now, in the Angel's memory. It was a note to be addressed later. For right now, he had to know the 'what before the why.'

Darzíel took a breath and was just beginning to speak when a loud crash sounded outside the very hall they stood in. They all turned at the noise. Sin'ka, Eźmeralda, and Ba'ile all snarled as they sensed the scent of what had caused the noise.

"Time to go!" Kaldär said even as he stepped back and slashed an arm through the air. "Darzíel, you're coming with me; I have questions I still need answers to."

"He's the enemy," Oníx complained.

"He was," Kaldär said. "He was the enemy. Right now, we have to go."

At that moment, the doors that led back to the dark garden crashed open. From them poured a hoard of demons, and it was like watching ants run out of an anthill.

Kaldär cursed. "Get through the Portal!" He jumped forwards and slammed his palms into the floor. Magic shot free of his fingers and traveled out to break free of the ground in waves. The solid fire rose high to merge with the ceiling, creating a barrier between them and the hoard. "Go," he shouted as he pumped magic into the barricade like water.

The man's maña didn't even weaken with the use of such large amounts. It was terrific, but as Kaiźer watched, three demons stepped forward to stand before the wall of magic. Much more massive than the others, they were humanoid and were covered in what looked to be demonic tattoos that had been carved into their very flesh.

"Generals, damn." Kaldär looked back at them. "I will follow, GO!"

Eźmeralda rallied them, assuring them all of his ability to give them the opening he had. He followed her but turned at the last second and looked out at Kaldär as he stood up, magic blooming in his hands.

"Come on, Kaiźer," Eźmeralda said. "He'll be fine. He's faced worse."

Looking at her, he nodded. She stepped through, and he followed with one final glance at Kaldär. The last thing he saw was lighting and fire as the barrier came down.

Stepping through the portal, Kaiźer emerged and immediately stumbled into someone standing right in front of the breach. Falling to the stone of the floor, he realized it was Oníx.

Looking around, he found the cause of her hesitation. Once she'd stepped through, the sight before her would have made even him pause.

Their destination had once been a sprawling mansion that of which now sat in ruins. The remains of a twin staircase hung shattered, suspended from the second floor by a few beams of wood that had survived the destruction. The foyer they had appeared in was littered with rubble. Also, what was left of the roof was little indeed. The first light of morning was visible on the horizon, and as he helped Oníx to her feet, he watched the sunrise above the mountains through the hole at the front of the mansion.

The entirety of the entrance had been blown to smithereens. Beans as thick as his torso lay splintered and scattered among stone that had been ground to dust. Something with an immense maña had passed through the house like a twister; the only question now was, was it still here?"

Sin'ka stood in the center of what had been her sizeable living area. However, when he started towards her, the scent of death assailed his senses. Drawing Kaín, he stepped through the rubble till he saw the carnage that had drawn Sin'ka's attention. The damage was fresh and reeked of demon magic.

~*Fucking Hell*~ Kaín groaned.

Hanging from the wall, their bodies suspended upside down, three women and two men had been strung up by their feet. Beneath them lay a sheet of broken glass, its outline wrapped in blood. The mirror's reflective surface was clean, and as he watched, a drop of blood fell from a finger of one of the women's hands to splash onto the surface. Just as quickly, the mirror soaked it up like a sponge, leaving the reflection as clean as before.

Ba'ile lost his stomach then and rushed outside. Eźmeralda followed; her face was slightly green, and Kaiźer soon heard both fall to the ground, heaving the contents of their guts onto the grass.

"What could have gone this?" Oníx asked him.

He had a hunch and found that he usually ended right when he listened to his gut. Now, based on the maña he sensed, the stench was undeniable. He told Oníx to take a whiff, and when she did, she wrinkled her nose in disgust with a cringe.

"Ugh, mirror demon, and not a puppet either," she said, but as she did, she froze. "But that's impossible."

Wait, one strike? ~Apparently not, because the thing clearly destroyed Sin'ka's home with a single strike~ Kaín said. Kaiźer turned and looked around at the structure. What he hadn't noticed before was, in fact, one origin of the damage. Only one strike indeed.

"Kaín, can you sense the bugger?" he asked.

~*Nope, he's long gone*~

Okay, that was a relief. Kaiźer turned back to the wall where the corpses hung pale, their eyes bulging slightly from hanging upside down for so long. Not even an hour had passed since they had entered the demon realm. Looking around, he realized that this had been intended as a message, but for what reason? Neither he nor Oníx had any connection to Sin'ka's staff besides James...

James! Kaiźer quickly spread his senses outward and searched the land surrounding the house. Almost instantly, he sensed an orb of energy. It was a barrier, and he recognized the magic. James had used Dragon Spirit Cradle to ward himself from the attack. Smart. Such a technique showed the boy's mastery and proved his skill.

~Oníx!~ he called. Oníx met his eye, and he relayed what he had gathered. *~he's just over the rise, near the lakeside but well hidden. He had his magic camouflaged; he's invisible to the naked eye~*

Oníx nodded at his telepathic message and took off into the morning light. He didn't watch her go, intent as he was on getting Sin'ka out of the room. He had to get her away from the scene before her. She had yet to move since he had arrived, and when he reached her, he noticed that her eyes were glazed slightly, and she had red stains on her cheeks. She was mourning and yet, had kept it silent.

"Sin'ka?" he called to her.

She stirred and looked at him with a dead expression. She had been lost in her own thoughts and was now feeling the truth of what was before her. He took her into his arms, and she went willingly, wrapping her arms around him and burying her face into his shoulder. Her chest heaved with silent tears, and as he led her outside, he heard her muffled cries through his shirt; he had traded his armor for civilian clothes before going to Sin'ka.

Leading Sin'ka slowly, he stepped from the ruins and set her on the lip of the fountain that sat before the house. By some miracle, it was whole, with only a tiny part of the base missing. It looked to him as if something had smashed through it. Despite that, he smiled at the beauty behind the design. Sin'ka had a good taste for art; he had seen her studio before they had left, and she was quite the artist. He thought it funny because Abika had been horrible when it came to fine art. She couldn't have drawn even if her life had depended on it. *Another fact to remind me is that they are not one and the same.*

Looking at the fountain, he saw something glimmer near the top. He would have missed it if the water had been running. It was a hilt. Activating his magical sight, he looked through the stone to gaze within. What he saw took his breath away. Hidden quite well was a mighty blade. It was plain-looking but clearly suffused with magic. The rock kept it sealed, and looking closer, he saw the wards that were weaved into the rocky structure. Did Sin'ka know this was here?

She still clung to him, but she had stopped crying and now only gave a shuddering heave here and there. She had her cheek rested on his shoulder, and as he watched, she rubbed a sleeve across her nose. She didn't dry her eyes though, the red stains still stood prominent along her cheeks. It was a little like mascara, he realized, bloody mascara.

~Don't tell her that~ Kaín said. *~She would kill you~*

~You're right, but any other time I might have. Besides, Sin'ka just lost her friends. I don't think this is a time for making jokes~ He wouldn't have even tried, even if it had made things better. He had seen whole villages put to the stake, but the mind tended to make people do crazy things when it was personal. Thankfully Sin'ka had simply broken down instead of becoming broken. It was times like this that made him wish he could read her thoughts. He had no way of knowing what she was truly feeling inside.

"Who am I to you?" Sin'ka asked suddenly.

So out of the blue was the question it took him a while to register her words.

"What do you mean?" he asked.

Sin'ka sat up. Her eyes were puffy, and her skin was flushed. The stain of her tears didn't do her justice; she looked miserable. And as she spoke, he ran his thumb along her cheek in an attempt to clear away the bloody streams.

"What I mean is; who am I to you?" Sin'ka asked again.

He stopped his hand and considered. Sin'ka's question had most likely been spawned from the emotional turmoil she'd just gone through, and after losing those she cared for, she was looking for a rock to keep her steady in the storm around her.

Love. That is who you are to me. A forbidden fruit I had thought to never taste again. I swore never to indulge in its nectar while never losing my craving for it. He took a deep breath to calm his beating heart. Sin'ka was breathing hard, but each rise and fall of her chest was solid and steady. She had pinned him in her gaze, and he could see fear and trepidation, as well as hope. He dropped his hand to the slim curve of her neck. "I learned of such no sooner than I had laid eyes on you that night at the club. You reminded me of"—he had to pause as his voice broke— "of someone I lost, many years ago, and when I saw you, I knew. You were the one I had said I would never seek. I guess fate had other ideas." He let out a soft chuckle, but it quickly died, and he dropped his hand and his gaze. "I knew you were the love of my life from the first moment I saw you."

Closing his eyes, he turned away from Sin'ka. *There, I said it.* He couldn't take it back now, and that scared him. Since Abika, he had yet to love a woman as his own. He felt a tear fall free and went to wipe it away, but a hand stopped his. He turned and, looking at Sin'ka, watched as she wiped his tears with a hand.

"About time, you dummy," she said.

Rising, she pulled him down and placed her lips against his in a soft kiss. He smiled and gave a soft chuckle, which made Sin'ka grin. She giggled, and he laughed, which only made her giggle fit worse.

"James..."

"What?" Kaiźer frowned at her words. Sin'ka had whispered the name against his lips. Pulling away, he looked at her.

"James," she said again. "I can sense him!"

Sin'ka shot to her feet and turned north. Following her gaze, he grinned. Oníx had reached him then. It would only be a matter of time now. Sensing something behind him, he turned to watch Darzíel step out of the ruins. The man's face was pained, but Kaiźer could see that he shook with anger.

Feeling his own rage heat, he strode towards the man. Darzíel saw him coming but did nothing as he approached. Kira appeared behind him but could do nothing as he struck.

Kaiźer's knuckles sank into the Angel's jaw, sending the man reeling. It was like he was striking stone. His hand thrummed from the impact, and he gave his arm a shake as Darzíel regained his balance.

"That was for Kurai," he snapped.

Darzíel met Kaiźer's eye. He was massaging his jaw, but at Kaiźer's words, his hand stilled. Kira had watched it all from the sidelines, and Kaiźer felt Sin'ka watching too. Drawing Kaín, he let the sword flash free. Kira drew a quick breath, but as he shot a quick glance at her, he buried the blade in the ground beside him.

~*Hey*~ Kaín snapped. ~*Watch it!*~

~*Oh, shut it; it's not like you'll rust*~ He looked back at Darzíel and let out a slow breath. The Angel stood there looking lost, and that made him angry. He knew this man was not to blame, but he still wanted to put a face to a name. Envy may have been driving, but Darzíel had always had his hands on the wheel. He may not have known what he was doing, but still, he had done it.

While he watched Darzíel, Eźmeralda and Ba'ile came into view to stand beside Sin'ka. Looking at them all, Darzíel wobbled on his feet. Stumbling back a step, his knees buckled, and he sat down on a wooden beam that had fallen from the second story. He let his head fall into his hands.

Kaiźer settled on the ground and waited. The Angel held his mind behind a sturdy barrier, and as he waited, he watched that barrier ripple. Like waves in a sea, it moved, giving off the impression of a calm breeze. Darzíel let out a long slow breath, and Kaiźer blinked as the man's mind became steady once again.

Looking up at him, Darzíel let his hands drop into his lap. "Half of me wants to remember, while the other half doesn't," he said. His voice was hoarse and sounded strained despite the calm of his mind. "I'm sure the memories will come; I was in the dark for..." —he looked at his hands— "for a long time and no time at all."

Kaiźer felt more than heard Oníx and James arrive. He gave them a momentary glance when Sin'ka rushed to James's side. She would take care of his injuries. He had Darzíel to worry about. Clear as day, the man was lost, looking between them all with a dead gaze.

"I... my mind is no longer blank, but neither is it clear. When I try to remember, it's all fuzzy." Darzíel cradled his head. "Only time will tell," he said after a long pause.

Oníx stood from attending Sin'ka with James and came to stand beside Kaiźer. Her hands were on her hips, and he got the feeling she was about to do something she shouldn't. Her eyes were cold and calculating in their depth and as she studied Darzíel, her mouth curved into a frown.

Suddenly, Darzíel shifted uncomfortably, and a look of discomfort overtook his face. Kaiźer leaned forward and let his senses open to incorporate all that was around him. His magical sight flared upon landing on Oníx and then more so when he reached Darzíel.

The Angel's mind was guarded, but as Kaiźer watched, the second layer of maña wrapped itself around the weave that protected Darzíel's consciousness. Kaiźer recognized Oníx's signature, but his questions died as he saw that the pure white weaves she was surrounding were falling apart. Like stone, they crumbled, and slowly but surely, holes in the man's resolve appeared, and as soon as they did, Oníx slipped through the cracks.

Pushing through, she set her attention on the man's memories. In the physical spectrum, Kaiźer watched sweat bead upon Darzíel's face. He was trapped by Oníx's magic, unable to even twitch a muscle. Kaiźer was amazed that he could even keep up a struggle with the amount of magic on which Oníx was pumping through him. It wouldn't be long now. He could see the man's mind weakening with each passing millisecond.

None too soon, Oníx's weaves shot free of Darzíel's mind, returning to their owner. Darzíel —like a puppet with its strings severed— fell to the ground in a jumble of tangled limbs. At the same time, Kira collapsed in a similar state. Kaiźer raced over to her and saw that just like Darzíel, she was breathing unsteadily; her eyes flickered around in a frenzy of motion behind closed eyelids.

"What happened?" Sin'ka said in shock.

Kaiźer rose to his feet and grabbed Kaín from where he had felt him.

~They were still linked?~ Kaín said, answering Sin'ka. *~What vestiges of the death chain that remained were connecting their minds. I feel she has been put into a similar state as the Angel~*

The dragon's voice was unsteady, and as Kaiźer relayed what the dragon said, he looked over at Oníx. As she bundled Kurai with a blanket, he noticed that despite her chest rising slow and steady, a thin sheen of sweat lay upon her skin. She had struggled then. He would have been surprised if she had done what she had with ease.

"But because of the link, I have a feeling she cured both of them..." he said slowly.

Sin'ka looked at Oníx but didn't ask any questions. As James let out a low groan, she went back to treating his wounds.

Based on the damage to the house, Kaiźer made a quick assumption. He had to guess James had been out near the lake at the time of the attack. It was second nature for him to run to the house. Which was when the strike that had obliterated the mansion had blown just shy of his path. The evidence showed on his skin. Half of his body was burnt, his left arm and leg shattered, ribs cracked. The white of his left eye was shot through with black, and the natural blue of his iris was stained reddish grey. He was lucky to be alive, and Kaiźer was sure the blast had thrown the boy back to the point he had located him. No way could he have moved with the amount of damage he had taken. It may have been the only thing that had saved him.

"When they wake," Oníx called his way. "Let me know."

Nodding, he turned back to where Darzíel lay in the dirt, his legs draped over the beam he had sat upon. With a chuckle, he went and sat beside where Oníx had laid Kira, watching as Ba'ile and Eźmeralda went and stood behind the Angel. They looked ready to give the guy a piece of their mind despite his state. Ba'ile's form rippled slightly, and beside him, Eźmeralda had a look in her eye that sent a shiver down his spine.

"I'm sure he won't be hurting anyone else anytime soon."

Looking up, both flushed when they saw him. Their eyes went wide in shock, and when he came looked their way, they shuffled back a few steps. He wondered what they would have done had he not spoken up when he did. Ba'ile had looked ready to shift, but Eźmeralda hadn't been so easy to read. The only visible sign he'd had were her pupils, which had been like daggered slits of black. He had little when it came to knowledge about feline shifters, so he couldn't know what she would have done.

Most shifters were immune to physic attacks, their minds being as they were. Odd enough, the thought caused Kaiźer to recall one of Maliki's lessons.

Three cycles before he disappeared from the Jackal's Court when the moon had sat smiling in the night sky, his master's voice had droned through another long lecture.

With his chin nestled in his hands, Kaiźer sat with his gaze locked onto the far horizon. Makili paced behind him as he watched for whatever the old man had told him to look for. It had been hours with no sign of anything happening, and he could feel his master's growing restlessness. The fire had gone out not minutes before. However, neither he nor his master had thought to light it again.

Kaiźer held back a massive yawn. He did not need Maliki lecturing him about alertness. Bored, he be, but not weary. He had too many bruises on his knuckles for him to think of letting his mind wander. As much as he hated it, his task would keep his belly empty till it was finished.

Hours before, his master had caught him in the stables, half-clothed, with a lady of the Court astride him. She had been very heated when Maliki had pulled her off of him, and he had given the woman credit when she'd stood her ground and tried to slap Maliki despite the state she was in. he let a smile escape against his brooding as he remembered how his master had grabbed them both by the ear and dragged them out into the moonlit street. Everyone else had succumbed to the dream realm long before, so the roads had been quiet, not a person being awake to see them.

Listening to his master's steps, he grimaced at the thought of why his knuckles throbbed. The pain still felt fresh despite the time that had passed. He did not need his master's help in gaining more aches and pains. The last few nights had yet to fade from his back and arms. Even against Meagän's skill with the blade, Maliki, with only a pole-staff, would wipe the floor with her. The pain in his fingers proved as much.

The memory passed as he listened to his surroundings. His master had started muttering; the words incoherent as he moved in tight circles around the high mountain clearing. The wind whistled through the peaks giving away a horrible case of paranoia, the sound just enough to put him on his toes. Ignoring the sound, he rubbed the back of his neck in frustration.

"I told you to keep watch."

"Come on, man, there aren't nothin' out there!"

"All the same," Maliki snapped. "Keep your eyes open! She's out there."

"Kaiźer doubted that. They had been out here for hours with not a single sin to collaborate the scouts' reports. If he had his way, the two would be back home, cozied up in front of the fire.

"I'm going home," he said finally.

"No, don't!" Maliki cried out.

Already standing, he didn't see the attack till it hit him in the face. As he had turned to look at his master, a female wolf-shifter had fallen from the tree beside him. He barely had a chance to widen his gaze before her fist smashed into his nose. Landing on his back, he tasted blood in his mouth and felt it fall down his face. She'd broken the bone with ease.

Getting up, he looked at Maliki and found him circling with the shifter. Summoning his magic, he crawled to his feet and tackled the shifter from behind. She cried out as she hit the hard-packed dirt, but as he struck at her mind, he found a natural block, which no magic had created, circling her mind.

She looked at him quizzically, and he realized he'd frozen in shock. Too late, she kneed him between the legs, and like a bomb, he felt like his balls had been blown to smithereens. His senses went blank, and his vision flashed white. He didn't even see the elbow that struck out to impact his chin. It was simply light out.

He awoke with a groan. Lifting a hand, Kaiźer grasped his jaw tenderly. Yeah, the bone was fractured, his face most likely puffy. Sitting up slowly, he found his hands and feet to be bound with thick rope.

With another look, he saw that he wasn't alone. Maliki sat across what appeared to be a small fire pit. Glaring at him, his master chewed on a length of rope that had been secured between his teeth. Looping behind his head, it looked uncomfortable.

They were in a small portable camp of sorts, he realized. A small tent was erected to the side of the clearing—the same clearing he had sat sentry in not... hours before? Yes, he was sure only a few hours had passed; it was still dark out. Wiggling around, he took his time, slowly transitioning his arms to his front. Starting at his butt, he slid down to his feet till the ropes strained, soon feeling the pressure release, his hands coming free before himself. With his arms free of his back, he moved towards the fire, intending to thrust the bonds into the flames. But just as he was nearing the fire, a lone wolf pushed into the clearing.

Usually, he wouldn't have stopped cold, but the sight of it was attention-grabbing. Padding up on all fours, the wolf was enormous, but as it looked at him, its fur rippled, and with a wave of light, the creature morphed into that of a tall, athletic woman. She had sharp greenish-gold eyes and fair skin with a thick head of maple brown hair—though her cheeks and shoulders were covered in freckles—and she... was nude! Covered in what looked like tribal tattoos, which he realized were made of fur, he could see that her figure was lean and... incredibly striking. He felt his face heat with embarrassment. He was keenly aware of where he was to her, but before he could do a thing, she saw him.

"Quite the agile one, aren't cha!" She didn't seem surprised to find him where he was. With a flick of her arm, she made a knife appear in hand. "I wouldn't do that if I were you."

Glaring up at the lady, he drew his hands away from the flames and sat back on his haunches. She nodded at him and put the knife away. It vanished from sight, and he wondered where she could have put it; he hadn't seen her pull on her magic. Maliki had yet to get into detail on the shifters. So, all of this was new to Kaiźer, and not in a good way, nudity aside.

The lady went over to Maliki and, shifting to watch her, Kaiźer eyed her figure as she bent down and rummaged in his master's pack. Pulling out a pair of hunting greys, she slipped them on and, pulling a strip of tanned leather from around her forearm, secured them around her waist. The wrap that would have held the pants secure was wrapped around her bust. She tied it in a knot between the generous swell of her breasts., and Kaiźer swallowed. Her femininity was embellished by such, and he looked away as she met his eye.

"So young and inexperienced." she chuckled. "If the boy can't hold his ground against a woman's beauty, how can he hope to defend against their retaliation?"

Kaiźer looked up at her when she spoke with an air of heated disagreement. He wasn't inexperienced; he'd been with plenty of women, just... not one who was so open with her beauty. Staring between her and Maliki, though, he kept his thoughts to himself, making sure to retain the guard on his mind; he couldn't have this lady prying into his mind uninvited.

"You were right; he is a strong one if stubborn." the lady said suddenly after a moment of silence. Kaiźer's eyes went wide at that. *You were right?* Looking between them once more, he sputtered as his emotional control finally snapped.

"You were—" he said, trailing off in irritation as he looked at Maliki. His master looked at him calmly, unmoving. "What was this, some kind of test?" he shouted.

The lady came up to him in a rush of supernatural motion. With a start, his head snapped to the side. She'd just slapped him!

"Quiet," she snapped. "I'd listen if I were you instead of trying to prove your stance in the matter." she glowered down at Kaiźer as she spoke, and he flushed in anger. She wasn't his master. As she was turning away, he struck out at her with his foot. But, at the last second, the lady moved. Instead of landing a hit, his leg was smashed into the dirt, the bone snapping on impact. He cried out in pain as her foot landed and groaned as she stepped away with a scowl. Looking at Maliki through blurred eyes, he couldn't keep his face from scrunching up in agony.

The man was stoic, unmoving, his hair moving slowly in the wind. Standing slowly, his master massaged his wrists. And as Kaiźer writhing in anguish, he looked at the lady who stood over him. They exchanged a glance, and the lady went over and undid his bonds.

"You didn't have to do them so tightly, Meagän? I could have acted trapped," he said, rolling his jaw experimentally.

The lady grinned at Maliki. "It wouldn't have felt real if I had." She looked at Kaiźer with curiosity painted on her face. "Besides, the boy I couldn't have held back on lest he knows the truth."

Maliki nodded in agreement but frowned at the bone that was protruding from his apprentice's calf. "But did you have to strike out like you did? He will have to heal normally; you know the rules of the Court."

Meagän flicked her hair over her shoulder nonchalantly and looked at him with a contemplating glance. "Who would know?" she said.

"I would." Maliki looked at Meagän with a frown. "And I cannot lie to my King, even for you."

"Back in the day, my father—"

"Your father would say the same thing if he were here." Maliki interrupted, cutting of Meagän mid-sentence. She scowled but kept quiet. Kaiźer let out a groan as he shifted slightly. His leg throbbed now, the pain only coming as a low thrum. He could feel the injury more now than before for some reason.

Looking at him then, Maliki and Meagän shared a look before coming over to his side. Holding his steady, his master gripped him under the arms in a way that wouldn't allow easy movement.

"Easy there, I apologize for this, but sometimes the best way to learn is the hard way," Maliki said as he nodded at Meagän. Looking at the shifter, Kaiźer felt confusion take hold but looking up at his master once more, he didn't see it till he felt it.

With a roar of pain, he tensed up against his master's hold, unable to move as, with a loud snapping sound, his leg was reset by Meagän. She fixed his leg quickly while his wits fell away, but as he settled down, the pain faded just as fast. His leg throbbed once again to a dull ache, and breathing heavy, he watched as Meagän moved away to snap two thick branches from the lower limbs of one of the surrounding trees. Maliki had her toss his pack to him, and the two of them proceeded to wrap his leg in a makeshift splint.

"What do you mean, learn the hard way?" he asked when he felt he could speak with a steady voice.

His master looked over at him and chuckled. Kaiźer was bewildered by that, but before he could shoot another question his way, Maliki spoke with calming tones.

"When faced with danger, a person will either fight to survive or simply give up." he tied off the cloth that he had pulled out of his pack, finishing off the splint. "But if facing a teacher, no one will show their true reaction, knowing that no matter what they do, they won't die. But in doing so, they don't learn what the teacher wants them to."

Kaiźer looked at his master for a second. As things began to make sense, he soon glanced over at Meagän as the meaning of the riddle dawned on him. Meagän wasn't just some random lady who knew his master like he'd initially thought, which meant she was either an informant or a Jackal herself.

"Good to see that you understand," Maliki said then. Standing, he helped Meagän lift him to his feet and cradling an arm over each shoulder; the two of them led him to a small rock that jutted out from the dirt near the fire. Breaking camp, they soon came back and helped him back up. Cradled between them, Kaiźer was woozy but alert as they headed east towards the keep.

A random thought came to the surface, and with a grunt, Kaiźer raised his head. "When I struck out at you before, your mind was blocked." he looked at Meagän. "But not from magic." the question was slight, and as she met his eye, a shadow of a smile crept along the edge of her mouth.

"What you experienced was a gift that shifters are born with. We don't have to think to block our minds. It happens naturally when another tries to get in uninvited." Meagän smiled at him then. "You're lucky all I did was knock you out."

He chuckled at the memory of his throbbing jaw. Granted, the pain of which had faded after what had happened with his leg. The pain he realized was well worth it to learn what he just had. His master was correct; he wouldn't have taken things seriously if he had known what would happen.

With the thought, Kaiźer chuckled. Ba'ile and Eźmeralda were so similar despite being of different species. Looking at them now, he saw their discomfort in proximity to Darzíel. He knelt over the Angel and, placing a finger against his neck, he checked the pulse. It was steady but weak. All the same, reaching out, he slapped the guy on the cheek, awakening him.

Darzíel gave a jolt upon becoming aware, but he fell back onto the dirt at the sight of him. Kaiźer went to stand but stopped when Darzíel gripped his ankle suddenly. Looking down, he saw the man's eyes.

Slightly misty, they stared up at him almost pleadingly. He wondered at the man's show of sentiment. *What could he be thinking of to cause such open emotion?*

"I remember it all...." Darzíel whispered.

Kaiźer's eyes went wide in shock. Looking over at Oníx, he balked. She'd cured him?! Looking back down at the Angel, he didn't say anything.

"I know what you must think of me but know that I didn't want any of it to happen upon anyone. I'm sorry...." The words seemed to pour out like a flood, each syllable laced with the strength of a thousand years of regret. "My only request is that you know I will do anything to prove to you that I am not the person you knew this whole time. I may have a few smudges myself, but I am not a bad person. Allow me to help you in any way I can, and you can do whatever you wish to me after." Kaiźer listened to if all, a growing sense of contentment filling him with each word voiced with a substantial dedication. He could feel the truth behind Darzíel's words; no magic was required to know that he would follow out his promises.

Leaning forward, he held out a hand. "If I am to accept your help, I expect you to hold to that promise!"

Staring at his hand, Darzíel grinned wide in relief. Grasping it with a firm grip, he let Kaiźer lift him to his feet. "You have my word," he stated, his eyes determined.

Kaiźer nodded, turning without another word to head for where Sin'ka was treating James with the help of Oníx. Standing up, Oníx faced him, and at the sight of Darzíel, she pursed her lips. Darzíel saw her, and a look of deep regret clouded his expression.

"You feel any better?" she asked him.

Running a hand through his hair, he smoothed the wild mane with a nod. Oníx looked on with a grim stare before turning without a word. He couldn't blame her, trust wasn't going to be easy for a while between Darzíel and them, which was to be expected, but so far, he could tell from the man's aura that he was not the same man as before. He looked at Darzíel from the corner of his eye when Sin'ka touched him on the shoulder with a slight grasp. Looking at her, he saw that her face was grim.

"What is it?" he asked.

Shaking her head, Sin'ka glanced over at James. Wrapped in a blanket, his head was the only thing visible, and what he saw was bandaged, tuffs of his hair protruding at odd angles.

"James is fine, but he seems to be in a coma. His body was severely damaged, and if we hadn't found him when we did, he probably wouldn't have made it." --She was trying not to cry and taking her in his arms, Kaiźer held her as she continued-- "We treated his body's burns, and what bones he broke are mending as we speak, but I don't think he——" Sin'ka's voice broke then, and he pulled her close as she fell into her tears.

"Shh," he whispered. "James will be alright; I know of someone who can heal him. We will have to watch him, though, as the journey will take time." He looked down at Sin'ka with a warm smile.

She smiled back, wiping her eyes of their bloody streaks with a silent curse. Fidgeting, she tried to hide her face from Kaiźer in embarrassment. Standing silent, he said nothing, but as she looked back up at him, he smiled wide, hiding his own discomfort. *Those tears of hers are something we will need to work on. She clearly hates crying in front of others, in front of me.*

As she looked up at him, her expression soon changed as if something had just dawned on her. Her eyes went wide, and a gasp escaped as she turned to face James. With a start, she hastily wiped at her face and swept her hair behind her ears.

"We need to go then!" she said quickly. Her words blended as one with the speed she spoke, and before he could figure out what she said, she was gone in a wave of supernatural speed. He blinked as she reappeared beside Oníx and knelt beside James. Coming up, he heard her talking with her and understood when they both shot into motion. Wrapping James up, Oníx began to erect a cradle for them to carry him in. She did the same for Kira as well, who apparently hadn't woken yet.

Standing with Darzíel, Ba'ile and Eźmeralda went to help, leaving him with the Angel alone once again.

"Where is it we will be going?" he asked.

Kaiźer looked over at the Angel's question. He didn't seem to have any ulterior motives in mind asking such, but the thought wasn't going to be easy to rid himself of after spending so many years with the man as an enemy. He could answer him for a change and not worry about what it would mean for those around him.

"A place that doesn't allow outsiders." Kaiźer crossed his arms and stood steady. "The only one who has the skill to heal James resides there, and I wouldn't go there unless I had to."

Darzíel looked at him expectantly, and Kaiźer realized he hadn't said where he was talking about. With a grim smile, he looked at the Angel. "We will be going to the lost city of *Ascaria*."

The Angel's eyes went wide.

Jag'ranica

Epilogue: True Fiend

My gaze is knowing, my breath intoxicating, and my blood boiling. And each I look upon knows my wrath through a reflecting soul of expiry.

The Mirror Demon
Unknown Age

Laying on a reflective stone layer, scaled and covered in its slimy exoskeleton, the mirror demon fumed. It had been too long—centuries, in fact. With the capture of the Dark General Greed, the demon's control over her had vanished.

With her first act, she'd gone after the ones who had imprisoned her. She'd been stuck with that despicable creature and its host for centuries. Starved and half-mad with rage, she hadn't cared about what or who had been in her way. She had torn through the veil to ravage the last place that she could sense her prey's aura.

Like fleas, those she'd stumbled upon had been crushed under her feet. Opening eyes of reptilian liquid, the bronze of their glow lit the area, and Jag'ranica hoisted herself up. The steady flow of dripping blood had stopped, which meant the corpses she'd erected had run dry, or they had been found by the ones she'd left them for.

The answer was given as the reflective stone floor shimmered to reveal the destruction she had left in her wake. In real-time, she watched her enemies arrive one by one. The last person to appear amid the rubble made a shiver run down her spine. Hot with rage, Jag'ranica clenched, clawed fists tightly. *Seeing your face now, all I want to do is tear it to shreds through teeth and claw!* The fire cooled to a calm blaze when she looked upon Darzíel, however. The fallen angel was powerless, his mind shattered, and she felt terrible for the guy for some reason. The feeling was foreign to her. It tasted of a mysterious flavor that made her typical emotional meal... zesty of all things. It was interesting.

She didn't like it. Letting the image fade from the rocks around herself, Jag'ranica left the scrying cave's dark depths.

Clothed in demon armor, she strode through the rubble on clawed feet, moving through the remains of what had once been a mighty fortress. Looking at the gray sky that made up the entirety of her realm, Jag'ranica scowled. Her home was a creation of the new gods, and they had done an excellent job in trapping her indeed.

Moving into the astral castle's ground level, she moved through the crumbling columns and towers to stand at the edge of the abyss. Floating among the Null-void, her clump of a home sat alone with only a few stray parts of the castle trailing weightless around the more massive rock.

The rocky mountain of rock dropped negative to a point, looking to have been torn from the very ground of its original resting place. Resting on its surface, the castle was a ruin. Surveying the open void around her, Jag'ranica contemplated. The tear in reality that she had opened had mended, and she had not the power to open it again, which meant her rage would rekindle till she was able to enact her revenge once more, for real this time. She didn't know what her enemy would do now. Although, the magician who had been with them before was missing from what she had seen. That meant he was trapped in the Underworld. How quaint.

"My revenge will burn you all!" she shouted at the empty sky. For her crown, the skulls of Kaiźer and Oníx would make a good fit. She would tear the celestials from their seats in the sky and use their bones as her throne. They would get what was coming for them, this she promised as she headed back into the depths of her entrapment with a glowering rage.

Find out more in my next novel

A Vow Unbroken (Part 1)

Coming sooner or later to a bookstore near you

Acknowledgments

I want to give thanks to those who helped in the creation of this book and all its characters. The first person who deserves thanks on my list is my mother. She gives me love and support each day and I cherish her guidance (even when I don't like it) for she means well and knows what's best for me. I told her once when I was very little that some day I would write a book. And I did just that. Thanks mom!

To everyone in the book club that I was in during the birth of the first chapters, many thanks for taking the time to listen to my creations as I worked on each part each week. I want to give thanks to my friend and ally Hopper for the creations and development of the Character Ryeznya. It was with your stubborn steadfast decisions that I was able to broaden his dark history and evil deeds into something worthy of the twisted personality you envisioned.

I also want to give thanks to Mrs. Gibson for listening to me as I proof read my chapters late into the night. It was with your guidance that my scribbles were able to go from an incongruous jumble of short chapters into a full, worthwhile Short Novel.

And to my best friend and fellow writing buddy, Stephen Blair, who argued and bickered with me about each chapter and what would and could be added to each. It was all thanks to you and the fact that you stood by your ideals that I got my book published and available to the public.

To all my family members who gave support and many years of encouragement to follow my dreams.

To Todd Brown, may he Rest In Peace, I give thanks for opening my eyes to the possibilities of adding illustrations to my stories. Your short novel series, "That Ghoul Ava" gave me many ideas and sparked many a light bulbs in my mind as to what the supernatural world has hidden within its dark shadows.

I will also give thanks to Emmalee Rusk for her fellowship and writing abilities. She first introduced me to the writing world and its possibilities with her own books during our high school days.

A special shout out will also go to Aimee Salter, who gave me guidance on how to get my book published and what would be needed to accomplish my goal. Thanks Aimee, your advice truly helped a ton!

I would also like to thank George Skurju for giving me the drive to get shit done! (mind my French). With your business mindset, I was able to think about the possibilities of what publishing a book could do for me mentally, emotionally, physically, and financially.

Thank you, all of you, for your support and love over the years. I couldn't have done it all by myself. It was because of all of the loving people in my life that I was able to achieve one of my childhood dreams.

Many Thanks

Levi Marshall Hyatt

Otherworlders / Humans

Abika Angelica von Morningstar: Deceased lover to Kaiźer; murdered by Ryeznya. Born of low birth, she was taken in by the Jackal's Court and trains beside Kaiźer in their ways. With a thick head of red fiery hair, porcelain skin, and fair features, she hails from across the sea. Utilizing the elemental of fire and water, she is both healer and destroyer.

Ba'ile: A canine shifter who is companion to Kaldär Morningstar. Sporting a lions main of silver hair, his face marred by an x-shaped scar across is left cheek, and a scar down across his left eye, he dresses in a pure black suit. Born with the elemental of acreage, he mastered all four elementals and learned the fifth power under the tutelage of Kaldär.

Eźmeralda Starlight: Feline Shifter, apprentice to Kaldär

Gũnder: a Friend of Kaiźer's, deceased Hunter

Helen Corinika, the immortal Seer: The Seer within the Garden Eternal. Age unknown, mother to Kaiźer, Maliki, as well as Ryeznya. Also the mother of Kaldär, each of her children's heritages have been the highest kept secret among all the celestials

James al Voinovich: Brother to Oníx Voinovich, protects Abika

Jessíca: A lady of the sheets at The Lovers Bite, water nymph

Jokahn: Blade Master to the House of Vermilian

Kaiźer von Morningstar: The brother of Kaldär, half demon half angel heritage, a Hunter of the Jackals Court.

Born in 2486 A.B. (1,435 years of age) refer to; Jackal, Jackals Court

Kaldär von Morningstar: One of the six True Immortals, brother to Kaiźer; lives within the heavens shard's lone mountain. Born in 87 B.B. (is 4,000 years of age)

Kiyle Ross: A friend of Kaiźer's; human acquaintance

Kusko— Top general to Lord Vermilion; murdered Kaldär's wife

Meagän: Friend of Kaiźer, deceased Hunter, a shifter

Oníx al Voinovich: Elemental mage of angelic heritage, companion of Kaiźer, Born in 2506 A.B. (20 years younger than Kaiźer)

Paris: Human host to the Deadly Sin; Greed

Ryeznya: Hunter nicknamed the Slayer, uncle to Kaiźer and Kaldär. Age unknown

Sara al Vore: Deceased lover to Kaldär; murdered, refer to; Kusco

Sin'ka Finsaria: Soul mate to Kaiźer, born in Londinium as a high lady but was turned by a vampire in 3700 A.B. now resides in Nypheriam as an herbalist. Born in 3683 A.B (is 217 years of age)

Skyler al Vermilian: prince to the kingdom of sand, he is the son of Lord Vermilian and Lady Sabrina

Kurai Aka Hoshi: Succubus who is slave to Darzíel

Jasmine: one of Kaiźer's friends during his time within the house Vermilian

Divine / Demonic Beings

Angels: Arcane beings that rule the heavens above the mortal realm, Resided in Nypheriam during the Age of Heroes

Darzíel: A fallen angel who is corrupted by a dark lord who has a grudge to pick against Kaiźer

Draghi: owner of the Red Fountain in Londinium, hidden informant to Darzíel aka Envy

Elves: Otherworlders with pointed ears and heightened senses. Called the fair folk for their beautiful features

Envy: One of the Seven Dark Lords, commandeered the angelic host, Darzíel

Gabriel, Archangel: Leader of the astral beings, refer to; Angels Coven, the

Gaia: Mother Nature, creator of the mortal realm.

Greed: One of the Seven Dark Lords, commandeered the human host, Paris

Guardian Angels: Immortal beings charged with the protection of a single mortal of their choosing. (Only a few let their charges know of their existence)

Kaín Algora: Black dragon trapped within a magic sword, familiar to Kaiźer

Lucifer: top general to the Unseen One, rules part of the netherworld

Pan: The god of Nature and all things derived from Gaia

Rakariage: a magical carriage that is summoned for fast travel across the five kingdoms, driven by a gremlin

Shadow-demon: a creature of darkness that resides within the Nix void

The Kraken: A mythical beast that usually resides in the deepest depths of the sea. Rarely comes to the surface

The Sea-Folk: underwater fairies who are renowned for their pure (indestructible) pearl creations

The Unseen One: ruler of the dark realm; the underworld

Vampire: undead begin that has been cursed with agelessness and has a thirst for blood, refer to; ShadowFolk, the

Devil hound: a dog that originates from the depths of the underworld, rotten skin and bones of stone make up the horrifying abomination made flesh

Titles / Terms

Death Dealer: An assassin for hire

Monoelemental: someone who can use one elemental magic

Bielemental: someone who can use two to three elemental magics

Polyelemental: someone who can use three to four elemental magics

Full Polylemental: someone who can control all four elementals and harness the power of light (the fifth).

Fey-Whisperer: a female magí (males can rarely gain the trust) who has been granted with the ability to talk with fairies; extremely rare to find

Demigod: half human half god, mortal man / woman who had one immortal parent

Druid: Protector of mother Gaia, they keep the balance

Folkweaver: a storyteller that travels the five kingdoms, performs for royalty and poor alike

Hunter: Term used for the Jackals for their tracking skills

Lady of the sheets: refers to; prostitute

Magician: Title given if a mortal gains the powers of an angel

Mermaid: Otherworlder that is half human half fish; underwater dweller that keeps the waters surrounding the elves territory (the Ascarian forest) free of foreigner ships

Nephilim: Title given to a mortal who is of immortal heritage, refer to; demigod

Otherworlder: Supernatural being that is not of the human realm

Prostitute: Someone who leverages sex to earn a living and to gain information, refer to; lady of the sheets

Seraphim: The highest ranking given to an angel

ShadowFolk, the: Residents of the Kingdom of Twilight, thought to be the offspring of, refer to; Kingdom of Twilight, the; Vampire

Shadowalker: term for the shadowfolk that reside in the land of twilight

Summer / Winter Solstice: a time in the year when all the realms are washed clean of unneeded maña; basically Gaia recycles the energy of the lands, purifying them

The Angels Coven: The organization of arcane beings that watch over the mortal realm

The Dark Lords: the term for the seven servants of the unseen one; greed, envy, lust, pride, gluttony, wrath, sloth

The Gentle Folk: Residents of Nypheriam, titled for their calm manner and old bloodlines

Those Who Dance with Thunder: Nickname for the ShadowFolk

Divine / Demonic Artifacts

Codex – a magical phonebook that is used to store a user's maña, can be used for many purposes

Death Daggers– firestone daggers created in Hell, designed to kill Hell Spawn

Dwarf Star alloy– the strongest metal within the five Kingdoms, Originally it came from the heavens, and it's the material that makes up all angelic artifacts

Excalibur– the ancient blade wielded by the archangel Gabriel

Heavens Bane– the black blade that holds Kaín Algora captive

Magic Shell– a flat seashell that is infused with all four of the elemental magick's. Is used as a communications device that uses the holders codex as its source of contact

Repidar– Ryeznya's magic dagger

Shadow dagger– a phantom dagger that can only be seen by the caster, Used for shadow travel

Tesseract— a divine artifact designed to transfer energy or matter to a secondary dimension

The Fore-Lorne Looking Glass— a portable passageway between Heaven and Hell

The Mirror of Retribution— a demonic artifact that allows the user to grant any wish they so desire but at the cost of the user's life. Takes two people to wield

The Pendent of Anubis— a Tesseract intended to mute demonic maña

The Seven Scarabs— seven colored jewels designed to purify black magic

Magic / Entities of the Universe

Arcane Maña— pure energy that has no form of purpose, It stands as a support for the structure that is the different realms

Magic— a power fueled by Maña. Broken into five categories. The first is acreage magic, which is the energy of the land. The next is fire magic. This is the arcane energy within the land. The third magic is wind magic. The fourth one is water magic, which is the arcane energy of the heavens. The last but not final magic is called the fifth power

Magic, Acreage— the energy of the land. When accessed, it gives the user the ability to manipulate the earth around them, how much so depends on their mental/ physical strength

Magic, Black— refer to; Magic, Demonic

Magic, Demonic— energies that belong to the Underworld, used by the demons and servants of the underworld it is a foul power that taints the user, refer to; Magic, Black

Magic, Fire— arcane energy within the land, wilder in nature it is harder to control and more volatile

Magic, Water— arcane energy within the heavens, more powerful, it takes someone skilled in magic to wield such power

Magic, Wind— the energy of the heavens. Once accessed allows the user to thicken the air around them or others, has an unlimited list of possibilities that is only limited by the user's imagination and physical/ mental strength

Maña — the power that runs through all living things. Comes in two forms; demonic and angelic

The Fifth Power— the spiritual energy the runs in all things, can only be gained through harmony of one's self and all that is living. Once gained, the user can control their own body allowing shape shifting abilities or self-healing (aside from those who are born with such abilities)

Magical / Physical Techniques

Banger spell— a magical firecracker that will go off when triggered

Divinejump— the ability to cross great distances in a single step, not teleportation; think hyperspace

Divinestep— the ability to walk on air, gives the user the gift of flight if only partly

Elemental Voodoo— a druid's use of the land around them, they can liquefy or solidify the land around them to whatever consistency they choose

Golden Blaze— magic ability used to travel great distances in seconds

Rumination — a form of mediation that allows the user to access the deepest recesses of their mind.

Shadowjump— the ability to cross a great distance in a single step, made easier with a shadow dagger to mark the area of travel

ShadowStep— the ability to merge the users figure with surrounding shadows, the darker it is the better the effect. Example: a dark corner of a room

Wings of the Azure– the physical representation of the power of all six of the seraphim that guard the heavens, only Ryeznya is known to have a link to such power

White divine— the act of calling down fire from the heavens. If white in color they are at their strongest. Oníx's are icy blue

Black Helix— same as White Divine, However the flames are black in color they are stronger but cannot be used as often

Warp— tears reality to shreds, the limit is only the imagination

Sky jump— divine teleportation technique designed for angels

Wings Of The Arcane— Oníx has inherited her mothers angelic gifts. White wing man of compressed light, making for a dazzling site in the form of for wings covered and shiny white feathers

Lands / Land Markers

Eternal pool– a gathering center for magic, Scattered throughout the five kingdoms in hidden underground caves from before the time of man.

Heaven – the astral plane ruled by the angels

Heavens Spire– an island out at sea, surrounded by raging waters. Named after its lone mountain that forms a spiral

The dark realm / The Netherworld– the hellfire plane ruled by the unseen one

Sal'kar– a small island south of Londinium, it's just off the coast

The Elder Mountains– a rocky divide that cuts through the Nypherian Kingdom, and the Kingdom of Dawn

The Elder Pass– a hidden valley through the elder mountains; guarded by the Jackals

The Enchanted Lagoon– a bay that is home to the Sea-folk and mermaids

The Forbidden Sands— an endless desert that stretches across the west side in the Kingdom of Twilight

The Garden Eternal- a realm that rests within the cracks of the living realms. Home to the immortal seer, refer to; Helen

The Great Spires— a mountain line directly through the center of the land, dividing the five kingdoms in half

The High Woodlands— main resource of lumber for the Nypherian Kingdom

The Lawless Land— no-man's land, a wasteland without water. The air is toxic because to the plants that grow in the lands barren soil

The Nix Void— a realm outside of time. No one knows what it is

The Shadow Realm— layer of reality under an actual living realm, think a shadow. Running at a slower pace it allows a traveler to pass a great distance in a tenth of the time it would take in the actual realm, refer to; ShadowStep

The Twin Isles— a small cluster of high walled islands. Only way of access is by air

Traders' Pass— a divide within the great spires; passage of trade between the two lands

The Great Forest— the woodland that makes up the entirety of the Kingdom of Light

Villages / Towns

Aquariadonis — the underwater city of the mere-folk

Ascaria— ancient city built during the Age of Heroes, held as the capital of the Kingdom of Light

Genesteria— the capital city within the Kingdom of Dawn, refer to; Starasix, Sterling, Starasix, Starleín

Londinium— the market city in the Kingdom of Sand; center of trade for the southern Kingdoms

Nypheriam— capital city within the Nypherian Kingdom, center of trade for the northern Kingdoms

Sanctuary — a tropical reservoir in the dry land within the Kingdom of Sand

Sha'arda— the lone city in the Kingdom of Twilight

The Chantry — a safe haven for those who seek sanctuary, Resides within the Kingdom of Light

The Forgotten Realm— a city hidden by mist within the Kingdom of Twilight

The Jackals Court— located in the Kingdom of Dawn, it is a hidden city where the Hunters reside

The Market city of Traiathica — the city that resides along the traders' pass that splits the Great Spires

Miscellaneous

Dragonstar Alloy — a metal that is from the heavens. Will not rust to the ravages of time and is impervious to damage or breakage. Can only be melted down once

Gandian Silk — a fabric from the Ancient city of Atlantis. As thin as silk but as strong as steel, and can take on any color you desire. Can even be made transparent

Lianica — part lion, part dragon, resides in the high mountains west of Nypheriam

Sea folk pearl — near indestructible material used for all kinds of things ranging from weapons to pottery.

The Lovers Bite — a house of Sin within the city of Nypheriam

The Red Fountain — an Inn within the city of Nypheriam.

The Five Kingdoms

The Kingdom of Light— home to the fair folk and the Chantry. Consists mainly of thick forests, wide rivers and streams

The Kingdom of Sand— home to the nomadic people

The Kingdom of Twilight— a dry land known for its culture and spicy foods. Home to the ShadowFolk

The Nypherian Kingdom— the Land of the Forefathers. Home to the royal house

The Kingdom of Dawn: home to the Jackals Court and the Lawless Lands.

The Five Ages

The Age of Heroes~ (3100 B.B. – 600 B.B.)

Heroes roamed and built their reputation. This was a time of kings and queens and it lasted for 25 hundred years since the first man arrived on the shores of Nypheriam.

The Age of Echelons~ (600 B.B. – 0 B.B.)

The land in oppressed. Foreign leaders hold power till they are overthrown from within, this cycle continues for 600 years. The world is broken.

The Age of Eternities~ (0 A.B. – 500 A.B.)

Darkness fell, and a famine overtook the land. A good percent of the world's people died; the only remembrance of the past is now written on page. This age lasts for five centuries.

The Enchanted Age~ 500 A.B. – 3500 A.B.)

Magic is discovered and the first woman leads the people. Technology is created, using magic and steel. Iron from the age of heroes can now be forged once again. Lasts for 3 thousand years

The Age of Knowledge~ (3500 A.B. – 3921 A.B.)

Everything since the age of eternities is stored in the great library within the capital city of Nypheriam. Magic is used for everything and the first artifacts from the age of heroes are being discovered. Has lasted for the past four centuries.

About the Author

A man of many talents, the author of The Chronicles of the Garden Eternal, has traveled through life trying to find a calling that would satisfy the itch that plagued his mind. It wasn't till a young lady, a friend of his, introduced him to the art of writing. Ever since that day, he has strived to write every thought, no matter how extravagant or irrelevant, in the hopes of publishing it. It is through her that he created this series and found his calling.

Made in United States
Troutdale, OR
09/29/2024